I0788432

changes
and
CHOCOLATES

Changes and Chocolates
Untouchable #2
Copyright © 2019 by Heather Long
Proofing: Meghan Leigh Daigle
Cover: Crimson Phoenix Designs
Formatting: Sloane Murphy

Changes and Chocolates/Heather Long – 1st ed.
ISBN-13 - 978-1-956264-04-3

Foreword & Dedication

When I first began Rules and Roses, I had no idea how much I would fall in love with Frankie, Coop, Jake, Ian, and Archie. Nor did I have any idea how much their day to day lives or how they were facing such tremendous upheaval in their personal relationships would come to mean to me.

Like the first book, Changes and Chocolates captivated and pushed me as Frankie struggles alternately made me laugh aloud, sniffle, and sometimes just get plain pissed off. Frankie is the kind of girl I'd have been friends with in high school and she's the kind I want to protect now.

This book wouldn't be complete without the enormous support of Blake Blessing and Rebecca Royce. They've been tremendous as cheerleaders, as sounding boards, and even pushing back in places where I needed to dig deeper and let me tell you, this book is so much the better for it.

Also a huge hats off to the readers who've left reviews or reached out to me or recommended Rules and Roses, you're the best and I adore you!

Finally, just a couple of housekeeping notes!

For those of you who have never read a reverse harem before, first let me thank you for picking this up and giving it a shot. Second, a reverse harem means the heroine will not make a choice in this book or any other between the guys in her life. It may take her a while to reach that conclusion, but it's the journey that drives it. There are many ways to frame this kind of relationship, currently reverse harem fits it very well.

Also, this is the second book in a series. If you haven't read Rules and Roses, I encourage you to pause here and go grab it. While there may be no specific happy endings at the end of each of these books, there will be one to the whole series, that I promise you. Some of these books will have cliffhangers, largely due to the size of the story, but the happy ending has to be earned as part of the journey.

Thank you again for reading Frankie's story and I truly hope you enjoy it!

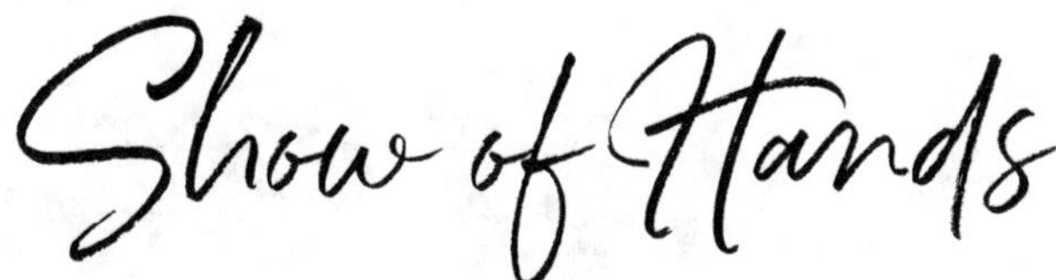

Show of Hands

Archie

> We need to talk.

Jake

> Now we need to talk? You've been dead quiet since yesterday.

Bubba

> Worse, you took off with Frankie. Nothing. No word.

Archie

> Are you done?

Bubba

> Hardly. Frankie isn't answering either.

Coop

> What did you do?

Jake

> I'm with Coop. What did you do?

Archie

> Told Frankie about the plan for Frenchy.

Jake

> ...

Coop

> Oh FFS

Bubba

I told you guys to leave it alone.

Archie

Bite me. It's bad enough about her mom, we don't need the French guy.

Jake

She's all right, isn't she?

Archie

Not really.

Coop

...

Jake

...

Bubba

Explian.

Archie

She spent the night. We talked. It was good. Told me she wasn't going to see Frenchy anymore. Done deal.

Coop

...

Archie

Was relieved. Told her we didn't have to do the thing.

Jake

...

Bubba

You have to be kidding me.

Archie

She was fine. But... that pissed her off.

Jake

...

Coop

...

Bubba

I told you to leave it alone.

Archie

Fuck you, Bubba. I was going for honesty

Jake

...

Coop

I'm still back at she spent the night.

Jake

Where is she now?

Archie

Home.

Bubba

Where are you?

Archie

Not there, she threw me out.

Jake

...

Coop

She's ignoring my messages.

Jake
And mine.

Bubba
Archie—you're a jackass.

Archie
This isn't done. And see above on the fuck you if you can't help.

Coop
Now you want our help?

Jake
...

Bubba
If she won't answer, we go to Mason's.

Jake
She hates that.

Coop
She really does

Bubba
I know, but it's harder for her to ignore us there.

Archie
Shit. Edward's back.

Jake
She with him?

Archie
Yeah. Jeremy said they'd be gone before party.

Coop

We should tell her.

Bubba

That won't help. I wish I didn't know.

Jake

Too late now.

Archie

I'm aware.

Jake

You're going to be in pain too.

Coop

Cause that helps.

Bubba

Stop. Frankie first.

Coop

Agreed. I'll go by her place.

Bubba

Don't. If she isn't answering the phone, it'll just be cornering her at the door.

Archie

So what? We wait?

Bubba

I was thinking grovel.

Jake

Yeah. Archie first.

Archie

Jake

Bubba

Coop

Jake

Archie

Chapter One
SUPER COOL PARTY PEOPLE

Mom's new boyfriend was Archie's dad. Archie's *married* dad. The guys knew. Had known. I—I couldn't deal with this.

"Wait," Archie said, tightening his arms around me. He pitched his voice low, probably a good plan to keep it from carrying out to the pair still locked together below.

Acid churned in my gut, and I think I threw up a little in my mouth. As much as I wanted to storm out, I didn't dare draw attention to myself. Not if it meant I had to talk to Mom right now in front of all of them.

The fact they'd known was bad enough.

My legs wobbled, and if not for Archie, I probably would have landed on my ass. As it was, I pushed away from him and crossed to one of the chairs they'd abandoned. They were farther back, invisible from below. There were four open beers on the table.

Well, good to know they started the party early.

Grabbing one, I took a long pull from it and grimaced.

That was so foul.

"Easy," Jake said as he crouched next to me. When he put a hand on my leg, I jerked my knee away, and he lifted his hands in surrender. One by one, the others sat down, and I tipped the bottle up and drained the rest of it, then shook my head at the horrible taste.

"Are they gone?"

Archie was the only one not sitting or crouching. He glanced over his shoulder, then back at me. "Almost."

"You knew." It wasn't a question.

"Caught them last week," he admitted.

Last week.

Caught them?

"That's why you weren't at school on Monday." I wiped the back of my hand against my mouth. The air was still cool, even if the sun was warm. The covered deck added to the chill racing over me. Had to explain the goosebumps somehow.

"Pretty much," Archie admitted.

"And when did you tell everyone else?"

Coop sighed. "Tuesday—when you were at lunch with Mathieu."

Okay. That fit.

My mom was having an affair with Archie's dad.

She wasn't out of town at all.

"Your parents were supposed to be out of town."

"Yeah well, not the first time Edward and Muriel made different plans." Archie crossed over to a small outdoor bucket I hadn't noticed. He pulled out a bottle of wine.

It looked pretty familiar, and heat scorched through me.

It was the same kind we'd had the night before. He retrieved a glass and carried it over.

"If you're going to drink, drink something you like. And give me your keys."

Ian had said nothing; he just sat forward, elbows on his thighs and hands clasped together as he stared at me. When I caught his gaze, he gave me a small smile. "I'm sorry we didn't tell you." I'd gone to his place on Tuesday. We'd… made out in the pool. "I didn't tell you later because—Frankie I have no idea how to tell you something like that about your mom."

Bottle open, Archie filled the glass halfway and held out the wine. "Keys."

If I took the wine, I was staying.

If I stood up right now, I could just leave.

"I know you're mad," Jake said quietly. "You can be as pissed at us as you want to be. We deserve it. But stay… we can cancel the stupid party. Just don't go away angry and having to choke on this."

"We're still your friends," Coop added. "Maybe not the best of friends right now, but we're yours, and you shouldn't be alone."

"For what it's worth," Archie said. "I got really blitzed, and I was hungover as fuck on Monday. I knew Edward was cheating. It's not like it's new. He's a serial cheater. But Muriel puts up with it. They left together. He came back alone, took a different bag and left again."

Mom had been dating for months. The whole time, I hadn't been talking to the guys. I stared at the wine glass for a beat longer. Shifting in the seat, I dug my keys out of my pocket and handed them to Coop. The corners of Archie's mouth tightened, but he gave me the wine.

"It's a little late to cancel the party," Archie said as he grabbed a fresh beer out of the bucket and popped the cap. "But the fact we're having it means they'll go, so it'll at least be a safe space here."

"I'm not sleeping in the pool house." The thought made my skin crawl.

"No problem," Archie said. "You can have my room."

"Hey," Ian said.

"I said she could have my room," Archie told him. "Not that I'd be in there with her. Course," he continued, glancing back at me. "That's entirely up to you."

My stomach bottomed out, and I took another swallow of wine. It was sweet, but more, it seemed to help calm down my jangling nerves. "You only found out last weekend?" Did I have that right?

"Yeah," Archie said. "I knew he had another—one." One was not the word he'd planned to use. He was editing himself for me. "But I didn't know it was her, Frankie. Bubba's right, I didn't know how to tell you."

But they'd all been so keenly aware of Mom's absence.

I scrubbed a hand over my face, and Jake tried again, this time just touching my arm. "Can I just hold you for a minute?"

The request floored me. Was he serious?

"Why?"

"Why?" He raised his eyebrows. "Because you just took your second sucker punch of the day—and I was part of one of them. You need a hug."

I snorted. "Yeah, that was what Marsha said."

"Her boss," Coop said, probably answering Ian or Archie, but I didn't look away from Jake. His pale blue eyes implored me to believe him, and the damn thing was, I wanted to believe all of them. But how was I supposed to do that? Really?

"This sucks."

"Yeah," Ian and Coop exhaled almost on the same breath.

"That's a word for it." Archie cut his gaze to Jake, and so did I.

"Okay," I told him and stood. When I set my glass on the table, he surged upward. He took the chair, and when I settled in his lap, he wrapped his arms around me. It was nice, and I sighed as I leaned my head against his. "Are they gone yet?"

Archie pulled out his phone and sent something. A minute later, his phone vibrated. "Jeremy says they've left."

I blew out a breath.

Jeremy knew.

This was… "I don't even know what to do with this."

"You don't have to do anything," Archie told me. "This isn't on you. It's on them."

That sounded a whole lot simpler than it was.

"Frankie," Ian said, drawing my attention to him. "You were right—you're worth a lot more than having us make some plan to get rid of a guy you liked. I'm not going to defend it. But…"

I raised my eyebrows.

"But hear me out this time?"

I nodded as Jake gave me a light squeeze. Since I was sitting with my back to his chest, his hands were over my abdomen, and I had mine resting on his. What had been nice a moment earlier set my nerves jangling. What was I doing?

"We like you. All of us." There was a small round of nods, and there was something absolutely unsettling about having this conversation with all four of them. "A lot," Ian continued. "But we don't want you to date someone else if you're dating us."

Us.

"Plural? All of you, plural?"

"Told you, Frankie," Coop said gently. "*We* like you."

"What happens if you decide you don't want me to date anyone but one of you?" I locked gazes with Archie though, because Jake was behind me. Last night, Archie and I had crossed and then torched the line between friends and what—lovers? Did we qualify as that? The bracelet on my wrist suddenly took on a whole new weight.

The silence was telling as the guys glanced at each other, and then Archie shrugged. "It's not a problem yet."

Yet.

I tapped Jake's hands, and he loosened his grip. It took me a minute to stand, and the wine I'd drunk along with the beer had already gone straight to my head, but I didn't stagger. I needed the distance.

"Hey…" Jake said, catching my hand, but I pulled free. "It's not a problem.

We argue. Some of us do stupid shit." He glared at Archie. "But we all agree on one thing."

It was all just too much.

"You," Coop supplied as he snagged a fifth chair and pulled it over for me. Perching on the edge of it, I was violently aware of the silence surrounding me.

"You hungry?" Ian asked.

"I don't know," I admitted. "I don't know how to do this."

"Well, that makes all of us," Jake told me, reaching out again, but he pulled his hand back when I shifted away. "Since it's us, I say we just do what feels right to us."

What did that even mean?

Coop glanced at his watch. "Party starts in thirty minutes. If we're feeding Frankie, we need to do it now."

"Yep," Archie agreed, his phone in his hand. "Jeremy is bringing food up."

My phone buzzed in my pocket, and I shifted to pull it out.

Mom

Breakfast tomorrow? Just you and me?

I didn't know how to do any of this.

"Want me to do the honors?" Coop offered, but I shook my head. She was my mother.

Me

Can't. Have plans with the guys.

Which was technically true, even if this had suddenly become the last place I wanted to be.

I waited for a long minute, the phone matching the silence of the guys around me. When it buzzed again, I almost dreaded whatever message she'd send. What new lie she'd spin.

Mom

Are you planning on being out all night?

It felt like she was judging me. There was a lot to judge at the moment. Or maybe she was trying to decide if she could bring the boyfriend home. The thought made me shudder.

Me

Don't know. At Archie's for a party.

There. Suck on that news. Not that I planned on staying here. Not long. But if I went home, that meant seeing her. I had no idea how ready I was for that at the moment.

Mom

Dinner?

Have you ever wished you didn't know what you did?

I could feel Jake's gaze on me, and I slanted a look at him. Then I sent.

Me

Have plans. Gotta go. Talk later.

I had plans every night this week. And into the weekend. Like a neat little box I'd walked into.

His smile was almost blinding, but I put the phone in do not disturb and shoved it back in my pocket. I still hadn't read all of their messages. Jeremy arrived with a tray of sandwiches and chips. He dropped off the food and didn't comment on the alcohol.

"You know what," Coop said. "Tonight—let's just be us. We'll party, maybe dance, have a few laughs, and when we kick everyone out, the five of us can crash and watch a movie. No pressure. No expectations."

"I don't know that I'm staying." I didn't want to go home. I had no idea where I could go. Maybe just get in the car and drive.

"I'll set the alarm," Archie said. "One of us can go with you to feed the cats and you don't have to see your mom alone if she's there."

If. That of course was the big question.

"Does she know you know?" Did I really want the answer to that question?

Archie shook his head slowly. For some reason, that helped. God only knew why. Mom had to know Archie's dad was married. Why?

Beyond that—the guys had still lied to me. They'd gone behind my back. I wasn't…

"Stay, Frankie," Coop said, a quiet plea in his voice. "You don't need to be alone, and I know it may not feel like it, but you're not…"

I glanced around at them. "Yes, I am."

"Frankie…" Ian began but I shook my head.

"Don't. I—really can't do this right now." I'd come over here with a plan. Establish boundaries. Make it clear I would not put up with this crap.

"Nothing has to happen," Jake said. "Coop's right, we're here for you. We're friends first. No pressure. No expectations. Don't—don't walk out." At the moment, walking out was pretty much my only option. I'd already surrendered my keys.

"To be perfectly clear, I'm game for more," Archie told me bluntly. "But you can put on the brakes at any time. Last night's rules apply."

Heat licked up my spine at that memory. He had let me dictate the speed and whether anything happened. Then again, he'd been playing with all the cards. If I'd known—if I'd forced the issue about Mathieu—and he'd told me the plan the night before? Would I have had sex with him?

Probably not. We'd probably have had the fight then.

"Guys, lay off," Ian said.

"Excuse me?" Archie slanted a look at him.

"You heard me, lay off. She's in shock, she doesn't need us telling her what to do." The firmness in Ian's voice got to me. Yeah, he was standing up for me, but… "Just—let her breathe."

"We're not doing anything," Jake said. "We're allowed to tell her we *want* her here. All of this started because we *assumed* she didn't want us, and now we know differently."

I twisted to look at Jake, but he was focused on Ian. Were they really…?

"Whether she wants us or not, she needs a moment," Coop said, apparently landing on Ian's side of the line. "She just found out about her mom, and I needed a shower after Archie told us."

I closed my eyes. If I'd known about my mom? God, had they been in the pool house while Archie and I were in the hot tub? Nauseated didn't begin to cover it.

"Her mom's a bit—" Archie cut himself off, but the sentiment echoed clearly. "It's another reason she should stay here. As long as the party is on, Edward and Ms. Curtis will be scarce. If she goes home, she's going to see her. Maybe. If Ms. Curtis went there…"

"C'mon, Arch," Ian said with a sigh.

Yeah. C'mon Arch… I opened my eyes, but none of them were looking at me.

"Seriously, Frankie," Ian said, finally meeting my gaze. "We want you here…I don't know if you can have fun. You can blow off the party and just go play video games or something inside. But, stay…"

"Ditto," Coop told me and bumped my shoulder. "Besides, you still have to meet your rose admirer."

Jake scowled. "You had to bring *that* up."

"Because we're her *friends*," Coop stressed. "And we're all *here*. So Frankie can feel safe about *meeting* them."

Not very zen, but also not subtle.

I wanted to laugh, but there was no humor in any of this. It wasn't funny. If I went home, and Mom was there… I'd have to face her knowing what I know. But here? With all of my *friends?* I had to face what they'd known and chosen to do. The rose guy had been the last thing on my mind, and now… He was going to find me here, if I took off, I left him hanging.

Granted, I didn't owe him a damn thing but those roses—they were bright, untainted spots in my week. What if meeting him ruined all that? My thoughts were like balls in a pinball machine stuck between two bumpers in a machine racking up crazy points, because I had to ask, "What are the chances none of you is going to hit him?"

With a groan, Jake said, "As long as he isn't a douche and doesn't expect anything, fine. He gets handsy, and I'm not promising I won't break them."

"C'mon," Coop said. "We won't punch the guy." The last he said to Jake. "Or try to set him up." That went to Archie. Then he looked at me. "You know you wanna. Besides…you gotta stay and dance with us, Frankie. Show off the bikini maybe?"

"She doesn't have to show that off to anyone else. We can save that for swimming later when people are gone," Archie suggested. "But if you decide you want to, you're just going to have to deal with a little more protectiveness. You're hot, and I don't want anyone getting the wrong idea."

It was like talking to four brick walls. "You know that's not as cute as you think it is."

"It's not about being cute," Archie retorted.

"He's not wrong," Ian said slowly. "You're stunning, Frankie. Absolutely stunning. People are gonna drink even if we don't supply it. So—we want you safe. Fair?"

"In what world is that *fair?*" I eyed them each, one at a time. Shoving the chair back, I stood. "I'll stay, but not for you. Not for any of you. I'm staying because right now, I can't go home. And I don't know what I'm going to do. But you're going to leave me alone." I snagged one of the sandwiches off the tray and looked at Coop. "Give me back my keys."

"You said you weren't leaving…"

"Not right now, I'm not. But I want the option to go when I decide, not you."

Hurt flickered in his eyes at the last comment. "Promise you're not leaving."

Promises meant something to me. "Like I said, I'm not leaving right now. Now give me my keys."

"You're being stubborn to be stubborn," Jake snapped.

"Well, stubborn is better than being an ass. I've never lied to you. Or tried to sabotage any of you. Not that you four can say the same." I shook my open palm at Coop, and he slid the keys out of his pocket before setting them in my hand. "Thank you."

With that, I walked away from them. Every step hurt. Not just because of what they did, but because everything had changed—*again.* I didn't see Jeremy or anyone else on my way to the patio doors. The hot tub was running, the water bubbling happily, and the lights were on in it again.

My gut knotted as I went wide around it and headed for one of the patio lounge chairs. The music was louder down here, and I pulled my sunglasses down as I finished my sandwich, aware that four sets of eyes were on me from above. The wine gave me some distance, but it didn't do a damn thing for the way my gut churned. The food helped soak up some of the mild buzz, but it served as a distraction for far too short a time.

The patio door slid open and Ian walked out, he was in swim trunks and an unbuttoned short-sleeved Hawaiian shirt. Beer in hand, he circled the pool to drop onto the lounge chair next to mine. His sunglasses shielded his eyes, though I only peeked at him as he passed me.

Neither of us spoke, and I couldn't figure out how I'd gone from magical Friday to miserable Saturday. Worse—I couldn't figure out how I was going to make it through the next hour, much less the whole party.

I already wanted to get the hell out of here. But high school parties were part the experience, right? I clung to the lame excuse, because I really had no idea where else I would go right now. The closest thing I could think of was to go back to Mason's and see if Marsha was there.

How humiliating would that be?

"Frankie," Ian began, and I held up a hand.

"Don't."

"You're mad…"

"Am I?" I crossed one ankle over the other. "Want to give me more details on my feelings and behaviors since you four all appear to be the experts on deciding what I get to do and to feel as well as know?"

He sighed. "Fine, maybe we deserve that."

"No maybe about it."

That seemed to shut him up. "Accepted. We deserve that." Not for long apparently. "I want to make excuses, but you were right. I knew that they were planning something, and I didn't say a word. I'm sorry." Well, at least he was talking for himself and not the others.

Not that it helped much.

The sliding door opened, letting the other three out, but I shifted my gaze to where the gate had opened and the first partygoers began arriving. Jeremy wasn't sending them through the house, but around it. I was almost grateful for the new arrivals and the distraction they offered.

The first couple of people were kids I recognized, but I didn't *know* them. Not far behind them were several members of the football team. Ian rose after a long moment and brushed my shoulder gently before he headed over to greet them. The sun had begun to dip, and the lights added a kind of moody glow over the area. In a little over thirty minutes, there must have been fifty people who'd shown up, including—and unsurprisingly—Rachel Manning and her little posse of girls. Maria, Patty, and Sharon arrived at some point.

I probably wouldn't have noticed, except Laura Zaverman came over and claimed the lounge chair Ian had abandoned. Holding a can of soda in one hand, she perched on the edge of the chair and the only way to avoid looking at her would have been to turn my back.

I'd made it thirty minutes.

Thirty more, and I'd ditch. I still had no idea where I'd go, but driving around in the car had to be better than this.

"Hi," Laura said.

"Hey." To be honest, I didn't know Laura. We had a grand total of maybe two classes together in the last five years. Maybe. That was a stretch. The only thing we had in common, I think, was Coop. Not really a way to open a conversation. Especially since a little over a week ago, she thought they were still dating.

Yeah. Cue uncomfortable silence. Particularly when the best thing I could think of was at least her sitting there was better than Patty or Maria who were both pissed at me, or Sharon, who probably wanted to punch me.

She lifted her soda and took a drink, her gaze skipping past me briefly then back. "I know this is kind of awkward, I don't think we've really ever talked before."

"Not much, no," I said, then because I didn't want to be more of an asshole than I already felt like, I dredged up a smile. "How are you?"

"I'm—confused."

Fuck. I just invited this conversation.

"I'm sorry. Confused is not fun." There, door closed.

"No," she said, then glanced past me again. The hopeful smile on her face was painful. More, it told me what, or more precisely, who was there. "Hey Coop."

I did not sigh or roll my eyes. He dropped to sit on the lounge chair next to me. "Hey Laura," he said, his tone cool. "I didn't know you were coming to the party."

"I didn't know I was coming either." She glanced from Coop to me, then back again. "But I'm glad I'm here. Do you think we can talk?"

"We're talking." Oh, I knew that tone. He was going to be an ass. "What's up?"

"I kind of meant…" Laura hesitated, glancing between us, and I elbowed

Coop.

"I can take off if you two need to talk." But before I could go anywhere, Coop latched onto my arm.

"No, you don't need to go anywhere," he said, then looked at Laura. "You can say anything you need to say in front of Frankie."

Oh. God.

I was going to kill him. "No, she can't, don't be a douche."

The harshness in my tone must have warned him, because he stared at me.

"Really? You aren't dense, Coop. If she wants to talk to you it's not because she feels like spilling her guts in front of me. So stop being a dick." This right here was what I'd meant.

Laura's eyes widened, and she wasn't alone. Coop frowned. "I'm not being a dick." But he cut his gaze to Laura. "Am I?"

"I think I should just go. I wasn't sure if you broke up with me because of Frankie, but now I think you did. Which—" She actually threw me an apologetic look. "I'm sorry, I wouldn't have bothered you if I'd known, but Sharon said you were with Bubba and Maria insists that it's Jake, so—I had to be sure."

"About what?" The tone shift in Coop's voice dipped toward a warning.

"Nothing," Laura said as she stood.

Dammit.

"Good job," I said with a sigh as she walked away.

"What?" Coop twisted to look at me. "I'm not going to go off and talk to her, we're done. I told her that. I came over here to talk to you."

Maybe he meant well. Maybe he didn't. "I don't want to talk to you."

He frowned. "C'mon, Frankie…"

"No," I said, then tugged my arm out of his grip. "I'm going to walk around."

I didn't wait for him to follow me. I didn't want him to. I felt bad for Laura. Folding my arms, I circled the pool to get away from not only him, but from where Ian was talking to his friends from football. I didn't see Archie or

Jake, but I wasn't trying to find them either. Unfortunately, my path took me right past the pool house.

Last place I wanted to be. The music around the pool cranked up, and a handful of the kids ended up in the water. Sharon cut a look from me to where Ian stood, then dove in the water. Call it an intellectual exercise, but I didn't miss the way she swam right over to where he was standing and asked for assistance getting out of the pool.

Rolling my eyes, I turned away and smacked right into Jake.

"Going somewhere?"

"Taking a walk." I side-stepped to go around him, and he hooked my arm.

"Frankie," he said, his voice low. "Come on, seriously? Don't—"

"Don't what? Make a decision for myself? Decide I'm worth more than you guys plotting behind my back? Decide that you keeping an epic secret from me because—what? You thought it would hurt me? Did it hurt me less finding out how I did?"

"First—I'm not apologizing for the Frenchy thing. I don't know that guy and more, I don't want to know him. I've wanted you for years. The first inclination you show toward dating, and you're going out with some *other* guy? Not happening. Not without making it clear I care, and I think I made it pretty damn clear and so did you."

Heat flooded my face. Yes, he had made it clear.

"That said, I'm glad we didn't have to do it. I never want to hurt you."

I scoffed.

"You think I'm lying…"

"I think you already hurt me."

He slid his hand down my arm and then closed over my hand, even as I curled it into a fist. "I'm sorry that it hurt you. That I can say sorry about. Hurting you wasn't the intention." Sighing, he glanced past me toward the pool. "Can we get out of here? Just you and me? I'll take you wherever you want to go."

I almost crumpled, right there. I just—I needed a hug. I needed someone to tell me this was all going to be okay. I wanted to go back to that floaty feeling I had that morning before Archie told me about the *plan* and before I'd seen my mom and Archie's dad.

"You missed us this summer," he reminded me. "We *missed* you. Please don't make me miss you again standing right there…"

My resolve wavered. I was mad but…

"Hey, Frankie." Rachel Manning calling me was probably the second to the last thing I wanted to happen right now. Jake scowled, but the other girl was a lifeline—whether she knew it or not—and I was drowning.

"Hey, Rachel," I said, turning and trying to tug my hand out of Jake's grasp. "What's up?"

She was solo. Where had her posse gone? Cheryl and the others were by the pool with Maria. Sharon was standing right amidst the other football players, dead in front of Ian, but his arms were folded, and he stared across the pool to where we were. Coop wasn't on my lounger, he'd moved to the patio and looked to be arguing with Archie.

What were they fighting about?

You know, no, I focused on Rachel, and finally Jake let me go, because I think he got the point that I wasn't going to stop. His sigh spoke volumes, though.

"Just thought I'd see if you had a minute. I know it's a party—but you think you have time to go over some poetry with me?"

Seriously? Homework help?

"It's a party, Manning," Jake said, scowling. "She's not your private tutor."

"I don't think I was talking to you, dickhead," Rachel retaliated. "And since she was trying to get away from you, maybe you should take a hint."

And okay… "Sure, I can give it a few minutes, but it's a party, and everyone else looks like they're having fun."

Rachel shrugged. "You're not, and I think you could use the break."

Well, she wasn't wrong.

"Frankie…"

"I'm going to talk to Rachel," I told him firmly and tried not to drown in those pale eyes. Jake never let me get away with anything, and he had to know I was bolting. It was written all over his face.

"Don't leave," he said, then added. "Please. Just don't take off?"

"No promises." It was the best I could do. I folded my arms again and faced Rachel. "Want to take a walk out in the garden? It's quieter. Probably be able to hear ourselves think." Because someone had cranked the music louder.

Jake loomed over us both, but Rachel ignored him. "Sure, sounds good. See you, dickhead."

"Bitch," Jake muttered under his breath as we walked away, and I shot him a look over my shoulder. Seriously? The impatient look he gave Rachel before he met my gaze answered that question. I wanted to reassure him, but Rachel bumped me, and I glanced at her.

"He's cranky. Sulking will do him some good. Besides, you really do look miserable."

I really was miserable.

Didn't mean I wanted to talk to her about it.

"Thanks," I said, not bothering to hide my sarcasm. "This is my best hair shirt look."

She grinned as she pushed open the gate. "Huh, maybe you need more Elizabeth Barrett Browning in your life," she said as I followed her into the low-lit garden, and the music faded behind us.

I needed something.

Chapter Two
HELP WANTED

The garden was really just a collection of shrubbery with some seasonal flowering plants, crepe myrtles—and they were already giving up their flowers—along with a pair of dogwoods, one in each far corner so their flowers didn't end up in the pool. But the ground lighting and the tall shrubs with the mismatched stone pavers and mulch gave it a kind of fantasy element.

If nothing else, the tall shrubs—particularly those lining the pool area—muted the sound. But you could still catch some of the lyrics. Arms folded, we walked several feet in silence. There were a couple of benches out here. The garden itself wasn't huge, but it was long, and you could meander like it was a maze.

"Did you really want to talk about poetry?" I asked Rachel.

"No. I mean, we can. You just looked like you needed an excuse to get away from Jake."

I had plenty of excuses to get away.

Plenty to stay, too.

"That obvious, huh?" And humiliating.

"Maybe not to everyone," Rachel said, then shrugged. "But you haven't been happy all evening, and you weren't at work this afternoon."

"Took a half-day." Not totally a lie. Marsha had sent me home early, so technically a half-day.

"Resting up for the party you're not enjoying?"

I shrugged and walked over to one of the benches. Sitting, I went to rub a hand over my face, but remembered I'd actually tried to look nice tonight, so stopped. "I'm just tired."

Also not a lie. I was exhausted.

"Then go home," Rachel said, sitting next to me and stretching her legs out. "You're not having fun, and you're tired. No one says you have to stay."

No, they didn't. I pulled my phone out of my pocket. There were a couple of messages on the screen. One from Archie, and the other from Jake.

Jake

Do not just take off.

Archie

If you need a break, go inside and make yourself comfortable. Party not allowed in there.

Make myself comfortable. I cleared away the messages and checked the time.

Ten more minutes.

Then I could figure out where to go. Maybe take myself to a movie, if I stayed out late enough, I could get in after Mom went to bed. All at once, that reality blanketed me again and I wanted to be sick. I just didn't get it. Why would Mom have an affair with a married guy? I wanted her to be happy…

"Frankie," Rachel's voice jerked me out of the reverie.

Oh. Shit.

"Sorry." The frown practically echoed in her voice. "Did you forget I was here?"

"Yes—no. Sorry, I'm just distracted." I set the phone down on the bench next to me so I could just hit it to check the time.

"I can see that." The dry tone helped. "Do you want to talk about it?"

Yes, I did. But I didn't have anyone to talk to about it. Rachel and I weren't that close. We kind of had been back in middle school, sorta. But not really. "Not right now," I said slowly. "But thanks for asking."

Sitting out here meant I had a break from the guys, but it also meant I wasn't where Mr. Thorns could find me. I had to stop calling him by that name. Maybe I should just go.

"I think I'm going to go…"

"Yeah?"

"Yeah." I glanced at her and found her watching me with a look of genuine concern. "Thanks for wanting to talk, but I'm—I'm in a mood, and I'm tired."

"It's okay. You all right to drive?"

I'd had the wine and the beer an hour ago. The distance and buzzy feeling were gone. If I'd really had them at all. They'd helped with the shock, but that wasn't saying much. "I should be fine, just need to figure out where I want to go."

It was too early to go home. If Mom was there—no way she would be asleep. Then again, I could drive by. If her car wasn't there… maybe she and Archie's dad went to a hotel or something.

"Home?" Rachel asked, and I couldn't help it, the thread of questioning curiosity in her voice tugged at me. "Or… we could go grab food, if you're hungry. I think the guys had snacks at the party. But I haven't eaten today."

"You didn't eat at Mason's?" Didn't she say she went by?

"I grabbed a shake," she said, shifting and smoothing the hair back behind her ears. "It was packed, and I didn't want to wait for a table."

Guilt swamped me. They'd been packed? And Marsha sent me home. Crap.

I should call her. "Was it that bad?"

"I don't know," Rachel said. "I mean, they were full and I mostly swung by to say hi since I was over there."

Really? I frowned.

"What?" Rachel grinned. "I've been to Mason's a lot over the last couple of months, you thought I was just going there for the burgers?"

Honestly, I hadn't really thought about it. But I supposed she was right. I had seen her a lot over the summer. "Sorry, I guess I've been living in my own bubble."

"It happens." Rachel let me right off the hook. "Course, now you can make it up to me and make my shake extra thick when I come in next time, because it's not for the food."

I laughed. "The shakes are already thick, if you want it that thick, I'll just scoop you some ice cream."

"That would work. I like ice cream."

We both grinned. It was ridiculous and funny, and maybe just what I needed to hear. "Where do you work?"

"Me?" She raised her brows. "Why?"

"Well, if you're going to stop by Mason's to see me, seems only fair, that I go harass you at work, too."

"Oh, so it's harassment now." Her voice warmed. "I see how it is."

"Well, depends, can I do my homework there?" God knew, I had a lot of it.

Rachel snort-laughed, and I snickered. "You can come by, but it's not glamorous."

"And working at Mason's is?" I raised my eyebrows. "I smell like burger grease and french fries at the end of every shift."

"But you love it," Rachel pointed out. "You're always smiling and nice, even when it's insane."

"That's the job," I told her. "People respond to happy." Even when I was dying on the inside. Course, it was harder to be happy then. "So where do you work?"

"The grocery store," Rachel admitted. "Three times a week, nothing big, you know. But it gives me extra cash. I didn't want to work retail, but I like the folks who shop at Dell's Grocery, and I get a discount. So if you ever need deli meat or something, I'm your girl."

I got a discount at Mason's, too. Technically a free meal each day I worked. Most of the time, I didn't take advantage of it, because who wanted to eat the same burgers over and over and over again?

"Good to know. I like Dell's, we don't go there as often cause they're expensive."

"Local places are—I mean, Mason's isn't a chain either." Which was true.

"What days do you work?"

Rachel grinned. "Hey, I never asked your schedule."

"What you stalked Mason's every day to find out when I worked?"

"No, because that would be creepy," she said easily. "I went in and asked when you'd be there next, and I heard you tell Coop that you were working weekends last spring."

Oh.

"Okay, that's way more reasonable."

"Right?" Rachel canted her head and looked back to where the pool was, not that we could see it. There were shrill screams of laughter punching through the darkness, and someone turned the music up. If they kept that up, the cops were going to be called.

It had happened before.

"You feel better?"

Leaning forward, I flattened my hands against the bench edge. Did I feel better? "I don't know. Maybe not so wound up." Laughing had helped—a little.

"Do you want to try and go back to the party? It sounds like the dancing's started. Might be fun." There was a hopeful note in her voice.

Going back meant seeing the guys. "I don't know," I said, and maybe that made me a broken record.

"Okay, well you can still go, or we can go grab something somewhere quieter. Unless you don't know about that, too."

I groaned and covered my face. "I'm sorry, Rachel. I'm terrible company."

"You're not so bad," she said far more easily than I deserved. "I don't mind hanging out here, it's comfortable." Though it had gotten a bit chillier, she wasn't wrong. "It's kind of nice to be near the party but not have to deal with the people."

"Since when don't you like people?" I sat up and then back. It was ten minutes past the hour. Course, if Mr. Thorns was there and I was hiding in the garden, it wasn't like he was going to find me out here.

"Since…"

Displaced and scattering mulch announced the new arrival before Coop popped around one of the taller pine shrubs. "There you are. Jesus, Frankie. Don't disappear."

"She didn't disappear," Rachel retorted. "She took a walk, and your buddy Jake saw her go, so don't pretend you didn't know where she went."

Wow. That was hostile, even for Rachel. Coop stared at her for a moment and, I gotta admit, so did I.

"You know what, Rachel…" Coop began.

"She does, actually," I told him. "And I didn't disappear. I took a break." Coop swung his gaze to me. "I also don't need a babysitter."

He sighed. "Frankie…"

"I'm not doing this right now." And I definitely wasn't doing it in front of Rachel.

"You don't have to do it at all, if you don't want," Rachel stated. "My original offer stands."

"What offer?" Coop asked, his eyes narrowed, then he shook his head. "Look, I just wanted to make sure you hadn't run into the flower guy and gotten in over your head." He winced.

Well, at least he had the grace to feel bad about that statement. "I'm fine,

Coop," I told him.

"Does that mean you already met him?"

"It means I'm fine." I met his stare and his shoulders deflated.

"Frankie…"

"Dude, do you need a sign?" Rachel asked, and I put a hand on her arm as Coop glared at her.

Coop just didn't do that. Though lately, he'd been doing a lot of things I would have said he didn't do.

"It's okay, Rachel, seriously, thanks for wanting to stand up for me. But I can handle it." I really didn't need or want her fighting my battles for me. It was kind of weird that she was offering to do it, and at the same time, I appreciated her.

Gripping my hand once, she said, "You really don't have to put up with them."

"You know, the only person here who wants your opinion, is you," Coop informed her. There it was, his temper fraying. Just because he was usually the easiest going guy around didn't mean he didn't have one. Not that I saw it often. Usually only in context with his dad.

"I think I'll listen to Frankie's opinion on that," Rachel countered with a smile. "Truth hurt, Coop?"

He stared at her. "You were the one who told her that crap."

"You mean the truth? That you guys wouldn't let anyone else get within a hundred yards? That you wanted to have your cake and eat it too?"

Okay, this was escalating.

"It was none of your damn business," Coop said. "Seriously, girl, get your own life and butt out of hers."

"I think she needs more people in her life, because if you all had your way, it would be the four of you and no one else…" Rachel stood up. "And I'm not afraid of you or Jake or Bubba or Archie. You're all a bunch of—"

I whistled. It was sharp and shrill, and they both turned to look at me.

"Now that I have your attention," I told them. "Knock it off. Rach—seriously, thank you, but I can handle this. And Coop—shut up. Rachel did me a favor. You don't like it, because I was righteously pissed at all of you." And hurt.

His expression shifted. He knew what I wasn't saying.

"You don't get to be mad at her for telling me the truth."

He blew out a breath and raked a hand through his hair.

Smiling faintly, Rachel glanced at me. "I'm going back to the party. Come find me when you're done, if you still want to get out of here."

"Thanks."

"Sure thing…" As she started away, Rachel pivoted. "I work on weekends and on a couple of afternoons after school. One of the perks of early release, I'm usually getting done with work when everyone else is getting home."

She had a point. "Cool."

Another smile, and then she was gone.

"I hate this," Coop said, his voice somber. "I really hate this, Frankie."

"Well that makes two of us."

"Three," Ian said as he slid around a collection of pine bush. "Sorry, I wasn't trying to eavesdrop, but I came out here to see if you were all right, and I guess Coop had the same thought."

"Coop wanted to make sure I hadn't escaped or snuck off with some other guy." The fact Coop grimaced said I wasn't too far off the mark.

"You're mad at us," Ian said quietly. "We deserve it. I'm sorry, I should have given you a head's up. Admittedly, when my friends do bonehead things, I try to talk them out of it. I was kind of hoping you'd never have to know because they'd change their minds." With a glance at Coop, Ian continued, "You should know Coop was the first one to tell them to back off."

"So it was basically Jake and Archie, that's what you're saying?"

"No," Coop offered. "It wasn't. We all knew. We all talked about it. Ian never backed off, I—did. After Thursday, I really, really want this shot. Now I think we blew our feet off."

I didn't have an answer for that, so I folded my arms and leaned back. I was so tired.

"I have to be able to trust you guys," I said slowly. "That's—that's why I told you what I wanted in the first place. I trusted you. I know I spent the summer not trusting you, and that sucked. What you did hurt—this hurts more. It's not just about Mathieu."

Coop rubbed the back of his neck. "We know. But what Ian said earlier is right, we didn't know how to tell you, or if we should. I mean—she's your mom."

Dropping to sit on the ground in front of the bench, Coop studied me. Ian glanced between us and then he eased down into the spot Rachel abandoned. "Do you mind if we just hang out here with you?"

I did and I didn't.

"Guys, I don't know what to do."

"Okay," Ian said on an exhale. "Want to try talking to us like we're just your best friends?"

"And not the guys I made out with?" Coop winced, but he nodded. "Trust circle?" His smile was weak but genuine.

"We were friends first. I beat up Robbie Gillerton for you."

I snorted. "I knocked out Maisy Jackson's tooth for you."

His eyes widened briefly, and then he burst out laughing. "Oh, God. I forgot about that."

"Who the hell was Maisy Jackson, and why did you knock out her tooth?" Ian glanced back and forth between us, some of the tension leaching out of his face.

Coop looked at me, and I grinned at the plea in his eyes. "Hey, you started it," I reminded him. "You brought up Robbie."

With a dramatic sigh, Coop looked at Ian. "In first grade, Maisy Jackson decided that she didn't like me. She was the little queen of the class, and she would announce daily who she liked and who didn't like."

Maisy had been a drama queen, and I hadn't seen her since sixth grade, so hopefully she'd gotten over herself.

"But every day, she didn't like me. Some days, she liked Frankie, but never me. Frankie and I still played together, but Maisy insisted Frankie couldn't play with me on the days she like Frankie."

Ian snorted. "She sounds like a treasure."

"She was a horror show, but we were six. I just didn't like that she wanted to tell me who I could play with, so I just agreed with her and did what I wanted to do. Then she threw a softball at Coop."

"Smacked me right in the face, knocked one of my teeth out," my best friend admitted with a sigh.

"And you…?" Ian looked at me.

"Threw the ball back at her. And the tooth I knocked out wasn't loose."

He put a hand over his face and just cracked up. Coop grinned. "We all went to the office, Frankie didn't miss a beat. The principal asked why she did it, and she said, and I quote, 'I thought she'd want it back. Since she threw it at us in the first place.'" His expression sobered a beat. "Us. Not me. Us."

I shrugged. "You were my best friend. I wasn't going to let her hurt you just cause she didn't like who I was playing with."

"I'm still your best friend," he said seriously. "Even if you don't want to acknowledge it right now."

That was probably true. The laughter dried up, and we were left sitting in the quiet with only the music and rising volume of the partygoers filtering through the night air.

I glanced at my phone. It was closing in on nine. I'd stayed way longer than I intended. "I should probably go walk through the party." Even if I had zero desire. "Then I think I'll go home."

"Frankie," Ian said, catching my hand. "Is there a way to fix this?"

"I don't know."

"Do you want to fix it?" Coop asked. "I know we're not being fair. This—

this is a lot, and we want you to say we can fix it, but do you want to fix it?"

"I had sex with Archie last night, I'd really like it to not be something I did and then—this."

Silence met my announcement.

I guess Archie didn't tell them everything.

"Maybe that changes your minds about me. Or maybe you get why I'm not really feeling it at the moment."

Ian tightened his grip. "Archie—are you okay?"

That wasn't the question I was expecting, but I stared at him. "No, Ian. I'm not okay."

"He meant with last night," Coop stated, his gaze intent.

"I was…I was feeling pretty great, until he told me about the plan." I sniffed, because there were tears clogging at the back of my throat, and I didn't want to do that here. I didn't want to do that at all. "I'm sorry if that disappoints you."

"It doesn't," Coop said rolling up onto his knees. "Frankie, nothing you've done is going to disappoint me. Do I like all of it? No. Do you have the right to be mad at us? Yes. Do I want you to let us try to fix this—yes."

"Maybe we don't try tonight." It was the closest to a concession I could come to. "And maybe—maybe don't be so mean to someone who was trying to be a friend to me."

"Rachel?" Skeptical didn't begin to cover it, and Coop shot a look at Ian.

"Didn't know you two were friends," Ian said slowly.

"Well, my circle has dwindled. You guys take a lot of time and effort."

A grin softened his mouth. "We like having your time."

"And your efforts," Coop tacked on.

"But," Ian continued and gave Coop a look before focusing on me again. "If she's your friend, we'll try not to be assholes. I think we can manage that."

"Yeah okay, I'll try," Coop said. "But I'm not promising anything for Archie or Jake."

Ian snorted. "You know they can make their own apologies."

Not likely, Jake already made it clear he wouldn't apologize for anything except hurting me.

"You going to be okay to go home?" Coop switched the subject.

"I have to see her sooner or later. Lately, she's never there, so…" I shrugged.

"Can I hitch a ride home with you?" Coop asked.

Ian frowned, then said, "Or I can follow you home. Or both. Just so we can make sure you get there, and if she is there, you have an escape route if you need it."

"Guys, she's not going to do anything. If she is home… I'll just tell her I'm tired and go to bed." If Archie's dad was there? I'd grab some stuff and go sleep in my car.

"Just looking out for my best friend… besides the party's kind of a bust."

Considering the noise level? I somehow doubted it.

"If you really need a ride, I'll take you home, but I'd rather just be on my own for a bit."

Coop sighed.

"I'll make sure he gets home," Ian offered. "Will you text us when you get there?"

"Please?" Coop added.

"Okay." I could do that. It was a plan at least.

Ian squeezed my hand, and then Coop stood up and motioned toward the far fence. "There's a way out over there, I can walk you up the driveway to your car, save you the trouble of having to go through the party."

"Can I call you tomorrow?" Ian asked. "Maybe before you go to work? Just to say hi?"

"Let me call you? If I'm up for it?" I barely knew how I felt right this second, I had no idea how I'd feel in the morning.

"Okay." He accepted it easily enough.

"And I'm not working tomorrow." I couldn't remember if I'd told Archie that or not. "I planned to take it off cause I was supposed to spend the night."

His expression fell. "And we screwed it all up."

The fact I wanted to comfort him messed with me a little. "I'll text when I get home."

He nodded before he started to reach out to me and then withdrew his hands and put them in the pockets of his trunks. "I'm looking forward to it."

Arms folded, I followed Coop along the path toward the fence, then we paralleled it. There was a gate, tucked there in the corner. I guess that made sense. The gardeners had to get in. It let us out on the small service path that circled the house. It shouldn't have surprised me when we emerged out front that the number of cars in the driveway had grown to a ridiculous number. There were easily a dozen between where I'd parked off to the side and where the driveway was down to a single lane to get out.

There was no way I was getting my car out any time soon.

Coop raked a hand through his hair as he glanced back down the driveway, then at my car. "This could be a problem."

"No kidding."

Crap.

I should have just left earlier.

"We'll figure it out," Coop promised. "I know who owns some of these cars, we'll just make them move them." Yeah, that would be difficult. Half those people were probably already trashed.

There was a note under the windshield wiper of my car, and it had my name on it. He frowned and hesitated as I reached for it.

"Do you want me to stay or should I give you some privacy?" The tight lines at the corners of his mouth promised me that wasn't what he wanted to offer, but he had offered it.

That meant something.

Maybe that was why I said, "It's okay."

I slit the envelope open, and there was a note inside in neat—not typed this time—lettering.

I wanted to talk to you tonight, but you seemed very sad. I don't know why and it's not my business. I like to believe that everything works out for a reason. Maybe we can try again soon. I hope you like the roses. I wish I'd planned ahead, then I would have brought you one. Next time. I promise.

"Well, I guess you don't have to worry about him," I told Coop, and he glanced from the note to me. Before he could respond though, there was a shout that echoed from the back. What the hell?

But Coop gripped my arm as the chant reached us.

"Fight! Fight! Fight!"

Oh. Crap.

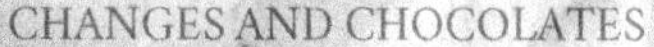

Chapter Three

P.S. I HA…

"**F**rankie wait…" Coop tried to stop me as I headed for the path to circle the house. The shouting had gotten louder, drowning out the music. Coop jogged next to me and caught my arm.

I hesitated and glanced at him as he caught my arm again.

"Not a good idea," he said. There were squeals, and then a shout.

That—that was Jake.

"Son of a bitch," Coop swore.

Jake was fighting, and a sudden fear swept through me. "Were you guys watching my car?" Had they seen someone who left the note?

"No," Coop told me firmly, but kept hold of my arm as we reached the gate to the pool. The partygoers were gathered in a half-circle, blocking our view of the covered porch. They were still chanting.

"Shut up," Jake bellowed again. "Dammit, Bubba—let him go."

Shock rippled through me. Ian?

The crowd scattered a little, but everyone had their phones out, and my phone buzzed in my pocket. So did Coop's. The noise level began to climb, and it gave me my first good view. Archie was sitting on the ground, his nose bloody and his face reddened and swelling. Jake had a hold of Ian and had dragged him a few feet back.

"C'mon," Coop said. "They can sort it out."

But my gaze locked with Archie's, and my heart squeezed. Ian had punched him. I knew why. I should have kept my mouth shut. "Coop, go help him."

My best friend stared at me. "You're kidding, right?"

"No, I'm not…" But Archie was already climbing to his feet, and I knew the moment Ian told Jake, because he swung his head to glare at Archie. With almost a smirk, Archie wiped at his nose and then picked a can out of one of the buckets and put it against his face.

"He's fine. Archie can take a hit. C'mon, I'll walk you back to the car, and then we can figure out how to get you out of the driveway."

"You know what—I'm fine. I'm going to leave the car here and just call a ride share." Guilt scraped through me as I pulled out my phone. The notifications were pictures from Instagram tagging the guys. And a text message with a video.

Coop said, "If you're taking a ride-share, then I'm definitely going with you."

A sigh speared through me. I could barely look away from Archie, and even as the partygoers scattered and the music climbed again, Archie, Jake, and Ian were still on the covered porch. "Coop…" My tone turned pleading as much as I hated to admit it. "I need air. Archie…"

"Got what he deserved, and like I said, he can handle a hit. You need a break, go back to your car. I'll haul people out there and make them move theirs. Or I go with you if you get in a stranger's car…"

"Why would she get in a stranger's car?" Cheryl's question made both of us jump. The blonde stood a couple of feet behind us, dressed in a tank top and shorts over what looked like a bikini. "Sorry, I had to run out, I forgot—something."

Something? You know, it didn't matter. "I'm blocked in, so Coop was going to get people to move their cars."

"Oh. I can help, Danny Galligan is parked right behind you, and Lars Cowen, I think he's right behind Danny…"

"They can keep their cars there, I'll take you home," Ian said from directly behind me. "I can get out no problem."

Coop sighed, and I glanced back to find Ian and Jake both staring at me.

"You sure?" Cheryl asked. "I mean it's no problem, I can just whip in there and get those guys moving. I think Rachel's in that line, too and Sharon."

"I'm sure," Ian said. I couldn't see Archie anymore, and Coop exhaled.

"The bike can get around the cars," Coop admitted.

"I'll bring you back to get your car later," Ian promised.

"Or I can," Jake said, but the tightness in his jaw worried me. "We're supposed to go out tomorrow night." The last came out as almost a soft reminder.

"Well, you're busy," Cheryl commented in a bubbly voice lacking any judgment. She gave me a side hug. "I'm going to rejoin the party if you're good." Still, one arm around me, she waited for me to let her off the hook.

"Yeah," I said slowly, trying not to notice the relief swimming across the guys' expressions, even Jake, who wore an air of aggravation. "Thanks, Cheryl."

"Anytime," she promised before giving me a squeeze. "See you later, guys!"

And then we were alone in our awkward little bubble.

"Does that mean you'll let me take you home? Or anywhere else you want to go?" Ian asked.

"Home would probably be best." Even if it meant coming back here the next day for my car, I could ride share back, none of them needed to know when.

Coop rubbed my arm once and nodded. "Text when you get there? Let me know you're okay?"

"Let *us* know you're okay," Jake said, turning the request into an order. "You *are* okay, right?"

"No," Coop told him before I could answer. "She's not. Don't be a dick right now."

"I'm not being a dick," Jake snapped, shooting Coop a dirty look. "I'm worried."

"We all are," Ian told him. "And I'm going to take her home."

"You coming back?" Coop asked.

"Undecided."

Jake frowned. "You're really not dressed to be on the bike. C'mon." Then he caught my hand and tugged me with him. We made it halfway back to the driveway before I got my hand free. "Sorry," he muttered. "But I have an extra jacket in my car. I think I might have some sweats, but you'd probably be swimming in them."

"I'm not going to race with her on the bike," Ian argued.

"I don't care. I don't want her hurt." Jake whirled and went toe to toe with Ian. "You should be careful with her, she's not dressed for your bike."

I had a headache.

Coop sighed, eyeing the pair before we locked gazes, then he rolled his eyes. I almost laughed, almost. As it was, a half-chuckle escaped. None of this was funny.

"You're just pissed because she said yes to letting me take her home," Ian countered. "Get over it…"

"You're an ass," Jake snorted.

"You're a prick," Ian countered. "What else is new?"

A throat clearing had all four of us turning. Jeremy stood there, his expression somewhat severe. "Miss Frankie, is everything well?"

No. No it wasn't, but I didn't want the guys to get into trouble. "Ian is taking me home, Jeremy, because I can't get my car out of the drive. I hope you don't mind if I leave it here for now."

"Of course not. Though I am happy to make up a room for you, away from everyone if you're looking for quiet, or I can call a car for you." Again, his focus was locked on me.

Ian shuffled. "I got it, Jeremy."

"I do not believe I was talking to you Mr. Bubba." The fact Jeremy could deliver that address in a straight face was a testament to his professionalism. We'd all cracked up the first time he'd greeted Ian that way, but over time—the formality stuck. "I believe Miss Frankie has had quite enough of you four at the moment."

He wasn't wrong, but the fact he included Archie in the *four* said no way did he not know I'd stayed the night before.

I was never escaping at the rate we were going.

"What if…" Ian began, and I twisted to glance at him. "What if I take you home, and if your mom is there, we come back and you can take Jeremy up on his offer?"

"What if she just stays?" Jake countered. "Then we don't have to worry about anything happening on the bike, and you can get some rest—though I don't blame you if you don't want to stay here."

"Guys…" Coop said with a sigh, and I held up a hand.

"Stop."

That pulled all their attention.

"Seriously, stop. I get it, you all care. You all want to fix this, and you all seem to think you can make decisions for me better than I can make them myself."

Jake opened his mouth to argue, but Coop elbowed him, earning a glare instead.

"I don't want to stay, I'd rather drive myself out of here and just be alone…"

Ian's face fell and guilt stabbed me all at once.

"Fine," Jake said. "Coop, grab people. They can move their damn cars." He pivoted and stalked off, Coop a half-step behind him.

Jeremy regarded me for a moment. "The offer for the car or the room stands, Miss Frankie. Would you like me to wait here with you until the young gentlemen have gotten the cars moved?"

The offer was sweet. "Thank you, Jeremy." Of everyone here, even knowing he had to have known, I didn't blame him. "But I'll be fine."

"As you say." He inclined his head. "I'll be just inside." The last he directed at Ian before he turned and re-entered the house, leaving Ian and I alone.

"We could just go right now," Ian offered.

The hell of it was, the idea tempted me. "I don't really think that's fair to you," I admitted.

"I don't care about fair to me," he said. "I care about you. I care that you're hurting and I'm part of the reason why." He held out his hand, and it was hard to miss the bruises on his knuckles.

"Did you have to hit him?" The earlier guilt swam up. As aggravated as I was with all of them, I didn't want them hurting, too. No, I didn't always understand myself.

"Yes," Ian said simply. "I did." He raised his brows, hand still outstretched. "I won't let anything happen to you."

I'd already stayed hours later than I'd planned. Tabbing open my phone, I went to messages and sent a group text.

Me

Ian is taking me home. Don't disrupt party.

Not that the sound level from the back had diminished.

Done, I pocketed my phone and took his hand. His bike was only a few steps away. He freed the second helmet and offered it to me as he pulled on his own. We were both in shorts. He opened one of the saddlebags and pulled out a jacket, then held it over to me.

I hesitated.

"It's going to be chilly on the bike." A weird thing to think, but it was cool out here. I slid it on as he straddled the bike. I could swim in the jacket, but I managed to push up the sleeves enough to free my hands, and then I climbed on behind him and wrapped my arms around him.

His whole body seemed to relax as he released a sigh. Pressing his hand over mine for a moment, he said, "Hang on." Three steps to back us up, and I barely caught sight of Archie standing just inside the alcove leading to his front door.

How long had he been standing there?

My heart wrenched, but Ian was already gliding between the cars and down the drive. In short order, we were on the road, and then I just held on as the breeze whipped over us. The engine rumbling beneath us was kind of soothing, and there was no one talking to me. Nothing to compete with the tangle of thoughts and knotty emotions binding me up. Even when we stopped for traffic lights, Ian would only put his hand over mine until the light changed, then he was reaching for the handlebars again. Yes, the air was cool against my legs, but I wasn't cold.

I'd never been at such an impasse before. I was furious with them and wanted to comfort them in the same breath. Hating the quiet disappointment on Archie's bruised face, even as I wanted to smack him for keeping the truth from me, twisted with the fact he'd discovered *his* dad was having an affair.

He claimed he was used to it, but how did you get used to one parent betraying another? I could barely wrap my mind around Mom dating a married man—an *obviously* married man. She'd met Archie's mother. There was no way she didn't know. At the same time, the guys kept making these choices for me, about me. My own guilt just made a total muck of it all. I wanted to throw up.

Ian slowed as we reached my apartment complex. The trip had taken too short a time, and in the same breath, it felt like years since I'd left. We coasted down the slight hill to where I usually parked.

Mom's car sat in the carport. I blew out a breath, my insides were shaky, but before I could get off the bike, Ian caught my hand. "Can I come up?"

With Mom there?

"That's not a good idea," I answered far more shakily than I cared to admit. I squeezed his hand once, then tugged. He let me go and I climbed off, then unbuckled the helmet.

He dropped the kickstand on his bike, shutting it off so it didn't continue to rumble, even if it was quiet. After stripping off his own helmet, he took mine then said, "Frankie…"

"Don't," I begged. Fuck, I'd been reduced to begging. "Please just let me go inside and hopefully just go to bed. I'm exhausted."

"I'm sorry," he whispered.

"I know."

The hell of it all. I believed him when he said he was sorry. Coop, too. Even Jake—despite the fact the only thing he was sorry about was that I got hurt.

Rising on my tiptoes, I pressed a kiss to his cheek, but pushed away when he would have turned his head. "Thank you for bringing me home. Please don't fight with Archie."

"He…"

"Didn't do anything I didn't want." I could admit that, and Ian sucked in a deep breath. "He was very clear in asking me, and he listened to everything I said. I'm mad because you guys kept things from me, and I'm angry with him because he knew what was happening and told all of you and not me. But I'm not angry at him for last night."

I wasn't that much of a hypocrite.

"Not sure I can say the same," Ian said. "But it doesn't change anything for me…I can dislike it, but never you. Call me tomorrow?"

Call him. Not he would call me.

"If I don't—will you let me have the time?"

"I can see you Monday," he said, though it clearly pained him to say it.

"Thank you."

"If you need a ride tomorrow—to get your car, tell me. No strings, I'll pick you up and take you over there and leave you alone."

"Ian…"

"I mean it." He studied me intently. "Nothing's changed for me, Frankie. I still want to take you to Homecoming. I still want to date. I still want you."

Tears burned in my eyes, and I had to look away. "You're killing me, Ian."

"No, I'm caring about you," he whispered, pressing a lingering kiss to my cheek. "Now go inside, I'm not leaving until I see you safely behind the door."

My heart still twisting, I made myself walk away. I made it all the way up the stone steps to the back door before I glanced back. As promised, Ian stood there, helmet in hand, watching me.

When he caught my gaze, he gave me a small smile. Tugging the keys from my pocket, I unlocked the door and gave him a little wave before I slipped inside and locked it behind me.

The kitchen was dark, save for a single low light over the stove. Tiddles trotted out to meet me and rubbed against my legs. Tory blinked at me from the sofa as I grabbed a soda out of the fridge and then headed toward my room. The living room was also dark with only a low light burning in the hall for navigation.

Mom's door was closed. There was no light under it. And no sounds drifted out—thank God. I had no idea if Archie's dad was there, and I really hoped he wasn't. To be honest, Mom might not even be in there, car or not. All three cats followed me into my room.

It hadn't changed since I left to go to the party, and at the same time, it seemed utterly different. After I changed into a tank top and sleep shorts, I crawled onto the bed and pulled out my phone to let the guys know I was home safe, and a series of messages and notifications were waiting on the screen.

Jake

You home safe?

Coop

Check in, okay?

Ian

I'm hanging out for another ten. Just in case.

Archie

...

My stomach cramped and I ran my hand over Tiddles as he bumped against me. Tabby had already claimed one of my pillows, and Tory jumped up into the window and began to groom. Tiddles crawled into my lap and purred as I stared at the messages.

Finally, I shook off the stupor and sent

Me

Home

to Jake and Coop.

To Ian, I typed

Me

It's quiet. I'm in bed. You can go. Thank you for the ride.

Jake

All good? No issues with Mom?

Coop

Not sure if we're staying tonight. Jake said he'd give me a ride home. Text if you need me.

Ian

Okay. I'm a phone call away. I mean it. Probably going home myself.

Me

Be safe

To Jake I just said

Coop didn't need an answer, but I sent a

anyway. That left Archie. Another notification popped up from Instagram, and I sighed. How many videos or pictures were there going to be of Ian punching Archie? I didn't want to know.

Archie's message still had three dots like he was typing something but hadn't sent it or wasn't done.

I took a long drink of my Coke, then typed in:

Time seemed to elongate, and I was debating switching over to my laptop and queuing up YouTube videos to watch until I could sleep, when the phone buzzed.

Chewing my lip, I stared at it.

Archie

Don't hate me, Frankie.

The last message wrenched me.

Me

I don't hate you.

Archie

Do you regret last night? Because I don't.

Did I? I told Ian I didn't, but I had to ask myself.

I nudged Tiddles off my lap and curled back against the pillows. It still smelled like Archie. One side of it. The other kind of smelled like Jake. I closed my eyes when I dragged the covers up because I could smell Archie on the sheets, too. It was almost like he was there, and it made me miss him.

I missed all of them.

As much as I hated their choices, I didn't want to fight with them.

Me

I don't. If you'd told me before—last night might not have happened. I'm still mad, but… no, I don't regret being with you.

Not when I could still feel him. That was the one sensation I hadn't been able to shake all night. The feel of him pushing into me, it was still there. The gentle ache of it. The way he'd wrapped around me after.

The best thing I should do was to stop talking to him.

Archie

Thank God. I can still taste you.

I groaned.

Archie

Fair warning. I'm not giving up on us. I like what we have and what we could be.

Me

Even if my mom is...

Archie

...

Archie

...

Archie

Your mom and my dad are their own problem. They aren't us. Don't let them define us.

But what about... my head hurt.

Me

How is your face?

A selfie popped onto the screen. The nosebleed was done, but there was a definite red mark on his cheekbone and just below his eye, another nearer to his nose.

Archie

How could you not adore this face?

I laughed. That was so Archie.

Archie

I think it gives me character.

Me

I think you're crazy.

Archie

About you.

Another image popped up. The one of the two of us in the living room getting ready to go out to dinner, and my breath caught in my throat. I hadn't realized he'd been looking at me. His expression was both intent and wondering as he smiled at me.

Archie

See?

Me

I'm going to sleep.

Archie

Night, Frankie. Call me tomorrow?

Me

No promises. Night, Archie. Feel better.

Archie

I'll feel better when you're not mad anymore.

Yeah, I didn't know how to answer that one, so I closed the messages and stared at the ceiling.

After putting the phone on silent and do not disturb, I turned it face down on the nightstand, then dragged my laptop up and loaded YouTube. I had no idea what I wanted to watch, so I just picked a channel and turned it on.

Movie flubs was as good as anything. But I barely saw the screen as Tiddles curled up next to me and I began to pet him. I was so tired.

But I wasn't going to sleep. When I turned my face toward the pillow and took a deep breath, I sighed.

I had no idea what to do.

None.

Not good.

Fightin' Words

Coop

She's home.

Jake

She texted. How was she, Bubba?

Bubba

How you'd expect. Her mom's car is here.
I'm staying in the parking lot for a few.

Coop

Good idea.

Jake

Coming back after?

Bubba

Probably not.

Jake

We all need to talk.

Coop

I think we said enough.

Jake

...

Coop

We did. We fucked up.

Bubba

Some of us more than others.

Archie

If you can punch me you can say my name.

Jake

Not now, Arch.

Archie

Now is good.

Coop

...

Jake

...

Bubba

If you're waiting for an apology, don't hold your breath.

Archie

Wouldn't dream of it.

Coop

...

Archie

Told you she spent the night.

Jake

...

Bubba

And skipped some key details.

Archie

It was and is none of your business.

Jake

Frankie is our business.

Coop

Yes, she is.

Bubba

You had sex with her. That explains so much about her reactions.

Archie

Fuck you, Bubba. I don't owe any of you explanations. Or do you want to ask Jake about his night with her?

Jake

...

Archie

Or what she and Coop got up to?

Coop

...

Archie

Here's one—what about you?

Bubba

What about me what?

Archie

You jealous because I got there first?

Jake

Don't be a dick.

Coop

Guys this isn't helping.

Jake

What happens with Frankie is private.

Bubba

Archie—you're a jackass.

Archie

That was my point. We don't talk about Frankie like this.

Coop

We're not starting it.

Archie

Too late.

Bubba

...

Jake

Guys...

Coop

Really not helping.

Bubba

Look, we said us. Fine. But you told her about your plans after sex. You...

Archie

Should have done what? Told her first?

Jake

Maybe.

Bubba

Well, let's see. Jake, did you bring it up at your slumber party?

Coop

You know what. It's done. Now we have to FIX it.

Bubba

She knows about her mom too.

Jake

Yeah. Don't know how to fix that one.

Archie

We can't. This is Edward's thing. The problem is when he dumps her mom.

Jake

One way of looking at it.

Coop

Cause that helps

Jake

She texted. That's something.

Archie

Yeah. I'll try to see her tomorrow.

Bubba

Don't. She needs space.

Jake

She and I have a date.

Bubba

When?

Jake

Tomorrow.

Archie

Good luck.

Jake

<middle finger emoji>

Bubba

She may not want to go.

Coop

And you can't make her.

Jake

Not losing her. Not after all this time.

Archie

Finally, you're speaking my language.

Coop

One other thing. Thorns.

Jake

He was a no show.

Coop

He was there.

Jake

?????

Archie

Bubba

Note on her car. He saw she was sad. So he gave her space. He said she'd hear From him soon.

Bubba

...

Bubba

On the upside, waiting for him meant she stuck around long enough for us to talk to her.

Jake

On the downside, there's some loser after our girl.

Archie

Key words there: our girl.

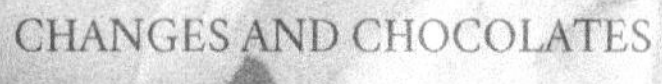

Chapter Four

LIKE MOTHER...

I'd had exactly one hangover in my life. On the one hand, I was aware my life hadn't been that long, but on the other hand, that single hangover was a miserable experience. The guys had gotten several boxes of wine, and while Archie complained about the quality, we all gave it a shot. I'm pretty sure I drank my body weight that day.

However, the biggest thing I remembered about drinking that wine was how exceptionally crappy I'd felt the next morning. I knew, logically, hangovers were about dehydration. Knowing and experiencing, however, were two totally different things.

When I woke up the Sunday morning after the party, my head pounded, my stomach churned, my mouth tasted like ass, and I felt like crap. There was no way the *single* glass of wine and that third of a bottle of beer that I had drunk had caused me a hangover. No, if anything, I'd been stone cold sober by the time I left with Ian. I'd definitely been stone cold sober while I was talking to the guys in text messages before I went to sleep.

No, this hangover had everything to do with raging disappointment.

Disappointment in the guys was bad enough. Worse was the disappointment in myself. And God help me, the disappointment in my mother.

As I stared at the sunlight filtering in underneath the blinds, a sinking realization hit me. I had to deal with my mother today. I guessed the cats understood how bad I felt. Because they hadn't woken me up at their normal 6 AM for breakfast. Once I opened my eyes and started shifting around, Tiddles' complaints suddenly increased in volume over wanting his breakfast. Tory and Tabby weren't much better. In fact, they were currently walking back and forth over my bladder, a surefire way to get me out of bed.

Pocketing the dread as much as I could, I dragged myself out of bed and made my way to the bathroom. The cats raced all around my feet and tried to hurry ahead. It wasn't long before they bumped the door after I closed it, probably disappointed when I didn't rush into the kitchen to open their can of food.

On the other hand, my bladder and I were having a disagreement. I lingered in the bathroom after, washing my hands and face, then brushing my teeth and then my hair. I lingered and kept waiting to hear Mom feeding the cats. I kind of needed some kind of clue as to whether she was home or not.

Since I'd told her I might not be home the night before, there was a possibility of running into Archie's dad in the kitchen.

Please, please don't let that happen.

Finally, I couldn't put off leaving the bathroom anymore. I had to get in there and do something. The cats needed to eat, or they were going to stage a full on revolt. As it was, they yowled as they raced around my path to the kitchen. The very quiet kitchen where no coffee waited and didn't even look like any coffee had been made. There were no dishes in the sink. Not a cup or a spoon. In fact, it looked exactly like I left it before I went to the party.

A little curl of dread began to tighten in my belly, but I didn't have time for that because the cats still needed to eat. I busied myself with that task. Soon, they were eating their food, happily ignoring me again. I got coffee started, because whether Mom was home or not, I really needed coffee. The sad truth was, Mom might be home. Archie's dad might be here.

In her bedroom.

What little appetite I'd developed fled. So I concentrated on what I could do. I made coffee, I checked the freezer for something for dinner, even as I thought about the fact that I was probably not going to be home for dinner it was probably a good idea to look.

The only reason I wouldn't be home was if I went out with Jake. My head pounded. Crap, I was supposed to go out with Jake later that evening. Or—at least spend the evening with him.

Was that still on? Did I want it to be on?

When the coffee finished brewing, I poured a huge mug full of it, uncaring whether or not I left enough coffee for Mom, because I had no idea if she was here or out. Maybe they were hiding in her bedroom because they heard me coming, I didn't know. Right now, I really didn't want to. The fact I couldn't stop thinking about where they were or what they were doing was going to make me crazy.

Coffee in hand, I made my way back to my bedroom, moving as quietly as I dared past Mom's door in the small hope that if they were in there and they were asleep, maybe I wouldn't wake them up. No, I didn't live in a fantasyland. I was, however, not eager for that particular conversation. What would I even say?

When I was twelve years old, my mother came into my bedroom while I'd been sprawled out reading a book.

She said, "Frankie, you need to make a phone call for me."

Wasn't the first time my mom had asked me to do something strange, and I'd made calls for her before—like for pizza and stuff. So I said, "Who do you want me to call?"

She said, "Kenny."

Mom had been dating Kenny for a long time. When I'd first met him, he'd been little more than a guy with a drawl and a kind smile. But he'd always been nice to me and did generous things for us. He once took me to the state fair up in

Dallas. Well, actually, he took me and Mom. But he'd taken me on all the rides, even the ones Mom wouldn't go on. He played the games and won me a stuffed bear. He was fun. He liked to play games. Even got along with my friends.

"Okay, why am I calling Kenny?" I'd asked. Someday, far into the future after that particular day, I'd learned to not ask that kind of question.

"I just need you to tell him I don't want to see him anymore. Tell him not to come around and not to call."

My heart sank. "Why?"

"I don't have to explain that to you. I just need you to call him."

"But if you don't want to see him, why do I have to call him? I like Kenny. He's fun, and he's supposed to take me to the movies this weekend with Coop and Bubba."

"Frankie, I don't need your opinion. I need you to do this for me. Don't ask questions, just take care of it, okay, sweetie? " Mom was insistent, and she wouldn't answer any other questions about it, so I did what I had to do.

She handed me her phone, and I chose his contact. When he answered, I said, "Hi, it's Frankie. I don't want to be the one calling to tell you this, but Mom doesn't want to see you anymore. She said you shouldn't call or come by to see us ever again."

And I wanted to cry. But I said it all perfectly, exactly how Mom had told me to say it. The dead silence on the other end of the phone choked me.

Had he heard what I said? Was I going to have to say it again? I didn't want to have to say it again. I didn't want to say it the first time.

"Sweetheart, it's okay," Kenny said, his now familiar drawl slow and sweet. "You take care of yourself and your mama, okay?"

And while Mom had said that was all I needed to say to him on the phone, I added, "I'm going to miss you, you're a good friend."

"I'll miss you too, kiddo. I wish it could be different. But sometimes you just gotta listen to your mom. You take care, okay?" I thought Kenny felt as bad for having to say that to me as I did for saying it to him. The whole time I was on the phone, Mom stood in the doorway to my room watching, listening, and not saying a word.

Into the quiet on the phone, I'd said, "Hey, Kenny?"

"Yeah, Frankie, I'm still here."

"I know I'm only twelve, but in six years I'll be eighteen, and if you still want to go to movies and stuff, you can still be my movie buddy." And I glared at my mother the entire time I said it.

He'd chuckled and said—something inane. What was he going to say to a twelve-year-old that just said she'd go out with him when she was eighteen? It had been a stupid thing to say, but I'd been so mad at my mom. I *liked* Kenny. I didn't always like the guys she dated, but I wanted her to be happy.

Why couldn't she have been happy with him?

After I got off the phone, Mom walked out of my room with her phone in hand and not saying a word.

I didn't really see her for the rest of the day. I had to tell Coop when he came over that we couldn't go to movies anymore because Kenny was gone. Then I had to tell him why.

He stared at me like I'd grown a second head. I couldn't blame him, because it kind of felt that way. Kenny was my friend. I thought Mom really liked him. They'd dated for over a year. They had dated long enough that he actually spent the night in the apartment every now and then. Not often. Mom was very strict about the fact the people she dated didn't stay at our place. Still, I never forgot him, and I hadn't seen him again. If Mom had?

Would I even know?

As I sat on the bed in my room drinking my coffee, that scene replayed itself over in my head, over and over and over again.

Did I have calling Archie's dad and breaking up with him for my mom to look forward to in my future?

Or worse, would he end up having those visiting privileges because they'd been seeing each other long enough?

Wait. How long had Mom and Archie's dad been seeing each other? She'd been dating someone since the end of my junior year. All those business trips over the summer—and part of the reason I hadn't been able to tour colleges—had they actually been business trips? Or had they been a way for her to go out with Archie's dad?

I hated the fact that I had to ask myself these questions.

By the time I finished my coffee, the residual drowsy, groggy, headachy, I felt like crap feeling had passed. I was just tired. It was still early, but I had laundry and homework to do because I hadn't done any Friday night, and nothing got done on Saturday. I had stuff that was due the following week. I was way behind on my study schedule. And I didn't have to go to work today.

That made my decision for me, I went to get my laundry sorted so I could take it over to get the clothes washed. As I was sorting it out, I found Archie's T-shirt and his sweats along with Jake's boxers.

I still had no idea what I was going to do.

Steeling my spine, I went ahead and sorted their clothes in with mine. It wasn't like they didn't need to be washed. That idea, however, took my attention to the bed. Technically, I should strip it and wash the bed sheets and comforter. But I really didn't want to wash the sheets, and I really didn't want to wash the pillowcases.

I was pathetic; I didn't want to wash them, because I didn't want to wash the scent off. I didn't know when the next time was that they would be over—if at all. It wasn't because of what they wanted, but because I didn't know what I wanted.

So I compromised. I pulled the comforter off to wash it and left everything else in place.

Laundry gathered in the basket, I slung on my backpack so I could take my homework with me and got quarters out of the jar I kept on my dresser. As I turned around, I paused and stared at the roses sitting on the desk by the window. The very first rose had begun to wilt. The second two had opened full, but were now starting to droop. The three were just now blooming, while the four and the five looked like they were going to any time now. I needed to refill their water when I came back up.

I thought about the note that I'd gotten the night before. The only reason I went to the party was to set the boundaries with the guys. To hold them accountable for what they had decided to do. The only reason I stayed was so that I could meet this person, because they said they were going to be there. Then, it turned out I was too sad for them to see. Hence the note.

Great, I went from being untouchable to being sad. Such an improvement.

Seizing my basket, I snagged my keys and headed for the door. I was halfway to the laundry room when it hit me; I still had to go get my damn car.

Laundry took a couple of hours. During that time, I managed to get most of my reading done for AP European history, about 1/3 of the paper for AP Lit drafted, I even had time to do some calculus. Three of the problems on the calculus homework made me pause, however, and I was half tempted to pick up my phone and text Ian, because they were the kind of problems that usually gave him issues.

The fact that my fingers twitched and itched to reach for my phone made me not do it. It was still on do not disturb from the night before, and I hadn't turned the sound on yet. Actually, I hadn't even looked at it. I was being chicken.

I was halfway through folding the last load when Coop appeared in the doorway.

That was predictable.

"Sorry," he said, eyeing me carefully. "You weren't answering your phone, or the text messages, and I got worried. So I thought I would check to see if you were here."

"Here I am," I told him as I continued folding the clothes. "I just haven't been up to dealing with my phone yet today. Wanted to get ahead on my homework before I got distracted."

His expression brightened, and he tilted his head. "So you were going to answer us later?"

"I don't know what I'm gonna do," I admitted. "It's the hardest part of this, Coop. I trusted you guys. I trusted you with everything. And now I'm sitting here wondering why. And then I hate myself for wondering why, because you guys are my friends. But if you are my friends, why would you do those things?"

It all spilled out of me in a rush, and I had to blink rapidly to keep the tears from pooling. I wasn't going to cry. I needed to find a way to deal with this that didn't involve yelling, screaming, or crying. Though all three sounded pretty good right now.

"I don't know how to fix it either," Coop admitted. "I just know that I want to. We were wrong. I don't know how else to tell you we were wrong. Did we want to protect you? Yes."

I stared at him and shook my head. "Isn't that what got us into trouble in the first place?"

"Because we told people they couldn't date you?"

"Because you wanted to 'protect me,' wasn't that what you said?"

"Yes, that is exactly what we said. Frankie, I can't apologize for wanting to protect you. I won't. I mean, I've been here, I've seen some of the crap that went down. I know that you don't talk about it, and you don't ever want to talk about it. But I know how lonely you get. I know the crap your mom has done."

I held up a hand. And narrowed my eyes. Coop blew out a breath and backed up a step. Discussing my mother and that part of my past was truly off-limits. I know the guys didn't understand, but she was my mom. Some days, I didn't even know if I liked her, but she was still my mom.

"Let's keep this about us," I said slowly. "The only part about my mom is the part where she is seeing Archie's dad." I really needed to find a new way to think about that. "You know what, I'm not even going to call it my mom seeing

Archie's dad. I want to call it bad meatloaf."

He raised his eyebrows and stared at me. "Bad meatloaf?"

"Yes, bad meatloaf. You know how it sits in your stomach like a rock, and it's dry, and tastes like ass, but you still have to eat it because it's the bad meatloaf that's for dinner, and you don't get to eat anything else?"

"Yeah, and I avoid that like the plague if I can," Coop said, a small smile forming on his lips. "That's what cereal for dinner is for."

I shrugged. "So that whole thing is bad meatloaf." That way, I didn't have to say my mom and Archie's dad so much or ever again, if at all possible.

"So, we didn't tell you about bad meatloaf," Coop said slowly, and for a moment, his lips twitched. And I have to admit, so did mine. "I can't change that now. I can honestly say that knowing what I know now that I wouldn't go back and tell you anyway. You're right, Frankie, she is your mom. How am I supposed to tell you something like that?"

The hell of it was, I didn't know. "I don't even know if I would've believed you guys if you *had* told me." For a moment, his shoulders sagged.

"I don't know if you would have believed us either. I know that you would hate to have heard it from us. You don't like telling us the bad stuff, I can imagine you don't want to hear it either."

I dropped the shirt I was folding into the basket and reached for the next one — it was Archie's — and Coop's eyes narrowed on it as I folded it. The flare of his nostrils told me the moment he noticed Jake's boxer shorts. Course, he might not have pinned them for Jake, but they were boxers, and I didn't own any except for an old faded pair of his.

I didn't comment on the clothing, and neither did he. I just kept folding.

"I don't know what I want to do," I told him again. "Everything just seems off. I'm supposed to go out with Jake later. Or maybe Jake was supposed to come over here." Oh God, that would be even worse, if Jake was here while my mom was here.

"I know, he's really hoping you don't back out."

I laughed a little, and then I blew out a breath. Because for a split second there, I thought about asking Coop to let Jake know I didn't want to go out. Not until I knew how I really felt.

But I wasn't my mother. If I was gonna let one of these guys down or tell them I wasn't going out with them, they were going to hear it from me.

"What are you thinking?"

"Thinking I'm a little messed up. And that I miss my best friends. I don't know how to make this so I can trust you guys again."

"Have you ever thought that maybe what we need is time?"

"Well, we have some of that," I told him. "The college applications are due, and Homecoming is around the corner, and you guys have my schedule all partitioned up for dates and I don't know whether I'm coming or going, and then there's the bad meatloaf."

"That meatloaf we could just throw out," Coop said flatly. "As for the rest of it, if you need time, you tell us you need time. Just *don't* stop talking to us." Then he took a step forward, and when I didn't withdraw or make any motion for him to stay back, he came all the way up to me.

I dropped the last piece of clothing I was holding in the basket and turned around, and when he opened his arms, I stepped right into them. Because this was Coop. This was my best friend. He was there through skinned knees and busted elbows and the first time I lost a tooth. He got into a fight for me, and I got into fights for him.

"Don't stop talking to me," he said. "Can you do that?"

Holding on, I rubbed my cheek against his shirt, and then I nodded. "I can try," I said. It wasn't quite a promise. "But I'm really hungry, and I need to go get my car."

Coop laughed. "Want to take a ride share with me, and then we'll grab lunch after we get your car?"

You know what? I did.

"This doesn't mean I'm not still mad," I warned him.

"Understood," he said, his expression serious. "This is just refueling."

I laughed. "Well, we do need to eat."

"That we do," he agreed with me, and then after a light squeeze, he released me. Turning, he snagged the basket. "I'm ready to go now, so let's just drop this off and I'll call the ride share?"

I gathered my stuff back into my backpack and eyed my leggings and tank top. I wasn't really dressed for going out out. Hell, I didn't even have a bra on.

"You look fine," Coop told me. "If you're scared of being seen in public, we can just get drive-thru and drive over to the lake and feed the ducks with the leftovers."

I snorted. We hadn't done that in years. "I still have a ton of homework to do," I told him. "So food and then probably back here."

He sighed. "You can't blame a guy for trying."

"No," I agreed with him. "I guess I can't."

His smile grew at that admission. "Good to know."

Chapter Five

FORGIVENESS AND STUFF

At the apartment, Coop waited outside while I carried the laundry in. It was still quiet. Apparently, I didn't have to worry about bad meatloaf this morning. Leaving the laundry basket and backpack in my room, I snagged my wallet and sunglasses before I headed back out. Coop straightened, phone in hand to show me how far away our ride was.

"Six minutes," he said.

"Cool." I locked the door, and we walked down to the parking lot to wait. It was hard to miss my mom's car, sitting there like a testament to the fact she wasn't home.

"So I was thinking," Coop said.

"That's dangerous," I reminded him, the retort as automatic as saying "bless you" or "gesundheit" when someone sneezed.

"I know, right?" He grinned, and before I knew it, I grinned, too.

"*Anyway*, you were thinking… and you should probably spit it out before it dies of loneliness."

His chuckle warmed me from head to toe. "Keep it up, Frankie."

"No, no. I'm good now."

"No, seriously. Keep it up, because I want to be able to plead self-defense for zinging you back."

Peeking up at him, I slid my sunglasses on and smiled. "I'm good now."

"You sure?"

"At least for the next five minutes." It was easy to settle into the banter. This was me and Coop, this was how we rolled. "After that, no promises."

"Good to know. *Anyway,*" he mimicked my earlier emphasis. "I was thinking about Halloween."

"Why?"

That was still a few weeks off. Not that everything wasn't closing in on us. We were barely three weeks out from Homecoming, Coop's birthday was around the corner, and we had to have our applications in at the first of October. We got a small breather, then Archie's birthday was right before Halloween. So much more going on than Halloween.

"Because—I want to go trick or treating."

Wait… what? I stared at him.

"Hear me out."

"I'm listening," I said, uncertain of whether I should be or not. This sounded like a trip to crazytown.

"You remember when we were kids, and we'd coordinate our costumes?"

"Yeah, I don't remember it as coordinating. We were supposed to be Jessie and Woody one year, but you decided you wanted to be Dash instead. The year after that, we were going to go as villains, but Mom didn't want me to dress up as the Queen of Hearts, so I got to be Alice and you were…" Wait, what was Coop dressed up as that year?

"A cop," he admitted with a wince. "And you painted your face white and became a zombie Alice."

"Right, oh—right." I'd even added blood and used oats from the oatmeal to create flecks of brain. My mom had not been amused. I giggled. People had been so grossed out, and Coop kept offering to arrest me.

"So, this year—we should coordinate. Maybe pick out something fun, we can do it and give out candy, or we can roam around like when we were kids and do it all over again."

I laughed. "Coop, most people get snotty when teenagers trick or treat." We'd kind of outgrown that, right?

"Screw 'em," he said with a shrug. "We can roam and have fun, be silly and relaxed. How many chances are we gonna have to be *kids* again after this? Next year, we're at college."

It loomed over us like a juggernaut on relentless approach. "Yeah…" I could concede that point. "Archie will probably throw a party though." He loved his parties. Well, he had loved them. Last night might have changed some of it. I winced. "It's also right around his birthday."

"So we go to the party after. C'mon, Frankie—just think about it?"

"What are we gonna dress up as?" It wasn't agreement, but I had to admit, the idea wasn't bad. Our ride pulled up before he could answer. Our driver was a woman named Yolanda, and she was really nice. She was older than Mom, but she chatted with us on the way to Archie's house, but with an audience, Coop and I put our earlier chat on hold.

We arrived all too swiftly, and she let us out at the base of the driveway.

"What about Green Arrow and Black Canary?" Coop suggested as we walked up the drive.

"From the show or the comic?" I hadn't read the comics in forever, but Coop had loved almost all of them.

"Fishnets, like the comic." His playful leer made me roll my eyes. "Or we could do cops and robbers. You can even be the cop this time."

I snorted.

"I know—Anakin and Padme."

"She had dark hair."

"Details," he said with a wave.

"Supergirl and you can be Jimmy Olsen."

"Ouch." He clutched at his chest. "Where's the love?"

The pack of cars from the night before was gone. My mouth went a little dry as I spotted my car, sitting by itself. "I'd say Violet and Dash, but again—I don't have dark hair."

"Well, we don't have to go as characters. We could go as Joy and Sadness."

I slanted a look at him. Yeah, I'd already been labeled the sad one. "Maybe not so meta."

He snorted. "John Wick and his dog?"

Okay. "Rude." I shoved him and he laughed.

The slap of shoes on the driveway had me turning, and my heart caught. Archie jogged toward us, his bare chest gleaming with sweat. His muscles flexed as he moved and rippled along his legs. There was a sweatshirt tied around his waist, and he tugged the ear buds off as he slowed.

"Hey," he said, his breath coming in little pants. The effect took me back to Friday, and I licked my lips. He really was gorgeous, even with the bruise darkening his cheek and just below his eye. It wasn't quite a black eye, but it looked like it hurt. His disheveled hair stuck up in places and clung to his damp forehead. While he wasn't as in to sports as Jake or Ian, he kept fit.

"Hi," I greeted him.

"Morning, Arch," Coop said as he leaned back against my car.

"Glad to see you made it," Archie said quietly. Guilt twisted in my gut. I'd planned to just grab my car and go. I was pretty sure Archie recognized that. But he didn't say anything other than, "Did you sleep okay?"

"Yeah," I admitted. "I think I was just exhausted." Which wasn't a lie. "Did you?" I'd left in the middle of his party.

He shrugged. "Not bad. Got to bed late, took us a while to get rid of everyone. Then Jake took Coop home."

Shame skated through me. Part of the plan had been all of us spending the night. At the same time, I couldn't have stayed, not after…

A car moved up the driveway, and my heart pounded like a fist against my ribs. The vehicle slowed, and Archie pivoted to face it. It was a sleek, black Town Car. The driver stepped out then moved around and opened the rear passenger door.

Muriel Standish exited in her all her graceful, poised glory, and my stomach plummeted. Archie's mom was gorgeous, self-possessed, and classy as hell. She was also the wife of the man my mom was screwing.

Bile coated the back of my throat.

"Archibald," his mother greeted him.

"Muriel," he said in the exact same cool tone she'd used. The driver was removing two suitcases from the trunk as Muriel eyed her son expectantly. With a sigh, Archie narrowed the distance and pressed a kiss to her cheek. He towered over her by a couple of inches, even while she was in heels.

"Do me a favor and take those in for Jeremy, yes?" Then she glanced past Archie to me and Coop. I had never wanted to be in a place less.

"Francesca," she said slowly, sweeping her gaze over me. I straightened, but there wasn't much I could do for the tank top and leggings, much less lack of bra. "Cooper."

"Mrs. Standish," Coop greeted her, and he wrapped an arm around my shoulders. "We were just heading out to grab food, I'm starving."

"Nonsense," she said, glancing at me again, and Archie straightened behind her, his eyes narrowing. "I haven't seen you kids in ages. We really must catch up. Francesca, sweetheart, come…" She held out her hand toward me. "I want to hear about those Harvard plans Archibald mentioned. Is that still in the offing?"

If I ignored the overture, I was rude. If I didn't—oh God, how did I do this?

"Muriel," Archie said. "They were just swinging by to drop some homework off. Not to visit."

"But they're hungry," Muriel said, and her gaze fixed on me. Did she know? Was that why…? "So come on, dear. I haven't seen you since last spring, it's been ages."

Dread curdling in my gut, I forced my hand to take hers, and she smiled.

"That's better." She tucked my arm through hers. "You were fond of Jeremy's French toast if I recall correctly."

"Um, yes, ma'am," I told her. "It's really good."

"Excellent."

There was quiet behind me, but as Jeremy opened the door to greet us all, Archie and Coop were right behind me.

"Good morning, madam," Jeremy greeted her. "Miss Frankie. Mr. Coop. Mr. Archie."

"Jeremy, darling, coffee please—at least two gallons, and breakfast for the children. Francesca prefers the French toast."

"Of course," he said.

"Archibald, you and Cooper take the bags up and then do go shower. You smell terrible."

"Uh huh," he grunted. "C'mon, Frankie, you and Coop can play video games while you wait for me."

But Mrs. Standish didn't release my hand. "Ah-ah," she said. "Francesca and I need to talk."

"Muriel…" Archie began, but she gave him a cool look and his mouth closed, even as his jaw tensed. I was going to throw up. "Do not be such a pill. Hurry, I'm not having Jeremy hold breakfast for you." Then with a dismissive look, she headed for the dining room and tugged me with her. Panicked, I threw a look at Coop but he was already following me.

Archie mouthed *sorry, I'll be right back* and half ran up the stairs. Once we were in the dining room, Mrs. Standish finally let me go, and she shrugged out of her jacket. She was dressed in a cool cream silk blouse and flowing dark blue pants. Seriously, she looked like she could have walked off the pages of some fashion magazine. Her hair was perfectly coifed and her cosmetics flawless.

She did not look like a woman who could possibly have an almost eighteen-year-old child. Dark hair and eyes so like Archie's, my guilt turned into ice that left me freezing. She smiled. "Sit down, children, and tell me all about Harvard." She motioned to the table with a well-manicured hand, the gold bracelets on her wrist jangled a little, and it was impossible to miss the pair of diamond rings on her left ring finger.

"I um…have my application all ready to go, I just have to finish the last essay, and then I can send it on the first." It sounded pretty weak to my own ears and without even an nth of confidence. Still, with no other choice, I sat down. Thankfully, Coop grabbed the chair next to mine as Mrs. Standish chose the chair at the head of the table to my left.

"Well that sounds dreadfully simple, what do you want to study?"

That was the ten thousand dollar question. "Writing, probably. Journalism is definitely on the list. But I'm a little torn—to be honest. I thought I'd spend the first couple of weeks testing out all the classes and finding the right fit."

"Well, that's certainly one strategy," she said, then glanced at Jeremy as he carried in a tray with mugs of coffee for each of us, me and Coop included.

"Breakfast will be ready in five minutes."

"Wonderful. You're such a dear. I've had a dreadfully long weekend with such terrible service. Glad to be back where I'm important again."

Jeremy gave her an indulgent smile, and while I didn't think the pointed comments were directed at me, they still landed. "You're home now," Jeremy soothed. "I'll make sure everything is just the way you like it."

I wrapped my hands around the coffee, desperate for any kind of warmth. Then Mrs. Standish focused on me.

"You should have at least a secondary field of study you feel passionate about. Journalism is all sound-bites these days and not much in the way of ethics or class."

Ouch.

"I don't think that's true of all journalists," I countered. "Granted, it's a click-bait driven world, but the facts still mean something. They would to me."

"Which is glorious, darling, but having scruples won't keep you warm at night. Going after what you want requires drive and conviction. You have to want it more than the next person and not care who it hurts in the process." She gave me a thoughtful look. "I don't know that you could handle that."

"Muriel," Archie said as he strode back into the room, his voice a warning and one I rarely heard out of him, much less in context with his parents. "Frankie's got more ethics in her pinky than some people we know, and she's damned determined. She can do whatever she wants."

"I'm sure she does." Though her tone said quite the opposite. "At least she seems prepared for her application, though Harvard is a challenging option for even the best of students. What are your safety schools?"

This was not a conversation I wanted to have. "NYU, Stanford, and UCLA."

I listed the schools we'd talked about a couple of weeks earlier.

"But Harvard has charm," Coop said. "We're all applying. Law of averages says one of us has to get in."

Mrs. Standish suddenly narrowed her eyes at Archie. "Since when are you applying to Harvard?"

"Since ninth grade," he told her bluntly and dragged out the chair opposite me, which put him to his mother's left. Jeremy carried in plates. "Doesn't mean I'm not applying to MIT or NYU or Stanford or UCLA. We're keeping our options open."

"I see," Mrs. Standish said, tapping a manicured nail against the side of her mug. "What does your mother think about you going so far away, Francesca?"

I froze, but Coop pressed his leg against mine as he leaned back for Jeremy to set a plate of French toast with eggs and bacon in front of him and another in front of me. There was already a ball of butter in a little dish next to the French toast on my plate, but Jeremy added a boat of syrup for us to share. Mrs. Standish was the only one not eating French toast, in fact, all she had was regular toast with some butter and jam.

"Probably the same thing you do, Muriel," Archie said with a smirk. "When will the bother be over so we can get out of the house?"

His mother scoffed. "It is no bother, Archie. We can afford to send you wherever you want to go."

Oh, that hit landed, and Coop stiffened next to me.

"Amazingly," Archie said without an ounce of niceness in his tone. "I can afford to go wherever I want and to take whoever I want with me. But let's not bore our guests with finances. It's rude."

Her eyes narrowed and her lips compressed, then the tight expression washed away to a veneer of politeness. "Very well, then tell me how many are we hosting for your birthday party in a few weeks? Amanda's girls are both seventeen and will be coming. I expect you to be nice to them. Either would make a great match."

Archie rolled his eyes. "Not having a party."

That surprised me, and I stared at him.

"Pretty much over parties…"

Mrs. Standish lifted a piece of her toast, then paused to stare at him. "Then you shouldn't throw hooligan parties. And dear, you had best cover up that bruise before tomorrow."

"I earned it," Archie said with a shrug and cut into his food. "And my hooligan parties are a blast with the right people." He cut a look at me, but it was brief, before he focused on his mother. "I'm going to do my birthday my way. So don't worry about the party."

Coop nudged my knee, and I glanced at him. He nodded to my food. My stomach was in knots. It smelled fantastic, but I wasn't sure I could choke any of it down.

"Archibald…"

"Nope," he said. "Not doing it, and I'll be eighteen, so you can't make me. If you want to throw a party so all your friends can congratulate you on having made it to the end of your sentencing and being free of me, go right ahead. I'm spending my birthday with my friends."

I shoved a bite of the French toast into my mouth. It was a crying shame that I could barely taste it. Jeremy made the best French toast ever. But the rest of the meal continued in this same vein with Mrs. Standish making these very polite, if snide observations, while asking pointed questions.

At one point, she reminded me that the average student graduated with hundreds of thousands of dollars in student debt that could put a chokehold on my life for the next thirty years, and I might consider downsizing my expectations to something more reasonable.

I had no idea how I ate the food. It sat in my stomach like a rock. Archie kept trying to distract her, but she would only be dissuaded for a few moments. Coop got her when he brought up studying psychology because he had plenty of material on family relationships to do a dozen different dissertations, and his pointed look at her actually shut her up.

That lasted five minutes.

But it was enough time for me to finish my food. Now, I needed to make excuses to get out of there. "Thank you so much for breakfast," I told her. "You really didn't need to go to all that much trouble."

"It was no trouble at all, Francesca. I am glad we were able to spend this time together."

I wanted desperately to say *me too* and sound like I meant it, but all I managed was. "I appreciate it." Which was a damn lie, but it was better than the alternative, which involved a lot of primal screaming. "But we need to go, I have a lot of homework to do…"

"Of course," Mrs. Standish said, rising from the table. Then she reached over and pressed her cheek to mine as she kissed the air. "Always so good to see you." Then, still gripping my hand, she said, "You know, it was good to see you, and I don't get to see you enough. You and your mother should come to dinner this week. All of us together. It will be lovely. I won't take no for an answer."

Yep. That did it. I wanted to die.

"Muriel, Frankie's got a really busy schedule," Archie said smoothly, and he covered our hands and then disengaged me from her. I clutched at his fingers almost desperately. "Tell you what, we'll have her let us know if she or her mom are free. Besides, I'm pretty sure you have at least three events on your calendar this week already."

"I can always make time for your friends, Archibald. And I haven't seen Madeline in even longer than the last time I saw Francesca. I'll be sure to call you dear, and do let your mother know."

Kill. Me.

"Thank you, Mrs. Standish."

Archie rolled his eyes and turned. His exit from the room pulled me with him, and I dug my nails into his hand. Coop was a half step right behind us. Then we were out the front door and the cooler air hit me like a slap in the face. I let go of Archie's hand and put both of mine over my face as I fought to catch my breath.

I didn't make it another step before Archie wrapped an arm around me and tugged me back against him. "Don't worry about the dinner, I'll shitcan that whole thing, and I'm so sorry Muriel is such a bitch."

"She knows, doesn't she?" God I was gonna be sick.

"Probably," Archie admitted. "Muriel and Edward are… well, neither of them are stupid. I hadn't really thought about what she knows or didn't, but after that little stunt? Yeah, she knows."

I dropped my hands to his arm and met Coop's worried gaze. Archie gave me a gentle squeeze, and I leaned back against him. He smelled like his soap and his shampoo.

"I'm sorry," he whispered against my ear. "I was trying to get her to knock it off. Next time, I'll just pick a fight. Trust me, I can piss her off like no one's business."

A laugh escaped me, but it was more a sound of disbelief than humor.

Coop flashed me a small smile.

"Take her home?" Archie asked, and he had to be looking at Coop. "Unless you need to go somewhere else—is your mom…"

"I don't know."

"Bad meatloaf," Coop said.

"Excuse me?" Archie grunted.

"That whole situation—we're calling it bad meatloaf." Coop grinned at me. "The really dry kind you get forced to eat because it's all there is for dinner."

Archie snorted, then pressed a kiss to the side of my head, almost nuzzling my hair. "You don't ever have to have bad meatloaf. That's an affront to the taste buds."

His arm around me helped. The hug grounded me and kept me on my feet at the same time. Gradually, the panic ebbed and I could take deeper breaths.

"So…is there bad meatloaf at home?" He sounded like he couldn't believe he was asking the question.

"I don't know, the kitchen was clean and there were no dishes when I got home last night."

"So fifty-fifty." Archie hummed.

"Hey, you can always come study at my place," Coop offered. "I'd say go to the library, but it's closed on Sundays."

True enough.

"Well, if I know Muriel, she's going to head up and sleep for the rest of the day soon. She always needs a good rest after she's been away. We could sneak back up to my wing, and you guys can hide there."

"You're both sweet," I admitted. "But I need to go home, I need to get this homework done, and I have to decide about Jake tonight."

"What about him?" Archie asked, not mentioning my sweet comment.

"She's got a date," Coop supplied. "Just not sure about going yet."

"You should," Archie said slowly, and when I twisted to look at him, he loosened his hold but didn't let me go completely. "Yeah, I know I can't believe

I'm saying it either. But going out would get you out of the house, and you know he cares."

I knew they all cared.

"We all want to make this right."

Coop had said the same thing.

"Time," I told him quietly. "I think I need time."

Archie nodded slowly. "Time we can do—but are we talking minutes? Hours? Days? Give me some frame of reference?"

"I don't know," I admitted except… "I want to forgive you. I want to forgive all of you."

Relief punched through his expression, and he pressed his forehead to mine. "Thank fuck."

I laughed, then brushed my fingers to his cheek. "I'm trying—but I need the time."

"You take whatever you need, Frankie. Just—don't disappear again. Please?"

Coop coughed once behind me, and Archie and I both glanced at him. He raised his eyebrows. "Same thing I asked. Just keep talking to us."

"I promise to try—can that be enough for now?"

I looked from one to the other.

"Hell yes, that's enough," Archie said. "Do you mind if I kiss you?"

I blinked. Well… "I'm still mad, Archie."

"That's fair, doesn't change my request."

He raised his eyebrows, and I leaned up and pressed a light kiss to his lips, but when he would have deepened it, I pulled away. Licking his lips once, he nodded. "Go on." Then he looked past me to Coop. "Look after her."

"Already planned on it."

Battling the strange reluctance, I let to go of Archie and headed to the car. He followed us, and closed the door for me as I started the engine. Rolling the window down, I looked up at him. "Are you going to be all right with your mom?"

He laughed. "Muriel isn't going to do anything to me, Frankie. Like I said in there, I don't need their money. They know it, too." He crouched so he could be on eye level with me. "You didn't do anything wrong. All of this crap is on them. The rest of it is on us. We fucked up. We'll fix it. They—you know what, let them deal with their mess. It's not our problem."

"Easier said than done," I admitted. Coop covered my hand on the gearshift.

"That's why you have us, even if you're still mad. That doesn't mean we can't help."

"What psycho boy said," Archie grinned, then looked past me to Coop. "Psychology? Seriously? That was a nice zing."

"I wasn't making it up," Coop told him. "I have been thinking about. That and film making."

Archie and I locked gazes, and we both grinned. "It's good to know we're all fixed on what we want to be in life," I said. "So much easier for planning."

"Nah," Archie countered. "We're flexible, and I think that makes us a much better fit." Then he leaned in and kissed me again, firm, but gentle and swift. "Take care of you, I'll see you in the morning with coffee. Hot or cold?"

"I know I said hot earlier, but I think iced would be better. Double the extra shot of espresso?"

"You got it," he said with a smile. "And go out with Jake. Tell him he can start making it up to you by making you smile."

Then he backed off and motioned us toward the driveway. I glanced at the rearview mirror to find him watching after us, and I raised my hand out the window to wave at him before I turned out.

The last hour and a half had been so surreal, but… "Coop?"

"Hmm?"

"Was that weird for you?"

"The breakfast? Hell yes, it was weird. That woman needs to be medicated."

I groaned. "No, that part was definitely weird. I meant—the part where Archie kissed me."

"You mean after you kissed him?" There was the faintest note of teasing in his voice.

With a sigh, I looked at him. "Yes."

"No," he told me. "Not really. It was kind of hot, and he was doing all the right things. Guy's got style, I'll give him that."

Oh. Relief threaded through me.

"Course, now I'm kind of hoping that my shot at getting a kiss just went up, too."

I couldn't help it.

I laughed.

"Maybe," I told him, and he grinned wider.

"Maybe is good." He clapped his hands together. "I'm good with maybe."

Afterboom

Bubba

Check Instagram. Now.

Jake

WTF?

Bubba

IKR?

Coop

What is it?

Jake

Someone posted pics.

Archie

No shit, it's Instagram. What pics?

Coop

In car. Gimme a minute.

Archie

They just left here.

Jake

...

Bubba

They?

Archie

She and Coop came to get car. Got stuck for here for food. Muriel came home.

Jake

Oh shit.

Bubba

I can't believe I'm asking this. Does she know?

Archie

I'll fill you in later. What the hell is this?

Coop

...

Archie

I'm gonna kill her.

Jake

Is Frankie okay?

Archie

No, obviously. This is going to make it worse.

Coop

Almost home.

Archie

We need her to take this down.

Jake

She isn't the only one who posted.

Coop

3 minutes.

Archie

Fuck me.

Bubba

Calling Sharon now.

Jake

Don't

Bubba

She needs to delete that.

Archie

Bubba, J is right. Don't.

Jake

She wants you to call.

Bubba

We need her to take it down.

Coop

...

Jake

If you're with Frankie, wait 'til you're home.
Don't call S, I'm going to call Maria.

Bubba

Bad idea.

Archie

Why don't I call them?

Jake

Worse idea. Make Coop do it.

Coop

Finally, home

Jake

You still with her?

Coop

No, she's gone up. No idea if mom is home.

Archie

Seriously?!?!?

Coop

Well I didn't see your dad.

Archie

Fuck

Bubba

Her car was there

Coop

Yeah, still here. Who am I calling?

Archie

Look at Instagram.

Coop

!!!!!!!

Archie

You need to call Sharon.

Coop

She doesn't care what I think.

Archie

She doesn't care what any of us think. But you are the nicest one

Coop

LOL That's Bubba.

Bubba

So I call.

Jake

Don't. I texted Maria. She's calling me in a minute.

Archie

Dude. Bad idea.

Coop

What is Maria gonna do?

Jake

She and Sharon are friends.

Archie

And they hate us.

Bubba

They don't hate us.

Coop

No, they hate you. But this is about Frankie.

Jake

No. Shit.

Bubba

Sharon's pissed.

Jake

We got that. M calling.

Archie

Good luck.

Bubba

Yeah, good luck.

Coop

Why are they doing this now?

Archie

You're not stupid.

Chapter Six

INFIDELITY

After we got back, I told Coop I'd see him the next day, and even though he glanced at my mouth, I didn't kiss him. I thought about it. At the same time, I was exhausted. I just wanted to go hide in my room. The apartment was as quiet as it had been when I left. Turning up the music, I finished straightening up my room, including getting the now clean comforter back on the bed and putting up my clothes.

Next, I got the roses watered and rearranged. I was almost sad the single lavender rose wouldn't make it the whole week, but I wasn't quite ready to toss it out yet. The last thing I did was run the vacuum around and make sure the litter box was clean before I grabbed a soda and headed back to my room to get ahead on my homework.

The busier I kept, the more I could keep my mind off of stuff. Breakfast at Archie's had verged on a nightmare. I felt bad for his mom. I felt bad for all of us really, but I didn't want to focus on any of the bad meatloaf.

Pulling out the journal I'd started for lit, I flipped open to the first blank page and wrote down the date. Ms. Fajardo said she didn't plan on reading the entries, here was hoping she meant it.

Titling it *Rules and Roses*, I tried to sum up the last two weeks and what it all meant. Fifteen pages and a hand cramp later, I still wasn't sure if I'd managed to capture all of it, but that was definitely enough pages to cover two weeks of journaling. I'd just pulled out my Calculus when my phone buzzed.

Mom

On my way home, in the mood for takeout. You home? What do you want?

I sighed. I wanted her to not be wherever she was. It was almost three though, and I hadn't really looked at my phone since I got in.

Me

Not really hungry. Whatever you want is fine.

Mom

You still going out tonight?

Was I?

Ugh.

I looked out the window. I didn't have a great view, but I could see some of the flower shrubs that lined the walk and a sliver of the pass between the buildings. The only upside was my window didn't face any other window directly, so I didn't have to worry about people staring in at me.

Me

Maybe. Homework first.

Mom

Let me know.

Yeah, I'd get right on that. Closing out of her message, I glanced at the messages with the guys. There were still a few I hadn't read. I'd talked to Archie and Coop today, and I'd talked to Ian the night before, but I hadn't really talked to Jake.

Not to do more than shut him down.

Tabbing to his, I stared at the last message he sent.

Jake

Talk to me? Pls?

The message yanked at me. Leaning back in the chair, I stared out at the other apartment building. Archie and Coop had both encouraged me to go out with Jake tonight, which besides being kind of weird, was also sweet. I don't think I'd have made it through breakfast without Coop and Archie there for help.

The hugs. The kiss. I was still mad. But...

Me

Setting the phone down, I flipped to the page with the calculus problems and pulled out clean notebook paper. I'd work them out first, then login to do the homework online. We had options, but numbers worked better for me if I was writing them. It wasn't until I finished the last problem and I heard the backdoor open that I glanced at my phone again.

No new messages.

It was still mid-afternoon. Jake could be busy.

"Frankie," Mom called, and I took a deep breath. Leaving my homework, I headed out to the living room.

"I'm here," I called. The scent of fried chicken hit like a hammer. Oh boy. Fried chicken buckets were usually reserved for the holidays. Unless we ended up getting invited somewhere, Mom and I made an annual KFC run and stocked up on all the goodies from the sides to the biscuits to all the fried chicken we could eat.

But it was for special occasions.

Mom was standing in the middle of the kitchen—alone. Oh. Thank God. Arms folded, I paused at the entrance and studied her. She was smiling. Genuinely smiling, and her eyes were shiny. Mom had dark hair where mine was blonde, but our eyes were the same.

"There's my girl."

"Yep. Here I am."

She was dressed in slacks, a pretty green blouse, and was just stepping out of her heels. There was an overnight bag by the door. Coming or going? You know, I didn't want to ask.

"You look happy."

Another grin lit her up, and she paused as if to consider my comment. "I am happy. Food's on the counter. I'm just going to change."

I scooted out of her way, and she brushed a kiss to the air next to my cheek.

Almost a week since I'd seen her, and that was at least familiar. We didn't go for the PDA here. "What's the occasion?" I called.

"Hmm?" Her door had opened and then closed again.

"What's the occasion? You got fried chicken." Maybe I should just swallow the questions. Did I really want the answers? It was hard to decide, really.

Damn, it smelled good though. I grabbed a couple of plates out of the cupboard and set them on the table, then went back for my soda. It was mostly empty, but I might as well finish the can. I checked my phone while I was in there. If I hadn't heard anything after food, I'd try again.

I told him I was pissed and I needed space, maybe he was giving it to me.

In the kitchen, I opened up the bags of food. Two buckets of fried chicken, all the sides I could want, fresh hot biscuits, and there was gravy for the mashed potatoes. My mouth was watering as I loaded the plate. The French toast I'd had that morning might have been amazing, but it had been a few hours earlier, and it hadn't been fun to eat while facing Mrs. Standish knowing what I knew.

"What did you ask?" Mom said as she re-entered the kitchen. Tory sat in the doorway behind her, tail swishing as she watched us. Tiddles had no such shame, he was already sitting on one of the chairs at the table and eyed the food as I served out my portion. He wouldn't get on the table, but he'd definitely mastered the "I'm starving and wasting away to nothing" expression.

Fortunately, I'd mastered ignoring it. Glancing at my mom, I said, "I asked what the occasion was…" I motioned to the chicken. "Thanksgiving isn't for another couple of months."

Mom said, "Does it have to be a special occasion?"

That wasn't an answer. "I guess not."

"Maybe I just felt like doing something fun to celebrate."

Yeah. Okay. "Mom, if we're celebrating, then it's a special occasion."

Rolling her eyes, Mom glanced at me and then turned to open the fridge. "True. Do you have time to talk?"

The dread curling my stomach suddenly developed volcanic properties, and my appetite evacuated. "I was doing homework, but—yeah."

"Don't sound so thrilled, I wouldn't want your excitement to overwhelm you." The dry teasing probably had the opposite effect of what she'd hoped for. I nudged Tiddles off the chair and sat down, then took a bite of the chicken. It was crispy perfect and a little greasy. The rich flavor turned to ash on my tongue, but I kept chewing.

At least if I was eating, I didn't have to say anything.

A bottle of water in one hand and a Coke in the other, she sat back at the table and put the Coke in front of me while she opened the water. "I met someone."

Oh. Please don't tell me. Please…

"I met him a while ago," she said. "He's—amazing. We've been dating since early last spring."

I almost choked. At my cough, Mom frowned but waited for me to take a drink before she continued.

"We kept it quiet, personal. I think he was as concerned as I was about whether this would work out. I haven't been the luckiest, you know."

Yeah.

I knew.

Blotting my lips with a napkin, I nodded.

"But he went with me these last few business trips…"

"Okay."

"Frankie—he's everything I ever wanted in someone. He's smart, accomplished, and he really respects me."

Were we talking about the same *married* man? Or had I missed something?

"Don't look at me that way, I know you don't understand. You can't. You don't have the best track record yourself."

Wouldn't she be surprised? "I haven't really had the time to date, Mom." Did that come out too bitchy?

"Fair. You're very driven. You remind me of me at your age."

The chicken sat like a rock in my gut, but I made myself take another bite as she served up her own dinner.

"Anyway, this last week…we made some decisions. That's why I called and told you part of me thought I needed to be there."

"So it wasn't a work thing at all, just a guy thing." Yep, that came out dismissive because her eyes narrowed. "Look, sorry…it's been a long week. You guys were trying to figure out what was the next step?"

Early last spring to now? That was probably pulling into the six-month category. We'd been there before.

That meant I got to meet him.

I so did not want the new introduction when I already knew him.

Hadn't Mrs. Standish still been wearing her wedding ring? The bright, shiny diamond ring?

"Is everything all right?"

"Yeah," I lied. "It's totally fine. Just had a long week."

"Oh, how was the party?" Her lips curled a little higher as she smiled.

A number of thoughts danced on my tongue, but none of them made it out of the wings. "It was okay. I didn't stay late."

"No? That's too bad. I thought you might be staying over."

"So did I." I shrugged. "Came home instead."

Her eyes widened. *Yeah, Mom. I know you weren't home.*

With a grimace, she reached over to cover my hand. "This is why I wanted to try and have dinner with you. I've just been gone so much, and I wouldn't have been, but this was important."

"Okay." I wasn't going to argue the point.

"Frankie, Edward and I…"

I was going to throw up.

"We're going to move in together."

They were what now?

"Edward is the boyfriend?" Yeah, that was exactly what came out of my mouth.

"Yes," she said, then she took a deep breath and braced her shoulders. "Edward Standish. Archie's father."

Fried chicken had just become the ultimate bad meatloaf.

"It may seem fast, I know. But you know Edward, and it really isn't—we've been so happy together. Oh, please be happy for us, Frankie. I know this is going to change things. But we'll have a bigger place…"

Bigger—we were leaving the apartments?

I stared at her.

"Isn't he married?"

All of the animation in Mom's face faded. "Okay. So we'll tackle the challenging part."

"Married isn't a challenge, Mom. It's a fact."

"I'm aware of that," she said, her lips compressing. "It's not like we planned to fall in love."

She went there. Oh God. "Or to lie to everyone in your lives?"

Because she'd *definitely* been lying to me.

"You can be upset, I respect your right to be angry about my choice to not involve you, but you know better. I don't involve you in my relationships if I can help it."

Except to break up with them…

Or to leave me covering the house and the cats while you do whatever…

Or when you want to catch a guy's eye…

But I didn't say any of those things.

"Archie's my friend, Mom. Mr. and Mrs. Standish," yes, I said both their names. "They're his parents."

"You and Archie are almost eighteen. I'm not going to discuss Edward's relationship, but suffice it to say, it's not been well in some time. He made the decision to divorce her this week, and he's asked us to move in. I told him we would." She clutched at my hand again, which was fine cause I wasn't using it. If I tried to eat anything, I'd probably be sick. As it was, I had to keep down what I'd already swallowed.

"So, done deal. They're divorced and we're moving."

"Frankie," she said with a sigh. "Please don't play dumb on purpose. You have an opinion, say it."

"You don't want my opinion." I pulled my hand out from under hers, and I rose to put up my food in Tupperware. No way I was finishing it.

"Of course, I do, this affects your life."

"If you wanted my opinion, Mom," I told her carefully, and I kept my tone even. "You wouldn't have kept him a secret for months. If you wanted my opinion… you wouldn't have lied to me." Sealing the lid, I turned around and met her gaze. "If you'd wanted my opinion, you would have asked before you committed me into leaving the apartment we've lived in for most of my life to move in with some guy who may or may not divorce his wife, but will certainly have some complicated legal process to jump through. Oh—and the guy in question just happens to be the father of one of my best friends, who will now have to deal with his parents going through a divorce."

I hadn't meant to yell, but there it was.

"If you'd *wanted* my opinion, you'd have told me you were having an affair with a married guy. But you *didn't*. You *hid* it."

My breath came out in panting little explosions of air. Did she really think he was going to leave his wife? Maybe he would. But—if a man cheats on one wife…

"Are you done?" She asked, all trace of the joy in her expression gone.

And I'd done that.

I'd rained on her happy parade.

"I guess," I said. Because I didn't really have anything else kind or good to say. My mom was the spoiler in a marriage, and she wanted to move in with the guy.

"Marriages," she said in the closest thing to a lecturing tone I'd ever heard out of her, and I had no idea how I didn't roll my eyes, "are complicated relationships. More complicated than you know. It takes being willing to compromise on both sides and valuing the happiness of your partner, sometimes above your own. They can also create ruts where you just stay because it's the only thing you've ever known, and it's scary to put yourself out there. You can be miserable and be married."

She sighed.

"I wish I could explain it to you. Eddie—he'd been deeply unhappy—"

"I don't care," I found myself saying as I held up my hand, and you'd have thought I slapped her. "I don't care about him or his feelings. I care that he's married. I care that you've been cheating and lying and sneaking around. I care that you're about to upend our whole life, and the only assurance you have is he told you he would—guess what, Mom? He told her he'd love, honor, and cherish her for the rest of their lives. How is that working out?"

I don't know which one of us moved first, but her hand cracked across my face and it stung like hell. Horror flickered in her eyes, but not enough to chase away the rage.

"You don't like it, fine. Don't like it. But you still have a few more months here, young lady, and you *will* be respectful."

Covering my cheek with my hand, I sucked in a breath and then said, "May I be excused?"

All of the fight went out of her. "Frankie..."

But I didn't capitulate. All she wanted was respect. Fine. If I wasn't supposed to care about her setting herself up for failure, then I wouldn't. We'd been down this road, and it wasn't like she'd ever been married.

She turned away from me and said in a shaky breath, "I'm sorry. I shouldn't have slapped you."

Yeah. You shouldn't have done a lot of things. But I kept my opinion to myself.

I waited her out.

"Yes," she said finally. "You're excused."

I grabbed my Coke and walked back to my room. I didn't slam the door—but God, I wanted to. No, I crossed over to the desk and picked up my phone.

No messages.

Tears burned in my eyes, and I unlocked the screen and did a swipe down to check the notifications. Sometimes when it was in do not disturb, it didn't display them all. There were numerous notifications from their messages. I cleared those—most of them I'd read, but a couple of them were apologies that I hadn't.

Nothing recent. Not since that morning.

There were—good lord, a hundred notifications from Instagram. I'd been tagged in a bunch of photos?

I'd check that in a minute. There were some Reddit thread updates, and a Snapchat from Cheryl. I hit that first because I had no idea how old it was.

"Hey girl! What color for the dress? I don't want to match. I want to do silver. I think."

I literally had no thoughts on that whatsoever, so I just closed snapchat out and went back to my messages. Tabbing into Jake's, I scanned to where I sent the *hey*.

Read. The timestamp was for less than a minute after I'd sent it.

But he hadn't answered.

Okay.

Thumb hovering over the keypad, I debated what I wanted to say. A hundred sentences entered and discarded immediately.

Finally, I went with the truth.

Me

I need to get out of here. Are we still on?

Maybe it was selfish. I'd shut him down the night before, and if he wanted to blow me off, fine. I had my car. My stomach hurt, and I stared at the homework I still needed to finish. The math was mostly done, I just needed to log in and do it online.

I'd take my bag with me.

Flopping back on the bed, I stared at the ceiling. My bedroom door was still open, but it was quiet beyond my room. Tiddles had followed me inside, and he jumped up to demand attention. I stroked his back as I stared at the message.

No read receipt.

The group chat was quiet, too.

I scrolled to Archie's text.

Me

Hey

Archie

Hey you. How you doing?

Me

Not great. Talked to Mom.

Archie

Do you want me to call?

What did I want him to do?

Me

She's still here.

Even if I hadn't heard her in the last few minutes, it didn't matter. My face hurt.

Archie

What can I do?

Me

I don't know.

How much did I tell him? I still couldn't wrap my mind around it.

Archie

I can be there in fifteen. Pick you up. Ice cream?

Archie

We can walk around the lake.

It wasn't raining out there.

Archie

Frankie?

I scrolled back to Jake's text message. Still no response. Still no read receipt.

Me

Do you know where Jake is?

His answer was a long moment coming.

Archie

He had to run an errand. I'll text him that you're with me.

Archie

Let me come get you?

I should say no, I shouldn't be selfish, and at the same time…

The television turned on in the living room.

Me

Yes please.

Archie

On my way. 15 mins.

I rolled off the bed and got changed. Clean leggings and an oversized shirt along with a bra, and then shoved my feet into my running shoes. Not that I planned on running, but better for going around the lake. I dug a hoodie out of the back of the closet—it was one of Ian's old ones. I borrowed it in sophomore year and never gave it back. I didn't think it was that cold, but better to have it than not.

Finger combing my hair, I pulled it up into a ponytail before I stuffed my homework and laptop back into my backpack. Wallet and keys in the bag, I flicked off the light and grabbed my phone before I headed out. I didn't bother making eye contact with Mom as I swung through the kitchen and headed to the back door.

"Leaving," I told her. "Back later."

"Frankie," Mom called, but I played the deaf and dumb card.

"Gotta go, in a hurry, bye." And I was out, I didn't bother to the lock the door. She was capable.

Down the steps and on my way to the parking lot, I wanted to be away from the apartment, and I didn't want her to catch me up.

Me

Walking up the hill. Be at the sign when you get here.

The sun seemed almost too bright, and as soon as I got to the apartment sign, I dug out my sunglasses. I still had at least six more minutes, so I checked Jake's message.

No read receipt. No answer.

Hopefully, everything was okay.

Flipping to Instagram, I half-expected to see pictures from the party. The first one—a close up of Ian hitting Archie made me wince. I scrolled past it and then my stomach bottomed out.

It was a black text box with letters in it.

Smart is the new dumb.

It was a story, and it had me tagged. The next image was Ian and Sharon making out at a party. His hands were down her pants, and she was on his lap. All it said in the caption was *Back to school party, 2 weeks ago.* The next image was Ian kissing me by my car. *Smart?* The image after that was Ian with Sharon again, only she was clearly topless, even if there was no boob showing. *Probably not.*

The next image was Archie and Patty, and based on the image—it was the same location. Archie's house. The swimming pool was visible. At least she wasn't in Archie's lap, though she was wrapped around him from the back with her hand down his swim trunks and his head tilted back to look up at her. *2 weeks ago.* The next image had to have been taken when me and Archie got to the football game, he had an arm around my shoulders, and he'd been telling me a story, whispering in my ear. *A week later.* Then another of Patty and Archie, only he had his hands covering her bared boobs, and she was laughing. It was a close up, but there were other people—in the hot tub with them.

The next image was Coop and Laura, Jake and Maria, Ian and Sharon, and finally Archie and Patty. *Makes you wonder, doesn't it?*

Then a series of photos with just the guys and me flicked past. Then back to Ian hitting Archie.

Smart? Nope. Guess the untouchable princess finally started putting out.

The photos were old but—not that old. And I knew all of it…except for the hot tub. The guys had lives before we talked about dating.

I knew this.

Didn't mean it didn't sting.

I didn't recognize the name who posted it, but they tagged just about everyone and hashtagged the senior class.

The number of likes and comments made me ill, and I scrolled away from it. I wasn't going to read those.

But I wasn't ready to see another Jake and Maria photo. They were at the wings place close to the high school, and it was posted only minutes before with the *#togetheragain*? on it.

The gentle honk of a horn pulled my head up, and I met Archie's gaze. He frowned, then leaned over and pushed open the passenger door. Feet dragging, I climbed in and he caught my backpack and put it behind the seat.

"Hey," he said, frowning. "What the hell did she say to you?"

"A lot…and then I saw this." I turned the phone over to show him.

With a sigh, he said, "That's not what it looks like."

When I scrolled up to the story, his expression darkened.

"But that is," I said, then clicked off the phone and leaned my head back against the seat.

"Buckle up," he told me, his tone almost brisk. "We're getting you out of here, and then we talk, okay?"

I nodded. At the moment, I'd do just about anything to make this sick, sinking feeling go away. "I'm sorry, Archie… you didn't have to come."

He wrapped a hand around my nape and nudged my head around, then he kissed me. Firm and real, even as he squeezed my nape. With a tug, he sucked on my lower lip, then nibbled another kiss.

"You feel that?" he murmured against my mouth. At my nod, he continued, "Good. I'm right where I want to be. You need me. I'm here. Hang on a little longer for me, babe. Can you do that?"

Licking my lips, I nodded. I had to get this together. I didn't just fall apart.

Dragging the seatbelt on, I clicked it into place and then pulled the door closed. Grasping my hand, Archie gave it a squeeze and rested my hand on his thigh before he shifted gears, but he covered my hand.

"Thank you for coming to get me." Pathetic as it sounded, I was grateful.

"Always," he promised. "Now just hang on. We're going to figure this out."

I didn't know whether to believe him or not, but I wanted to.

That was something, right?

Chapter Seven

RUN TO YOU

Archie held my hand all the way to the drive-thru at the Braums. He picked up two pints of ice cream and a couple of burgers and fries. Then we snagged coffee from Starbuck's. When he turned back toward his place, I stiffened.

"Easy," he murmured, catching my hand again. "Muriel's already gone. She stayed a whole hour after you left before she took off. This time, she's going to the spa for a couple of days."

I licked my lips. "What about your dad?" I really didn't want to see him.

"Call Jeremy," he said, and his phone began ringing via the speakers.

"Yes, Mr. Archie?" Jeremy answered the phone.

"Hey, has Edward shown up, or is he still MIA?"

"I have not seen him, but I could check if you would prefer."

Archie glanced at me, and I mouthed *please* and he nodded. "Yeah, if you would. Check to see if the Beamer is back, that was the car he went out in."

"Give me a moment."

"If he's there, I have a plan B," Archie said, then squeezed my hand.

"Okay?"

I nodded. "Thank you. Sorry to be difficult."

Chuckling, he shook his head. "Babe, you are not being difficult. I don't want to see him either, especially after Muriel was such a bitch this morning."

With a grimace, I sighed.

"Drink your coffee, it helps—a little." The coaxing note in his voice lulled me. I really was much better than this. Why the hell I was so off-center, I really didn't know. I couldn't get past the knots in my stomach. It was ten times worse than when Archie told me their plan for Mathieu.

That had only been the day before. How could so much happen in twenty-four hours?

"Mr. Archie?" Jeremy's voice startled me. I half-forgot he was still on the phone. "Mr. Edward is not on the estate as far as I can tell, and the BMW is not in the garage. I believe if you return and head to your wing, you will not encounter him, and I can warn you if he arrives."

"Thanks, Jeremy."

"My pleasure, sir."

Then the line disconnected. "That work for you?"

A shiver went through me, but I nodded.

"Okay, almost there, babe."

Once we were back at his place, it seemed almost surreal. My fourth time there in forty-eight hours. Friday night. Saturday evening. Sunday morning. Now.

Two of the three had ended okay, so maybe this would, too. I hoped so.

Archie snagged my backpack, and I carried the ice cream and coffee while he also got the food. We didn't encounter anyone—not even Jeremy—on our way up. There was a mini fridge and freezer in the game room where he shoved the ice cream, and then we retreated into his bedroom and he locked the door.

"Voila, privacy."

A little laugh escaped at his grand sweeping gesture as he spread his arms.

"Better?"

"A little," I admitted.

"Let's get comfy and eat, then we'll talk—but first…" He pulled his phone out and hit a number then put it on speaker. It rang, and finally Jake answered on the third ring.

"What the hell man—" My heart did a little flip-flop at his voice.

"Frankie's here with me," Archie said, meeting my gaze.

"Shit…"

I bit my lip.

"And someone there is documenting your visit with Maria."

"Excuse me?" A darker, edgier note crested in his voice.

"You were tagged on Instagram," I said, refusing to play coward. "Just you and Maria and hashtagging whether you guys are together again—and you weren't answering my texts."

"I'm sorry," he said. "Seriously, I am trying to get her and Sharon to…"

At his hesitation, Archie said, "She saw it."

"I'm pretty sure the whole senior class has seen it." I shrugged.

"Fuck me. Give me an hour? Frankie? I'm going to wrap this up. She's either going to help or not. But I'm not interested in them hurting you. If they keep this up…" Well, he didn't clarify, but then, he didn't have to. I could already read the resolve on Archie's face.

"Where are you two?"

"At my place," Archie said. "Frankie needed to get away from her mom, so now you know. Deal with Maria and then get out of there." He hung up without waiting for his response. "We were trying to get rid of it before you saw it."

"Okay." I believed him. His expression tightened as he studied me. "Not going to lie, the pictures hurt—the dates on them, but—I knew you guys dated and weren't virgins. So…" I spread my hands.

"Yeah, those pictures don't mean a damn thing." He sighed. "I'm just sorry she did that."

"She's hurt." Was I defending Sharon?

"That doesn't mean she gets to lash out at you."

I didn't really want to talk about Sharon. "It doesn't really matter. People are going to believe what they believe. And it's not like there isn't some truth to it." I took a sip of the coffee and looked around, but before I could sit on the floor, Archie caught my arm and tugged me toward the bed. He set the food bags down and waved me on.

A shiver went through me as I looked at the sheets, then at him.

"I promise, yes I want you, no, I'm not doing this to get in your pants, no matter what you just said." The last came out on a hard edge.

"Archie… you guys are all technically dating me because I *decided* I wanted to date."

"I don't care, Frankie. Everything about that post says we dumped them because now we have you, and to be honest, three of us were already history."

"Like I said, I know this." Coop had to break up with Laura—again— though only Coop could end up accidentally dating someone. Of course, after tripping into all four of them, I really couldn't talk.

Shoes off, I crawled onto the bed and he fluffed the pillows up and held my coffee until I was settled. Then he sat right next to me and spread our food on our laps.

"Okay," he said. "We're safe. We're locked in. You know the picture about Jake and Maria is bullshit. What did your mom do?"

Stomach still in knots, I stared down at my burger. Finally, I dragged my gaze up and met his. "Well, first she told me how happy she was with Eddie."

His expression of distaste had to match my own.

"Bear in mind, she brought home fried chicken to celebrate with."

A frown tensed his brow, and he twisted so we could face each other. "Celebrate what?"

"Bad meatloaf," I told him. "Apparently, they're moving in together. Or correction, we're moving in with him."

Archie's brows skyrocketed. "She said he asked her to move in?"

"She said they made some decisions—they've been seeing each other for months." I hated everything about this. "Archie—she said he and your mom are gonna get divorced."

"No they're not." He almost laughed, but seemed to think better of it. "I mean, I suppose they could, I have no doubt there's an iron-clad prenup floating around, but—Edward's…" He winced. "Frankie, this is not his first affair."

"I know. I tried to kind of point that out, but that didn't go well." I set the burger back down. I didn't know if I could eat it, so I reclaimed my coffee instead. "I don't want to move—I mean, I do eventually. But… where are we going to move in? Here? Where your mom still lives?"

The corners of his mouth curved. "I'd love it if you lived with me, the guys might have cow. But I'd like it."

"Please be serious…"

"I am being serious," he promised. Then he reached over and curled the end of my ponytail around his hand. "Frankie, I don't know what's going on with them, and honestly—I don't want to know. Edward's… he's done this a lot. He never leaves Muriel. Toxic or not, they are this volatile chemical mixture that just keeps churning."

Which meant my mom was going to end up getting hurt, again. I sighed.

"Look, I don't know what he said or what she wants to do, but it's not a done deal yet, and hey—" He nudged a finger under my chin to lift my gaze to meet his. "Whatever happens, that's on them. Not us."

"But whatever they decide is going to affect me—affect you."

"Not for long," he said. "A few months and we graduate, and then we get the hell out of here. We go north, you go to Harvard…"

"If I get in."

"*When* you get in. You know what, if you end up taking a skip year, fine, then we'll go see Europe and get as far away from the drama as possible."

It all sounded great… "Arch, we live in the real world."

"Pfft, overrated. I much prefer my fantasies as long as you're a part of it."

I laughed, but it wasn't that funny. It was hard to dredge up the humor when it felt like I waged a war against tears. "My mom really likes him," I told him. "She does this, I know she does…she falls for guys, and it never works out. But I've only seen her this happy a couple of times, and I made her mad—because I pointed out he was still married."

"You have a right," Archie said. He'd eaten some of his burger, and he motioned to mine. "You need to eat."

"I'm not hungry." I was still nursing the peppermint mocha. There was ice cream.

"You have to be hungry, there's ice cream and wallowing to be had." All the teasing in the world wasn't going to make this better. When that didn't work, he moved all the food—including my coffee—and dragged an arm around me to pull me close.

Closing my eyes, I buried my face against his neck and just held on.

"It's going to be alright, Frankie," he said. "I know you hate this, and I know you're worried about your mom. It's going to be alright."

Yeah. She had plenty of breakup experience. Didn't make it any easier.

"You know what I hate most about this…"

"No, but I'm hoping you'll tell me," he said, his tone dry. "I hate trying to guess."

I laughed. Okay. That was funny. Lifting my head, I looked at him and he grinned. When his gaze dipped to my mouth, I don't know which of us moved first, but then he was kissing me, or I was kissing him. Heat bloomed in my belly, dislodging the heavy rock there, and it flared outward as I clung to him and he fisted my hair. The kiss hadn't started gentle, and it didn't seem headed that way.

The scrape of his teeth sent a jolt over my skin, and my nipples tightened as I shifted on his lap. Then he sucked on my lower lip, dragging it out before releasing it with a pop. "Hi…"

My breath came in little pants. "Hi."

"You were telling me something."

I had been, but I was tracking the way his lips glistened and when I leaned in, he opened his mouth to meet my kiss and let me trace my tongue against his as he slid a hand under my shirt. His fingers were so cool against my skin, it sent another race of goosebumps over me.

His erection stiffened against my ass where I ground against him lightly, then he tugged my hair, breaking the kiss. "Frankie."

He was right. What was I doing?

"Not upset in the slightest, but I'm interested in getting rid of these clothes if we're going to keep this up," he warned.

Heat unspooled from my belly, and I clenched my thighs against his legs as I straddled his lap. The gleam in his eyes reminded me of Friday, and it would be so easy. Just focus on feeling good…

"But nothing has to happen. I didn't bring you back here to make out— sadly." Then he made a face, and another laugh swelled up through me. "Not saying no, just saying you don't have to worry."

"I wasn't worried," I admitted. "A little amazed that I can be mad at you and want you at the same time."

His grin grew brighter. "You want me."

My face heated. "I thought I made that clear on Friday."

"Oh yeah," he said. "But it's not Friday, and you're right, you were mad."

"I'm still mad."

"No, you're not," he said, then soothed his hands down my sides. "You're hurt, and that's a thousand percent worse. But if you were mad at me, you'd never have texted me for help."

He had a point.

"I don't think I've forgiven you yet."

"But you want to, which we also covered." He slid his hands under my shirt and continued his slow soothing strokes. I swayed a little at the contact, it eased some of the want simmering in my system and made me want to lean into him more.

The quiet elongated, and he nuzzled a kiss to the corner of my lips before easing his hands up to my bra.

"Can I?"

A shudder passed through me.

"I've been thinking about your tits since Friday, I want to play with them again, and I want to eat you out… You remember what I said about all the different ways I want to fuck you?"

I did, and I didn't pretend otherwise. When he kissed me this time, I pressed right into him and he unhooked my bra, the next time we broke apart, my shirt came off and then bra. He tugged his up and off.

"Fair is fair," he said with a grin, and then I was on my back and he was kissing me again. All I wanted to do was hold onto him, feel the way my breasts rubbed against his chest, and I ached for more as he rubbed at my pussy through my pants.

Every kiss he gave me was like a drug and left me craving more. Every touch sucked me out of my head and left only Archie and where we touched. I dragged my hands down his back and slid my hands against his shorts. He let out a little groan when I pushed him up. As I reached between us to undo the button and zipper, he studied me.

The earlier chill was gone. So was the vague sense of nauseating disquiet and uneasiness. I didn't care about our parents or the shit the girls pulled. I just wanted this.

I needed this.

As soon as I got the zipper open, he shoved his shorts off, leaning back and up until they were gone along with his boxer briefs. He hooked his fingers into the waistband of my leggings and at my nod, he dragged them off. Then there was nothing but bare skin, and when he came back, I met him, mouths fusing together. He rocked against me, and everywhere his skin rubbed against mine, I wanted more.

The first nudge of his cock against my entrance, and I pulled back, panting. Archie swore and reached over to the drawer. He yanked it out and pulled out the condom. Sitting up, he had it open and ready to roll on, when I wrapped my hand around his cock, and he froze. His expression went from hurried to strained, and he stared at me as I stroked him from base to tip.

"I didn't really get to touch you on Friday," I admitted, and he let out a little groan.

"Fuck, you feel good, babe." He was hot and smooth; the skin was so soft and yet, pulled taut. I rolled my thumb around the tip and wondered if I could do that, could I put my mouth there and… "Frankie." He dragged out my name, his voice hoarse. So I helped him roll on the condom and then he had my thigh up and eased inside of me.

The pressure was perfect and exactly what I wanted. I abandoned trying to reason or catalog anything. Just focused on feeling as he began to thrust. Every push sent a rush through my system. Hot and heavy against me, he deepened our kiss until his tongue thrust against mine with the same force as he snapped his hips. The grind sent sparks up my spine, and the spiraling tension coiled so tight, I thought I was going to burst.

The hairs on his legs tickled mine, and he dug his fingers into my leg as he braced his weight on his other arm. When he lifted his head, he stared right into my eyes as he increased the tempo. All I could do was fight to keep up with him, and then heat burst out. I almost sobbed, it felt so good. Another three snaps of his hips, and his pace stuttered as he came. I fought to keep my eyes open to watch his blissed out expression.

When he collapsed against me, I was shaking, or maybe it was him. Either way, I clung to him and held on. Gradually, my breathing returned to normal and his little panted breaths against my throat slowed. With a groan, he pushed upward and then eased out of me while keeping a hand on the condom.

"I'll be right back," he promised, nuzzling a kiss to the corner of my eye.

Oh, I was aching again. But it was so worth it. The drowsiness sweeping over me made me want to curl up and sleep. Little by little, the fact that light came in the windows sank in, and I let out a little laugh as I could hear Archie peeing.

So—weird.

So, normal.

I shuddered and pushed myself up on my elbows and then glanced at the disheveled bed and our strewn clothes. There was still an empty paper bag lying on the bed.

Sitting up, I reached over for my coffee because it was a lot closer than my clothes. I just lifted it for a sip when Archie came out of the bathroom, and he grinned.

"Now that's a sight I can get used to…"

Heat scorched my face and my chest, but what the hell? He'd just been in me. Looking shouldn't be such a big deal, and at the same time—I couldn't really pull my gaze away from him. The well-defined arms, the hint of his abs, and the spark in his eyes. Even the bruise gave him a kind of rakish air.

Archie made me feel beautiful when he looked at me like that.

"Feel better?" he asked as he came to sit on the bed again, but facing me and with one hand massaging my thigh.

I thought about that, turning it over to examine the idea. "Yeah," I admitted. "I do."

"Good." Then he squeezed my leg. "No regrets?"

"Nope," I said. "Thank you."

He chuckled. "My pleasure, babe. Seriously. I'm never going to get enough of you." He ran his hand over the inside of my thigh and teased a finger over my labia. A shiver sent goosebumps racing out, and my nipples tightened. "Definitely never tired of that."

But instead of continuing his caress, he settled his hand back on my thigh. The distraction helped. It had given me a little distance, and I didn't feel quite so—awful.

"What's the part you hate the most?" Archie prompted me, and I sighed.

"I want Mom to be happy. She *seems* happy right now, but it feels like another lie in a sea of them. I hurt her feelings today, pointing out that *Eddie…*" I grimaced and Archie winced. "Pointing out that your dad is still married, and that what she wanted me to celebrate was your family breaking up."

His expression gentled. "You were worried about me?"

"You weren't worried about me when you found out about them?"

"Fuck yes, I was worried about you because your mother wasn't around and…" He sighed.

I covered his hand on my leg. "So, yes, I was worried about you. I still am."

"Don't," he said, meeting my gaze. "Whether Edward and Muriel stay together or not—" He shrugged. "I don't care. Maybe they'd even be happier apart. God knows they make each other and me miserable. We've never been that happy television family, babe."

"Like I don't know what that's like?" I pointed out. "Mom and I are not posters for well-adjusted."

He chuckled. "You're pretty fucking awesome despite that."

"I think you're the awesome one."

"Well, we're a mutual admiration society, but since I founded it, you win awesome hands down."

I smiled. "We'll agree to disagree…"

"Frankie?" He leaned forward. "Forgive me yet?"

I sighed. After the last twenty-four hours? "Yeah," I exhaled. "Don't keep secrets like that again… don't…"

"Don't plan to get rid of some guy who thinks he can waltz in and take off with my girl?" He raised his eyebrows.

"Maybe just trust me." A thrill went through me at being called his girl.

"I do trust you. I trust the guys. That's a small circle, babe."

His phone buzzed and we both glanced around for it, and he finally reached to the floor and pulled it out of his discarded shorts.

Jake's name was on the screen.

"You're on speaker," he told him as he answered.

"Frankie's still there?"

"Oh yeah," Archie said, grinning at me, and heat washed over my face, and I set the coffee aside to go find my shirt and bra, but Archie tugged me back. When he slid his hand down to cup my pussy, I raised my brows and his grin grew almost devilish. "Maria get her to do it?"

There was a long sigh. "No," Jake admitted. "So, I warned her we can fight fire with fire. She can take it down, or I'll make sure she gets burned, too. I'm on my way to your place now."

My eyes widened at the declaration, but Archie just teased his hand against my pussy.

"Don't recall inviting you," he said absently as he touched a finger to my entrance and raised his brows. My gut went taut, and all the earlier desire pooled again. Oh crap. I spread my legs a little for him, and he eased his finger inside, and I tensed. Everything was so sensitive.

"Rule #2," Jake said.

What the hell was rule number 2? No sooner did that thought take root than Archie added a second finger to the first, and he began to thrust gently, skating his thumb against my clit. An embarrassing amount of dampness slicked around his fingers, and his grin grew.

"Frankie." Jake saying my name pulled me back from the edge, and I clutched at the sheets, but Archie kept his hand in motion and I strained upward with my hips. Fuck, that felt good.

"Yeah?" I managed to push the single word out.

"I'm sorry I didn't answer you earlier, I didn't want to give her fuel for the fire."

Who?

"And I know you're still mad but—think we could still have our date tonight?"

Our date.

Fuck, I was so close, and the combination of Archie's shit-eating grin and bruised face was just adding to it as he pushed me harder. His cock was stiffening with every stroke of his hand against me, and I licked my lips.

Going to answer him? Archie mouthed, and I shook as I teetered on the edge, and Archie slowed his touch.

Bastard. I mouthed, and his grin just grew wider.

"Can we talk about it when you're here?" I finally managed to get my brain to produce a reasonable sentence.

"Yes," Jake said, and the relief in his voice almost instantly made me feel guilty. He was all worried about whether I'd want to see him, and I was about to get off—again. "I'll be there in fifteen. Maybe ten if I hurry."

"Don't hurry," Archie said. "Take your time. We need about twenty more minutes."

"You asshole…" Jake said, but Archie had already hung up.

"That was mean," I told Archie, but he eased his fingers out from my pussy and licked them off. I think a brain cell shorted when he did that.

"What was mean was he ignored you, good cause or not," he retorted. "So a little punishment is good for him. I took care of that for you."

I groaned, and he had another condom on, and then he tumbled me over onto my stomach and the simmering tension hovered right at the edge of boiling.

"Now I'm going to take care of this for us…" He eased my thighs apart. "Yes?"

Fuck. "Yes," I panted as he pushed in, and the angle sent him deeper.

"That's my girl," he whispered as he urged me up, and then we were rocking together, and I spiraled up and over the edge as the tension burst. He chased my orgasm and came with his lips on my shoulder and his hand on my clit, pulling another orgasm out of me. When we collapsed this time, I was fucking boneless.

And Jake was on his way.

"We still have at least ten more minutes," Archie murmured. "Can I see if I can make you come again?"

For real?

I glanced up at him. "I don't know if I can." Not after all that.

"Oh… that's a challenge I want to win."

I was on my back and his mouth was on my pussy and my brain melted.

I don't know if I came, or if I ever stopped coming, but I was a wreck by the time Jake texted to say he was there, and we still needed to pull our clothes back on.

Chapter Eight
THERE ARE STRINGS

"Take a shower," Archie suggested as he dragged on his shorts. "I'll take Jake into the entertainment room. Come find us there?"

"Sure," I said, still on the boneless side, and then Archie leaned forward and kissed me again. "Arch…" I caught his hand when he pulled back. "Thank you."

He grinned. "Always." Another kiss, and then he had his shirt and tugged it on before using both hands to finger comb his hair. He didn't leave via the door to his room, but through the door to the adjoining guest room. "Locking this," he called, then he was out.

Sitting in the middle of the rumpled bed, I pulled my knees up and groaned. Oh, I was aching a little more than I had been on Friday. It was a good ache, but it made me leery of moving fast. Ten minutes and some fantastic water pressure later, I pulled my damp hair back into a ponytail.

The shower had helped. Dressed, I gathered up the leftovers of our burgers and fries along with the rest of my coffee, and then let myself out of Archie's room to go in search of them.

Jake's voice carried. "Are you serious right now?"

"As a heart attack," Archie said. "You're just bitching because she called me."

"I'm bitching because half of what's wrong is your damn fault. If you hadn't said anything to her…"

I sighed. Nudging the half-open door wider, I slid into the room. Jake and Archie sat on opposite sofas. Archie leaned back, expression—well the best description for it was relaxed and not giving a fuck, but not Jake. He leaned forward, scowling.

"If he hadn't said anything to me about your plan for Mathieu," I pointed out. "It wouldn't have changed the fact you were planning to do something you shouldn't."

Jake jerked and stood. He was pale beneath his tan, and there were bruises under his eyes, like he hadn't slept. I hadn't really looked at that photo of him and Maria earlier. Not closely. But it didn't look like he'd shaved today either "Frankie…"

Holding up a hand, I continued, "That's not okay, Jake."

"He still shouldn't have dropped a bomb on you and left. If—if all of that hadn't happened, last night might have gone differently."

"Yeah, maybe I wouldn't have seen bad meatloaf when I came here to yell at you guys, but it wouldn't change what you were planning to do. He left because I threw him out. I didn't want him there. Archie telling me the truth—it hurt. But his telling me wasn't the thing you guys did *wrong*. Please tell me you see that."

Groaning, he tipped his head back. "I hated the idea of you dating Frenchy."

"I got that," I told him, and pushed farther into the room. "So when does it become you hate me seeing Archie?"

Both of them stilled.

"Or Archie hates that Coop wants to see me. Or Ian. When does this… become all of us breaking up?"

Because that would suck. I would have officially torpedoed the one really great part of my life. Their friendships meant everything to me.

"That's not going to happen," Archie said quietly.

"You don't know that," I said, meeting his gaze. "Or maybe it's just that I don't." I set the food and the coffee on the table and rubbed my hands over my face.

"So we work hard to make sure it doesn't happen, and whoever you end up with—we all agree, no hard feelings." The offer was right there in Jake's voice. "I told you I wanted to date you, even if you are seeing all of them. What happened with Archie Friday night doesn't change that."

"Sex, Jake, you can say sex," Archie corrected him, and Jake just gave him a baleful look.

"You want me to give you a second black eye?"

"And now you're proving her point," Archie countered, almost smug. I smacked his shoulder as I passed him to sit on the other sofa. "Ow."

"Be nice," I told him as Jake dropped onto the seat next to me.

"I was being nice, I'm being supportive." But he dropped the smug act, then reached over and put a hand on my knee. "I'm—happy about Friday. I'm not happy about the stuff that followed on Saturday, but I'm really happy about Friday."

It was hard to argue the sentiment when I felt the same way. Especially after the last couple of hours.

"Frankie." Jake pulled my attention, and when he covered my hand, I threaded our fingers together. The tight frown gathering his brows eased a little as he stroked his thumb against the back of my hand. "I'm sorry. I tried to get Maria to get Sharon to take that crap down."

"I don't care, it's fine," I told him.

"It's not fine," he said.

"In the laundry list of things that bother me right now? It's fine. I don't have to look at it. And—even if they took it down, everyone has probably seen it anyway." I should probably call Coop and Ian. The quiet stretched between us, but Jake didn't let go of my hand.

Archie nudged the food toward me again when Jake said, "I know this is probably bad timing… but it's Sunday."

"I know," I said, and Archie gave me an encouraging look. He'd already told me I shouldn't cancel the date. "Our date."

"Yeah." Jake gave me a little smile and squeezed my hand. "I get that you may not want to go out. But… I'd still like to spend the evening with you."

"I'm going to grab us some water," Archie volunteered, and gave my ponytail a little tug as he stood. "You two hang out for a minute."

Then he was gone, closing the door behind him. Shifting to sit sideways, I half-faced Jake and the hopeful, but worried look in his eyes set off a pang in my chest. "I don't like fighting with you guys."

"Yeah you do—just not about when we do stupid shit," Jake teased. "Unless it's the time we all jumped off the bridge into the creek."

"That was not stupid," I pointed out. "That was insane. You could have broken something."

"But we didn't," he murmured. "Ahhh… Frankie, I'm sorry. I'm sorry we pissed you off and more sorry we hurt you."

"I'm not mad… not anymore. I was, don't get me wrong. I was really mad. But mostly hurt and confused. You guys have to let me make my own choices. Even if you don't like them."

His jaw tightened. "Can I agree to work on it?"

"Yeah." I couldn't ask him to do much more, not really. Even if I'd like it if they just promised to never do it again. That might be unreasonable.

"Then I promise, I'll work on it. Can we hang out tonight? Or… did you just want to stay here?"

"I promised you time." That was what he'd wanted. Just us. "But not really sure where we can go. I—I don't know if Mom is still home, and I think it might be weird if I took a boy home after today." It also meant seeing her, and I wasn't ready for that, either.

The corner of his mouth kicked up. "Weird, maybe. But it wouldn't be our first time. I wanted to take you out out, so… if you're game, I'd still like to."

I still had all that homework to do, but… "Okay."

Relief poured off of him.

"*But*," I began, and he seemed to brace. "I have a ton of homework I haven't done." It was still mid-afternoon. "When did you want to go?"

"Now?" He grinned. "We'll grab your stuff, go back to my house. Not sure where Mom and the girls are, but we can study in my room and I'll grab a shower and get changed—maybe shave. Then we can take it from there?"

The door opened, and Archie came back carrying bottles of water. "So what did we vote on?"

Jake raised his brows at me. A part of me kind of just wanted to stay here and hide, but it wasn't like I was really hiding. Half of bad meatloaf lived here.

"We're gonna go back to his place and do homework, then probably go out and do…" I had no idea what we were going to do.

"Cool," Archie said, handing over the water bottles. "You don't have to leave to do homework though. We could—make a big study group right here." At Jake's dark look, Archie held up his hands. "I said study, that doesn't mean I'm inviting myself along on whatever your date is."

Slanting a look at me, Jake said, "Up to Frankie. I can stay here, my crap is down in the car. I never took it out on Friday."

"I'm sorry about your game," I said abruptly. It had been canceled, and then Archie and I hadn't picked up our phones.

"No biggie," he said, still holding my hand. "Bubba and I dragged Coop out to a movie."

"What did you see?" None of them had mentioned that, and Jake gave me a blank look.

"When you went out to a movie, dude," Archie supplied.

"I dunno—that thing with the robots. It was—*bad*. We left about halfway through it."

"So, maybe we don't go see that tonight?" I kind of wanted him to smile, particularly because I was bringing everyone down and we could cut the awkwardness in the room with a knife. Or maybe that was me.

"Well, if we did see it tonight, we wouldn't miss anything by making out all the way through it." A glint flashed in Jake's eyes.

Heat flooded my face, even as I grinned. Archie snorted. "You don't need to go to see a bad movie to make out."

"I dunno, Frankie said she wanted the dating experiences. Making out in a movie theater is on that list."

"Wait—there's a list?" I eyed them. "Is that what rule number two is?" That little tidbit had come up when he'd been on the phone, but I had been way too distracted to latch onto it for long.

"There's probably a dating list somewhere," Archie commented, cracking his water bottle open. He nodded to mine and said, "Check Buzzfeed? And do you want me to open that?"

"I got it." Jake lifted my bottle and twisted it open. "Arch is right. Check Buzzfeed or just do an internet search."

"Though, I'm surprised at you, Frankie—you don't have a list of your own?"

I knew they were teasing and it was funny, but my face caught fire. It had been warm earlier, but it was scorching now. "I make a lot of lists."

"So you made a dating one?" Jake poked me. "Are you holding out on us?"

"Well… no. I never wrote it down, specifically."

"But you have a list," Archie challenged, eyebrows raised. "Are we supposed to guess what's on it? Is that how we pass or fail?"

"I'm not grading you," I protested. Good grief. I'd wanted to make Jake smile, not encourage them to gang up on me.

"But you're not telling us what's on the list, so we're flying blind here."

Jake had let go of my hand to open the water bottle, and I dug out my phone and took a long swig of water before googling ten best date ideas for teens and ignored Jake's snort. "She's looking it up."

"Of course, she is. She always does her homework…"

I flipped Archie off, it was automatic. "Right now, I'm doing your homework."

"Well, you do his homework, too." Jake bumped my shoulder, and I laughed. Because it was true.

"Not just mine," Archie argued.

"Ha," Jake retorted.

I clicked the first website and read off the list.

"Make dinner together." I made a face.

"Well, we've done that…"

"We get takeout," I said. "I kind of made dinner for Coop."

"Potato skins and mozzarella sticks," Archie said. "That counts. So big fat check there."

I laughed. The next one would be a little harder. "Go on a bike ride together." They meant bicycle, but… "I rode with Ian."

"Then check," Jake said, leaning back on the sofa next to me and stretching his legs out.

"Scoot over." Archie nudged me, and I almost ended up in Jake's lap, not that he complained. As it was, they pretty much squished me between them. "Okay, what's next?" He peered at the phone seriously.

"Sing karaoke."

They burst out laughing, and I shook my head.

"I'm pretty sure since you did that with all of us, we can call that a check, right?" Jake teased.

My face had probably turned a prominent shade of crimson, but I pushed on and just laughed. "I think so, because you're never getting me up there again."

"That's a challenge," Archie murmured.

"Hmm-hmm."

I didn't even have to glance up to know they were plotting something.

"Next," I said. "Go to a weird museum."

"Weird museum?" Jake leaned in, and the stubble on his face brushed my cheek. It prickled and a shiver raced through me. "Define weird?"

Archie pulled out his phone. "Weird museums in Texas gets us—the Cockroach Museum."

"Ewww." I gaped at him.

"Hey, they dress them up in costumes." Then at my continued gagging noise, he said, "It says weird museum, this is definitely weird."

"That's a hard no," Jake commented. "What else do they have?"

Still laughing, Archie read off his list, "The Toilet Seat Museum, the guy there will tell you the stories of where they came from."

"Ugh." I shuddered. "That's disgusting."

"I'm assuming they're clean," Archie offered.

"Don't assume," Jake suggested, wrapping an arm around my shoulders and pulling me back against him.

"Point. Devil's Rope Barbed Wire Museum."

"Is that real?" I know the list said weird museum, but why would there be a museum for barbed wire?

"Yup," Archie assured me, and showed me a picture on his phone. "So is the Salt Palace Museum—not only do they give you the history of salt, the building is made out of salt."

"That could be kind of cool," Jake muttered. "Maybe."

"For kind of cool we have the Art Car Museum or the Garage Mahal as they call it. Oh, the Texas Prison Museum. Hey, we can get a picture taken in a real jail cell. Museum of the Weird—well that should be number one—if shrunken heads are your thing."

I giggled. "Shrunken heads are not my thing."

"Good to know," Jake said, pressing a kiss right behind my ear. I ran a hand over his arm where he had it wrapped against my chest. Archie glanced up from the phone, then met my gaze and smiled.

"National Museum of Funeral History? Nah. Here we go, the Creation Evidence Museum, it's right next door to Dinosaur Valley State Park."

Laughter rolled through Jake and shook me as I grinned.

"That brings us down to—the West of Pecos Museum, where they have an actual animatronic bartender."

"A little too *Westworld*," I suggested, and Archie made a face.

"Only if they have the hot saloon chicks, too." Then he paused and glanced at me. "But we'd have you, so we don't need their hot chicks."

"Nice save," Jake murmured. "Idiot."

And I laughed.

"Ha!" Archie held up a hand. "Got it—the Munster Mansion in Waxahachie. Look." He showed us the picture. "These people completely designed the house to be the Munster mansion from the old show."

That show was ancient, and it used to be on TVLand when we were little.

"What do you think? Which one qualifies for your weird museum date?"

"Yeah?" Jake asked, stroking his fingers lightly against my collarbone. "Which one?"

"Um… maybe we can just—skip the weird museum date."

"Nope," he said. "No can do. You wanted the full dating experience. That list says weird museum date, we gotta pick one."

"You liked the salt one. And Archie likes the Munsters."

"I like the fact it's a long drive and I get you alone in a car," Archie teased, and I rolled my eyes.

"Huh… not if we all go."

"If we all go, it doesn't count as a date," Archie retaliated.

"Karaoke counted," I pointed out. "So you guys ask Coop and Ian, and I'll let you four pick, as long as it isn't toilet seats or roaches." I shuddered.

"Fair enough," Jake said. "What's next?"

I lifted my phone, and there was a message from Ian on it.

Ian

Hey, just checking on you.

I flipped from the webpage to his text message to answer.

Me

I'm okay. With Archie and Jake at Archie's. Had to get out of apt.

After I hit send, I considered it a moment, then added:

Me

Thank you for asking. Are you okay?

Almost at once, Archie and Jake's phones buzzed. "Busted," Jake said, and he eased me forward to pull out his own phone.

There was a group text on his screen, cause it said *guys*.

And Coop's name popped up.

Bubba

Sharon didn't take down pics. No one told me they got Frankie.

Coop

You got Frankie?

Archie

She's sitting right here. Getting ready to do homework.

Jake

Why don't you grab Coop and come join us?

Surprise unraveled through me, and I glanced up as Jake typed. "This is…"

"Yep, it's my date," he said. "But you're relaxing right now, and I want to see you keep relaxing, and we didn't get to hang out last night like we all wanted. So homework? Hang out? Arch doesn't mind, do you?"

"Nope, and there's still time for you two to go out later if you want—we can finish that list while we wait for Bubba and Coop, then we'll be all earnest and shit and do our homework. Frankie can rap us with a ruler if we get out of line."

"That's hot," Jake commented, and I groaned.

They both grinned as Jake's phone buzzed.

Bubba

On our way.

"See," Jake said before he closed the message and pulled me back against him so I could face Archie again, and Archie tugged my feet into his lap. "Let's finish that dating list. Weird museums are on the to be decided list. What's next?"

Ian

See you soon.

Biting back a smile, I switched screens. Jake inviting them to come over and then planning to stay here was exceptionally sweet. I hadn't enjoyed seeing them the night before—so much had been going on, and I missed them. I'd made up with Archie. Coop and I were in an okay place, but we could be better. Jake and I were apparently okay, or at least we were *trying*. But Ian deserved better than he'd gotten from me, and he'd been great the night before in the end, and he'd taken me home and hadn't put any pressure on me.

Archie squeezed my foot, dragging my attention back to the present. "Sorry—um…next is bowling."

"Not it," they said in unison, and I laughed.

"What's wrong with bowling?"

"Not a damn thing, get Bubba to take you. He likes it," Archie said.

"I don't mind it, but we're all pretty competitive, or are you not remembering ninth grade? Josh Traynor's birthday party at the bowling alley?" Jake reminded me, and I frowned.

"Did I go to Josh's birthday party?"

"No," Archie said suddenly. "You didn't. You had the flu."

"Oh shit. That's right." Jake snapped his fingers. "You were sick, you had a fever or something, and we sent cake home with Coop for you, but he said you couldn't eat it."

I had literally no memory of that. But I'd had like Type A flu or some crap and I'd been dead to the world for a week. The guys had all gotten my homework for me, and when I started to feel better, they went out of their way to help me get caught up.

"So you guys got competitive at the party over bowling?"

"Yeah." They sounded like a pair of guilty kids.

"What did you do?"

"Maybe we save that embarrassing bit of our history for another day," Archie suggested. "Get Bubba to take you bowling. You'll have fun. What's next?"

"I'll tell you later," Jake whispered in my ear, ignoring Archie's glare. "Archie just acted like a dick and doesn't like to be reminded of how much of a dick he was."

"Bite me, Jake," Archie snorted, then tipped his bottle up for a drink and motioned to my phone.

Curious, I squirmed a little, and Jake picked me up and sat me on his lap more properly, and I squeaked. But—it was more comfortable. Clearing my throat, I read off, "Have a picnic in the park." Which we had all actually done.

"Check," they answered, and I grinned wider.

"Play mini-golf."

Archie just stared at me, and the corners of his mouth began to twitch, and I cracked up.

"You guys definitely have that covered. How many weekends did you go?" Jake asked.

"A lot." Archie emphasized. "But Frankie likes it, so that can go back on the list."

"So can video games," I reminded him, and he saluted me. "Board game night."

"Cards Against Humanity," Jake said. "That counts."

"Agreed."

"Roller rink?" I raised my brows.

"Nope," Archie said, shaking his head. "They play disco music."

Jake just laughed.

"The last one is a nature hike."

"I'll take you on one," Jake offered. "I like hiking."

I smiled. "Me, too." I had done a lot of these things. Not as dates specifically, but with the guys.

"There has to be more lists," Archie said. "So—when the guys get here, we all write down date ideas on individual pieces of paper, we put them all in a bowl, and then Frankie gets to pick one each week, and one of us has to do it if not all of us until we empty the bowl."

Oh.

I *liked* that idea.

"Weird," Jake said. "But doable. Just have to time it when Frankie's not working, and it doesn't interrupt someone else's date."

"You guys are a little crazy," I told them.

"About you," Archie said, then winked. "Okay, I like this list better…" He showed us his phone. "Parties, movies, dinner, dancing…"

I grinned. "Check. Check. Check and…very soon, check."

"There's also beach, stargazing, bungee jumping…"

"Bungee jumping?" I straightened a little. That was on the dangerous side.

"I wouldn't mind doing that," Jake admitted. "Or going skydiving."

"I've never even been on a plane, and you want to jump out of one?" I twisted to look at Jake, and he grinned.

"Sure, it'll be fun."

"We can do it," Archie said. "We can do all of it. You game?"

To do crazy stunts? "I think we should do homework now." Because the butterflies in my stomach suddenly had butterflies.

Jake chuckled. "We'll keep it on the maybe list." His phone buzzed, and so did mine and Archie's.

"They're here," Archie said. "C'mon, Jake, let's go get your stuff. Frankie, go grab yours from my room, and everyone back here for a meeting of the study buddies, and no one gets to snuggle Frankie until homework is done."

Groaning, Jake flopped back. "That's a crappy plan, I'd much rather snuggle Frankie."

"Then get done with your homework first," Archie said with a smirk. The bet was funny, even I laughed. It wasn't long before they were all back, and the unease and distress of the day faded even more.

I still had no idea what I was going to do about my mom, or even how we were all going to make this work, but they were all here for me. When Ian and I sat shoulder to shoulder while working on calculus, or Coop and I puppy piled over the Lit assignment, or Archie pulled me over to sit with him on government, or Jake and I took turns quizzing each other on European History—I wasn't alone.

Not even a little bit.

My best friends were right there, and for once, I didn't want to examine that too closely. I just let them be there for me.

And I did my damnedest to be there for them.

Chapter Nine

RED LIGHT

"**P**izza?" Coop suggested a little before seven. I was finishing up the last couple of paragraphs of a paper for French.

"Sounds good," Ian said, stretched out behind me on the sofa. He'd finished his homework first, but I needed to type on my laptop so he'd settled there while I wrote.

"I could eat," Archie groaned. The burgers and fries we'd gotten earlier had all been consumed over the course of the study session. Never get between teen boys and calories, even when they were cold.

"Jake?" Coop asked, but instead of answering, Jake bumped my foot.

"One sec," I said, holding up a finger before typing in my last couple of thoughts. At least writing in French had gotten dramatically easier the last year or so. I could speak it with a fair amount of accuracy, but reading it had been harder until sometime in junior year, and it clicked over in my brain. As I finished the last period and hit save, I glanced up. "What?"

Chuckling, Jake said, "The guys want pizza. Do you want to stay here and eat, or ditch and go do something else?"

The weight of three other stares pressed in around me, but I studied Jake. The last couple of hours had actually been great. I'd focused on the work and not on anything else. "What do you want to do?"

"Take you out," he said easily.

Archie snorted. "Easy answer there."

"Okay," Coop said slowly, pulling my attention. "But I still want pizza."

It took a few minutes to get everything packed away, and they were all helping, which actually made it take longer. Then Coop tugged me in for a hug, and I closed my eyes as I held him tight. He kept his voice low as he murmured, "Call if you need me okay? I'm right there."

"I will," I promised. Then he let me go, and Ian held out his hand, and I walked right into his hug. "Thank you," I told him. "For taking me home last night and for not pushing."

"Always here for you. We still on for Tuesday?"

A laugh escaped. It was a little easier. The sense of doom and gloom wasn't quite so pervasive. It couldn't choke me out. "Yep," I said. "Applications open next week." We had to get his audition tape made.

He let me go with a smile, and then Archie wrapped his arms around me from the back, and my whole body seemed to sigh. I could really get used to all this hugging. "Coffee order still the same for the morning?"

"Yes please, though have them throw two extra shots of espresso in it?" After the last couple of days, I really didn't know how I'd sleep tonight.

"You got it," he pressed a kiss right behind my ear. Then he held my backpack out to Jake who gripped it easily.

Following Jake to the door, it was kind of weird to leave the other guys, I glanced back to find them all watching me go. "We're okay," I said slowly, hand on the doorframe. "Right?"

"We're fine," Ian assured me.

"Yep," Coop said.

"Not a problem here, babe," Archie tacked on. "Just jealous you're leaving with Jake."

Coop and Ian exhaled an almost simultaneous, "yeah." But Ian added, "We'll see you tomorrow—but answer your texts, okay? Don't vanish down another rabbit hole."

"I'll do my best."

Jake linked his hand with mine and then we were heading out. It occurred to me as we descended the steps that we might run into Archie's dad, but Jeremy hadn't warned us that he was home, so I kept my fingers crossed all the way out to Jake's yellow SUV.

Inside, he started the engine and glanced at me. "Trust me?"

"That's not a leading question at all."

He grinned. "That wasn't an answer to the question."

"True." Did I trust him? I wanted to. I really wanted to trust all of them. "Yes."

"Thank you," he said, then reached over to squeeze my knee once before he curved to glance back as he reversed to turn the SUV around. "You wanna talk about what happened that you needed Archie to come get you? It's not like you to not just take your car and go."

It wasn't. Since I'd gotten the car, I'd craved my independence. Spring semester, sophomore year. It had been *awesome* to be able to drive to school. Until then, the guys—sans Coop—had been giving us rides. Then I could take Coop.

"Mom told me about Mr. Standish," I admitted. "It was—uncomfortable and weird. We kind of fought. I was just upset. I know you want to ask a lot of questions, but… I really don't want to talk about it anymore. At least not right now." I was kind of talked out. Especially the whole moving idea.

"No problem," Jake said. "You need to talk about it to someone. You have too much stuff you sit and stew over."

The characteristic bluntness was more of a comfort than I cared to admit. "I talked to Archie."

His knuckles went white on the steering wheel, and I turned my attention back to the passenger window. We were heading toward the highway. Not my place. Not Jake's.

After a long pause, Jake said, "Okay. I'm glad you talked to someone."

"Do you want to talk about why you thought seeing Maria would get her to talk Sharon into taking the pictures down?"

"Not really," he admitted.

"See, you should probably talk to someone, too. You know she still likes you. That's kind of cold to use those feelings against her."

"I didn't lie to her," he swore. "I didn't tell her I was there because I wanted to see her again. I told her I needed her help. That was true. I thought she'd be more invested, considering she's in some of those pictures."

The topless ones? Yeah, I'd guessed. Had they had some kind of an orgy in the hot tub?

There was an image that wouldn't go away.

"Frankie, you believe me, right?"

"You don't usually lie to me, so yeah. I believe you. I just don't get why you thought she'd want to help when… you dumped her."

"She's your friend."

"Hmm…" I made a so-so motion. "A lot of my friends have fallen off the last year or so, I think that might be my fault." As uncomfortable a truth as that might be to swallow. "And even if she was, I broke girl code."

"Girl code?"

"You guys have a bro code, technically girls have a girl code. You don't go after your friend's boyfriend."

There was a beat of silence.

"You didn't."

"Doesn't look that way right now, does it?" I slid a glance at him sideways and he sighed.

"Fuck, I hate high school. When we graduate, we don't have to do this crap anymore. I don't *care* what they think. I care what *you* think."

"Then I think they're hurt, and they're going to lash out at what they think hurt them. In this case—you guys and me."

"But you didn't do anything to them."

"I'm dating you, Jake, and Maria wants to still be dating you. Ian made a big production of inviting me to Homecoming…" It had been so sweet. Tilting my head against the window, I laughed. "Everyone saw it, and I don't think I've been more embarrassed or flattered in my life." He sang in public for me. Ian, who kept his passion for music very quiet from the majority and rarely even performed in front of our friends, had done that so I would have an ask to remember.

"He didn't do so bad," Jake admitted. "But that doesn't excuse Sharon."

"Didn't say it did, but two weeks ago, you guys were all with other girls—in one form or another. Whether you were 'dating' them or not. Right or wrong?"

"Frankie…"

"Right or wrong?" Really, if I had to live with this crap, then so did they.

"You're talking about the end of the summer bash." It wasn't a question, and we were definitely going somewhere farther out. We'd left town behind and were heading north.

"I'm talking about the topless pics in the hot tub… and the fact that Sharon told me if I'd been at the end of the summer party, then I'd realize just how new all of this is. Not like I didn't already know that."

Jake flinched. "Truth? Even if it's painful?"

"Better than lies." Or secrets.

"Then yeah, a couple of weeks ago, at the bash, we all got out of hand. It was—end of the summer, senior year, craziness ensued."

Pretty much what I thought.

"I don't know about the others, we didn't really discuss it," Jake continued. "But yeah, Maria and I hooked up, and it wasn't anything. But Sharon and Bubba might have. I don't know. Don't know about Archie and Patty or Coop and Laura, though I can guess."

So could I.

"Okay."

He blew out a breath. "That's it?"

"What do you want me to do? Yell?" I slipped my shoes off and propped my feet against the dashboard, since apparently, we were driving hell and gone. The sun was dipping on the horizon, but it wasn't dark yet. I could have put on my sunglasses, if I wanted to dig them out of my backpack. Instead, I just looped the end of my ponytail around one finger. The hair had mostly dried.

He didn't say anything for a couple of minutes. "Fuck, it feels like we're not okay again."

"I'm sorry, maybe… maybe going out was a bad idea. I was fine while we were all talking and I was doing homework."

"Would yelling help?"

"I can't yell at you guys for having lives before. Not only would that be dumb, it would be hypocritical. I knew you were dating."

"Yeah, but most of that wasn't dating, at least not by that party."

He didn't have to tell me that, I'd gotten it already.

"I can tell you about baking a cake with Mathieu, but I'm afraid there really aren't any topless pictures."

His expression turned incredulous as he shot a look at me. "Good."

I couldn't help it, I laughed, and he shook his head.

"Seriously, Frankie…"

"Well, I've got nothing else to compare it too—except Archie, and I don't want to talk about that. Mathieu's the only guy I even pseudo dated outside of you guys."

"We can keep it that way," Jake said firmly. "Just like I'm not dating Maria or anyone else."

"Still seems hypocritical to expect that when I'm…" dating everyone else?

"You're not expecting or demanding it," he reminded me. "This is me making a promise." When he put his hand on my leg, I covered it. "I want to make this okay again, Friday you were… you were happy, and then the next time I see you…"

The world had crashed in.

"I was happy Friday. I was happy for a little while earlier, too."

"Yeah?"

"When we were going over the dating list… that was fun. Speaking of which—*where* are we going?"

"Took you long enough to ask. I'm kidnapping you."

Rolling my head to stare at him, I raised my brows. "Explain?"

"Taking you away from the crazy for a little while. You remember when we were kids, and we wanted to go to the Gemini?"

"The drive-in, but no one ever wanted to take us, and it's closed now. Most drive-in theaters are."

"Most," Jake agreed. "Not all. When we were doing homework, I did a little research. Movie dates were on that list, and so was weird, so I thought I'd combine the two with a little nostalgia. There's a drive-in Lynchgate and they have a double-feature tonight."

A double feature. "Lynchgate is like ninety minutes away."

"Worth it," he said, switching his grip so he was holding my hand. "Miles away from home, the crap at school, your mom, all of it. Just you and me and a couple of movies."

"At a drive-in?"

He nodded.

"It's not the robot movie, is it?"

Snorting, he said, "If it is, I promise to make out with you in all the boring parts."

"I'm going to guess it's the whole movie."

His grin grew. "Maybe." Sobering, he added, "But if you don't want to go, I'll turn us around. We'll be late."

I hoped Mom had still been home to feed the cats, and it wasn't like I had a curfew.

"Okay," I told him. "I'd love to go to the drive-in with you, but I want Twizzlers and popcorn—and a soda…"

"And a hot dog and nachos. Yes, your bottomless pit will be fed, I promise."

I smacked his arm, but he just grinned.

"You are a bottomless pit. I've taken you to movies before and tried to share popcorn."

"I am not that bad," I complained.

"No, you're adorably the worst, but it's why I like taking you."

Nose wrinkled, I stuck my tongue out at him, and he chuckled. The bubble of tension pressing in on us just—evaporated, and I could take a deep breath. "Adorably the worst… I think I need that on a t-shirt."

"And on a coffee mug."

We shared a grin, and it was my turn to squeeze his hand. "What were we going to do before? Since you looked it up while we were doing homework?"

He cast me a sheepish look. "Well, I was kind of hoping we'd do a movie night at your place, but that was kind of shot to hell."

Translation, he'd hoped we'd have sex. Yeah, not commenting on that seemed to be prudent. "I like the idea of a drive-in," I said. "Actually, I kind of love it. It's a first, and we need more of those things we've never done."

"Yeah?" He glanced at me, the tilt of his lips curving toward a hopeful smile.

"Yeah." On impulse, I ran my knuckles over his cheek. "I even kind of like you scruffy. But if you get sleepy on the way back, let me drive, okay?"

Catching my hand, he kissed my palm, and the bristles scraping against it tickled. "Scruffy I can also do."

"It suits you."

"What does that mean?"

I grinned. "I don't know…but there's something about a rumpled Jake, who's scruffy, that I like."

"Noted." He winked. "And I'll be fine for the drive. We can always get coffee on the way back."

We spent the rest of the ride like that, trading idle comments, teasing, and relaxing. The tension bled out of the car, and it wasn't awkward—at least, not stilted anymore. By the time we got to the drive-in, I'd actually gotten excited, and we had a bet on what we were going to see.

It was fully dark when we got there, and the first showings began in twenty minutes, so we'd made good time. We only had to pay one fee for the car, which was cool, and our options were a double-feature of horror movies or a double-feature of murder mystery and a psychological thriller.

Jake grimaced and looked at me. "Definitely not the horror."

"Nope. But the other two sound cool."

"You sure?" The tense little worried frown he wore was adorable. "We can skip out on the thriller if it's too much."

"Or make out," I pointed out to him. "I promise to not try and break your arm."

"You can break anything you want, if we're gonna make out." The playful grin softened his frown. He drove us in and got a good spot in front of our screen. It was a mostly wide open field, devoid of grass and a little dusty. The picture screen was huge, and we were the only people here so far. Maybe Sunday nights weren't busy.

I went with Jake to get concessions and to use the bathroom. When I came out, he had a pizza, nachos, hot dogs, popcorn, Twizzlers, *and* a pretzel. My stomach growled at the sight. He told me to wait while he ran and used the restroom, then he came back for the food, and I took the sodas. A few more cars had trickled in, but no one parked right next to us. He got the radio tuned to the station for the sound, and then we started divvying up the food. It was a feast, and I was starving for the first time that day.

Every other meal had been punctuated by discomfort or grief. Jake laughed when I even shared some of the pretzel.

"Well now, I really feel special."

"I share," I reminded him.

"I know, but it's still fun to tease you." Then he leaned over and kissed me. It was a light brush that sparked hotter the second our lips touched. He put a hand on the pizza box to keep it still as he tilted his head and teased at my lips with his tongue. My hands were full or I'd have been touching him too, then he leaned back slowly, a grin pulling at his lips. "Definitely fun to tease you."

A shiver raced up my spine, and I took another bite of the pretzel before I said something dumb. Still, my system hummed from the kiss, and my lips tingled. When he offered me a bite of pizza, I took it, and then we started feeding each other... even after the movie started. When he sucked my fingers against his lips, another shudder went through me.

The murder mystery was good—though I think I missed more than a few clues between stolen kisses and Jake making sure he sucked on each of my fingers. He was making me a little crazy. Course, the fact I got him to shudder when I grazed my teeth then my tongue over the tips of his finger was definitely something I never wanted to forget.

Eventually, he leaned back in his seat, but he kept a hold of my hand, and I tried to desperately follow who had done what to whom—thankfully, this one was something of a comedy, so they laid it all out at the end. When the movie was over, I went from my seat to Jake's as he shoved his seat away from the steering wheel. There wasn't a lot of room until he pulled the lever, and his seat went back to lay nearly flat.

Sprawling on his lap and chest, I studied him. "Hi..."

"Hey, we have ten minutes before the next one starts. Need a bathroom break?"

"Nope."

"Awesome." Hand around my nape, he pulled me to him, and then he was all lips, teeth, and tongue. The bristle on his face stung mine, but I couldn't bring myself to care. I had my hands in his hair, and he had a hand on my ass. I was still achy from earlier, but the tension winding through my body promised me we'd get over it.

When the sound of the movie kicked up announcing the second one, Jake groaned. I lifted my head and stared down at him in the dark with only the flickering light from the movie screen beyond to highlight him. We were a thousand miles away here.

"Not in the car," he whispered. "I want to—but not here. I don't want to be squirming to find an angle, and I definitely don't want anyone else looking at your ass."

I nuzzled another kiss and then climbed off him carefully to slide back into my seat. He lay there for a moment, and I'd be lying if I said I didn't notice the erection pressing at the front of his shorts. Finally, he sat up and adjusted himself, then grinned at me.

"I could always—you know…" I held up my hand. "I have some practice from before."

"Fuck," he groaned. "You're killing me. I'm going to be good." He caught my hand and about all we'd missed were previews. Jake liked to hold my hand. He did it all the time, and while it had been weird at first, as with all the hugs earlier, I liked it.

I liked the constant contact.

The making out was good, too.

The second movie captured our attention far more effectively than the first. The murder mystery might have been quirky and funny, but the psychological thriller strung me tense. I couldn't look away from the screen. Even when Jake unpeeled my hand from his arm and covered it with both of his hands.

At the end, I was so wound up that when Jake tugged me in for another kiss, I didn't hesitate. Panting by the time we broke apart, I said, "That was insane."

"Yeah. Thrillers go off the list with horrors."

"Awww… I meant insane in a good way."

He grinned. "You were taking out my throwing arm."

Dipping my head, I kissed the nail indentations I'd left on his skin. "Sorry."

"It's okay… c'mon, let's clean out the trash and hit the bathrooms before we head back." It was late, the first film started at eight-thirty, and it was well after midnight. We wouldn't be home until two, maybe a little earlier.

A few more cars had come in while we watched, but we still had plenty of space. Jake was waiting for me when I came out though and walked me back to the car, despite the fact most of the others had left and the staff was closing up.

"You good to drive?" I checked. I'd been exhausted earlier in the day, but after the movie and the making out—and maybe all the sugar I consumed when I killed the Twizzlers—I was wide-awake.

"I'm good," he promised.

Getting back took longer than we planned though. There was some big accident on the highway, and they'd shut it down. The GPS alternate routes were going to take us hell and gone. Jake scowled as he drummed his hands on the steering wheel. "We can try this, but—it's gonna add another hour, or we can try to wait this out, once we get past, we're still an hour away, but I can make up time."

"Give it fifteen minutes? If this isn't moving, we try to get off?" We weren't the only ones stuck here, the traffic behind us had begun to back up, and it didn't matter that it was late.

"Sorry, Frankie." He checked his phone. "Oh, yeah—let me tell the guys. I told them we were going to the movies, but I didn't say where." He grinned.

Oh, crap. My phone was in my backpack, so I wiggled to reach into the backseat and snagged my phone out of the side pocket. It was deader than a doornail.

Pfft.

"I'm no help."

He chuckled. "You're all the help in the world. Soon as mine's charged back up, you can plug in." His was at ten percent.

We got lucky, at thirteen minutes, the traffic started to trickle past the cop cars and fire trucks with their flashing lights. It gave me a good view of the accident. Truck versus car versus—oh, it had been a motorcycle. There were ambulances pulling away earlier, someone had been hurt. The car was totaled, and the truck looked like it had hit the side rails as well as the car, but the bike… it was a disaster. There was some big wet stain the flashing lights kept catching, and it took a second for the fact that it was blood to register.

My heart hurt for those people.

"I hope nobody died," I whispered.

"Yeah," Jake said as he took hold of my hand again. Tired began to ease into my bones, and I was half-asleep when we pulled into my apartments. Jake pulled up behind my mom's car, and we both stared at it for a minute. Twisting, I leaned over and kissed him.

"Thank you for tonight, Jake."

"Even if it took forever to get back?"

"Even if." Another kiss as I cupped his cheek. "You okay to drive home?"

"If I'm exhausted, can I come sleep with you?" It was a tease, but I was pretty sure if I said yes, he'd park in a heartbeat.

"Mom's here."

"Yeah." He gave me another kiss. "Okay, get your stuff and go in, I'm staying until I see you inside. Don't forget to charge your phone."

"I won't." Another kiss stolen before I stripped off my seatbelt. As I slid out of the car, he pulled my backpack up and held it out to me.

"Night, Frankie."

"Night… text me when you're home?"

"I will."

I was exhausted as I walked up the steps. My feet were lead weights and added a hundred pounds. But I got the key in the lock and the door opened. I waved back toward the car and then slid inside and locked up behind me.

Tiddles let out an annoyed meow from where he sat on the kitchen table, tail thrashing. Yeah, I was late.

"C'mon, off," I told him, scooting him off the table. It was almost three. If I was lucky, I could get three hours of sleep.

I made it to the edge of the kitchen, when the light snapped on in the living room and almost blinded me.

"Where the hell have you been?"

Mom.

Well, so much for being lucky.

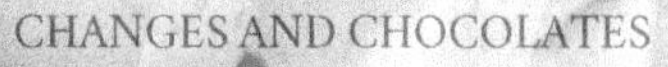

Chapter Ten

GLASS HOUSE

Two and a half hours of sleep was not enough. My eyes were gritty, my head hurt, and all I wanted to do was crawl back in the bed and sleep for another eight hours. Not that it could happen. No matter how much I wanted it. A shower helped. Brushing my teeth helped. Coffee in the kitchen helped more. My mother sat at the kitchen table, dressed for work, an overnight bag by the backdoor, and a cup of coffee next to her.

She wore the exact same expression she'd had when I walked in at three. One part irritated, one part resting bitch face, and one part—I had no idea how to define it. I hesitated to call it concerned. But her eyes tensed as she focused on me.

I poured the rest of the coffee into the travel tumbler before capping it. "Do I need to put more coffee on?" Eight more words than I'd spoken to her before. I hadn't answered her question. Instead, I'd just crashed.

"No, I'm leaving in five minutes."

I took a long gulp of the coffee, then rinsed out the carafe and set it to the side to dry before emptying the grinds into the trash and leaving the top open to air out the condensation left behind.

Another swallow of coffee, and I shouldered my backpack and headed for the door.

"Frankie…"

So close.

I paused with one hand on the door.

"I'm going out of town today."

Not really wanting to have this conversation, I waited.

"I have to be in Los Angeles for the next three days, I probably won't be back until Friday, but I might stay over."

Still, I didn't turn.

"Are you going to talk to me?"

I considered my answer. Then pivoted to face her. "What would you like to talk about?"

Sighing, she said, "Nothing, I suppose. I'm moving money to your account. I didn't get to the shopping this weekend."

Color me not surprised.

It was hard to meet her gaze and not glare. I didn't understand her choices. I didn't even *like* them. And had no say in them.

"All right," I managed finally when she said nothing else. With a sigh, Mom picked up her coffee and cradled her mug.

"Have a good day. I'll text you once I'm in L.A."

I wouldn't hold my breath. With a nod, I turned to grasp the door, when she added, "And if you were out late because you were having sex with one of those boys, please be sure you're being careful about it. The last thing you want is an unplanned pregnancy derailing your life."

Ice crawled up my spine, and I damn near bit a hole in my tongue to keep from telling her to do the same thing. I didn't slam the door, no matter how satisfying it might have been.

Coop was waiting at my car when I got there.

"Hey," he said, pushing away from the driver's side door. "What's wrong?"

"Nothing." I motioned toward the car. "We need to go. I need to review for a test this morning." My brain was currently mush, and the chill of my mom's words left cold in my veins.

"You sure?" He put a hand to my cheek, but I pulled away.

"Yes, I'm sure. Just tired. We were out late. Can we go?" I shoved my backpack in the back, and Coop held his hands up before he circled the car.

"Sure."

The drive to school passed quickly, and I wasn't really in the mood to talk. I didn't even want to head to our table. Ian's bike was parked in the spot next to where I usually parked. My gut tightened. The bike last night hadn't looked like his, but I never wanted to picture him in an accident like that.

My phone had started buzzing as we headed inside. Aware of the looks Coop kept casting me, I avoided meeting his gaze. I didn't want to talk about any of it. I wanted to focus on school. Just had to get through the next few hours, and then I could crash early tonight.

The hum of conversation in the cafeteria was on the rise as we headed through. Archie was sprawled back in a chair at our table, his feet up with his phone in his hand.

He glanced at us with a grin, but it faded. "What's wrong?"

"I asked the same thing," Coop said, but I just shook my head.

Sliding into a chair, I opened my backpack and pulled out my notebook. "Nothing. Just tired, and I have a test today. "

Standing, Archie nudged the coffee over to me and then moved to sit in the chair next to me while Coop took the one on the other side.

"Thank you," I said, taking a drink of the coffee. The long, icy cold slug hit my system like a bullet. Hopefully, it would do more than the coffee I shotgunned on the way in.

Focusing my sore-eyed gaze on my notebook, I flipped straight to French and started mentally reviewing the material. I had submitted the paper the night before, but the test would have more essay questions.

My phone buzzed again, and I dragged it out of my pocket.

A half-dozen photos of me had been tagged on Instagram. Oh, yay. I just dismissed the notification.

There were two texts from Rachel.

Rachel

You okay?

Rachel

Don't worry about Patty. I already clapped back for you.

Patty?

"What the fuck?" Archie asked, and I caught him looking at my phone. "What'd she do?"

"I don't know. And right now, I don't have time to care."

Me

Thanks.

I sent it back to Rachel, then locked the phone and put it face down and took another drink of the coffee.

"Crap," Coop muttered, and he pushed out from his chair and circled me to sit on Archie's other side. I spared a look for where he was showing Archie something on his phone. Yeah, no time to focus on that.

By the time Jake and Ian got there, I was over half-done with the review.

"Hey, Frankie," Ian slid into the chair Coop had abandoned.

"Hi," I told him. "Sorry, studying." I tossed a smile to Jake. He looked almost as tired as me. He dropped into the chair opposite me and slid his foot over to nudge mine, I pulled my feet back, and tucked them under my chair as I kept reading.

"Yeah, Frankie has a test," Coop said. "So she's not in the mood to talk."

"So I see," Jake said. The noise level in the cafeteria continued to rise as more students poured in. The guys shifted positions so they could talk, but they didn't abandon the table. Once, when I glanced up, Jake scowled at his phone.

I was on the last page of my review when someone walking past the table sneezed *"slut."* The words on the page wavered in front of me, but Jake was up and moving.

"Fuck," Coop muttered. I winced at the sound of flesh slamming into flesh, and I twisted in the chair to see Jake take the guy all the way to the floor. Ian and Archie waded in with Coop to try and separate them, but Jake was pounding the guy.

Holy crap.

Like everyone else, I was on my feet. The volume climbed, and Ian just got Jake off of—was that Rodney? I couldn't tell. I thought it might be Rodney Dial. But his nose was a bloody mess, and he was almost in a fetal position.

The school SRO was there, and Mr. Davis, the principal. Crap.

Coop backed over toward me. Jake's expression was filled with hostility as he glared at Rodney. The SRO was escorting him away, and Mr. Davis along with Ms. Ryerson was helping Rodney up. A whistle cut through the air as Coach Dodd sent people back to their tables. Nearly half the room had crowded around. Sharon bumped me on her way past, and I caught Maria staring off after Jake.

Locking on Ian's pained gaze, I said, "Is he going to be okay?"

"I don't know," Archie answered, raking a hand through his hair. His knuckles were a little reddened. Had he hit Rodney or Jake? "C'mon, let's get to class."

I glanced over at the coach, then back at Ian. "Jake's gonna get in trouble with the team."

"Maybe," Ian soothed, rubbing my shoulder. "Maybe not. It depends."

On what? He just attacked Rodney, and yeah, Rodney did that stupid sneeze thing, but… the unsaid part of it all was Jake went after the guy for me.

"Go with Arch," Coop said. "I'm going to swing by the SRO office, see if I can see him."

I almost hated to ask. "Should we call his mom?" Jake's mom was an involved mom.

"I don't think that one is going to be up to us," Ian said, his expression turning stiff and angry. He wasn't looking at me though, and when I twisted, I caught Sharon turning away.

"Don't," I told him, covering his hand with mine. "Don't pick a fight for me."

"She hasn't taken them down," Ian warned.

"Ignore her." It was my only advice as I squeezed his hand once, then went to stuff my notebook back into my backpack. No way I was going to study anymore after that. "Trust me. She wants your attention. Ignoring her will hurt more."

I spoke from a lot of experience.

Ian studied me a beat. "Are you okay?"

"I'm fine. Just worried about Jake now." The more I lied about it, the easier it was. I did not want to talk about Mom or bad meatloaf or anything. "And tired."

"You guys were out late," he said quietly. "Did you at least have fun?"

"Yeah," I admitted. "We went to a drive-in movie. It was a lot of fun."

"Good." His expression gentled, and his smile widened. "Go on." The noise volume in the cafeteria was louder, and I wasn't the only one catching the looks being thrown our way.

Archie and I caught a few more looks and comments on the way to class, including Dobie Masterson slinging an arm around me and asking if I could juggle an extra guy.

I elbowed him in the gut and got between him and Archie before Archie threw a fist.

"Assholes," he snarled as Dobie laughed and walked away, all the while saying, "Just curious."

Dick.

First period wasn't so bad. The walk from first to second was a joy. I had to swing by my locker, and there was a lovely slut note taped to the front. I tugged it off and crumpled it up. Rachel bumped the locker next to mine as I opened the door.

"Don't let them get to you. They're just a bunch of sharks scenting blood in the water."

"Yeah, it's fine," I told her. "Thanks for—the thing with Patty."

"Anytime," Rachel said, smiling. "You good to get to class, or do you want me to be a bitch on wheels for you?"

I laughed. "I'm good. I'll see you later."

"Count on it."

Ian was waiting for me outside of class. "Jake's still in the SRO office, and his mom is on the way."

Crap.

"I talked to my dad, too. He said he could come up. Might help, but he was gonna call Jake's mom." Even that reassurance wasn't a bright spot.

I'd checked my phone a dozen times in class, but nothing from Jake. He probably couldn't text, and I didn't want to distract him.

Calculus sucked, and it was all I could do to focus on the numbers and the formulas. It didn't help that two of the girls on the other side of the room kept up a whispering commentary with pointed looks at me. Maybe I was just being paranoid. Ian walked with me to French, his determined expression seemed to hold some of the comments at bay, or I was overreacting.

Mathieu smiled when he saw me and nodded to Ian. "I'll keep an eye on her," he promised, and I frowned.

"I can look after myself," I told them both. "I'll see you at lunch?" The last was to Ian, and he nodded, then gave my hand a squeeze before he looked at Mathieu.

"Thanks, man."

"Of course."

The test in French should have been easy, but it was hard to focus, and took me longer than usual to work my way through it and the two essay questions. I had maybe ten minutes at the end of it, and I was exhausted.

At least the test kept people quiet. The walk from French to AP Lit brought me eye to eye with Patty, who opened her mouth then shut it abruptly as Rachel bumped my hip and smirked at her.

"Yeah, I didn't think you wanted to say anything," Rachel said as we continued past her. Great. They were all pissed at me. After we were down the hall and around the corner, she glanced at me. "Keep your chin up. Haters are going to hate."

"I noticed… thanks."

"You're welcome." She gave me another bump. "See you later." She continued up the hall as I diverted into AP Lit. Coop shot me a smile as I walked in.

"Frankie," Ms. Fajardo said as she rose from her desk. "Can I have a word?" She motioned me back to the door, and I nodded. Worry and guilt collided in my gut. Had I forgotten something else? Ms. Fajardo didn't usually pull me aside—at least, not before class. Though we talked a lot the mornings I'd hung out in here. Coop tracked us with a worried look as I squeezed past two students to get out of the room.

"Everyone take your seats, and if you haven't done the chapter reading for today, get to it. If you have, then pull out your journals. No talking." Then she closed the door as the bell rang, leaving us in the deserted hallway. Worry filled her eyes. "Are you all right?"

"I'm fine," I said slowly. Other than being worried about Jake, while also being labeled a slut, and having to endure kids I didn't know whispering about me, and some of my former friends treating me like a pariah. Discounting all of that, I was awesome.

"Well, I was informed about the online bullying, and your counselor has asked that you come down and speak to the student support advocate, and then she'll go with you to see the SRO to give a statement."

Was she kidding?

"Really?" That was the last thing I wanted to do.

"We have zero tolerance policy for a reason, Frankie. I'm sorry that this happened to you. But—go on down to see Dr. Miller?

"If I'm not the one complaining, do I still have to go?"

"Yes," Mrs. Fajardo said. "I'll make sure Coop has a copy of the notes for you, and I'll email you any assignments. I know you don't like to make a big deal out of these things, but it is a big deal."

Oh, shoot me.

"Okay."

She gave me a pat on the arm and then returned to the classroom. My phone buzzed, and I fished it out.

Coop

????

Me

I have to go see the Student Advocate and the SRO.

Coop

Why?

Me

Post. No big deal. See you at lunch.

I checked my messages with Jake and then sent him one.

Me

You okay?

I wasn't expecting him to answer right away, and he didn't. The counselor's office was hell and gone from Mrs. Fajardo's room, so I made the hike. The receptionist glanced up when I came in, and she smiled.

"Frankie Curtis," I said. "I was told I had to see Dr. Miller."

"Have a seat, I'll let her know you're here."

I wasn't the only one sitting in the office. There were two other students present, one waiting like me, and the other one a student aide. As soon as I sat down, she had her phone out to text.

Great.

Yep, I was definitely getting paranoid. I was too tired for this. It took twenty minutes before the receptionist sent me back to Dr. Miller's office. The woman in question was about my height, and had light brown hair pulled back into a neat ponytail. She had to be in her late twenties, but she looked unsettlingly closer to my age, which made having to talk to her even weirder.

The fact she was an actual licensed psychologist didn't help. Like I said, Curtises didn't go to therapy.

This was as close as I ever intended to get, and I was not here of my own volition.

"Mrs. Fajardo told me you needed to see me," I said, lobbing the ball firmly in her court.

"Yes," she said, kindness practically perfuming the air around her. "Have a seat." She waved me toward the chairs and closed the door. Then she picked up files from one of the chairs and moved them around the credenza behind her desk.

Reluctantly, I perched on the edge of one chair, and I didn't take the backpack off. I had zero intentions of staying here very long.

"First, let me say it's very nice to meet you, Frankie—I can call you Frankie?"

"Yeah, that's fine." I flattened my palms against my knees, even as I started to bounce one foot.

"Thank you. I find it's easier if you just call me Diane, rather than Dr. Miller. Doctor is so formal."

Yeah, I didn't have a problem with formal. Still, I nodded. It wasn't a big deal to not argue that point.

Exhaling, she studied me as she leaned her elbows on the desk. "I'm sure this has been a tough morning."

"Not really." I gave her what I hoped was a bland smile. "Gonna be tougher tonight when I have to make up for missing my class."

"Mrs. Fajardo understood, and you'll be allowed to make up the work. I understand if you're uncomfortable…"

Foot bouncing regularly now, I kept my gaze fixed just to the right of hers. It let me look like I was staring right at her and avoiding meeting her eyes all at once.

"Cyber-bullying is a very important issue…and like all forms of bullying, it takes its toll on someone. The post on Instagram was reported to the principal this morning. It was also flagged yesterday to the attention of the counselors."

Oh. God. "Okay."

"You do know the post I'm talking about?"

"Yep." Because it had to be the *I'm stupid* one. Or I was supposed to be the smart one. Whatever.

"Frankie," she continued when I didn't add anything more. "There are a couple of things you need to understand. One, this was done to you—you're not in trouble. Two, it's okay to be upset. Bottling every emotion isn't healthy."

"No offense, Diane. But I'm fine. I can't change other people's opinions." I couldn't even change my mother's, what hope did I have of anyone else? "And what they think doesn't really matter to me."

"You can tell yourself that, but it doesn't mean the situation isn't uncomfortable for you."

"This," I pointed out. "This is uncomfortable for me. Being pulled out of my class where everyone sees that I'm gone and then wonders where I am. Some student aide sends out a message that says I'm here and people start to speculate. That just adds more whispers to it. I didn't ask to come here, I didn't report this—I'm *fine*."

"Be that as it may, we still need to report this, you still need to know you have options, and you need to know this is a safe space where you don't have to be fine and no one is going to gossip about it." She sounded like she meant well, but I shrugged.

"Consider me informed. What happens next?"

"Well, I'd like it if you would consider sitting and talking to me for a few minutes."

"More than I already have?"

"You haven't really spoken to me." Hands clasped, she leaned back in the chair. "I get it, it's weird to talk to a psychologist. I wasn't comfortable the first time I spoke to one."

"Did you want to talk to them?"

"I suppose yes," she said with some careful consideration. "Though not excited about doing it. I needed help, and I was hoping she could help me."

"There's the difference," I said. "I don't want help." I didn't want to talk about my mom or school or the guys or the girls—none of it. "I just want to go to class, get my work done, and graduate."

"That fits. You're an overachiever. You filled your schedule with challenging courses, and you're taking nearly a full load. You added a TA opportunity to your schedule. You have a stellar transcript, and my understanding is that four separate teachers have offered to write you recommendations, and you're planning on applying to Harvard."

"You know a lot."

"I try to make sure I know who I'm talking to, particularly when I don't think they want to talk to me. I don't take it personally. Trust takes time. You don't have to trust me right now. But I am on your side."

"Aren't you on the side of every student here?" That was her job, right?

"Yes, I am," she admitted. "But I am not choosing one side over another. Do you think you can talk to me for a few minutes about the posting?"

"I don't really have anything to say." I shrugged. "There's nothing to say."

"Can you tell me how it made you feel?"

"I can, but I don't want to. Look, Diane, I appreciate that this is what you have to do, cause it's the rules. But you've talked to me, and I'm fine."

"Except that knee hasn't stopped bouncing since you sat down. You're on the edge of your seat, ready to run. You're throwing up barriers to conversations and shutting everything down with answers designed to block follow-up questions. That doesn't say fine."

Stilling my leg, I scooted back an inch in the chair and met her gaze. "I have to pee."

A hint of a smile appeared on her face. "Well, you may use the restroom here in the office at the end of the hall while I call your mother. I need to let her know what's going on, or I can wait for you to call, and I'll sit here with you."

"Mom's on a flight to California," I informed her as I stood. "You can call, but you'll probably get voicemail."

"I see." The advocate frowned. "I'll leave her a message. Go use the restroom, and then if you are truly unwilling to discuss this any further, I'll walk with you to the SRO, and you can make a small statement there."

"If I don't want to make a statement?"

"Then you can tell the officer you have no statement to make. That's your prerogative. I would urge you to reconsider, as you have the right to report this bullying."

"Someone else has already reported it, so you don't really need me." But I wasn't going to keep debating it. Letting myself out, I made a beeline for the bathroom. I did actually have to pee. Inside, I shut the door and leaned back against it.

I checked my phone.

Jake

All good. Might make lunch. Definitely don't want to miss study hall.

Archie

What's going on? Coop said you got
pulled from class.

Ian

You okay?

Coop

Lunch in ten minutes. You gonna make it?

I had no idea.

An alert popped up on my phone. Another tag on Instagram.

Wonderful.

Tabbing to the picture, I stared at it. It wasn't a post—it was a DM. There were several of them. All from different accounts. All of them anonymous. One was a photo of Patty and Archie making out. Boy that one was old—but the bikini was familiar. It was captioned: *He gets around.*

The next was one of me and Jake in the hall, holding hands, followed by Ian holding my hand, and another with me and Coop. *You are running out of hands.*

Another was just some white lettering on a black background.

Heard Patty and Archie made out @Sat Party. #hot

Shaking my head, I scrolled to the last one.

You know everyone hates you right now, don't you?

Closing the app, I pushed away from the door and stuffed my phone in my pocket, then used the restroom before washing my hands. I couldn't linger in there anymore.

Diane was waiting for me in the hallway, wearing an encouraging smile. She led the way, then insisted on walking next to me. It wasn't a short jaunt to the SRO's office. It didn't help that the bell rang for lunch before we were halfway there.

I should have just stayed in bed this morning.

Hanging by a Moment

Archie

Any news? Jake or Frankie?

Coop

No.

Bubba

None. Dad is here though.

Archie

Any updates from him?

Bubba

He just told me to hang tight.

Coop

Frankie stopped talking.

Archie

Head to SRO or Student Advocate at lunch?

Bubba

IDK – split? Go to both?

Archie

SRO. F just got here.

Coop

Bell rings in five.

Bubba

We'll be there.

Archie

Anyone feel like ditching after?

Coop

Yes.

Jake

...

Bubba

Maybe. A. Did you see P's post?

Jake

...

Archie

Yes.

Coop

Did they have a meeting or something?

Bubba

We need to fix.

Archie

Sure. How?

Jake

...

Bubba

J we know you can't talk. Fill us in after.

Jake

K

Bubba

U don't have a plan, Arch?

Archie

Bubba won't like my plan.

Bubba

Share. I might be fine with it now.

Archie

Pissed?

Bubba

Yes.

Archie

Good.

Coop

Bell in 2.

Archie

Talk soon.

Bubba

SRO?

Archie

SRO

Chapter Eleven

CRASH COURSE

Dragging my feet wouldn't make the trip to the SRO's office any easier, so I did my best to hit a brisk pace. I could only wish avoiding prying eyes was possible. Jake and his mom were sitting in the office when we got there, and my gaze locked on his.

He frowned, then glanced past me to the student advocate. Ian's dad was talking to Officer Jennings. Our school had three resource officers, two were usually always on site.

Mr. Rhys frowned at my arrival. "Hey, Frankie, what's going on?"

"Hi, Mr. Rhys," I said, looping my fingers through my backpack straps. I really didn't want to discuss this with anyone, much less the guys' parents.

"Ms. Curtis, if you'll come this way." Officer Lester stepped out of an office and beckoned to me. She was the only female SRO, so I suppose that was a perk. Diane was right behind me.

"Wait," Mr. Rhys called. "Why is Frankie in here?" His voice carried a lot of authority. Most of the time, like his wife, Mr. Rhys was so laid back and friendly. At the moment, however, his attitude reminded me of his military service.

Jake sat forward, but it was Diane who said, "It's an unrelated matter," she stated. "And also not one we can discuss with you, because you're not Frankie's parent."

Oh, if only the floor would swallow me up.

"Actually, Sarah and I are both on the list of emergency contacts if you can't reach Maddy."

They were?

Since when?

Mrs. Brennen was—Coop's mom and mine had been swapping out for both of us for years, but when did Mom add Ian's parents?

Officer Lester cleared her throat. "We need to check on that. For now, Frankie come in here, will you?"

Jake lifted his chin toward me, and I gave him a little smile before following the officer. Diane didn't join me immediately. The officer closed the door, shutting us in before she circled the desk. The dark-skinned woman had a genuinely nice smile, and she cast me a sympathetic look as she took a seat.

"Frankie, before I look this up, do you want Mr. Rhys in here?"

"I don't know why I would need him. You just want me to make a statement about the posting, and I really don't want to make a statement or even have one to make. I told Diane, I didn't report it."

"I know you didn't," she said, her expression sober. Leaning forward, she held my gaze. "Frankie, bullying seems like a trial to report. A lot of people feel like they are admitting to doing something they shouldn't have done, and that's why they are being treated this way. We used to tell kids to ignore it, and it would go away. Then bullies found new ways to pile on. Everyone can be a bully, it's not just one person—it's an attitude. It's an attitude of entitlement that allows one side to strike out against another."

"We discussed that in psych class," I told her. "The problem is—what happens when you report bullying? Really? The kids who did it might get disciplined, but then they're pissed off because they get called on the carpet for it. Doesn't that just make them lash out harder?"

"It can also set a boundary, because not responding indicates that the behavior is acceptable. It's not. The post? The photos? All of it? It's not acceptable. You were targeted. Several people agree on this issue, and having reviewed it…"

Embarrassment crawled through me. "You looked at it?"

"I'm afraid so. It's public. The tags are public. We've had to screen shot all of it so we have a record of it. There will be discipline—however—the poster's identity is anonymous, and we're trying to identify who did it, and we've reached out to the company."

Seriously?

"There were names in the complaints, but I'd like to hear from you…"

At a knock on the door, I flinched. Officer Lester gave me a small smile before she said, "Yes?"

Diane opened the door. "Mr. Rhys is listed on the emergency contacts, and he tried to call Ms. Curtis, but as I explained to him, she's on a flight to California at the moment. All our calls are going to voicemail."

The officer looked at me, and I leaned back in the chair as much as I could with the backpack still on. I didn't want to take it off or act like I was comfortable. I just wanted to get this over with so I could leave. "I still don't want to make a statement."

Lester curled her fingers, and the door opened wider to let Diane and Mr. Rhys in. When I glanced back, I caught Jake's frown, and then twisted to look down at my lap. The sooner we got this over with, the better.

Dropping a hand on my shoulder, Mr. Rhys said, "Does this have anything to do with Jake and Rodney?"

"Yes and no," Officer Lester said. "Jake's statement made it clear what precipitated the fight."

Mr. Rhys gave my shoulder a squeeze, and a horrifying burn started in my eyes that I blinked away.

"This, however, is a separate incident." Officer Lester gave me another encouraging smile. "Frankie's not in trouble. Far from it. Frankie was targeted on social media with a bullying post. It was reported to the school by several sources, and we have reviewed the post and found it to be objectionable and actionable."

Oh, please don't ask to see it...

"I'm really sorry to hear that," he said quietly. "How are you feeling, Frankie?"

"Like I don't want to be here," I admitted. "And I think this isn't necessary."

"I'd like to see the post, and I'm sure your mother would, but if the officer and Dr. Miller feel this warrants action, then I'm going to lean on agreeing with them."

Of course, he would.

I didn't pull out my phone or volunteer the post, but I didn't have to. Officer Lester pulled it up on her computer screen and turned it around. I kept my gaze fixed on my hands. I really didn't need to see the images again. Showing Ian's dad was only going to create more problems for the guys on top of everything else.

"As you can see," Officer Lester said. "Some of these photos are fairly explicit. The language is also keyed to targeting Ms. Curtis, as are the implications in the following images."

My face was on fire, and I needed to file my nails. There were nicks in a couple of them. I also needed some lotion. The skin was dry. Did I not rub lotion over my hands after the shower that morning? A dull ache settled behind my eyes, weighing heavier and heavier with each tap of the space bar on the officer's computer.

Finally, the show and tell portion ended, and Mr. Rhys sat down in the chair next to me. I stole a look at him, and the sympathy on his face just made me want to crawl into a hole. "Do you know who posted it, Frankie?"

"Not for certain, no." That wasn't a lie. I was pretty sure it was Sharon. The screen name she used was close to her own. Course, Sharon was in some of those pictures. She'd been the one to make the comment in the bathroom, too.

"Are you just saying that because you want this to go away, or do you really not know?" The question didn't quite accuse me of lying, but the suggestion was there.

"I'm saying it because I don't know. I don't know the name it was posted under. I was just tagged in it."

He nodded, and then gave my shoulder another squeeze before he focused on the officer. "Are we getting those images taken down?"

"We've made some calls, but it's a process. In the meanwhile, it's obviously had a lot of hits. If we can identify the student, then we can also approach them and their parents to remove the post."

"Everyone has pretty much seen it, so what does removing it do?" Maybe I should have just shut up, but they dragged me in here for this less than comfortable discussion.

"I know it seems very after the fact," Officer Lester said. "However, documenting a pattern of behavior and perhaps nipping it in the bud may help prevent future incidents. We also want our students exercising better judgment when it comes to their social media behavior. As you know, colleges look at your social media footprint during the evaluation process."

Great.

"And while you didn't post this…"

It still had my name all over it. "I really don't know. I can guess, but that would be pointing a finger blind. It could be someone else entirely who just wants to cause trouble."

Mr. Rhys scratched his jaw thoughtfully. "We could reach out to the parents of all the other students pictured here. Particularly those at the party in some of the images." His mouth tightened, and I winced. "I would imagine they would know who was there and had access to these photos."

"It's the internet," I pointed out. "It takes less than three seconds to share a photo with someone else."

"I'm afraid that Frankie has a point," Diane said from where she'd been quietly leaning against the wall. "That said, we would like you to make a statement. You're the affected party. With or without your statement, we are going to investigate it because cyber-bullying is a serious offense that could have legal implications down the road, but is definitely in violation of the school's code of conduct."

For some reason, that made me want to laugh. No one cared about the code of conduct. We all had to sign it every year, and I doubted anyone had read it from front to back.

I hadn't.

It was ten pages long of basically common sense rules. We knew the important one: *don't be an asshole.*

"Maybe just tell us how this affects you," the officer suggested.

"I don't care what they think. The pictures paint an image, they're designed to make me question my friends. To feel bad. I don't." Which was mostly true. "It mostly makes me feel tired."

"Have you received any other contact from the poster? We looked at your Instagram, but we didn't find too many other tagged photos of a similar nature. Maybe ones sent through DMs?"

"No," I lied.

"What other social media platforms are you on?"

"The usual ones," I said with a shrug. "I don't usually do that much. I've been busy." Then with a look at Diane, I added, "I have five AP classes I'm taking, and I have a job."

"Frankie is probably one of the most conscientious students I've ever met. She's good for Ian. She shoulders a tremendous amount of responsibility, maybe even more than she should at her age." Was that judgment in Mr. Rhys' voice?

"I see." Officer Lester studied me for a moment. "Is there anything else that's happened in the last few days that may have precipitated this?"

Oh. I'd been making out with my best friends, had sex with one of them, fought with them, found out my mother was having an affair with one of their dads, and had a fight with my mom. While all of that was true, Ian inviting me to homecoming was the most likely trigger. "Not that I can think of."

Diane sighed, but she nodded to me and, Officer Lester said, "Thank you for coming in, Frankie. If you run into any other issues, I encourage you to come back and talk to us. Please."

"Go on and wait for me out there," Mr. Rhys said, and it took everything I had not to grimace. "It's not bad," he was quick to assure. "I promise. Just wait a couple of minutes for me? I'd like to talk to Dr. Miller and the officer."

"Sure thing." I was up and out of the chair. I'd not taken off my backpack the whole time, and as soon as I was out, I found Jake waiting by himself.

"Hey…" The door closing behind me seemed louder than it was.

"Hey." He stood up and glanced past me. "You okay?"

Shrugging, I said, "Pretty sure I should be asking you that."

I took the chair next to where he'd been seated, and he dropped to sit next to me. There was a faint bruise on his jaw, and his knuckles were raw on both fists.

"Eh, well, I'm not suspended yet. But I might have to sit out a couple of games."

Oh crap. "Jake…"

"No biggie," he said, catching my hand. "Seriously. Totally worth it. Punk had a mouth on him."

"People are going to give us shit…"

"Then they can give shit to us," Jake said firmly. "They don't get to say shit to you."

"I don't want you losing out on scouts seeing the games."

He shrugged. "I really don't care. I'm not going to college for football anyway. Bubba deserves any scholarship money there is." Which was great, but that wasn't what Ian wanted to go to college for either. "The guys are outside," he said. "Waiting for us. You got your phone?"

"Yeah, it's in my backpack. I had to talk to Diane, and then she brought me up here."

Jake pulled his phone out and texted something, then looked at me. "Can you go?"

"Mr. Rhys asked me to wait," I said with a long sigh. "I can't believe he sat through that. They showed him the pictures, Jake."

"Fuck." He grimaced, then tapped something else on his phone. "You all right?"

"I'm fine." I'd said that statement so many times today, it didn't have any meaning.

"No you're not," Jake countered. "But we'll talk about this after." The warmth in his pale blue eyes steadied me. He still hadn't shaved. It took me this long to even make that belated realization. Tired hung around his eyes, but his smile chased some of that away. The urge to run my fingers over the stubble on his cheek left my hand twitching.

"Okay," I conceded, and his smile grew. A minute later, I laughed, it was a hysterical little giggle, but he bumped my shoulder. When one of the doors opened, the humor faded, and we both glanced to where Mr. Rhys exited the office with Diane and Officer Lester behind him. Almost a heartbeat later, the other office door opened letting, Mrs. Benton out, followed by Officer Jennings.

Mrs. Benton looked irked. More than she had when I got here earlier. Jake stood when his mother reached him. "You can leave for the rest of the day," she told him. "They aren't suspending you. But you will have to talk to Dr. Miller this week about some anger management."

He nodded.

"You're also going to apologize to that boy."

Mutiny appeared in Jake's eyes. But before he could open his mouth, Mr. Rhys said, "Let's discuss it later and not here."

Mrs. Benton nodded, then turned to me. "Frankie, sweetheart, are you all right?"

"I'm fine," I told her. Yep, it didn't gain an ounce of truth, no matter how often I said it.

"Frankie," Mr. Rhys said. "I'm going to sign you out for the rest of the day, if you want to just call it and go home." At this point, I'd missed most of lunch, and Jake wouldn't be there for Euro or Study Hall. I really was worn out…

"I actually won't say no to that." I was tired of people overall. I could go home and hide under the covers.

"Then go on," he said with a smile. "I'll take care of it. I left a message for your mom, so I'll talk to her as soon as she calls back. Don't worry about any of this."

Fine by me.

"Thanks."

"And Frankie," Diane said. "My door is always open."

Well that was one way to let a draft in. But I just nodded. When I stood, Jake said, "I'm going to go now then…" He looked at his mother. "Maybe take Frankie to get something to eat. We missed lunch."

"That's fine, I need to get back to work, but I want to talk to you later. Understood?"

He bobbed his head. "I'll be home later. You need me to do anything?"

"No, Rebecca and Blake are going out after school, and Louisa has dance. I should be able to pick her up when I'm off. So you're free—for now." The last she said with emphasis, and I winced internally. At least Jake wasn't grounded, yet.

"Thanks, Mom, Joe." Jake nodded to Mr. Rhys. I never called him by his first name, but then, he hadn't asked me to, either. "C'mon."

I wasn't going to look a good escape in the mouth, Jake pulled open the door and, I slid out. As promised, Archie, Coop, and Ian were waiting a half-dozen steps away.

"We're out of here," Jake said. "Bubba's dad is signing Frankie out."

"Where to?" Archie asked as Coop wrapped an arm around my shoulders. I was tired, but we needed to dial back the PDA at school, no matter how much I enjoyed it.

I ducked out from under Coop's arm and said, "Sorry. Talk about it out of here, okay?"

"No problem." He searched my eyes, but his gray-green ones were a storm of worry.

Ian glanced past us at the closed office door. "Food," he said before he looked at us. "Coop, you ride with Frankie, I'm taking the bike."

"Everyone take your cars," Jake said. "Then somewhere quiet to eat."

Even as we headed away from the SRO hall, I said, "Guys, I don't really want to go out. I'm exhausted. I'd rather go home and sleep." At least there wasn't anyone there to stare at me or whisper or give terrifically awful advice. The whole day sat on me like a too many heavy sacks, and I was tired of carrying all of them.

"We'll pick food up and come over?" Jake offered.

The hopeful looks on their faces were hard to ignore. "Okay, but if I fall asleep, you guys just have to deal with it."

"No problem."

We split up with Coop and Ian falling in on either side of me as we headed for the exit closer to my car and Ian's bike. Lunch was over in five minutes, and I was a total coward, I took a different hallway so I didn't have to go through the cafeteria.

If Ian or Coop noticed, they didn't say anything. Outside, it was sticky and humid. The clouds were back, but the air was torpid. That just added to my bad mood. A note was stuck to my car, right under a windshield wiper, and I sighed internally.

"I got it," Coop said. Even if everything else left on or by my car lately had been sweet—this morning really hadn't been.

The cats were all different kinds of disgruntled because I'd disturbed them.

Someone had rearranged the roses too and combined them in one vase with fresh water. I stared at that for a long moment, then shook my head. Just not going there. They'd been sweet, even with the roses.

Light on, I dragged my backpack onto the bed with me and then checked my messages while I ate my sandwich.

There were three voicemails.

Fun.

The first voicemail was, surprisingly, from my mom. "Frankie, I had several calls from Joe, regarding an incident both at the school and online. I spoke to him a little while ago, and he filled me in. Why didn't you tell me? I had no idea! Are you all right? I've spoken to Eddie about it, and he's having his attorney contact the site to get that post removed. Call me when you get this message."

I just sort of sat there and stared at the phone for a minute. It was probably the most caring thing she'd said to me in a while. Although her tone when she asked why hadn't I told her sounded more aggrieved than it did concerned. Maybe Mr. Rhys's calls hadn't annoyed her as much as I thought it might.

The second message was from Cheryl. "Holy crap, girl!" At the first screech over the phone, I had to hold it away some. Sweet girl, but way too loud. "I saw the post. *Everyone* has seen it. Wicked bad. You still going to Homecoming with Ian? Even if you're not, we should still get dresses. You could totally go with me. It's fun to go to these things with friends if you can't find a date." No it wasn't, but nice effort for trying. I had been to plenty sans date. I was looking forward to doing this with Ian. "Anyway, I want to get together and pick out dresses. Hit me up."

Yeah. Cheryl could wait till tomorrow, although that was a really kind message. In her way. I'd text her the next day.

The last message caught me off guard. "Frankie, it's Rachel. You disappeared before lunch today, and the fight Jake got into with Rodney was the talk of lunch. I swung out to check on your car but it was also gone. Let me know that you're okay. Worried about you."

One, since when did Rachel check on my car? Two, she was worried about me? We had a kind of love-hate relationship and had for a really long time. Then again, she seemed to have been on my side more often than not lately. When Patty posted the little nastygram on one of my photos from junior year, Rachel immediately clapped back on it. I just deleted the photo to get rid of both comments, but still.

I sent a text to Cheryl that I'd reach out later that week, I had a lot of stuff on my plate to do, and I needed to get it finished.

Then I sent a text to Rachel and told her I was fine, just buried. We had to get our college applications ready, and that included scores, essays, and transcripts. She didn't hit me back, so hopefully that solved that. Speaking of applications, I needed to check the mail. Shoving off the bed, I headed to the front door but there was a whole stack of mail sitting on the table just inside the door. The mail key hung in its spot.

Coop.

He knew which box was ours, just like I knew his.

It was really weird that they were all doing all of this stuff for me. I was so used to having to do it all for myself.

Weird, but nice.

I went through the stack, pulling out the dozen or so different college brochures and postcards all saying *check me out, you want to go here!*

Newsflash, no I didn't. Somewhere right around the end of my junior year, the mail avalanches started coming in. Most of it ended up in the recycle bin, and I couldn't quite figure out how to tell them to stop sending me so much junk.

As it was, I found two bills, both of which I knew were on auto pay so I didn't worry about them, and the last was a letter hand-addressed to my mom with no return address on the corner and a New York postmark. I didn't open Mom's mail, so I just carried that one to the desk in her room where I was supposed to leave her mail. The stack I'd put there the week before sat untouched, and the letter went on the top.

I paused, just standing in her room. I didn't come in here often. Not cluttered, but not barren. It was just—hollow feeling in here. Maybe because she was gone.

Though it smelled different from the rest of the house, and then it dawned on me it might have something to do with Archie's dad, and I left. Closing the door behind me, I headed straight back to my room after dumping the rest of the mail into the recycle bin.

Sitting back on the bed, I stared at my phone for a minute and then fired off messages to let the guys know I was awake and thanked them for what they'd done, then added I needed to check homework to see what we missed, and to Coop, I sent a private apology.

His message in return was funny.

Coop

It's no big deal. You were really tired. I'm glad that we could give you a good night. And it would have turned out to be a boring date, since I have to babysit. Don't worry about my mom, she got the notice and laughed it off. Said boys will be boys. On the one hand, that's good news, right? On the other hand, not sure I want us just to be labeled as boys will be boys. Thoughts?

Oh God, Coop was in a philosophical mood.

My reply was pretty succinct:

Me

I don't have any thoughts. I can't brain today. I haz the dumb.

I got a series of crying and laughing face emojis in return.

Everyone else seemed to be doing okay. Jake wasn't grounded. Thank God. His mother was still not pleased with him, but she said that she had discussed it with Ian's father, and that she felt his actions were somewhat justified, however, she "encouraged" him to use alternative methods, rather than fighting.

Personally, I agreed with his mom. However, he was still on the hook for the anger management with Diane, and I felt bad about that. He was also on the hook for sitting out a couple of games. Still, he summed it all up with a final *worth it!*

What was I going to do with these guys?

Ian said he had a long talk with his dad after he got home, and that everything was going to be okay. Said his dad was worried about *me*, well, that could be good. So was his mom. He followed it up with *we're still on for working on the song tomorrow night?*

Me

Yep

I sent back.

Me

Need to get the audition recorded. Also need essays written. Gonna write one tonight. Want to see it when I'm done?

Ian

Absolutely. And I'm just sitting here working on some chords. Call if you want to talk.

Me

I can't believe I fell asleep on you.

Ian

Kind of liked it. You snore, just the tiniest bit. It's cute.

My face flamed.

Me

Snoring is not cute.

Ian

It is when you do it, and the guys have to sit there and watch me cuddle you. Definitely liked that part, too. You feel better?

Did I?

Me

Undecided. But I'm not falling down tired, and I can think. That's better.

Ian

So if I ask what was wrong this morning, will you tell me?

I stared at the message.

Me

Mom stuff. And I really was tired.

Ian

Ugh. Sorry. Go do your essay. You'll feel better.

I chuckled. He wasn't wrong.

Me

Can I ask you something?

Ian

Always.

Me

If I said no more PDAs at school, would that bother you?

He didn't answer for a long moment. That worried me. A little.

Ian

We've always put our arms around you.

True.

Ian

Hugs were okay, too.

He wasn't wrong. In fact, more than once that had annoyed the then flavors of the month, because they would hug me or tease me. One of them always slung an arm around my shoulders as we walked. I'd craved the contact and taken a lot of comfort from it.

Me

You didn't kiss me.

Ian

Ahh. I like kissing you.

A shiver rippled through me

Me

I like kissing you, too. But—if you kiss me and Jake kisses me and Coop and Archie...

Ian

So then only one of us kisses you at school. That would solve that.

Me

That seems a little unfair, and how do we even decide who?

Ian

I volunteer as tribute...

Laughing, I hit answer when he called almost hot on the heels of that comment. "Since we're talking and you're not working on your essay, I thought this would be faster." A smile lit his words. "And I like hearing your voice."

"Hi," I greeted him, and he chuckled.

"Hi."

"So you volunteer as tribute, huh?"

"Well, I am taking you to Homecoming, and I absolutely intend to kiss you at the dance. Just seems to make sense that I can kiss you at school."

"How do you propose we tell the guys that?"

A moment later, my phone vibrated and I pulled it away to see a message to the group chat with all of us.

Ian

Heads up. No more PDAs at school. I'm the only one who can kiss her there.

Eyes widening, I had to smother another laugh, even as I put Ian on speaker. "I can't believe you just did that."

"Why not? You snooze, you lose." Laughter eddied to the surface in his voice as my phone began to vibrate and his echoed over the open line. "Oh yeah, see—they get it."

Jake

No fucking way. Who called that?

Coop

Ha ha, very funny.

Archie

You jumped on asking her to Homecoming. You don't get to do that.

My face had to be hot, but under the embarrassment was a current of delight.

Ian

You snooze. You lose. Frankie called it.

"Hey now…" I corrected him and typed my reply.

Me

What I said was I thought we should dial back on the PDAs at school and Ian asked me to define the PDAs.

"Aww, you're going to rain on my fun," he teased, but there was no real recrimination in his voice.

Ian

Hugging her and putting an arm around her is normal, but all of us kissing her she's not sure she wants to flaunt that.

"Okay, I didn't actually say that."

"No," he agreed. "But it's what you meant. It's what's got you worried. We kiss you, other people see it and comment. Then we get posts like what Sharon did."

I grimaced. "Does that make me awful? I'm not ashamed of any of you but…"

"But dating all four of us no matter how we try to swing it right now is weird," Ian said. "I get it, Frankie. Just like…I know you made out with the other guys, and not a huge fan, but it doesn't make me wanting to kiss you any less intense."

I licked my lips.

Coop

Then no one kisses. That's fair.

Ian

I'm taking her to Homecoming. I'm kissing her at Homecoming.

"Everyone deserves that kiss pic, besides..." Ian said. "I reiterate my earlier point, I like kissing you."

"You were my first real kiss." It just slipped right out. I couldn't even remember if I'd mentioned it before, but the phone's vibrations punctuated the silence.

Jake

> If you're not comfortable with all of us kissing at school, then Coop's right, none of us. Might be easier on you with the bitch squad.

Archie

> It's up to Frankie. What do you want to do, babe?

"See, you say something like that, and I want to kiss you again—right now. But you're all the way over there."

"Tomorrow," I promised him. "I'll be over there tomorrow. Get to ride on the bike, too."

"You bet," he said. "And ugh...fine. If you want to keep the PDAs down, it just means we might need extra when we're away from school. We can do the down payment tomorrow."

I laughed, and my second line rang. "Hang on a sec, Jake's calling."

Answering it, I said, "Hey, I have Ian on the other line, gonna conference."

"Cool."

I conferenced it in. "Hey, I got Jake with me."

"I found Coop," Ian said drolly.

"I already had Archie," Jake said, and we all laughed.

"Conference call, nice. Sorry I fell asleep on all of you."

"No problem," Archie said. "You were beat. You snore really cutely."

"Oh my god," I groaned.

"See!" Ian chortled.

"You do, Frankie. Course, I've also heard you snore like a bear in winter, so I'll take the cute one."

"Coop, you're close enough for me to come find you and hit you."

"True," he said, almost bemused. "That might be my secret plan. Besides, you snore. It's a fact."

Archie chuckled. "It's really not that bad."

"I hate you all."

"Awww, I didn't mind it at all," Jake promised. "You're super snuggly, too."

I rolled my eyes.

"She is very snuggly, I noticed that." Archie was not helping with the conversation.

"Well, I'll have to let you know," Ian said. "But I have a good feeling about it."

Tingles swept me from head to foot, and before Coop could pipe in, I said, "*Anyway...*I just think it might be easier on all of us if we don't—play it up at school. Jake's already gotta talk to Dr. Miller, and everyone apparently was talking about the post today. I just don't want that much attention focused on us—especially not while we're applying to colleges."

The laughter still present evaporated.

"Yeah," Jake said slowly. "Schools look at our social media."

"Exactly," I reminded them. "So if you're thinking about *getting even,* don't."

"That's what an anonymous account is for," Archie suggested. "I didn't see her posting it under her own name."

"Yeah well, apparently your dad's lawyers are gonna talk to the site, or that's what Mom said, so don't be so sure that anonymous is anonymous anymore."

Archie snorted. "Got it. Look, we're not going to do anything right *now.*"

"Unless she doesn't back off," Jake continued.

I sighed.

"I told you, I'm not letting anyone treat you like crap," he said to the rumbled agreements of the others. "So if you want PDAs off the table at school, we can go back to just being friendly, but that means holding your hand and tickling you. Tickling you has always been fair game."

"Oh," Coop said. "He has a point—tickling is definitely not PDA."

"No," I groaned. "It's torture."

Ian chuckled.

"Since we're on the phone," Archie said, clearing his throat. "Maybe we should also lay down some ground rules… like no more two a.m. dates on school nights."

"Bite me," Jake said. "We needed the break, and we had fun."

That we had. "It was not fun to wake up this morning though."

"Nope," Jake retorted. "But I don't care, I'd do it again."

Yeah. "Me, too."

More groans. "Okay so let's say midnight on school nights? Frankie works hard enough, we don't want to break her."

"See," Coop said. "We're involving you in this discussion."

I had noticed. "Thank you," I said, still smiling before I opened up my bottle of water. "And on that note, I am going to hang up and actually write my college essay. We have like ten days left before they open applications. I want to get as many of these written ahead of time as I can, because we don't know what the essay questions will be exactly."

"There she goes being all over-prepared," Coop teased. "Go. Write. Be a genius. Show us how it's done. Then maybe write one for me?"

They were still laughing when I hung up.

Ian

Still thinking I like being your first kiss.

I grinned.

Me

I know I liked you being my first. It was awesome.

Ian

I really like you, Frankie.

Ian

So how long does the no PDA rule extend after school?

Me

I really like you, too.

Ian

Got it. Kiss your ears first.

He added a laughing emoji, and I grinned.

Me

Go away, funny guy. I need to use my brain now.

Ian

Be kind to that brain, it's one of the sexiest things about you.

Okay, that sent a wave of heat crashing through me and set my face on fire. Groaning, I put the phone in do not disturb and got my crap out of my backpack. It was just after ten when I finished my final draft. I'd knocked out some homework and took care of the lit reading assignment Coop sent over. He'd added his notes, but it was all basic stuff.

I emailed Mr. G to let him know why I was absent from AP Euro, but I was already ahead on my reading for there, and it wasn't like it was a grade. Calculus took ten minutes. But the rest of the time, I spent on the essay. I read it four times, corrected some minor typos, and then sent it over to Ian.

There was an essay from him in the inbox, too. He'd chosen the *any topic* and written about falling in love with music. It was deep and it was passionate.

Suddenly, mine seemed like so much garbage. I'd written about my job and trying to balance school with working twenty-five hours a week. Discussed how hard it could be to make sure I had enough money for gas or unexpected repairs, while still saving to offset the cost of college when I got there.

When you find the perfect minor chord between two majors, you can live there for a moment. It's the perfect note. The perfect beat. That's where songs are born. But it's also where the emotion we experience when we exist in that place between is my homework done and I wish my friends were here. It's a place of inexplicable joy. Every song has that one note, finding where it resonates with you is the key.

Mine was so—ordinary. Here Ian was writing about the passion in a note of music, and how coaxing genuine songs from an instrument was almost a seduction of his senses, because that was how he felt it.

It was… gorgeous.

I made a couple of minor corrections as I went through, shifted a comma and broke up a run-on sentence, but the last paragraph captivated me.

Music is another world for me, a place I can journey whenever the mood strikes. It doesn't matter how I played on the field, what my grades are, or if my parents are so busy helping others, they don't have time for me. With my music, I'm never alone. I've only ever felt this way with one other person, and she's nearly as magical as the notes. It's a good thing she likes to listen to my music, because she's as much my muse as music is my passion.

"Wow," I breathed, and then looked up. "Mine *really* sucks."

I glanced at the clock. I sent back Ian's with the notes and told him how beautiful it was. I read it again because I could almost hear the music in the words, and that—that was impressive. He really did need to let himself invest in his music. He was *so* good at it. Opening up a fresh document, I turned the prompts over in my head. The random one had seemed like a good place to start, but Ian found magic in his music.

He finds magic in me!

That feeling ballooned in my chest, but I shook my head and focused. I needed to figure this out. Staring at the blank screen where the cursor blinked away like a countdown to doom, I asked myself the same question over and over again.

What was magical in my life?

Chapter Thirteen

I WONDER…

Tuesday dawned almost normal. I fed the cats, showered, got dressed, found the requisite texts from the guys on my phone, and savored it all while I ate cereal over the sink. I'd just rinsed out my dish when Coop showed up and let himself in. The smirk on his face made me laugh.

"Sorry, I'm early," he murmured before he pinned me to the fridge. We had five minutes of solid making out that left my body humming and my heart racing. Lifting his head, he traced his thumb against my lower lip and I sighed.

"You know, I've never endorsed skipping school."

"I know," he said, the wistful note not lost on me.

"You're making it damn tempting though."

Then his grin spread. "Glad to hear it. But we missed yesterday afternoon, and you're going to have an anxiety attack before third period if you miss any more classes."

"I'm not that bad," I countered.

"No," he agreed with a crooked grin. "You're much worse."

Mouth agape, I gave him a little shove. "You suck."

He laughed. "But I'm not wrong." I pushed him again, easing out from between him and the fridge. "Aww…" He followed behind and wrapped his arms around me. "Don't be mad."

"I'm not mad, dork," I told him as I peeled his hands off. "We have to get to school."

"Blegh, and here I thought I almost had you talked in to calling out today."

Rolling my eyes, I shook my head. "We can't—well, I can't."

"Yeah," he said with a deep sigh, barely hiding his grin. "I know."

"Ass," I muttered as I pulled on my backpack and grabbed my keys.

"So you have said," he teased before opening the door for me. "But I think the lady likes my ass, or she wouldn't put up with me."

Canting my head to the side, I indulged myself with a good look at his butt. Admittedly, he looked good in those shorts. They seemed to emphasize a firm set of gluteal muscles. Considering I'd had my hands on his ass a few days ago, I could attest to the tone. "I'd give it a seven," I told him before locking the door and heading for the stairs.

"A seven?" Coop almost squawked, and I was grinning as he dogged my steps. "On what scale? Cause if it's seven out of seven, then I'm awesome, but if it's out of ten, that's closer to average. But if it's out of five, then I'm golden."

Rolling my eyes, I tossed the backpack in the car.

"What about the guys?" Coop persisted as we climbed in. "Give me some basis for comparison."

As tempted as I might be, I kept my own counsel. Still, Coop remained undeterred.

"Fine, let's talk actors on a scale of Robert Downey Jr. to America's Ass, where do I rate?"

"What's wrong with RDJ's ass?" I had to know.

"I haven't really looked at it, but it's not *America's* ass, you know?"

With a snort, I countered, "And why are they the scale? Have you seen Thor? Or The Winter Soldier?" I made a little swooning sound, and that got me such an outraged glare, I giggled all the way to school.

Coop didn't let it go, even when we reached the table in the cafeteria. "Seriously, you're just going to leave me dangling?"

We'd actually beat Archie, which was a bummer cause I was dying for coffee. Still, I dug into my backpack to pull out my notebook. "Just give me your lit notes," I said. "Then you can resume debating with yourself what seven means."

"I'm not debating it with myself," Coop said with a glare that held absolutely no heat. "I'm trying to get a straight answer out of you."

"I was pretty straight with my answer," I deadpanned, and he groaned. "Notes?"

He pulled them out. "You didn't miss much. You're ahead on the reading, right? So she gave us another practice essay, no grade, so you won't have to make it up, and then we discussed allusions for the rest of the class."

"Thank you." I was a little grumpy about missing the practice essay. The AP exams weren't for the faint of heart. Still, it could be worse. I copied over Coop's notes, and thankfully, he always took pretty concise ones and I could read his shorthand.

"Already have your head in a book," Archie said by way of greeting, and I grinned as he passed me coffee. His gaze went to my wrist and the charm bracelet I'd worn today. He'd given it to me on Friday, and I'd put it on this morning as more of a whim, but the expression on his face was more than worth it. Smile nudging a little wider, he said, "Feel better?"

"Eh," I admitted. "Just focused on getting through today." Which was better. I hadn't called my mom back, and maybe it made me a coward, but by the time I was done rewriting my practice essay for the third time, I'd been tired again, so I crashed after sending the last one to Ian.

He liked the first one and the second one. His comments had all been really kind, but it sort of felt like he was humoring me. Or maybe just too nice to tell me they sucked.

"Arch, ask Frankie about your butt."

Archie and I both looked at Coop, but I was pretty sure I wore the more incredulous expression.

With a shrug, Archie slanted a sideways look at me. "What about my butt?"

"I hate you," I told Coop, then took a sip of my coffee before focusing back on my notes. "Nothing. He has decided that I like his ass, or I wouldn't put up with him. I'm beginning to question that judgment."

Coop snorted. "She gave me a seven."

"On a scale of?" Archie asked.

"She won't *tell* me."

Archie laughed, and I got to the end of the page then re-read the notes I'd copied over. "That's because you're obsessed… and annoying."

"Wounded," Coop gasped, clutching his chest. "You wound me."

Snickering, Archie shook his head. "Do we all get ratings, or just Coop?"

And I knew this would happen. I closed Coop's notebook and passed it to him. "See…"

"Hey, if you'd just given me a scale, I wouldn't have brought it up," Coop declared.

"Bullshit," I told him cheerfully. "You'd have been bragging or complaining one way or the other."

"That is also true." At least he didn't deny it. "So, going to tell Archie, or do I have to enlist Jake and Bubba to get it out of you?"

"No and no, the subject is closed." I shut my own notebook and tucked it back into the backpack.

"I don't know," Archie said, giving me an amused look. "It could be fun."

"Fun would be if she gave us a scale." Coop pouted. "Please, Frankie?" The puppy dog eyes were adorable, but I was immune.

Mostly.

"Actually," I admitted. "This is a lot of fun, too."

He groaned. "My misery is fun."

"He's in a dramatic mood today," Archie commented, propping his chin in his hand as he studied me then Coop.

"He was philosophical last night."

Archie's shudder echoed my thoughts from the night before, and Coop glared at us both.

"Philosophy is dangerous," Archie advised him.

"Nope," Coop said. "Not going to get to me."

"Well, that's one way of looking at it," I said with a grin. "But there's always another point of view."

Coop fixed me with a look. "Are you declaring war, Frankie?"

I laughed. "That's an extreme view."

"Depends on your point of view," he countered. "You're being mean to me today."

Considering my lips still tingled from our rather enthusiastic make out session, I didn't mind the accusation in the least. "I could be meaner."

"She could," Archie agreed. "Absolutely she could, and we agree with that so she doesn't *prove* it."

Laughter bubbled out of us as more kids streamed into the cafeteria. It was hard to miss the looks tossed my way, but I kept my chin up. The last thing I wanted was to be the center of attention or the source of gossip. If I could just ride it all out, it would go away. The guys were acting like the guys—well, two of the four so far—and they'd promised no more kissing at school.

Maybe if we could just downplay it all, then we could avoid issues. Of course, Patty making a beeline for our table suggested we may not be that lucky. The strawberry-blonde wore a determined expression. But it wasn't Archie she was looking at.

It was me.

"Oh for fuck's sake," Archie muttered. Yep, he'd seen her too, and Coop twisted to track her progress.

Ignoring both of them, she circled the table until she stood near me. "Can I borrow you?"

I raised my brows but before I could say anything, Archie said, "What do you want, Patty?"

But she didn't look at him, she kept her attention on me. "It'll only take a few minutes."

"Depends," I said, holding up a hand when Archie opened his mouth. "Where is it you want to borrow me to?"

She regarded me with her pale brown eyes, and they were kind of creepy when she stared like that, wholly focused on me like she could mentally and physically block out that I was sitting with Coop and Archie.

"Just over there," she said nodding toward the other side of the cafeteria, like the vague, general direction was enough of an answer. "Please?"

"You don't have to," Archie said, his tone clipped.

I gave him a quick grin and shifted my backpack to my chair and grabbed my coffee. "I'll be right back." Practice should have been over by now, so hopefully Jake and Ian would be there soon. For now, I followed Patty across the cafeteria.

Twice I heard my name mentioned in a whisper and laughter afterward. Whatever. Better to ignore it. If I told myself that enough, I might even start to believe it.

The table Patty led me to wasn't empty. Maria sat there, and she blew out a long breath as we arrived. While we were far from alone, they'd taken a table on the near opposite side from where the guys and I usually sat, and there were still a couple of empty tables between us and the rest of those already in the cafeteria. But people were constantly streaming in, and we had maybe twenty minutes before the first bell.

"Thanks," Patty said as she pulled out a chair and I debated sitting.

Maria leaned forward, folded arms on the table. "Hey, Frankie."

"Hey," I said. "What's up?" I glanced from one to the other.

"Sit down?" At least Patty phrased it as a question.

Still debating it, I decided to go with at least some conciliation. If we could make peace, then maybe they would get off the guys' backs.

"Please?" Patty added. "We probably have five minutes if we're lucky before one of your watchdogs shows up."

"Patty," Maria said.

"Well it's true." Patty scowled then shook her head. "Sorry."

I waved off the apology and pulled out a chair. "What's up?"

"Thank you," Maria said. "I feel like we should… talk after the thing this weekend."

"We don't have to," I told her.

She grimaced. "Don't be nice about it."

"I'm not being nice about it." I shrugged. "You didn't do it."

The look the pair exchanged, however, suggested otherwise. "Well…" Patty said slowly. "Maybe we didn't post them but…"

"We shared our pictures," Maria admitted. "Don't get me wrong, I'm pissed at them—pissed at Jake. He's a dick. The others aren't much better, even Bubba, who I thought more of before he pulled that shit last week." The heat in her voice spoke volumes, despite the fact she wasn't shouting. "But I didn't agree with what was posted about you."

"To be honest," Patty added. "I don't really like you but I don't hate you."

"Glad we cleared that up," I said. "Is there a point to this conversation? Because I didn't need to come over here to listen to you talk about the guys."

"Of course not," Maria said. "You've always taken their side—in everything. Even when they weren't taking yours."

"Our history is our history." I spread my hands. "Not much I can do to change that. I'm sorry you got hurt. Both of you."

"You actually mean that," Patty said, disbelief etched into every syllable.

"We used to be friends," I reminded them. "That's changed, I get it."

Maria sighed. "Stop being so damn nice, just slap us and get it over with, then we can all go back to icy silences.”

I laughed.

Seriously, I laughed, and they both stared at me.

“Sorry, girls. Look—this issue you have, I can’t fix it.”

“You could if you told them no and walked away,” Patty muttered and folded her arms as she slumped back in the chair.

“You think if I wasn’t around they’d be back asking you out?” Did they genuinely believe that?

“Maybe,” Maria said. “Not that I want to really have him back, it would just be nice to be wanted.”

Patty scoffed. Yeah. I didn’t believe Maria either.

“Well I do want Archie back. I spent all of junior year trying to get his attention, and when I finally get it, he dumps me for you. I should have known, the other girls he dated all said the same thing,” Patty stated. “So could you just pick one of them and leave the rest for us?”

Wow.

“I’m pretty sure if Archie wanted to still be dating you, he would be. I don’t make decisions for them.” Even if they’d made them for me.

“You can’t say they don’t do that to you,” Maria echoed my own internal thoughts. “C’mon, Frankie. You’re not blind. Between the four of them, they’ve dated half the girls in our class.”

I was aware.

“And?”

“Do you seriously want to be that girl?” Maria stared at me. “You’ve *never* been that girl. Even if you were always in the way, you were… at least decent.”

“What do you want me to say, Maria?”

But instead of answering, she focused behind me, and that was my only warning.

“Yeah,” Jake said from behind me. “What do you want her to say, Maria?”

“You weren’t invited to this conversation,” Patty said, frowning.

"Good to know, not here for you," Jake retorted, then glanced down at me. "Hey, Frankie…"

"Hey," I said. "I'll be back over at the table in a minute."

"You can blow them off now, Bubba and I just got out of practice…"

"Wow, Jake," Maria drawled. "Nice."

"I can be," he said with the fakest smile I'd ever seen him wear. "Want to see me when I'm not?"

"Pretty sure you're going to get suspended if you get not nice again," Patty said. "Be a damn shame if someone complained, wouldn't it…"

Maria glared at her briefly, then looked at me. "Can you just think about it?"

"Nothing to think about," I told her, and if we were done, I was heading back to our table. "I get where you're coming from. But this isn't something that you need me to do. It's something you want me to make happen, and I can't—no matter what the circumstances are." I couldn't push the guys to do something they didn't want to do.

"Well…" Patty said, drawing a finger in a line against the table. "If you change your mind… might just make the year a little easier."

"You—"

I slapped a hand against Jake's chest and shook my head. "See you girls later."

"Yeah, later," Maria said as Jake transferred his glare to me.

I hoped my expression said *don't* as much as my head screamed it. His jaw tightened, but he nodded and backed up a step so I could pass him. It took him a minute to follow me, and then he fell into step.

"You alright?" he asked as we circled the other tables. Sharon was just entering the room, and she glared at me.

Yeah, no pretense there.

Good to know.

"I'm fine," I told him. See, I'd gotten that phrase down. "They wanted to talk. We talked. All good. How was practice?"

Cause that had to have sucked.

He made a face. "It was practice, boring as fuck sitting there watching everyone else. But Coach figures it will be good to teach me some patience."

"I'm sorry..."

"Eh," he said with a shrug. "I'll live. I might even nap if he stops checking on me." The last he added with a wink.

At our table, the others all gave me a quick look. "All good?" Ian asked. "Since Mr. Impatience there couldn't wait for you to finish your conversation."

"Eat me, you weren't thrilled about her being over there either," Jake retaliated as he pulled out my chair and moved my backpack so I could sit.

"But I, at least, was able to control myself and wait," Ian retorted with a smirk.

"Frankie thinks my ass is a seven, but won't give me a scale. Discuss."

I groaned as Coop utterly derailed them and I was the sudden focus of two sets of blue eyes. "What does that make us?" Jake asked.

"Yeah," Ian said slowly. "Kind of curious about that."

"Good luck, she won't give me a score either," Archie stated. "And I asked first."

I shot Coop my middle finger, and he beamed at me.

Ass.

By lunchtime, we had new subjects to discuss—like the huge lit project Coop and I just picked up, the upcoming test in calculus, and Archie and Jake were having a heated debate about their robotics project. It was kind of surreal to discuss genre while at the same time they were arguing the laws of robotics as written by Asimov, and Ian made notes on his song list under the guise of asking me calculus questions.

It was hilarious and relaxing after a day of whispered conversations, stares, and really less than subtle finger pointing. I was not looking forward to study hall in the library. Jake and I were usually left alone, but that didn't seem as likely today, and he was already grumpy.

Eating off-campus had just been the safer option. Back at school, we checked in with the study hall proctor before we headed to the library. It was the first time we'd been alone, really, since Sunday night. The time in the SRO's office didn't count; we hadn't been able to talk.

Even though we had our books open to read, catching up on the day before, we kept glancing at each other. Pressing his foot against mine, he asked, "Are we still keeping PDAs to a minimum at school?"

I grinned. "Yes."

"Damn," he whisper-grumbled. "You're looking particularly adorable at the moment."

"What does particularly adorable look like?"

"It looks like you, silly, what did I just say?" He rolled his eyes then nudged my book. "Get caught up. You don't need to have a meltdown this week if you realize your calendar's off."

"Ugh, you and Coop both."

"Me and Coop both, what?" Curious, he glanced at me again.

"He was giving me hell about having an anxiety attack if I'd skipped school today."

"Well…" The corner of Jake's mouth kicked up.

"I am *not* that bad."

"C'mon, Frankie, let's be real. You're the straight A student who had perfect attendance in three grades, and the only reason you didn't have it in ninth was because you had the flu. It takes an actual emergency for you to miss class."

"Well I skipped class yesterday." I made a face.

"Technically, you skipped your TA period, study hall, and a class we're voluntarily taking for no grade so we can take the AP exam and get the credits. Not quite the same thing."

I stuck my tongue out at him, and he grinned.

"Seriously, what bugged you more yesterday? That you had to talk to Dr. Miller and the SRO, or that you had to miss AP Lit?"

"I'm not talking to you anymore," I grumbled and went back to my book. Asses. They were all asses. I was not so predictable.

"Sure you are," Jake said, a smile in his voice. "Because you'd miss me if you didn't."

I gave him a dirty look, and he grinned.

"See, now I really want to kiss you."

Rolling my eyes, I sighed. He bumped my shoulder, then tapped the page.

"Read. Time for us to play later."

Sighing, I propped my head on my hand and tried to focus on the words, but now I was thinking about kissing. Stealing a glance at Jake, I caught him staring at me.

His eyes twinkled, and I stuck my tongue out at him, but I couldn't stop my own grin and he chuckled.

Fine, he was right about the fact I couldn't not talk to him. But they were wrong. I could totally skip classes.

After I made sure all my assignments were turned in and then hope there wasn't a pop quiz or test. Then again, lectures were important, and French was as much about participation as it was the homework.

So I could skip the afternoon, but not the morning.

Only G did have stuff for us to study in AP Euro, and I'd feel bad if I skipped out on my TA stuff, most of the time it was just hanging out, but she did have things for me to do.

"I hate you," I muttered.

"What did I do now?" Jake asked.

"Skipping would be stressful."

And what did he do? He just laughed and rubbed my back.

"That's why you don't do it, Frankie."

Ugh.

By the end of the day, I was tired, but I was also thrilled school was over. Jake and I headed out to the parking lot. "Hey," he said. "Were there roses yesterday? None of you said."

"No," I told him. "I haven't heard from…" Oh wait.

"You haven't heard from him?" Jake clarified. "Since the party?"

"No, there was an envelope on the windshield yesterday, but with everything going on—I thought it might be something else." Then I'd utterly forgotten about it.

"Do you still have it?" Jake asked as he pushed the door open.

"Not sure, actually." It might be in the car. Or Coop might have it.

Coop and Ian were already there. And Coop had a big envelope in his hand that he tapped against his thigh.

"Is that from yesterday?" Jake asked.

"Nope," Coop said. "Today. You want me to get rid of this one, too?" The last he directed at me.

"Did you throw out yesterday's?" Guilt hit me, it never occurred to me it might have been from Mr. Thorns.

"No," Coop said with a sigh. "It's still in my backpack."

After unlocking my car and shoving my backpack inside, I held out my hand and Coop passed them over.

Ian moved to stand at my shoulder while Jake leaned against the car and looked down at the envelopes.

"Just in case," Jake offered. "Solidarity."

"Yeah," Ian said. "Solidarity."

The first was just a greeting card with the picture of a bar of chocolate on the front. Inside it said: *The supply of available swear words is insufficient to meet the demands, but chocolate is forever. Have some on me. Keep your chin up.*

It had a gift card to a frozen yogurt place not far from the school.

I laughed. "Okay." The second card was similar to the first, only there were chocolate roses on the front and inside they'd written: *Don't be so serious. If you can't laugh at yourself, call me... I'll laugh at you. Better yet, laugh at everyone else or eat chocolate. Trust me, you're awesome, choose chocolate.*

The gift card was for Starbuck's, and I glanced at the guys.

"I really want to know who this is…"

"Me too," Coop said. "Cause he made you laugh."

"Yeah," Ian exhaled. "That's pretty awesome."

"Still not any of you?" I verified, and they shook their heads one at a time. I glanced around the lot and then tucked the cards away. Whoever my admirer was, they had all the power. But maybe I could get a message to them.

"You following us?" I checked with Ian, and he smiled.

"Can't wait."

Neither could I, but I really wanted to talk to Mr. Thorns, if for no other reason than to say thank you. He had been a bright spot over the last few days, and he was still doing it.

That was pretty awesome.

Chapter Fourteen

JUST WANT TO KISS YOU

Instead of heading directly back to his place, Ian took us for a ride around the lake. Between the wind against my face, the rumble of the motorcycle between my legs, and the ripple of his muscles under my hands as we flew down the winding road, the day kind of faded away. Not that it had been a bad day, but by the end of it, I'd been exhausted.

I told myself that the other kids talking about me didn't matter. It didn't. In a few months, I'd graduate, and then I was out of here. I'd be on my way to college—*c'mon Harvard, get me in!*—I'd be living in a whole new city, having a whole new life, and who cared what the kids at Robertson High thought?

If I was lucky, the guys would be going to Harvard too, or MIT for Jake and Archie. They'd be close by, and if not—well, we'd find a way to stay in touch. It wasn't like we didn't text sixty times a day. It would be fine. Mom would do—well, whatever she was going to do, and I'd have my own life separate from having to worry about her. I shuttled her to the side, I hadn't called her back, and she hadn't texted or reached out again, and I kind of hoped it stayed that way.

I wasn't ready to really talk to her.

Eyes closed, I drank in the sensation of the ride and only opened them when Ian slowed us down and then came to a stop. We were parked on one of the pseudo bluffs overlooking the lake. The whole area was dotted with them; little turn offs that offered some privacy from the road and ideal for picnicking or photos. Come spring, everyone and their brother would be out here for graduation pics.

Ugh. There was another thing I didn't want to think about. Even though we stopped, I didn't let go of him until he twisted a little, and then it was only to lean back so I could meet his gaze.

"Hi," he murmured, and his husky tenor rolled right over me like a hug in motion. The sunglasses hid his deep blue eyes, but I didn't need to see them to know the smile curving his lips definitely filled them. Ian seemed to smile with his whole being. It was one of the things I'd always adored about him.

"Hi," I answered, rubbing my thumb idly against his side since I had only dropped my hands to his waist rather than let him go entirely.

"Would you agree we're not at school anymore?" He quirked his brows high, and I laughed.

"Definitely not at school—" He twisted, one arm snaking around my waist, and then his mouth closed over mine and I forgot the rest of the sentence. The slow, even massage of his caress teased me. Firm, yet soft, and then he stroked his tongue along the seam of my lips and I opened to him.

Heat swept me from head to toe. Kissing Ian was like taking a deep dive into a perfectly crystal pool. The depths were so much more than I expected, and the sensations unraveling had me digging my fingers into him as he sucked on my tongue. Then just as swiftly as he deepened the kiss, he eased it down with light nipping kisses, drawing on my lower lip and then whispering them away before nuzzling the corner of my mouth.

Coils of tension looped around me in an ever-shrinking circumference until I plastered against his side, my thighs against his, and he lifted his head with a sigh that I echoed.

"I've been waiting to do that all day," he told me, and I shuddered.

"Yeah?"

"Well, since the last time you let me kiss you really—but that seems like eons ago."

It did. I licked my lips and lifted a hand to cup his cheek. "I'm sorry."

"For what?" He shut off the bike and the rumbling noise ceased abruptly, leaving us in a quiet punctuated only by a breeze off the lake and the hum of traffic on the loop beyond the trees.

"For saying no more PDAs at school," I said. "It's been a lot the last few days, and then I told everyone they couldn't kiss me."

"No," he said, rubbing his hand in a slow circle against my back. "You don't have to apologize for telling us what you need. Always tell me what's going on, seriously. If we talked like this before—maybe we could have avoided some of our issues."

I laughed, even if it wasn't terrifically funny. "I used to think we were always honest with each other. We always talked."

"I know," he promised, head forward so his helmet rested against mine. They made a little thunk noise that pulled another giggle out of me. "Me, too. Then I found out we're all a little hard-headed." His grin widened, and I laughed again.

"Only a little?"

"Well, I think we're learning." The breeze helped to dispel some of the humid air and the heat. The rain might have washed out their game, but it had a nice cooling effect on the weekend. But the sticky air and warmer temps returned. We were probably still in for a few weeks more of overwarm weather.

"I hope so," I admitted. "I don't know that I want any more whack me in the back of the head lessons." If nothing else, the past weekend had left me reeling with its incredible peaks and desperate valleys. "I just want—I want to write the perfect essay. I want to finish school with the right GPA, and if I have to, I'll take the SAT again."

"Frankie, you got a 1550, you don't need to take it again. That's a good score."

"But it's not the highest score, and I need all the help I can get."

"Your essays are good, and you have notebooks of writing you can submit as a portfolio. You've been writing some of the best pieces since freshman year. You've got good grades, you've got life experience, they would be fools to turn you down." The absolute confidence in his voice buoyed me.

"You're really good for my ego," I said.

"Good. You ready to head back to my place, or want to ride around the lake some more?"

Both were tempting. "I'm good with either," I admitted. "But first…" I leaned forward and he met me halfway. This time, I initiated the kiss, nibbling against his lower lip before teasing my tongue against his. His mouth opened so generously, and it was like falling and being caught in the same breath.

My stomach clenched as the tingles radiated out from where our mouths connected, and I leaned into him. Ian flexed his hand against my side and let out a low groan, before lifting his head. "I think back to my place where I can kiss you in comfort."

I laughed. "We still have homework."

"I know," he agreed, nuzzling little kisses to my mouth. "But we also have a pool and swimming together is a good thing."

Another shudder passed through me at the memory of being in his lap in the pool. Licking my lips, I tilted my head back and let him kiss past the strap of the helmet to my neck. The problem was the helmet was heavy, and I started to tip.

Chuckling, he balanced me and nudged my head up. "Definitely home. I don't want you to get hurt."

"Injured in make-out accident," I intoned, eyes widening. "We'd never live that down."

"Well, Bob, we're down here at the lakefront where two teens decided that sitting astride a motorcycle while wearing their helmets was the perfect spot to re-enact every teen movie ever—except the sun was still up, there is no backseat, and our intrepid heroine fell over because the helmet she was wearing weighed too much. Fortunately, the helmet also protected her head from the hit it could have taken. So keep in mind kids, when we say safe sex, this wasn't what we had in mind, but it is effective."

I gaped for all of about three seconds before laughter swamped me. It was both horrifying and hilarious. Ian's grin spread, infectious in its brightness, and he squeezed me closer.

He let out a happy sigh and then brushed my lips with another kiss before turning to start the bike. I settled against his back, arms around him and relaxed in a way I hadn't been. Some of the day lifted away as he got us moving, and we did another circuit of the lake before he cut away and toward his place.

Unlike the last few times, his parents were already gone when we got there. Relief invaded me as he cruised the bike into the garage. Climbing off, I loosened my helmet. Fast on the heels of relief came guilt. Ian's dad had done me a solid, even if it had been humiliating to have him see those pictures.

After hooking our helmets onto his bike, Ian slid his arms around me again. This time when he dipped his head, I could wrap my arms around his neck. He was all solid muscle and enthusiasm. With every lick of his tongue against mine, I clung tighter. This close, there was no way to miss the press of his erection or my own response. My nipples tightened as fever and chill raced in equal measure over my skin.

I was aware of everything. The spicy hint of the aftershave he used, the way his clothes smelled like him, the warmth of his skin, the faint rasp of stubble beginning to grace his jaw. The way our clothes rustled as we rubbed against each other. The solid grip of his hands as they clamped on my hips, then he lifted me—backpack and all—so I wasn't tilting my head back or straining. Thighs hitched to his hips, I sank into the kiss.

I needed to breathe, but I didn't care. One brief break for a rush of air, and then his mouth was open to mine again. My heart beat out a rapid cadence when he dragged his teeth lightly over my lower lip. Finally, we broke the kiss, but his forehead pressed to mine and we were panting in tandem.

Even in the shadows of the garage, his blue eyes were intense and his pupils huge. I had no idea what mine looked like, but I ached from kissing and wanted more in equal measure.

"Much better," he managed in a rough voice that sent shivers eddying through me. Somewhere in all of that, he'd cupped his hands on my ass and held me in place. "Hey, Frankie," he whispered.

"Hey, Ian." I ran my fingers through his hair, unwilling to take my hands off of him, even if we needed to move. Honestly, I lost track of time, and if not for the fact I'd started to sweat, I might have been content to just stay there, staring at him as we tried to get our breathing under control.

"Hi, Angel," he said as he carefully set me down. A thrill went through me at the nickname. After a briefer, but no less heated kiss, he turned me around and gave me a little nudge. "Go on inside and give me a minute."

I paused to glance at him. "Are you okay?"

"Yep," he said. "But I think I need about fifty laps in the pool."

Oh.

I bit my lower lip, but before I could say anything, he made a shooing motion. "Go find a suit and get changed. We can swim and cool off," he said before adding in a low mutter, "in more ways than one."

Not wanting to make him more uncomfortable, I headed upstairs. I stared at the door to his room for a minute, then the guest room. It would be just as easy to walk in there, strip off, and let him walk in and find me, or I could do what he asked me to do.

The fact I was even considering the first washed over me, and my skin lit up. Wanting any of them was not a problem. Every single kiss pushed me closer, but Archie and I had already crossed that line, and what did it say about me if I did with all of them? Even if they knew about each other. Ian punched Archie about Friday night, but he wasn't pulling away from me.

Eddies from earlier turned into a churn, and I diverted to the guest room. If I couldn't answer that question without gut-wrenching nerves, then I didn't need to be asking it yet. Ian was the one who said he needed a minute to get himself under control. And it wasn't like I'd been pushing him away.

Stripping off the backpack, I set it on the guest bed. Then walked into the guest bathroom to check my face. My lips were swollen, and there was a little redness around my mouth and cheek—from his stubble. The fact I could see it gave me another little thrill. The hickeys I had courtesy of Jake and Coop were still there, faded—save for the one Jake added to Sunday night.

Fortunately, he'd kept it lower so I could hide it under my clothes. It was going to be very visible in a suit though. So would the ones on my thighs. Nerves practically vibrated in my stomach, and I pulled my hair down and ran my fingers through it.

Maybe it had been a bad idea to bring my suit. I'd worn it Saturday but hadn't really gotten to show it off. The day had gone so epically sideways. The sound of Ian's heavier tread on the stairs reached me, and I rolled my eyes at myself.

Friends, first. We'd all been friends first. Stripping, I changed into the bikini I'd picked up for myself and ran a comb through my hair before leaving my clothes folded neatly to put back on. Then snagging my backpack, I opened the door and found Ian standing just outside his bedroom door, arms folded.

He hadn't changed yet.

His eyes flared as our gazes locked. "Wow…" Licking his lips, he lingered on my suit for a minute before blowing out a breath. "Really wow."

"I got this last spring, I just… never wore it." The look on his face made me wonder why I'd always been so reticent about bikinis. At the same time, I was happy I'd gone with it, even as my nerves decided to put on a fresh appearance. It was like being in a tug of war with a spring-loaded yo-yo. My emotions were all over the place.

"I like it." He straightened. "And that answers that question."

"What question?"

"Whether you wanted to just hang out in my room or go swimming…"

Did he mean? "If you want…"

"No, I mean—I do want. But I think swimming is better. Then homework, then music. Sound good?"

My stomach let out a gurgle, and Ian burst out laughing.

My face was probably the color of a cherry tomato. My gut was not known for its ladylike behavior.

"And food," he promised. "Give me a sec."

He was already pulling his shirt off as he walked into his room. When he didn't close the door, it was like every cell in my body yearned to follow him in there. Shaking my head, I made myself turn to go down the stairs. Just because he hadn't closed the door, didn't mean he'd left it open for me to ogle him.

I got to do that enough by the pool. The fact I had sex on the brain wasn't lost on me. Downstairs, I got us sodas from the fridge. There was a note on the counter from Ian's mom with some cash. It said to order pizza and have a good night—they would be late getting back.

Date night.

That was right. His parents had a date night once a week. Sometimes his mom worked evening shifts, but they'd been heading out on a date last week. I left the note and cash where it was and took the sodas outside with my backpack. The umbrella was already opened over the table, so I set out my stuff.

Cheryl had messaged me about dress shopping again, and I groaned.

Me

Cheryl

Girl, you gotta do the whole experience and trying on all the dresses together is part of that. When do you work this weekend?

Me

10 to 6 Sat and Sun. Always 10 to 6.

Cheryl

Ugh. Fine. Saturday evening. Mitch will just have to do without me. You and I, Rockdale Mall, seven. Want me to pick you up?

I made a face.

Me

Can I think about it?

Cheryl

Absolutely not. You need a great dress, and the key is to have the right wingwoman. Lucky for you, I'm amazing and I know you'll tell me if something makes me look like a creampuff.

I couldn't help it, I laughed.

Me

I swear, I won't let you look like a creampuff.

Cheryl

Thank you! So am I getting you girl or you meeting me?

Me

I'll meet you. Where at Rockdale?

Cheryl

Big fountain entrance next to Maggie's.

Maggie's was a really nice boutique and catastrophically out of my price range. But she did say we were going to be looking.

Me

Deal. I'll be there.

The door to the house opened, and Ian stepped outside in his trunks. The taper of his waist and the very clear lines where his abdomen descended into his Adonis belt had my mouth watering.

"You're smiling," he said.

"Yeah—Cheryl wants me to go dress shopping with her, and she's hijacking my Saturday night."

"What color are you getting?" He set his backpack on the table and reached for the Coke.

"I don't know… do you have a preference since it's your Homecoming date, too?"

"Whatever you wanna wear. I don't think there's a color that looks bad on you." The ease of that compliment had my toes curling. "Just make sure you tell me so I can match you."

"I promise," I told him, then took a drink.

"Swim?" He curled his hand in invitation.

"You just want to make out in the pool again," I teased him.

"I didn't hear you complaining," he retorted as we linked our fingers together.

"And you won't—" I might have spoken too soon because he tugged me to him, and then we were airborne before plunging into the water. Even though the water was far from cold, it was definitely cooler than the air, and I came up spluttering as he laughed. With a growl, I launched toward him and he let out a shout as I managed to land on his shoulders and just barely dunked his head.

Before I could streak away though, he caught my leg and towed me back to him. Then he lifted me up and tossed me. Laughing when I came up this time, I pursued him across the pool. We spent the next hour laughing, dunking, and wrestling in the water, until I finally moved over to the steps and sat there, panting.

All the earlier nervous energy had been burned away, and my muscles protested the vigorous play, but I didn't care. It had been fun. When Ian came to sit next to me, I leaned my head on his shoulder and closed my eyes as we just rested there.

"Feel better?" The quiet question nudged me from my near-doze state.

"How did you know?"

"You've been pretty wired the last few days," Ian said. "Yesterday when you crashed out like that, I knew you'd probably had enough, and you worked so hard today at not letting anything bother you."

I sighed. "Apparently not hard enough."

"I pay attention," he said, trailing his fingers up and down my arm soothingly. "I'm trying to anyway, and you have a way of smiling when it's the last thing you want to be doing."

Lifting my head, I twisted to face him. "I do?"

"Yeah. The smile is here," he murmured, tracing my lips with his finger before gliding his touch up to brush against the corner of my eyes. "But it doesn't reach here. You distract people because you can be solemn and you get harried and busy, so you don't have to focus on any one thing. I still saw it."

I swallowed. I wasn't sure I wanted to be seen like that.

"I'm not going to dig at you. This weekend had some epic suck moments."

Yeah, it had.

"But," he continued, cupping my face. "I think it had some good ones, too."

"Sunday was nice—later. Sorta—I mean it was, but later in the day. Not first thing. That was…" I wasn't sure I wanted to talk about the stuff with my mom. I'd told Archie because it was about his dad, too. But the rest?

"I'm glad," he continued, then tugged my wet hair gently. "If you ever need to talk, you know you can talk to me, right? About anything? Even—even the other guys."

"You punched Archie when I talked to you about what happened, even when I said I was fine with it."

He met my gaze unflinchingly. "He deserved that hit, and he'd be the first one to tell you he did."

"So if I tell you about Jake or Coop, are you going to hit them, too?"

"If they're dumber than a box of rocks, probably." He blew out a breath. "But I will try to restrain it to those times when they really deserve it. And before you get started winding yourself up about that, I fully expect Jake or Archie or Coop to knock me on my ass if I'm stupid where you're concerned."

"So… when do I knock you guys on your ass when you're stupid? Or who knocks me on mine?" Because I was genuinely curious.

Ian chuckled. "You're the smart one, Frankie. You can very effectively knock us on our ass. As I recall—you flat out told us to get out. You said there were boundaries. And you said you wanted to date." He coiled a lock of hair around his finger and tugged. "And no one is knocking you on your ass." Then he reeled me closer and nuzzled a kiss. "Because anyone who tries to knock you down is going to have to get past us."

I sighed as he teased kisses down my throat.

"Now," he murmured against my throat. "We better get out of the pool, and I need to order the pizza."

Laughter eddied through the shivers of his breath whispering against my skin. "We have a lot of homework to do."

"Hmm-hmm…and I want to play you the new song and see what you think."

"I love it," I told him, and he lifted his head.

"You haven't heard it yet."

I shrugged. "Doesn't matter. You have an amazing voice, and I love listening to you."

Arms wrapped around me, he chuckled. "You're good for my ego. I may have to keep you."

"Oh, the horror," I mock groaned.

"The horror, huh?" Then he had me up and I eyed him.

"Ian!"

"Oh, but it's the horror…" And he tossed me into the water, and it was even chillier against my sun-warmed skin. When I resurfaced, he was standing on the side, hands on his hips—looking *damn* good. "So—pineapple?"

A delightful shiver went through my whole body at the look in his eyes. "Yes please."

And it was my turn to do laps. Because all I wanted to do was climb him like a pole. When I finally abandoned the pool, he hauled me out and handed me a towel.

The next hour we actually spent on homework, but he kept my feet in his lap and would occasionally put a warm hand on my ankle while we worked through the calculus problems. The only break we took was for pizza, and then he dragged my feet back to rest against his thigh.

"Want to grab a shower and change before we head up to my room?"

I'd like a lot of things, but I'd settle for a shower. "Meet in your room when I'm done?"

"Hmm-hmm… unless you want to use my shower," he offered.

"With you?"

He squeezed my ankle. "I'm not in a rush."

Surprise flickered through me.

"Don't get me wrong—I *like* making out with you, and I *like* having you here and I want to do more, but I'm not rushing anything. You're important enough for me to take my time. You're worth more than a rush."

Warmth bloomed in my chest. Valued. Appreciated. Wanted. It was—a weirdly wonderful feeling. After another squeeze to my ankle, he started packing up his stuff.

"Besides," he said as he stood and raked his gaze over me, smile teasing. "Anticipation is half the fun."

"So you're saying we'd only have half-as-much fun if we rushed it?" I raised my eyebrows.

He opened his mouth, then closed it again. Head tilted, he squinted at me. "Definitely not saying that, but I still want to take my time. Enjoy every aspect of it. That's okay, right?"

"Yes," I answered swiftly. "It's more than okay." But he hadn't taken his time with… Nope, I shoved her name unmentioned out of my head. She didn't get to be a part of this.

And he just said I was more important and worth taking his time. "Thank you."

"For what?"

"For saying I'm worth it."

The look he gave me sent another wave of warmth through me. "Hell, Frankie… if you need me to tell you that every day, then you better get ready to be sick of it." When he held out an arm, I slid right against him and he hugged me tight, whispering, "You're the best. Never forget that."

It was easy when he was holding me and telling me.

It really was.

So I savored the moment. "Pizza. Compliments. Kisses. Now songs. I think you're pretty perfect, too."

Sprawled on his bed an hour later while he worked through the minor key change in "Message in a Bottle", I confirmed my earlier opinion. Ian had a gift.

Even more, we had the right song. Poignant. Haunting. Memorable.

And all him.

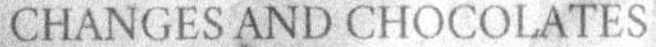

Chapter Fifteen

GAMES TEENS PLAY

Wednesday included a special assembly for all seniors. Every year they had an assembly for the various grades, but this one was different. This was about expectations for the year and about what we should plan for, from ordering caps and gowns, to senior pictures, to big events, to fundraisers, and more.

Sandwiched between Jake and Ian, I only half-listened. Most of this we knew. In fact, most of the dates the principal discussed I already had in my calendar. Every day we drew a little bit closer to the finish line. Instead of listening, I skimmed shopping sites on my phone. Coop's birthday was coming up. Archie wasn't that far behind him.

Jake slanted his head to look over my shoulder, and he tapped a game system and grinned with a thumb up. I rolled my eyes. They did not need more game systems. Ian tapped the screen to back up to the list, then scrolled down to the books on Eastern philosophy.

It was Jake's turn to make a face, and when he reached toward my phone again, I slapped his fingers. They both snorted laughing.

Idiots.

"…I know many of you have special schedules which allow you to come in late or leave early. In the interests of maintaining campus security…"

Yeah, I tuned him out again and continued to skim down the lists. Coop wasn't usually difficult to shop for. Though I hadn't been dating Coop before.

Archie

What's so funny?

Me

Nothing. Just window shopping.

Archie

Oo, find anything good?

Me

Nope.

Buying for my best friends always made sense. I just found stuff they liked. This wasn't any different, and yet, it seemed a thousand times harder. I glanced at the bracelet on my wrist. The A and the F gleamed in the light periodically.

Archie had never given me jewelry before either. No one had. It wasn't even on my radar as a kind of gift that I'd want. So was that part of the deal when you dated? You had to find something they didn't know they wanted? Or would like? If I had a girlfriend, I could ask her. I used to have a wider circle of friends, I got along with almost everyone. Correction, I had gotten along with nearly everyone. Part of me had begun to question those friendships—or lack thereof. Had those girls only wanted to get closer to the guys?

Cheryl? She'd always been nice, a little flighty, but nice. Her relentless cheerfulness and insistence that we get dresses together was kind of nice. Somewhere along the line, my only friends had become the guys and they were great. But I did miss having a girlfriend. While that used to be Sharon, Maria, and even Patty at one point, I didn't have anyone I could call for advice except the guys, and it was awkward to ask Ian about Archie or Jake about Coop or Coop about Ian or Archie about Jake. It just…wouldn't work.

The night before, Ian got me home around nine, though we diverted to take another ride around the lake. It was even nicer at night than it had been during the day. Though still humid, the air had been cooler. He'd even walked me to my door and then given me another long, deep, and very thorough kiss before nudging me inside. Only after I locked up did he leave.

I sent him a text before he got back to his bike.

Me

Thank you for this afternoon and evening. I had fun.

Ian

Me too, Angel. Text you when I get home.

The guys had been chattering while we'd been hanging out, nothing huge. But when I answered, my phone blew up with comments. It was warm and welcoming and made the apartment less lonely in a way. I finally sucked it up and sent my mom a text, too.

Me

I'm fine. The school is handling it. Mr. Rhys was great. Don't worry. Thank you to Mr. Standish if his lawyers took care of it.

The last part had been difficult to write, but it was the right thing to say. Not that I wanted to encourage her. Archie didn't think it was a problem for his parents. But that would make it a problem for Mom. The last thing I wanted to see was her hurt.

She didn't answer, but I didn't expect one.

And whether I had a girlfriend or not wouldn't help there. I didn't like to talk about Mom and me with others. In light of the affair, it would be even harder to bring it up to the guys—even Archie, who was in the middle of this with me.

"Other dates you should be aware of," the principal droned one as he listed the testing dates for lower grades. When Coop's birthday date was mentioned, I focused a little more. "On all of these days, seniors, you are excused from classes. We will need the space to spread out for testing. You will be responsible for any homework assignments and due dates if your teachers do not adjust them."

Had they all just gotten Coop's birthday off?

Coop

You're still taking that night off work, right?

I grinned.

Me

Absolutely. Wouldn't miss it. Happy birthday to you.

Ian chuckled and Jake smirked before he showed me his phone.

Coop

Ha! I get Frankie on my birthday suckers, all day!

Archie

Just means we can all do something big for your birthday.

Coop

Could be fun. Talk at lunch.

Archie

Whatever we do, I want to spend the evening with her.

Jake lowered the phone, and I smiled again. Ian bumped my shoulder as I checked my calendar and added the dates the principal had given us for testing. There was already a notification for B-DAY WITH COOP waiting for me to accept and it had the whole day blocked off.

There was also a reminder of a date with Coop on Saturday.

Crap.

I had to meet Cheryl at the mall, and I already had a date with Coop. I chewed my lower lip. I'd talk to Coop first, but I told him yes before I told Cheryl. Somehow, I couldn't imagine Coop going dress shopping with us...

Then again, the image of trying on all those dresses while he gave me a yay or a nay sounded kind of fun, too. We used to do that for Halloween costumes.

Would that be weird?

Filing that thought away, I let out the same sigh of relief as everyone else when the principal ended the talk but held us for dismissal. We just had to wait for the bell to ring. We'd missed second and third, so we'd head straight to fourth. Jake twisted in his seat. "So you work tonight, right?"

"Hmm-hmm." For once, I really wasn't looking forward to it. I didn't love my job, but I had enjoyed it. More, I'd enjoyed the freedom it offered because of the money I could save. "Normal schedule this week. Though I'm taking next Thursday off."

"Yeah, we all are," Ian said with a grin.

"Yeah, I meant the evening, too."

"Ahh," Jake exhaled. "Lucky Coop. Are you taking Archie's birthday and mine off, too?"

"Of course, I am," I said easily. At his smirk, I added, "Just remind me when that is again?"

Ian burst out laughing, and I grinned. Eyes narrowed, Jake reached over and tweaked my nose. The volume around us climbed, because we weren't the only ones talking.

"We'll come by after practice," Jake said as the bell rang. "Meet at my car for lunch?"

"Yep!"

The nice thing about walking out with Jake and Ian included the fact they folded around me so I didn't get pushed or shoved in the close quarters. Our class might not be huge, but five hundred of us squeezed into one spot slowed our exodus. Coop caught me just outside the doors.

"Tag," he said to the guys. "I'm it!" One arm slung around my shoulders, he grinned as I waved to Ian and Jake heading to their classes. "We have my birthday off."

"I seem to have heard something about that," I teased him.

"Heh," he chuckled. "I'm looking forward to it. The big 18."

"Alas, you'll be older than me for a few months. But only a few."

"No matter how old you get, I'm always going to be older."

"This is true…should we start counting the gray hairs now?"

He swatted at me as I tugged lightly against his sandy blond hair. "Evil, twisted… meanie."

I snorted at the last, but then we were at our classroom and Ms. Fajardo gestured to the board.

Timed essay.

Oh joy.

Coop on the other hand groaned. "You're trying to kill us, Ms. Fajardo."

"Nah," she said with an easy grin. "But you are going to be so used to these by AP time, it's going to be relaxing."

More than a few other students echoed his snort. I slid into my desk and pulled out fresh notebook paper as Coop dropped into his backpack on the floor next to him.

"You got extra?" he asked.

Used to it, I passed him several sheets and then offered him a pen.

"Thank you," he murmured, and I leaned back to wait for the bell to ring and for Ms. Fajardo to call time. She hadn't written how much time we would have or the subject. Since they varied the times on the test, so did she for the timed writing in the room.

The bell rang as the last student eeked in the door. He made his way to his seat as Ms. Fajardo walked to the front of the room. Everyone had their notebook paper and pens out.

"Under each of your desks is a face down sheet of paper. Pull it out and keep it facedown." I found mine and put it in place. "I have given each of you a different excerpt, the author and book title are included as well as the year published. When I say go and start the clock, you will have forty minutes to carefully read your excerpt then in a well-constructed essay, analyze how the author portrays the complex experience of the characters and their environment or setting. You may wish to consider such literary elements of style, tone, and selection of detail." She gave us all a once over. "Any questions?"

When no one raised their hands, she glanced at her watch, wrote 40 on the board, and then said, "Go," before she wrote the start time on the board.

I flipped mine over and stared at the excerpt. It was from Nathaniel Hawthorne's *The Scarlet Letter*. At the bottom the words *Fitting for you, don't you think?* were scrawled in pencil.

A hot chill spread under my skin. The comment wasn't kind, but how would anyone know this would be the paper I'd get? And who would have had access?

I must have stared at the comment for five minutes because the scratching of chalk pulled my gaze up and Ms. Fajardo had changed the time to 35 minutes.

Putting my hand over the words to block them, I focused on the text on the page. I'd already lost five minutes and I still had to write the essay. The minutes ticked by as I worked painfully slow. I couldn't seem to focus on a cohesive thought for the style of the writing or the intent of the characters beyond being miserable bastards.

Pretty sure that was just me projecting about the unwelcome commentary on the bottom. I was writing right up until Ms. Fajardo announced one minute.

Two more sentences.

A part of me was aware of Coop frowning at me, and when I put my pen down just as Ms. Fajardo called time, I caught her giving me a concerned look, too.

I stacked the essay together with the reading selection on the bottom. I'd rather just trash that, but we had to turn them in. With Coop a half-step behind me, I turned it in.

The last ten minutes of class, I made a concerted effort to focus on Ms. Fajardo's mini-lecture. It was more about active reading and why we needed to understand when a piece had been written in order to wring the most from the words. Culture and time period very much affected the prose. Though there were some genres that seemed exempt—like early science fiction.

So she issued a challenge, each of us was to find a work—long or short—of early science fiction published no later than 1940. That got a few gasps. We needed to read it, analyze it, and turn it in. Then we would be sharing with the class.

This was on top of the big project we already had.

Normally, the idea would excite me, but at the moment, I just wanted class to be over. When the bell rang, we were all ready to get out of there. Coop was at my side in a heartbeat.

"What's wrong?"

"Nothing," I said as I pulled on my backpack.

"Uh huh." Falling into step with me as I headed out of the room, he bumped my shoulder gently. "You never take that long to write an essay."

"I had a lot to say."

When he didn't retort, I hoped that would be the end of it. We'd had enough drama the last few days. I didn't want any more. Once we were outside though, he tossed an arm around me and said, "Talk to me."

"Coop…it took me a minute to get going."

"Frankie, why are you lying?" The question scraped over me, and I stopped dead to pull away and look at him.

The sun slanted across my eyes, almost giving him a halo. Coop was a lot of things—funny, wicked sense of humor, warm, huggable, and downright entertaining—but he was definitely not an angel. The hot cold feeling under my skin spread out everywhere. "It was a timed essay, what's the big deal?"

My stomach did rolls.

"The big deal is you're avoiding talking about whatever it was, and something upset you. You stared at that page like you hadn't seen words before for a long time, and you didn't twitch until Fajardo changed the time on the board."

"Why the hell were you watching me and not doing your own essay?"

He let out a slow sigh, but instead of irritation he frowned. Worry filled his eyes. "Frankie… talk to me."

Tipping my head back, I stared at the sky, then winced and dug into my backpack for my sunglasses. After I slid them on, I said, "Someone wrote something on the bottom of the page. It threw me."

"Okay, what did they write?"

A horn honked somewhere behind us, and Coop raised his hand and waved. Was that Jake…? As I started to turn, Coop caught my arm and turned me back to him.

"Just said, 'fitting for you, don't you think?'" I tried to downplay it, but his eyes narrowed and the discomfort in my gut threatened to turn into cramps.

"Fajardo wrote that?" Suspicion edged every word.

"No," I said, running my hands along my backpack straps. It hadn't been her writing.

Jake pulled up next us. "What the hell you two? Get in the car."

"Sec," Coop said, still focused on me. "So what was your excerpt?"

"If I tell you, will you let it go so we can go eat?" It didn't need to be a big deal. It was done. Someone wanted to mess with my head, well they succeeded. Congratulations. But I still finished my essay, so they could go suck it.

"Sure," Coop said. "We'll go with that."

"What's wrong?" Ian asked, he was sitting in the back of Jake's SUV and Archie leaned over from the passenger side to look out the window. All of them were staring at me.

"Nothing," I said. "Coop's just being nosy."

"Well, let him be nosy in air conditioning. We're starving," Archie called. "And it's hard to hear all the way over here."

I laughed at Archie's complaint, even if I wasn't feeling the humor, and circled the SUV with Coop right at my heels. Just before I opened the door, I said, "It was *The Scarlet Letter*. Happy?"

"No," he said quietly, opening the door for me. "I'm definitely not happy about that."

I passed my backpack to Ian and he shoved it into the back for me and Coop's followed. Then we were all in.

"Thank you," Archie said. "Let's move it. We've already wasted time waiting for slowpokes."

"You could have left without us," Coop said dryly. Despite the tone, I could feel his gaze on me. "Frankie and I could get lunch on our own."

"In your dreams," Jake said over his shoulder.

Ian caught my hand and threaded our fingers together. At the touch, I glanced at him. Concern reflected in his eyes, but I summoned up a smile. Probably one that didn't touch my eyes, if his expression was anything to judge by.

"Tell me something good about your day." Tell me anything so I could change the subject in my head.

"Well I almost got a two-hour nap but the principal wouldn't shut up," Archie said. "And my girl was sitting with these two bozos and didn't save me a seat."

Ian snorted. "You snooze, you lose."

"Ha ha," Archie said with a grin and winked at me. "Jake got news."

"Yeah, Jake got maybe news," Jake said. "And we're not going to jinx it."

"Man, it's good news," Archie argued, and Jake shook his head.

"It's maybe news, and we're *not* jinxing it," he repeated, and then we were pulling into the parking lot for food.

"Fine," Archie said, waving his hands as we got out of the car. "We're not jinxing it. Bubba? Coop? Good news?"

"Just got my birthday off from school," Coop said, though his tone wasn't that up beat.

"Yeah, we need to decide what to do with the time…" Ian said. He held my hand for a beat longer after we got out of the SUV, then let it go so we could walk inside.

Making plans for Coop's birthday sucked up all of lunch. A fact for which I was grateful, even if I caught him studying me. I was even more thankful he didn't bring up the essay again. Hopefully, he'd let it go, as unlikely a scenario as that was. Coop might not hammer on it right now, but I had a feeling we'd be discussing it again and soon. Fingers crossed, he wouldn't tell the guys because they weren't that patient. Back at school, we split up with Jake walking with me to study hall. We ran into Maria in the hallway, but she didn't even look at us. That worked. Fortunately, I didn't really notice anyone else.

In the library, I left Jake at our table while I went on a hunt for the science fiction project. I knew that we had a book of short stories from that period, so I just had to check it out.

By the time I was back at the table though, Jake had his phone out and was reading through something on the screen. He closed it when I got there and then smiled. "So…"

"So?" I raised my brows as I packed the book in with my stuff. Other than the lit projects, I didn't have any homework, since two of my classes were missed for the assembly.

"Is it okay if I come over after work tonight?"

It was a replay of last week. And all of a sudden, it hit me that I forgot to talk to Coop about Saturday.

Crap.

"Um…"

"Your mom is still gone, right?"

"Yeah," I said. "Probably until the weekend." If she didn't extend it. That seemed to be a recurring theme.

He ran a finger down my arm. "We had fun last week."

My face heated. "We did," I agreed, then bit my lower lip. "You planning on spending the night?"

"I'd love to," he said with a grin. "Course… that really was an accident."

"It was an accident that you curled up with me?"

"No, that we both fell asleep and then I didn't want to go." He tapped his foot against mine. "No strings, Frankie. I just wanna come over and hang out. We had fun on Sunday, yeah?"

We really had. "The not getting in until three kind of sucked," I said.

"No lie," Jake said. "This time, we'll already be home. Catch up on more videos, hang out. I'll bring dinner…whatever you want."

"If I'm really tired after work…"

"Then I won't hang out long—or I will, but we can just crash." He kept his voice low. "I liked sleeping there."

A shiver skated up my spine. I'd liked him sleeping there, too. Enough that I hadn't washed the sheets cause they still smelled like him a little. So did the pillowcase. He and Archie both.

Hmm, maybe I should change them before I went to work.

"You're incorrigible," I teased him. "Will you tell me the maybe good news if I say yes?"

"You don't have to say yes for me to tell you," he answered, his expression solemn. "But I'd like to wait until I'm sure."

That I understood. "Fair enough."

He grinned. "So, yes?"

I rolled my eyes. "Yes."

"Excellent." He bumped my foot again. "What do you want to eat?"

"Surprise me," I said. "Just not…"

"Burgers. Yeah, I know."

The conversation with Jake helped. I made it through sixth period with no issues, and swung by my locker to make sure I had everything before I went to seventh. There was a note inside—just a folded up piece of paper, no envelope, and it read:

*Rumor has it that one of your boyfriends has a secret. Do you know **who** all they did last summer?*

Wow.

I crumpled the note up, then shoved it to the back of the locker. After I grabbed the last two books I needed, I shut it and headed straight for Mr. G's room. Jake was already there when I arrived, as was Mr. G. He had another practice quiz for us.

Yay.

My phone started vibrating before the class was even over. But I couldn't check it until after I finished the quiz and it had a hundred questions. It was designed to run out the clock, but I managed to finish a split second before Jake, and I raised my hands even as the bell rang with him a heartbeat behind me.

Laughing, we high-fived and Mr. G just shook his head at us as he took the scantrons. "Get out of here, you two. See you tomorrow."

"Bye."

"Ha," Jake said as we cruised out of the room. "That was not fun."

I grimaced. "No, I feel like he took an icepick to my brain."

My phone vibrated again, and I shifted my backpack to dig it out of my pocket. Jake already had his out, and he scowled at his phone. "C'mon."

"What?"

"Just—c'mon." He grasped my hand in his.

I followed him as he cut through the hallways, shouldering people aside if they clustered too tight. We weren't quite running, but when we got to the doors leading out to where I parked, nothing could have prepared me for the sight of my car.

It was covered in condoms.

"Hey," Coop said as he headed for us. "We can't touch it. Mr. Obermeyer was already over here, and the SROs are coming. We have to wait for them."

My stomach lurched. Ian's expression was forbidding, so was Jake's for that matter.

Some of the condoms were in packages, a lot were out. Someone had gone to a lot of trouble to plaster them all over my car. I had to get to work. I already had to leave early on Saturday and then I missed Sunday—I mean, Marsha had given me the day off, but this…

Jake squeezed my hand. "Did anyone see?"

"You don't think I wouldn't have tackled the asshole?" Coop asked. "No, I didn't see. It looked like that when I got here and before you ask…" He glanced at me. "If there was a note, it's gone."

The note.

I'd never been more grateful that I forgot to write the note and leave it for Mr. Thorns that morning. I'd been distracted when I got home last night and tired when I got up that morning.

The hot/cold feeling was back again, and I sucked in a breath. Laughter erupted from another group. And a couple of kids paused to take pictures. Well, more than a couple.

"Guys…" I pulled my hand out of Jake's and pushed the hair back from my face. "I have to go to work. I have to feed the cats and go to work—"

"It's gonna be fine," Coop said. "Call Marsha, just tell her you might be a little late. Hopefully, the SROs will be here soon."

"I'm gonna kill the asshole who did this," Jake muttered.

"No, you're not. Just—don't get in any more fights. It's just—a lot of condoms."

Coop grimaced, but Ian shook his head. I glanced from the car back to the school. A virtual parade of cars was passing by, and there was more laughter and photos.

I would not cry.

I wasn't sure whether I was pissed or I was upset.

Or both.

"We gotta hit practice," Ian said, and there was an apology in his eyes. "I'll run over and tell Coach what's going on and that I need to be here."

"You can't miss practice, you have a game on Friday."

"I don't," Jake said. "I can stay."

"But you're already in trouble," I reminded him.

"What. The. Fuck." Archie had pulled up behind my car. "I thought you were kidding!" He cut off his car and slammed out of it.

Great. Now they were all here to see this.

"Don't touch it," Ian said. "SROs are coming."

That got us more looks, and a couple of kids came out the doors behind us and trailed past slowly looking at me and then at my car.

"Frankie," Coop caught my arm. "Call Marsha, tell her you're having car trouble. Soon as the SRO is done, we'll get that stuff off, and I can run your car to a carwash if you want."

If I wanted?

"I can take you to work," Archie said.

Nauseated didn't cover it. The icy hot feeling ran up and down my spine. "I'll call her… you guys have to go."

Jake opened his mouth to protest, so did Ian.

"Don't get in any more trouble over me. Coop's here. Archie's here. And really, what are the condoms going to do? Look ickie at me?"

It didn't even generate a smile. Jake gave me a hug, then pressed a kiss to my forehead. "You call me," he said at my ear. "You hear me? Text me when this is done and call me. I'll see you at work after practice."

I nodded. Ian threw me a pained smile, and then he gave me a hug. "It's going to be fine, Frankie. Whatever jackass did this poked the wrong bear. Archie and Jake are going to have so much fun getting even."

That *almost* made me laugh, which had to be the intention.

Then they were going, and I hated to see them leave, but it was better. Archie and Coop were right there and nudged me back toward the shade.

"You can sit in my car, if you want," Archie offered. "Air conditioning."

It was hot and sticky, and I almost didn't care about that at the moment. I couldn't even work up the words to say I was fine.

I looked down at my phone and the tags showing up on Instagram in my notifications.

"Don't look," Coop advised.

Not right now, no. I dialed Mason's and closed my eyes when Marsha answered.

I so did not want to tell her I was going to be late.

From reliable to irresponsible in four easy steps.

Today sucked.

Take Our Time

Jake

What's going on?

Coop

Still waiting on Obermeyer and the SRO

Bubba

Ugh. Is Frankie freaking out?

Archie

No, she's talking to Marsha.

Bubba

Good talk? Bad talk?

Coop

Bad, she's trying not to cry.

Jake

Fuck. I'm coming back.

Archie

Stay there. She wanted you to not get in anymore trouble.

Jake

...

Coop

A is right. SROs just got here.

Bubba

Tell us what happens.

Archie

Will do.

A little later...

Jake

Bubba's on the field.

Archie

SRO finished report. Has to photograph. Filing with cops.

Coop

A taking Frankie home. Then work. I'll get her car cleaned.

Jake

...

Coop

Yeah, it's bad.

Archie

She'll be okay. We got her.

Jake

Taking her car to her after?

Coop

Yes. Okay, A just left with F.

Jake

...

Coop

Who is targeting her?

Jake

Sharon did Instagram thing. Why?
Something else happen?

Coop

Gotta talk to SRO, gimme a few.

A little later...

Archie

Frankie at work.

Jake

B still on field. How is she?

Archie

Not happy. Hanging here for a bit.
What other thing happened?

Jake

Waiting on Coop.

Coop

Just got to detail place. Took time
to clear the windshield.

Jake

Fuck.

Archie

Spill. What did we miss?

Coop

5 mins. Want to get her car in.

Archie

I like her boss.

Jake

Yeah?

Archie

Gave her a hug when she got here.

Jake

Yeah?

Archie

Ok. Arch, don't let F see your phone.

Archie

Ooookay.

Coop

Yeah. Probably.

Archie

Sharon? Maria? Patty? Laura? Who?

Coop

I don't think it's Laura.

Jake

If you say she's too nice, I may hit you.

Coop

No, just—it wasn't a bad breakup.

Archie

Girls never tell you when it's bad.

Jake

No they dont.

Archie

Sharon's already out for her

Jake

Maybe.

Bubba

It's not that Thorns person is it?

Coop

Because of the posts over the weekend?

Coop

We need to catch them.

Archie

We need to do something. Staying at Masons.

Bubba

Be there after practice.

Jake

Ditto.

Coop

Be there when car is clean.

Archie

Think of who else might target her cause of us

Jake

It is us, isn't it?

Archie

Yeah. And they are going to regret it.

Chapter Sixteen

WHAT ARE YOU WILLING TO LOSE?

The fact I had to leave my car with Coop irked. Archie had been great on the drive to my place, he didn't nag or try to pry things out of me. All he did was say, "What do you need?"

While he fed the cats, I got changed into my uniform and washed my face. The burning urge to cry was almost as humiliating as what they'd done to my car. The Instagram tags kept coming, so I went into the app long enough to shut off notifications.

When I came back out, Archie slipped his phone into his back pocket before he held out his arms. Call me weak, but I wanted that hug. I leaned on him and closed my eyes for about thirty seconds. Then we had to go, I was already late.

Marsha had been fantastic. Despite the fact I'd worked at Mason's for two years and had my routines down to a fine art, I was so off-center for my shift. It took me twice as long to get shakes pulled, I had to double-check every order I took, and more than once, I caught myself examining every student I recognized and those that were in the right age range to be at our school.

Were they the ones who painted my car in condoms?

There were obvious picks—Sharon? Maria? Patty? But I didn't want to accuse anyone. Sharon had posted the pictures. As bad as those were, I even understood why she did it. That did not paint her the villain of any story, much less my own.

Archie parked himself at a table in the corner of my station and had his homework out. But every time I glanced over at him, he was either watching me or studying the customers. Paranoia could be contagious. Though, whenever our gazes collided, he'd give me an encouraging smile and it helped.

It helped a lot.

Coop slid into the booth when I was in the back pulling fresh ice cream tubs. The grin he tossed me when I caught sight of him squeezed me like a warm hug. I glanced outside, and there was my baby, parked neatly next to Archie's Ferrari, all cleaned up and sparkling.

Relief flooded over me. No sign of the sticky mess or the condoms. I owed Coop a huge kiss and a hug. As it was, I made him a strawberry shake and delivered it before I took his order.

"On me," I told him.

"Nah," Archie said. "I insist."

He'd already insisted on covering the cleaning. "Yes, but I control the check, so you don't get to." I stuck my tongue out at him, and he laughed.

"Well, I'm starving, so I'll take the Big and Thick, since you already brought me the thick." He winked before taking a drink from his straw.

"Smartass," I teased, then looked at Archie. "You want anything else?"

"Grab me a Coke?" Leaning forward on his elbows, he said, "I'm probably going to be here a while."

"Me, too," Coop said as he passed me my keys and then started opening his backpack.

"You got it." I pocketed the keys, then grabbed Archie's finished plate. "Thanks for taking care of her for me, Coop."

"Anytime," he said, the corners of his mouth curving. "You know that."

Funnily enough, I kind of did. It was Coop. He never minded helping me out, even when I didn't want to ask. I owed him.

Thirty minutes later, Rachel arrived and grabbed a spot at the end of the counter. "Hey," I greeted her. I hadn't really seen her that day.

"Hey," she said, giving me a narrow-eyed study. "You have your chin up and you can still smile, good."

I'd almost managed to stop thinking about my car for five minutes until she said that. "Girl's gotta eat," I tried to keep it light.

"Yes, she does. And I'm starving, so the usual for me, and if you have time, I have more poetry homework." The hopeful look in her eyes made me laugh.

"I'm starting to think the only reason you're talking to me is for help with your homework."

"We can fix that," Rachel suggested. "Pick a night, and we can grab a movie or something."

The offer was so smooth, I blinked. "Really?"

"Why not? You're pretty smart. I imagine you have to have at least semi-decent taste, and while I truly appreciate the homework help, it's not the only reason I'm talking to you."

Well, now I felt like an ass. "Sorry, I guess that did come out kind of bitchy."

"Not even a little," Rachel said easily. "You're always busy, but you have my new number right?"

"Actually… I don't know if I do."

She held out her phone. "Put yours in, and I'll text you, then you'll have mine. And don't worry about when you're free, just pick a day. We'll make it happen."

The offer shouldn't have thrown me, but it kind of did. "Thanks." I plugged in my number and added my name to the contact, then hit save before I passed it back to her. "I'll get your order in."

"Cool," Rachel answered. "There, sent you a text."

Then the number of people coming in began to pick up, so I only got to talk to Rachel a handful of times. Once to deliver her shake, then her food, and once more to answer her question on the poetry assessment she was writing. The funny thing was, she seemed to have a good handle on it. I wasn't sure if it was lack of confidence or what that had her asking for help.

Ian and Jake arrived during the chaos as a good half of the football team, their girlfriends, and more poured in the door. The volume climbed, and I was on the move. I barely had time to think, which was probably a good thing because I couldn't focus on Sharon and Maria taking over a table on my side, or that they were brittle and polite when I came to get their order.

However, the fact that I had four gazes laser focused in my direction while I spoke to them was a little unnerving. "Surprised you made it in today," Sharon said. "Then again, nothing really slows you down, does it?" She winced and snapped a look at Maria, who just glared at her. "Fine." The last huffed word was not directed at me.

"Thanks, Frankie," Maria said with a faint, if genuine smile.

"You know, at least she has stock in condoms, that should keep them busy for a week," Patty said as I walked away from the table. Sharon laughed, but Maria groaned.

"Shut up," she said. "That was nasty, whoever did it."

Well, score one for Maria. Of the three, I had always liked her best, anyway. They were lucky I wasn't the type to spit on their food or in their shakes. The idea was gross period, but I had to admit, it made me smile.

Throughout the rush though, the guys never left and Rachel held up her end of the counter, and it was like I had two bastions of safety in the place because I had begun to dread every table I approached. Some had smirks. Some snickered. Still, others didn't seem to give a damn one way or the other.

Not that it made me feel much better.

The fact all four of them were waiting for me when I walked out of Mason's was enough to pull a tired smile. I don't think I'd ever been this exhausted. Coop leaned against the back of my car, while the other three stood, forming a loose circle.

"There she is," Ian said, stretching out an arm, and I slid against him as he wrapped it around my shoulders and pressed a kiss to the top of my head. "You look beat."

"I am beat," I admitted. "I think even the aches on my feet have aches."

"You were running your ass off," Archie said. "How you feeling otherwise?"

"Tired." I leaned into Ian for another sweet moment, and then made myself straighten up. "Now I still have homework to do and cats to herd."

Coop snorted at the herding comment, but it was Jake whose gaze I caught. I could see the question in his eyes. Did I want him to come over? I did and I didn't. But all the reasons I did were about me, and all the reasons I didn't were about what other people had been doing.

So tonight, I was picking me and I nodded. He gave me a small thumbs up and a smile.

"Go home, call or text when you get there?" Ian asked, and I nodded. He brushed a kiss to my forehead before he let me go.

"I'm hitching with you," Coop said as he headed for the passenger seat. Archie snorted, then stole a hug and pressed a kiss just behind my ear.

"Call me if anything else goes wrong," he said, and it was in this stern voice. "Or if you just need to talk. Capiche?"

I gave him a little shove. "I'll be fine, thank you for everything today. You were a hero."

"Heh," he said, his grin growing. "See, I was a hero."

Rolling my eyes, I added, "Coop was a hero, too."

"I offered to blow off practice," Jake argued.

"I know," I soothed, giving him a sideways hug. "You and Ian are heroes, in my book. All of you are."

"Well, fine, I'll share the title with them," Archie grumbled, but his grin didn't diminish. "Go on, sleeping beauty, go get some rest. We'll see you in the morning."

"Yep. Thank you again, Archie."

Neither Jake nor I mentioned Jake coming over.

Ian peeled off for his bike, and Archie slid into his car. Jake waited for them to start moving before he said, "Pizza? Chinese? What are you in the mood for?"

"Wings," I admitted. "Spicy barbecue wings."

"Got it." He grinned. "Be there soon."

"I'll leave the door unlocked, I need a shower."

"And now I have incentive to hurry." His grin grew, and I laughed.

"That wasn't quite what I meant."

He winked, but didn't argue.

On the drive home, Coop didn't waste time. "I want to say something, and I want you to listen to it. Then I want you to think about it before you respond, okay?"

"Okay," I agreed. I'd been all kinds of tense since discovering what had been done to my car. The fact I'd ended up leaving her with Coop while Archie got me home and then to work had thrown me all evening. Behind the wheel of my baby again, though, I was more me. The stiffness in my muscles bled away even as the aches in my feet became more pronounced. We really had been busy as hell.

"You didn't want to tell me about the comment on the essay thing earlier. It really upset you. And don't try to tell me it didn't. I've known you a long time, I know when something is off." He paused for a beat. "It bothers me that you didn't want to tell me. I thought—yeah, Frankie doesn't like to make waves. You never have. You always go along to get along. It's one of the things that is sometimes adorable about you, and utterly frustrating."

Glad we were clear on that.

It was dark so that even when I glanced at him, I couldn't quite make out his full expression.

"But the thing is… someone hurt you, and you were just going to let them hurt you and not let any of us help. I had to basically coerce it out of you, and then you didn't want to talk about it. I get that you have that right, but, Frankie, there's so many times someone has hurt you that you shut down and you won't let me help."

There weren't that many times.

"Usually it's about your mom."

Okay, he might have a point there.

"But this is different… this is happening because of choices I made, choices the guys made."

I opened my mouth to protest, and he clucked his tongue.

"Listen, please. Listen to all of it, then think about it before you tell me to shove it."

I didn't mean to laugh, but I couldn't help it. While I hadn't necessarily intended to tell him to shove it, that had occurred previously.

"The point is—the post on Instagram, the thing with your car—those are big things that we see. The note on the essay in class? If you don't tell us, if you don't tell me, I can't help you and, Frankie, the very last thing I want is for you to be in pain or to be hurting in some way and I am not helping you. That's already happened once. You cut us all off because we were hurting you, and you didn't tell us we were. While, yes, we deserve some of that blame, I don't want to wake up one day and find out I could have done something but you didn't let me."

With that, he exhaled.

"Friend or boyfriend, I'm on your side," he said, twisting in the seat. "I need to know you know that."

We were almost to the apartment turn. "Is it okay for me to answer now?"

"Yes," he said. "Thank you for letting me say that."

A reluctant smile tugged at my lips. Coop was so sweet when he wanted to be. "I do know you're on my side. I know I was stubborn this summer, and my choices hurt all of us."

"Our choices hurt all of us," he corrected. "You might have made the call, but we definitely pushed you."

"Okay, so our choices weren't great."

"Accepted," he murmured, and slid a hand to my thigh.

"The thing with the note today…" I really didn't want to think about the note or what it said. It had stung. "There was another one."

"On the essay?"

"In my locker."

He tightened his grip, his hand flexing before it relaxed again as I turned into the complex and followed the parking lot down to where I usually parked.

"It was just a piece of notebook paper with the question, did I know who all you did this summer."

"Son of a bitch," Coop swore.

"So I crumpled it up, grabbed my books, and just went on to Mr. G's class."

"Crumpled it up—did you throw it away?"

It was on the tip of my tongue to tell him yes, I did. But we had all had enough half-truths and lies between us. "No, I just tossed it back into the locker under some of the books."

"Can I see it tomorrow?"

Parked, I stared at him. "Why?"

"Well one, I want to know if I recognize the writing. Two, I want to know exactly what it says. Three, someone keeps coming after you, they're going to find all of us in the way. I don't like you being hurt."

"Anonymous notes and vague threats aren't hurting me."

"What they did to your car *did* hurt you."

I couldn't argue with that. "We don't know it was the same person." Or if there had been a note on my car that they'd taken. I could only hope Mr. Thorns was at least vaguely aware, because I did not want him getting caught in the blowback.

The reality of that thought settled in my bones. I didn't know who he was, but I cared about Mr. Thorns because he'd been nothing but kind to me in those notes and even in not meeting on Saturday night. The evening had already been a shitshow, and in a way, I was kind of glad he kept his distance.

"Do you really think it matters if it was the same person or not?" Coop made no attempt to leave the car.

Covering his hand on my thigh with mine, I shook my head. "I just want it to go away."

"Me, too," he promised. "But I need you to tell us, to trust us to help and to protect you."

"You make it sound like we're in some grand drama. What do you think they're going to do, Coop? Dump a bucket of blood on me at Homecoming?"

"God, I hope not," he muttered.

"I was kidding." And being dramatic.

"Well, I'm not, that's the thing. What they did to your car is an escalation. What Sharon did on Instagram was an escalation. Those notes? Putting them on your work—did you even tell Ms. Fajardo?"

I hung my head. "You know I didn't."

"Will you tell her?"

"It's not like she won't see it." She had the sheets, we had to turn them back in.

"Frankie."

That was it. Just my name. Leaning my head back against the headrest, I said, "I'll think about it, okay? I'm tired. I want to go inside and shower…"

A knock on my window had me jerk and spin. Jake stood just outside the car with a concerned look on his face.

I unlocked the car and opened the door, heart racing. The adrenaline dump was not fun.

"Didn't mean to scare you," he said, leaning down. The scent of barbecue wings flooded the car, and my stomach growled. "Everything all right?"

"Yeah," Coop said. "We were talking about the note thing."

"You told them?" I shifted my stare to him.

"Yes," Jake answered instead of Coop. "He did. We needed to know, Frankie."

Another groan slipped out of me. Once we were both out of the car, I locked it and faced the pair of them. "I told Coop I'd think about talking to Ms. Fajardo tomorrow. I don't want to make a big deal out of any of this." No doubt, my car had made its stunning and wretched debut on social media, and probably with lots of humorous comments to entertain the masses.

"Okay, but it is a big deal," Jake said, almost echoing Coop. "You're important to us. Pretending it didn't happen won't make it go away. The stupid idea of ignoring a bully will just make him bored is so damn dumb, it makes me hurt to even say it."

"Can we talk about anything else tonight? Please?"

His expression softened and so did Coop's. "C'mere," Coop said, and he wound his arms around me. I leaned into the hug, and he ran his hands up and down my back. "You matter, Frankie. Talk to us, and I'll try not to be a pain in the ass about this."

A little laugh escaped me.

"I'm not making that promise," Jake said. "But you do matter. I totally plan to be a pain in someone's ass as soon as I figure out what asshole did it."

"But he's going to give it a rest tonight," Coop said, a warning in his tone. "So he doesn't worry you."

That would be nice.

"Yeah, okay," Jake relented. "C'mon, sweetheart. Let's go up, and you can shower and then eat. I'll help with any homework, too."

"Homework," Coop snorted, and I glanced up in time to see Jake give

Coop a look. He smirked and raised his hands. Then turned to me and dipped his head. The first brush of his lips was almost tentative, but it lasted all of three seconds before his mouth firmed against mine. The sweep of his tongue requesting entrance had me almost sighing. A part of me recognized Jake was right there, a quick kiss was one thing, but this… this was something else altogether.

This wasn't like the kiss where Coop had stormed through all my defenses while trapping me against the fridge, or the hungry kiss he'd devoured me with on the sofa. This was all sweet heat and gentle promise. Tingles raced over my skin and left a trail of goosebumps in their wake, and when he sucked on my tongue, my toes curled and I had to fist his shirt to keep from falling.

When he lifted his head, he smiled and I shivered. "Goodnight, Frankie."

"Night, Coop." My whole system hummed from that kiss, and a lot of my tired evaporated.

"You know, I'd punch you except that was hot," Jake commented dryly, and I jumped. Oh crap, I'd almost forgotten Jake was there for a second. I'd known he was there, and his watching had actually turned me on even more. Guilt pierced me, but then his words registered in the same moment as his slow smile.

"Yeah well, just remember Frankie needs to sleep," Coop said. "Don't stay too late."

"I've got her," Jake retorted, wrapping an arm around me. "C'mon, we're going inside. Night, Coop."

I stole one look back, and Coop grinned then blew me a kiss. Some of my guilt evaporated, and I glanced up at Jake. "That really didn't bother you?"

"You kissing Coop? Or should I say, Coop melting your panties with that kiss?" The droll comment made me laugh because he wasn't wrong with that assessment.

"Yeah."

At my door, he let me go so I could unlock it and then he followed me inside. He locked the door before he set the bag on the table, and I found myself swept up into another embrace. Only this time, it was Jake's hard chest I impacted against as he fisted my hair, and then his mouth closed over mine. The embers Coop ignited flared to life, and heat swept through me as Jake massaged my lips apart.

With one stroke of his tongue, I was shuddering. The keys fell with a jingle and a thud. Then I had my hands on his shoulders before sliding them up to his hair. It was so soft against my fingers. He made a low sound in his throat as he delved deeper, and there was no mistaking the erection pressing against me where his hips ground against mine. The angle was a little off, and then Jake picked me up and I was sitting on the table. He nudged my legs apart as he lifted his head for a moment. His pale blue eyes were like icy fire, and my nipples tightened at that single look.

"That kiss didn't bother me in the slightest," he said in a thick voice. "It was hot, like I said. Kissing you myself is hotter, but watching you melt into him? Yeah, I liked that."

He skimmed his fingers down my sides, and my breath caught as he nudged my shirt up to tease against my skin.

"Did you like kissing Coop while I watched, Frankie?"

The more I thought about it, yeah, I kind of did. I licked my lips. "Is it crazy to say yes?"

"Not at all." He traced his thumb across my abdomen. "I like knowing what turns you on." When he nuzzled a kiss behind my ear and then down along my throat, I groaned. "I also know you wanted a shower," he whispered at my ear. "You said something about homework."

Yeah. I had.

When Jake started to pull away, I gripped his shirt and dragged myself forward, even as I yanked him back. "You know what else I like?"

He raised his brows.

"You."

Then I reeled him down for a kiss, his mouth was open, hot, and wet when

I teased his tongue with mine. Everything in me ached and it had been a shitty day, but all of that fell away. The guys being there had helped. Coop had chased some of it away with his talk and his goodnight kiss. But Jake turned the rest of it to ash.

When his fingers tugged at my shirt, I pulled back long enough to shed the uniform top and meet his gaze.

The confident sexy smirk had turned into something of a wondering expression. "Yes?"

I knew exactly what he was asking.

"Do you have condoms?" Because—yes, I recognized the irony after today—I really needed to get some.

"Hell yes," he said, his breath coming in the same heated pants as my own.

"Then yes." And I didn't have to say another word because his arm was a steel band around me, and he lifted me up as I wrapped my arms around his neck again. He kissed me again with one hand on my ass, and suddenly I was burning up. We had on way too many clothes, and I was really going to do this.

Need consumed trepidation, but when I tugged Jake's hair, he broke the kiss to meet my gaze.

"I have a bed."

"You have a bed," he said with a hint of delight. "Yes, you do." Then he was striding through the apartment to my room. I was only half aware of the cats scattering. I'd make it up to them later, and I still had homework to do.

But Jake was here right now.

When I landed on the bed, I got a front row seat to him pulling out his wallet before he stripped off his shirt and then the rest of his clothes followed.

It didn't matter that I'd seen him naked before.

Nothing mattered except right here and right now.

Chapter Seventeen

WHEN DID YOU SLEEP LAST NIGHT?

f I'd thought I was burning up before, it had nothing on the heat sweeping through me as I stared at a naked Jake. I'd seen him naked the week before. We'd showered together. We'd done a lot of things together, and it had been mind-blowing. At the same time, this was different. I had a much better idea of what I had to look forward to and a far more precise idea of what I wanted to do.

My nipples were hard as marble beneath the cups of my bra. My mouth watered, and the shivers racing over my skin reminded me of the way he trailed his fingers along my arm. Clamping my thighs together against the need surging through me, I lifted my gaze to meet his. The harsh sound of our breathing rippled through the silence of the room.

"Can I…" I licked my lips, and Jake raised his brows.

"Can you what, baby girl?"

That was a whole new affection, and it settled over me like a lazy caress and sank into my bones. The roughness of his voice added to the strokes teasing me, and we weren't even touching each other. Why weren't we touching each other?

I pushed to the end of the bed, reaching behind me to undo my bra. "Can I put my mouth on you?" The awkwardness in the question echoed against me and my face was on fire, but I didn't look away as Jake grinned.

The bra slipped down, and Jake trailed his gaze over me, before stepping forward and sliding his hands to my hips. "You want to suck me off?"

The response sent another shudder through me. This close, it was hard to ignore the thick, swollen length of his erection. It was a ruddy color, redder than the rest of him. The tan on his chest and legs was from spending so much time outside, but his hips and buttocks weren't pale. His skin tone was deeper than mine. But his cock was red, the tip swollen and shiny, the mushroom shaped head engorging the more I stared at him.

I nodded slowly, aware of the flush spreading from my face to my chest. "I do, never done it before…"

He chuckled, and the low, baritone quality went straight to my pussy, and I clenched as everything went low and hot. "Baby girl, just watch your teeth, and I will happily let you learn whatever you want to on me, but it's killing me not touching you at the moment."

I stood up as he hooked his fingers into my pants, the button flicked open, and the zipper descended. Not once did he look away from me. The warmth of his hands on my skin before he began shoving them down—panties and all—had me sighing.

"Should I pinch myself?" The question slipped out as he crouched, and I had to brace a hand on his shoulder as he tugged off my shoes, and then I was stepping out of the pants.

With a light scrape of his teeth, he kissed my thigh and then nuzzled his nose right between them, and another bolt of lust shot through me.

"I'll take care of the pinching," he said lazily, before sucking a kiss to the inside of my thigh almost exactly where Archie had, and I slid my fingers into his hair a second before he swiped his tongue from my entrance to my clit.

On wobbling legs, I almost fell, but Jake kept me steady as I sank onto the bed. He never lost contact as he wedged his shoulders between my legs and deepened that carnal kiss. The rasp of stubble stung, even as he sucked tightly against my clit. The coiled tension ratcheted higher. A whining note escaped my throat as he spread his hot hands against my legs and pushed them higher and wider.

I was embarrassingly wet, but the discomfort faded under the sucking kisses and deep, tongue thrusting probes. The low moaning sounds he made vibrated against me, and all of a sudden, it hit me. Jake enjoyed what he was doing, this wasn't just about how wonderful it felt to me. Gratitude swelled in me, curving alongside delight. Tonguing me was giving Jake pleasure, and I wanted to give him more.

"Fuck…" I groaned as I fell back against the bed and arched my pelvis. I couldn't get any purchase with my feet, and still, I strained toward the orgasm rapidly unraveling. One minute I was on the edge, and the next, I swore I squirted a little as I fisted my comforter. Every muscle in my body seemed to go rigid, and I couldn't catch my breath.

Jake laughed against my pussy as he slowed his nuzzling caresses, and I glanced down the length of me to find him watching me with hot eyes. The moment our gazes met, he stroked my clit again and an aftershock rolled through me, and I think I might have screamed a little.

"I love that sound." Every word vibrated to my core, and then he was crawling up me, pausing to kiss and lick a path to my breasts. He sucked on one nipple, hard, fierce, and biting. Clasping my hands to his shoulders, I let out another cry. He ground his hips against mine, the length of his cock snug against my still fluttering pussy, and then Jake kissed me.

Cupping his face, I slid my fingers into his hair as I licked the taste of myself from his lips, and he teased my tongue with his. The hot weight of him blanketing me helped to quiet the jolts still rocketing through my system. Bit by bit, I tried to pull myself back together.

When I flattened my hands to his shoulders, he dragged his head up and stared down at me with lazy, heated eyes. "I love how you taste."

I went up in flames all over again. Need and want were so closely twinned, I didn't think I would survive if I wasn't touching him at the moment. He slid his fingers into my hair and tilted my head. Then he kissed me again, slow, nibbling bites, long strokes of his tongue, and then sucking nips as he pulled at my lower lip.

"Jake," I whispered in a raw voice, like I'd been shouting for hours. "My turn." The smile on his lips sent another wave of longing through me as he rolled his hips and his cock nestled even tighter against me. If he moved just a quarter of inch lower, he'd have thrust into me.

"If you put your mouth on me," he whispered. "I'm not going to last."

"That's okay," I promised. I'd never done this, hell, I'd heard horror stories of what it would taste like, but I didn't care. This was Jake. "We have time."

The crinkles at the corners of his eyes deepened at the mention of "time."

When he dipped his head and kissed my throat, then trailed those kisses down to my breast, I knew it was coming before he sucked the skin up and left a bruising mark. They loved leaving those damn things on me. A laugh bubbled up as I gripped his hair and tugged.

"Please, Jake?"

I don't know if it was my voice or the fact I said please, but his whole expression softened. He nuzzled another kiss to my lips before he rolled over and carried me with him. The grind of his cock teasing my too sensitive clit almost had my eyes rolling.

"Torture me all you want, baby girl," he whispered in that sexy voice.

Licking my lips, I trailed my fingers down his torso. He was so ripped. It wasn't hard to see the all the hours he'd put into physical training. From his broad shoulders to his thick chest, to the way his abs dimpled against his midsection. I pressed a kiss to his chest, savoring the salt on his skin and the tease to us both as I slid lower on his thighs and his cock dragged against my belly. The thud of his heart pounding seemed to echo the race of mine. I traced one of his nipples with my tongue as he stroked a hand through my hair, gathering it together so he could fist it into a ponytail. Staring up at him, I smiled when his gaze zeroed in on mine.

I slid lower, this time tracing the path with my fingers and tongue as I outlined his abs and then reached his cock. This close, I couldn't miss the faintly musky scent of him. The hair around his cock was a little damp, and that was all me. For some reason, that sent a thrill to spike through me as I curled the hair around one finger.

A quiver settled into my belly as I studied the length of his cock. Heat seemed to eddy off of it, it was still swollen and thick. There was a vein running along the underside of it, and I tested it with my tongue. Hints of salt and me coated him.

Apparently, that flavor wasn't a deterrent, and I traced the line of the vein with my tongue until I reached the mushroom-shaped head. A bead of moisture shimmered on the fat head. Jake flexed his fingers in my hair, but he didn't pull it or shove me closer. There was a hiss of air escaping him as I slid my lips over the top.

I wanted to be careful, the last thing I wanted to do was hurt him. My pussy stretched for Archie, and I'd be able to take Jake, but could I get all of him in my mouth?

The question floated through me on a little wave of laughter as I sucked against the head. The drop of moisture was a little bitter, but I didn't hate it. It was Jake, and another thrill skated up my spine as I wrapped my hand around the base of his cock, adjusting the angle.

One swipe of my tongue, then another, and his cock gave a little jerk. When I swallowed him deeper, taking as much as I could, the buck of his hips said I did something right, as did his groan.

Stealing a look up, I nearly forgot to breathe. Jake's whole face was tight, his expression torn between a grimace and a grin. The hand not in my hair was fisted against the comforter.

I dragged back, sucking against him as I pulled him out, and he let out another sound, low and guttural. Thrilling to each little cry, I worked to keep the rhythm even and matched the pace with the stroke of my hand, since I couldn't take all of him. I got him a little deeper with each stroke. My jaw had started to hurt almost immediately, but I really wanted to make this good for him.

Every thrust had my breasts rubbing against the comforter. The fabric rasped over my nipples, and my pussy clenched at nothing. Another dribble of the bitterness escaped the head of his cock, and I sucked it down. It took me a minute to figure out how to breathe through my nose each time I slid him out.

Jake's hips thrust up, and his fist in my hair tightened. He bumped the back of my throat, and I fought against the gag.

"Sorry," he said in a harsh tone. "Fuck."

Eyes watering, I wouldn't let him pull me off as I hummed against him. I could do this. I wanted to do this.

"Jesus—Frankie…I'm not going to last…" The warning was appropriate because the next pull, and he let out another shout. The first stream was hot and sticky. The bitterness hit my mouth, and I tried to swallow it as the spit gathered around my tongue. His groan was a continuous thing as his back bowed and he pushed upward. I relaxed my jaw, ignoring the dribble as I swallowed.

The emotions playing across Jake's features were absolutely captivating. He was so utterly wrecked, and I'd *felt* that way, and now I'd done it to him. It was a most heady sensation.

He hissed finally as the spurt trickled off. When he tugged my hair this time, I let him pull me free, and he slipped from my lips with a little pop.

Jake stared at me with blown pupils and a red face. Shuddering, he pulled me up, and then I was kissing him and I swore he was trying to lick himself off my lips. The ache in my jaw faded as his hands ran over my back and down to my ass. He clenched me to him, and then we were both groaning.

From hot and wet to slow and languorous, we kept trading kisses as he touched me everywhere. Rolling us to our sides, he slid his knee right between my legs. The soft hairs teased and tickled. When he began to rock me with it, I figured out he was trying to get me off again.

A sigh escaped me and I let him play, glorying in running my hands over his arms and his chest. I wanted to know every inch of him. Rolling my hips in time to his rubs sent shivers eddying over my skin. When he replaced his knee with his hand, I groaned against his mouth. Two fingers inside of me with the heel of his palm against my clit, and I came in about thirty seconds.

He swallowed my cries as he pushed me through the orgasm, then chuckled when he finally released me to half-collapse against him. There was a sheen of sweat on my skin, and his was equally damp. My hands slid against him, but I didn't want to move.

Dragging his fingers from my pussy, he trailed them up my side, but I was too replete to be tickled. Then he dipped and took one sensitive nipple between his lips, and I almost came again. It was too much, but he sucked against one as he caught the other in a pinch and twist that had the heat coiling again.

I was all wanting, and all I wanted to do was touch and play with him, even half exhausted. When I wrapped my hand around his cock, I delighted to find him half-hard and growing stiffer by the minute. On my back again, I stared up at him as he moved to brace an elbow on either side of me before he swooped in for another kiss.

Kissing Jake was something like a cross between the electrical charge in the air of an incoming thunderstorm, and the big fall at the beginning of a waterslide—intoxicating and breath-stealing. I dug my fingers into his back. My lips and my tongue felt swollen, and I still couldn't get enough. He peeled away from me abruptly, leaving me gasping as he fumbled behind him, and then he had his wallet and out came a couple of condoms.

Oh.

Yeah.

Dazed, I pushed the hair away from my face as the foil ripped. Jake's hot eyes never shifted away as he stared down at me. I ached as he rolled the condom on, and then the foil fell away from his fingers as he pushed my thigh a little higher and positioned himself.

Panting for air, I was burning up.

"Frankie," he said, dragging my attention back to him. "You and Archie—you did this, right?"

The question seemed to come out of nowhere, and guilt prickled little icy shivers down my spine. Was that going to be a problem? "I…"

"It's okay, baby girl," he soothed in that sweet voice of his. "I just want to know how careful I need to be. It's okay. It's not a judgment, I promise."

He wavered as tears filled my eyes. It was one of the sweetest things he'd ever said to me. "Yes," I admitted. "A couple of times."

"Okay, then we're still going to be careful." The dark promise in those words sent another blast of heat through my system. "I don't want to hurt you."

"You couldn't," I whispered. Jake had always been careful with me, more aware of his strength than I was, and I loved it when he eased forward, the first push stretching me. There was the faintest of burns as he thrust in, slow and continuous, moving until he blanketed me again. Sliding his hands under, he hooked my shoulders and then kissed me as he seated, the fullness of him seeming to split me in two. Suddenly, I was grateful for how wet I was and how easily he fit me. Hitching my thighs to his hips, I pressed a foot against the back of his leg, and he groaned.

Against my mouth, he said, "I love how flexible you are."

"Yeah?" I panted as he rolled his hips, striking fresh sparks in me. We'd shredded all the lines, the feel of him inside me made me wonder why I'd waited so long for this. I ached from wanting, and it wasn't like we hadn't both come, and I'd come more than once. But suddenly, I wanted more.

"Oh yeah," Jake murmured as I cupped my hands against his ass, and when he rocked his hips, we rocked together. I clenched around him, needing to feel him, and then he began to really move as he kissed me again.

There were no words for this. Just skin slipping on skin, grinding together.

When he slid a hand down to push a thigh up, he shifted the whole angle and I couldn't catch my breath. If I'd thought I was sensitive earlier, every drag of his cock through my pussy as he pushed in and pulled out set my nerves on fire.

The hairs on his chest teased my nipples. The electric touch of his tongue on mine sent charges through me, and I was fighting to stay with him, even as I strained toward my orgasm. It hit hard and fast as he pumped his hips at an almost bruising force. Every strike sent sparks through me. I was crying, or maybe Jake was. There were tears on my face and I was on fire, then all the tension just expanded out and my vision went a little white and fuzzy around the edges.

He pumped his hips another three times and then let out a shout of his own. The grip of his hand on my leg and my shoulder tightened. I was shaking, or maybe Jake was. I couldn't tell. When he collapsed against me, I savored the weight and held onto him like I would drown if he went away.

Time seemed to blur, and I had no idea how long we lay there. My hair was damp, and so was his. The slide of his skin on mine set off a fresh wave of tingles. He was softening inside of me, but he made no move to pull out until he started to slip free.

With a soft grunt, he rolled away and I almost whined, barely swallowing the sound before it escaped.

"Shh," he whispered as if he'd heard me anyway, and he cupped my face as he kept a grip on the condom. "I'll be right back."

Then he was up, and I slumped back against the pillows. I didn't want to move, but I hated the idea I couldn't see him. He walked out of the bedroom and down the hall. The world seemed to expand a little from our narrow little corner.

When Jake came back, he leaned against the doorframe. "I turned on the shower," he said. "Can you make it, or do I get to carry you?"

"How can you even walk?" I mean, I hadn't even stopped trembling yet, and I wasn't sure my legs would hold me at all.

He grinned. "Don't ask me, I feel drunk. You're everything, Frankie."

Soft. Even shaking, I went soft, and something of it must have shown on my face, because Jake's eyes gentled. He crossed over and slid his arms under me, then lifted me like I weighed nothing. I looped my arms around his neck. When he kissed me this time, it wasn't passion, but sweetness, and he nuzzled my lips, just holding me.

"Thank you," I whispered when he lifted his head.

"Ha," he said, a grin quirking his lips. "Thank *you*. That was—everything I could have ever hoped for and more. I'm already thinking about all the things I want to do with you."

Carding my fingers through his hair, I shivered again. The delicious little shocks kept coming. Jake carried me down the hall to my bathroom, and I was glad he was there when he stepped us into the shower together. The warm water on my skin was a caress all its own.

Somehow, we managed to get clean. Though I was half-tempted to try and suck him off again, I had no idea if I could even maintain my balance long enough. I was sore in all the right ways.

He frowned at one point and kissed my shoulder gently. "I bruised you."

Glancing down at it, I grinned. "I liked it."

With a scowl, he gave my ass a light swat. "I never want to hurt you." The heat of his palm striking my butt sent another flurry of feeling through me.

"Even when I like it?" I dared him.

Eyes narrowed, he said, "We'd have to discuss that ahead of time."

"Jake…" It was my turn to soothe him. I hugged him and stroked his back until he huffed out a breath.

"Promise me if I ever grip you too hard or something actually hurts, you'll tell me?" He pressed another kiss to my shoulder.

"I promise," I said easily. "I trust you, Jake."

I did. Despite everything—or maybe because of it—I did trust Jake. He was blunt and charged full steam ahead, but I had no doubts about his feelings. Especially not now that I paid attention to all the little things I hadn't noticed before. Jake always put himself between any perceived threat and me. He wouldn't let me pull away without a fight. Of all of them, he'd been the most persistent over the summer. Even when I didn't answer him, he called and left messages.

In the last couple of weeks, as soon as he learned what I wanted, he'd been all in, regardless of the fact I was dating the other guys. He wanted me. "But I'll tell you," I assured him.

"Good," he said, letting out a little sigh of relief as he pressed his forehead to mine. We lingered under the water for a little longer, and then we took our time toweling each other off and exchanging kisses.

He hung out in the bathroom as I dried my hair, my avid audience. Then he pulled on just his boxers, and it tickled me to pull on the ones he'd left behind last week. They were clean after all.

The grin he sported as I tugged them on and tightened them with a little drawstring made me laugh. The tank top was pale and did little to hide my nipples, and attracted his attention to them even more than when I'd been bare-chested.

We finally went in search of the food he'd brought because I was starving. After devouring the wings and having drinks, I belatedly remembered I hadn't messaged any of the guys.

They were gonna kill me.

Sure enough, there were messages from each of them, though Coop's had me blushing.

Reading over my shoulder, Jake laughed.

Coop

So in the interest of not ruining your evening, I told Bubba and Archie you were home safe and sound, and that Jake was there so you might be distracted. Yes, I know, I am awesome. I will see you in the morning. Sweet dreams.

Biting my lip, I glanced up at Jake. "They're going to know."

"Doesn't bother me in the slightest," he said, looping his arms around my waist. "Are you okay with it?"

I was…. Kind of. "Ian wanted to wait."

"That's Bubba's call," Jake said, rubbing his thumb against my belly where he'd rucked up the tank top. "I guarantee you, Coop is not going to."

Another blush scalded my cheeks.

"And that's okay with you?"

"As long as it's okay with you," Jake said. "I can live with them. No one else though." There was just a hint of warning in his tone. "Anyone else looks at you sideways, and I'm going to take their head off."

Okay, that kind of thing shouldn't turn me on, but it so did.

Leaning my head back against his shoulder, I closed my eyes. The fact Jake was okay with the others just added to the euphoria of the evening. "I don't want to do homework," I admitted.

"I know," he said. "But we have to—and if we get it all done, I'm going to eat you out again."

Talk about incentive. "If you get done first, I'm giving you another blow job." The dare in the words pulled a laugh from him as he dipped his hand into my boxers and cupped my pussy.

"I'm torn between taking my time so I can eat you out and winning so I can feel your mouth again. Fuck that was awesome."

"Well, we can always try both at the same time." Who was I, and where did these suggestions come from? Even blushing, I couldn't help but be even more turned on by the image.

Jake groaned and then sucked against my earlobe. "Deal." Then he slid his hand out of my shorts and gave my ass another smack. The heat from it sent a tremor zinging through me, and I might have moaned.

The smirk he suddenly sported sent a frisson of awareness through me. "You do like it," he said softly. "We are so going to have to explore."

Facing him, I raised my eyebrows. "Right now?"

He laughed. "No, baby girl, we're doing homework now because it's almost midnight, and you need sleep and to not stress about your homework. I have just the thing to relax you when we're done."

Sprawled together on my bed, I got my homework done at lightning speed. By one, we were entwined again, and it took a little maneuvering, but we managed another round and we definitely fit the sixty-nine model. By the time he curled up around me and I went to sleep, I was boneless and safe.

It was just about perfect.

Chapter Eighteen
EVERY PICTURE TELLS A STORY

Waking up to Jake still being there seemed *right* in a way that defied definition. The alarm hadn't gone off yet, and the cats were sprawled around the bed. Tiddles was actually curled up on my stomach, just below Jake's arm. Jake was sleeping on his stomach, his face turned away, but he had an arm over me. The room was still cast mostly in shadows.

I ached. Marvelously so. My shoulder twinged, and there was a hint of soreness between my thighs. Stretching slowly, I ignored Tiddles's meow of complaint as he leapt off of me. Jake curled his arm as if to tug me closer as I pointed my toes and raised my arms. A laugh escaped me, but I tried to smother it with a hand, not wanting to wake him.

When he shifted in his sleep and turned over to cuddle closer, I studied his sleeping face. Even in the dim light leaking around the edges of the shades, I could make out the stubble on his jaw and the tousle of his hair. The week before, I'd likened him to rumpled Jake, rugged and unpolished, and I might just have to add unapologetically sexy to that list.

His eyes opened slowly, and I rolled onto my side to face him. Stroking a hand down to my hip, he offered me a drowsy, if delighted smile. "I could get used to this," he whispered in a husky, sleep-drenched voice. "Best thing I've seen since last night."

Another laugh escaped me. "I was just going to say the same thing."

"Hmm," he murmured, then leaned in to brush a featherlight kiss to my lips. "Still early, sleep."

Carding my fingers through his hair gently, I couldn't seem to stop smiling. "You sleep, I'm fine right here."

Eyes flickering open again, he raised his brows. "Staring at me?"

"Hmm-hmm." I gave a little nod. I didn't think I'd ever get tired of looking at him. When he slid his hand down to my back and wrapped his arm around me, I was ready for the tug as he pulled me closer, breast to chest, and eased a thigh between mine. The heavy weight of his erection was right there, pressing against my belly.

This was where we'd gone off script the week before. Not that I was complaining. I skated my nails lightly over his scalp, and he made a small humming noise before nuzzling another gentle kiss. Morning breath was a thing, but it didn't seem to bother Jake, and when he teased my lips apart with his tongue, I fisted his hair. One hand on my ass, he squeezed, then tilted my leg higher.

Lazy kisses grew fiercer, and then he kissed a path down my throat. The bite of his stubble stung, even as his lips soothed. Groaning, I dragged his head back, then nuzzled my own licking, biting kisses to his throat. When I began to suck a spot right over his pulse, I swore Jake growled.

He speared two fingers into me, but I was more than wet enough, even if I was still sensitive and swollen. The languid heat pooling in my middle caught fire, and I bit down on his shoulder.

His quiet, but emphatic "Fuck" sent a pulse straight through me. He curled his fingers and traced his thumb over my clit. It didn't take much to edge me higher. Then he pulled his hand away, and I whined.

"Easy, baby girl, I know," he promised me and pressed his fingers to my lips. I opened right up to take them, sucking them clean, and he stared at me blankly for a long moment before releasing another, emphatic "Fuck."

He tumbled me on my back as he reached over, and I realized he'd snagged his wallet.

"Fuck."

No more condoms.

"I'll buy some today." I promised as I kissed a path down his chest.

"Wait…yes!" He let out a whoop and showed me a condom tucked right behind his driver's license. I raised my brows. "And you don't have to buy them, baby girl. I've got a whole box at home. I'm just going to put them in the car from now on."

A delightful shudder went through me as he tore the foil. I enjoyed the way he slid the condom into place, and then he nudged at me, pushing my thigh higher before sinking in one long, continuous thrust.

This time, my eyes definitely rolled back in my head. All I could feel was Jake, filling me to the brim. His expression tightened, and then he threaded his hands with mine and pushed them over my head. One hungry kiss later, he began to rock into me and I thrust up to meet him.

The intensity of the night before had been blunted, but I wanted him no less and eddied higher and higher on coiled tension as his chest scraped against my nipples. His hips ground against mine, and his cock impaled me as though fighting to get deeper. Every kiss stole my breath, and when the orgasm hit, I wasn't expecting it. I just kind of splintered over in warmth as it flooded out of me, and Jake bit off another curse as his rhythm stuttered, and then he buried his face against my throat as he shuddered.

I savored the way he felt as my inner muscles fluttered around him. The weight of him bearing down, the way he clung to me, and the soft press of his lips while he kissed his way back to reclaiming his breath. The bristling sting of his stubble only added to the myriad of sensations swirling through me.

Despite the lack of hurry, neither of us had lasted long. When he finally loosened his grip on my hands I dragged them up to rub up and down his back. "I don't want to go to school," I admitted, the words slipping out of me.

"Me neither," he agreed in a muffled voice. The huff of his breath against my neck tickled. Dragging his head up, he looked at me with a smile. "But we have to go."

I groaned and closed my eyes. "Why?"

"Hey," he whispered, his voice softening, and I opened my eyes to find him studying me with a concerned frown. "Why don't you and Coop ride with me today?"

"Because I have a car and you have football practice after school," I reminded him, even if I winced at the reminder he couldn't play yet. He brushed his bruised knuckles down my cheek lightly.

"Yeah, but Archie can run you two home after, then you can take your car to work." He lulled me with his gentle voice and I wanted to say yes, but at the same time… "And you won't have to worry about your car at school. We're going to split our time, make sure one of us is always with you. No more of this crap at school. You won't have to worry about anything."

"Okay, I'm not scared of what they did to my car." It came out harsh, and maybe I was trying to convince myself. Then again… "That pissed me off."

"Me, too," he agreed. "I don't want anyone messing with you."

"But running away isn't going to do anything other than make them think they're right about us." I lifted my shoulders. "And I guess, in a way, they kind of are."

He scowled. "No, they're not. You—are perfect. They're a bunch of assholes."

"We also don't know who *they* are."

"Yeah we do," he said with a snort, then eased up as he slipped out of me, and we both groaned a little. As he rolled off the bed to dispose of the condom, I sat up and blew out a breath.

"We really don't," I called after him.

"Then that means we need to be more cautious," he said as he came back. "Not less."

I really didn't want to go to school. Pulling my knees up, I rested my arms on them. "I don't want to give whoever it is any more ammunition. I don't want them to decide to target your car or Archie's… you're already benched. What happens if Ian is?"

"I'm benched because of what *I* did." He crossed over to the bed and caught my hands and tugged me up until I was kneeling on the bed, and he could drop a kiss on my lips. "The only thing I regret is that jackass said anything in the first place."

"Jake…"

"Let us watch your back?" He was holding my hands in his, the grip firm yet gentle. "Please?"

"You already talked to Coop, Archie, and Ian, didn't you?"

"Yeah," he said. "We talked about it yesterday." He tucked my hair back away from my face. "None of us want to see you getting any more crap."

If I didn't take my car, Mr. Thorns was going to have to find a new way to send me a message.

"Okay," I said, then put a finger to his lips at his sudden smile. "*But* only for a couple of days. I like my…"

"Your independence. Trust me, we know."

My alarm went off on my phone, and Tiddles popped up with a meow. "Duty calls," I said, and he grinned.

"Then breakfast."

Then breakfast.

As much as I didn't want to get up or shower again or even get dressed, I made myself do it. The reluctance to go to school was new, and Jake thought it had to do with the car. Maybe it did. Or maybe it was the fact I liked just being held, and we really couldn't do that at school.

Making a face, I shoved off the bed. Better get started, or I'd never leave.

Coop leaned against the fridge when I came out, Jake had gotten dressed faster than I. In fact, he'd even brought clothes with him last night. I'd missed that part, the extra clothes in his backpack. His smirk had been almost adorable, as was the kiss he left me with in the bathroom before heading out to pour cereal.

The shit-eating grin Coop wore had my face heating. "Did you two have fun?"

"Don't be an ass," Jake warned as he passed me a cereal bowl.

"Hey," Coop said, spreading his arms. "Genuine question here. We're still BFFs, and Frankie needs someone to talk to about these things. You know, compare notes and get advice."

Oh. My. God.

I stared at Coop, even as Jake thumped him. He did *not* just say that. Coop's laughter filled the kitchen.

"Ass," Jake muttered, then looked at me. "Ignore him."

Still blushing, I said, "I planned to." Then stuffed a spoonful of cereal in my mouth as Coop chuckled. He joined us at the table and hooked one of his feet against mine.

"You know you're still my favorite," he assured me. "Right?"

Jake snorted, but I had to smile.

"Yes," I admitted. "I do."

"And I'm always here if you need to confide in me. Especially if anyone isn't up to snuff…"

"I am going to beat your ass," Jake threatened without any real heat, and I laughed for real this time.

"Ha, see, I can still make her smile." Coop winked at me. "Besides, Frankie and I have a date on Saturday."

Saturday.

"Fuck."

At the exclamation, they both stared at me and I winced.

"Sorry, Saturday. Cheryl is being really insistent that we go get Homecoming dresses together, and when I couldn't come up with a better time, she decided Saturday at seven was perfect." I winced again. "I can cancel on her," I said. "But I kind of don't want to, and at the same time, I do need a dress, but I said we could go out…"

"I'll go with you." Coop said. "Problem solved. We'll find you a pretty dress, ditch the ditz, then go have fun on our own."

"She's not a ditz," I argued. "And really? You'd go with me to pick out a dress?"

"Why not?" He propped his chin on his fist. "It's hanging out with you, right? You need a dress. I get to see it before anyone else. Oh, I'm definitely in."

On that sentence, Jake scowled. "I want to see it, too."

"And you will," Coop told him, almost smug. "After me."

"Where are you going shopping?" Jake asked as he turned to me.

"Nope," Coop said. "It's also a date, that means…"

Means?

Jake made another face.

"What does it mean?"

"Nothing," Jake muttered. "We just agreed we wouldn't step on each other's dates."

They'd discussed this?

Embarrassment flooded me for a whole new reason. Mostly because I liked the idea they'd actually discussed me, right?

I caught them both watching me, a hint of worry in their eyes, and I smiled. "That's—really kind of sweet."

Relief filtered through Jake's smile, and Coop exhaled. It was sweet. I couldn't believe they'd worked it out. I hadn't wanted them to fight. Did this mean it really wasn't a problem for me to date them all?

Could I *really* have all of it?

Dates with all of them, making out while still being friends? Hanging out like we always did, just with even more benefits? Was that all something I could have?

Seriously?

My chest grew tight. It seemed far too good to be true.

"We should get going." Jake's words jolted me out of the mental spiral, and I sucked down the milk in the bowl. It took me two minutes to rinse it out, then grab my backpack. On my way back to the door, Coop caught me in a hug, and then his mouth claimed mine.

I barely had time to brace my hands against his chest, when he stroked his tongue against mine. Dizzy, I gripped his shirt for balance as he seemed to sample me with these even, gentle strokes, and then coaxed my tongue forward. The heated suck of his mouth sent a shiver all the way to my core.

The sensual ache between my thighs echoed the pull, and I was pretty sure the blush scalding my face covered other parts of my anatomy. Awareness of Jake behind me—even as Coop deepened the kiss—made me shudder all over again.

There weren't enough swear words for the topsy-turvy in my system. Dragging out my lower lip, Coop lifted his head. His gray-green eyes were a lot darker at the moment, and his heart hammered beneath my hand. "Needed a good morning kiss." Running his thumb over my lower lip, he smiled. "Good morning."

"Hi," I answered, then nipped his thumb, and his grin grew.

Jake let out a little sigh. "That's still hot."

"I liked it," Coop said, loosening his hold gradually. "Wouldn't mind just staying here today…"

My thoughts exactly.

"Unfortunately," Jake said. "We can't."

"Buzzkill," I muttered, and he laughed as he slid his hand over my ass and then wrapped an arm around my middle, pulling me neatly away from Coop.

"I'll make it up to you," Jake said before giving me a kiss that had me curling my toes and panting. They were turning me into a mess and expected me to go to school.

I think I hated them.

"I promise," he finished before nibbling another kiss at the corner of my mouth. "Maybe even over lunch if you wanna ditch the guys?"

"Hey," Coop protested. "Foul ball. Also—I see what you mean, that was definitely hot."

Jake chuckled, looping an arm over my shoulders as I swayed a little. Everything in my system hummed from those kisses. Hell, it hummed from the last several hours.

"Just saying, the backseats lay down."

Coop stared at him, but I gave Jake a shove as I laughed. "I am not going to be a cliché, thank you very much. It's bad enough I let you talk me into driving me to school while you all babysit me."

"Awww," Coop switched gears, slipping his arm around my shoulders after I scooted away from Jake. "Don't be like that, Frankie. That's on all of us. Remember what we talked about?" And as light and effortless as his voice was, I did remember.

He wanted me to trust them to protect me, and to do that, I needed to keep them in the loop. I hadn't expected it to be like a closing of the guard around me. "Yes," I said. "I do. But we're going to be late if we keep loitering." Though skipping school sounded better and better.

The butterflies in my stomach had butterflies all the way to school, even with Coop sitting in the middle of the backseat and leaning forward to talk to both of us. The tension from the kisses diminished some at least, until I noticed the hickey I'd left on Jake was clearly on display.

Crap.

Hopefully my hair covered the fact my ears were burning. What had been vital to me while we were wrapped around each other in my bed seemed almost out of bounds in broad daylight. As we pulled into the parking lot, Jake reached over and caught my hand.

"We didn't do anything wrong," he said quietly, and I cut a look at him. I was so wound up, I was going to make this bad for Jake.

"I know," I said, then blew out a breath. "I have no idea why I'm so nervous."

"Cause you're Frankie," Coop said lightly. "You think through everything you do at least fifteen times, and you are always revising your plan to be the most effective."

I made a face and looked at Coop. "I sound awful."

"Nah," he teased. "You sound like you. We like you just how you are."

"Yep," Jake said, parking and then turning to face me. "And because we have to behave when we get out, baby girl, believe me when I say I like every part of you. The overachiever to the cuddly girl to the friend I know likes the same damn dorky videos I do. Got it?"

Hard not to.

"Got it." I bit my lip because I wanted to kiss him. But we couldn't do that here. So I tried to lighten the mood. "Still not going for a lunchtime quickie in the back of your SUV."

A smile sparkled in his eyes, and he gave my hand a squeeze before shutting off the engine. "Damn, there went my cunning plan."

Coop snorted. "Not really that cunning."

And since I could pile on, I said, "Or a plan," as I got out. "But I like your enthusiasm."

Jake and Coop paused a beat, and then they both cracked up. It helped to settle the butterflies. Not as much as I would have liked, but it did help. A glance across the parking lot to where I usually parked made me a tad wistful. Ian's bike wasn't there either. He'd parked up closer in one of the smaller spots he could easily fit in. I guess they'd confirmed the plan.

It didn't take us long to find Archie and Ian inside, or the coffee and chocolate covered donuts waiting for us—along with my preferred apple fritters. Damn, they were going to spoil me.

No one commented on Jake spending the night, though Archie studied me pretty close for a few minutes. There were spots of laughter in the cafeteria as I walked across it. But I told myself it was paranoid to think it was about me.

Breakfast conversation turned to Friday night's game. Ian worried Jake being out was going to weaken their defensive line. Not that they could do much about it. Coop teased them about going dress shopping with me, and Archie wore much the same expression Jake had on the subject, but Ian looked bemused.

"Just make sure I know what color," he said, not rising to Coop's bait. Gaze lingering on mine for a long moment, Ian smiled. "I already know I'm going with the best girl."

Dammit, and I had just gotten my blushing under control. Then the conversation devolved to a new video game coming out the following week. When Coop suggested we spend part of his birthday playing the new one, I didn't make a face.

It was his birthday.

Archie winked at me when he said, "Let's not make it an all day thing though, yeah?"

I could have kissed him for that. Course, Coop said, "Nope, I was thinking we could all go to mini golf, or maybe drive up to the big amusement park."

Laughter eddied around the table, but Archie just shook his head in amusement at the mini golf. It wasn't long before we had to pack it in, and true to their word, the guys didn't let me go anywhere alone. Coop and Archie walked with me to my locker, and I gave them the note that had been inside.

If they recognized the handwriting, they didn't say anything. After, Archie walked me to first period, and then halfway to second where Ian hooked up with us in the hall for the hand-off, and it was very much that. After a second, Ian walked me to French, then reminded me to wait for Coop, he'd pick me up on the way to lit.

That was insane. Coop's third period was in the complete opposite direction, but I didn't argue. Mathieu pulled me aside in French to ask me if I was all right.

That was a little mortifying. Apparently, my bad fortune had definitely been making the rounds. Madame also wanted to talk to me, quietly, and in the hall. She offered me a card for a psychologist—not the one at the school. It took me a minute to realize she was worried about the bullying on other levels. Like my work slipping a little over the last week.

I'd gotten a B on an assignment.

I never got Bs.

Stomach churning, I promised her I'd get my focus back and I would be fine. The last thing I wanted to talk about was anything more to do with the car vandalizing or Instagram, or anything else.

As embarrassing as that encounter was, it was a little more when Coop waited for me outside the bathroom. Even after all these years, there were some things I could definitely live without them being intimately aware of—maybe even especially now.

The fact my stomach was in knots didn't help my focus in Lit. Coop's stare drilled into me all through class, but I waited until the bell rang before I headed up to talk to Ms. Fajardo with Coop hot on my heels. Getting the words out was a challenge, but I managed to keep my voice calm. When I explained it to her, she pulled out the file of ungraded essays and flipped through it to the sheet in question.

"Why didn't you say something yesterday?" Ms. Fajardo asked as Coop twisted to look at the sheet, and I barely caught the movement of his hand as he snapped a picture with his phone.

Forcing my gaze to stay on our teacher's, I shrugged a little. "I didn't want to make a big deal out of it. But with everything else that's happened, I've been advised that might not be the best course."

"I agree with whomever gave you the advice." She flicked a look to Coop.

"I'll take care of this one."

She knew who'd done it.

Coop got that, too. "You don't have a TA for our period."

"No, but I will handle it. I'm sorry you had to deal with this, Frankie. In the future, alert me immediately, please. Though I am hoping there is no future event to worry about."

Her and me both.

"I will," I said. "I'd really like to just focus on getting the work done."

"I know you would, but we have a zero tolerance policy for a reason. Now, you two go to lunch, all right?"

There was a reason I really liked her. She was no nonsense, but also fun. As teachers went, she listened and she could tease even as she taught. We headed out to meet the guys, and they were waiting—patiently—in Jake's SUV. Archie and Ian had the backseat and Ian slid out to let me climb in the middle while Coop got shotgun.

"It's not the same writing," he said rather abruptly as we left the lot.

"What—the thing on the essay?" That was why he took a photo?

"Yeah," he said, holding his phone toward us while Archie unfolded the paper. "It doesn't match the note."

They didn't match. I hadn't really thought to compare them, but the person who wrote the note used loopy cursive, and the person who left the nasty-gram on the test printed it neatly, if a little slanted.

"Well, I don't recognize it," Archie complained as he handed both over to Ian. "You?"

"No," he said. "But I'll be honest, I don't really pay attention to how people write. I'd know Frankie's handwriting, but I've been reading her class notes for years."

"Ditto," Coop said as Archie chuckled.

"I'll look at it when we get to the fish place."

Leaning my head back against the seat, I sighed. Archie caught my left hand and Ian my right. I glanced from one to the other and dredged up a smile. As much as I wanted to enjoy lunch, I kept turning the two different notes over in my mind. To be honest, I hadn't really focused on whether they'd been written by the same person or not—now though? Now, I wondered just how many people I'd managed to piss off.

Coop seemed convinced it was because of them, and maybe it was, but I was part of this, too. We were all friends, and if someone was coming after them the way they were me, I'd probably be a hell of a lot angrier.

So, why wasn't I angry for me?

That particular question buzzed around in my head all the way through lunch, even when I tried to laugh and smile at the conversation. It all felt forced, and I don't think I was the only one distracted. The guys kept sharing these looks, like they were having an entirely separate conversation.

"Before we go back…" I said after a while. "Is there something I should ask about with regard to the summer?"

Silence blanketed the table. They glanced at each other, then me.

"Pretty sure I told you about mine," Archie stated.

"Yours didn't include the Instagram pictures." Even if I tried to keep the accusation out of my voice, I couldn't quite mask the fact those pictures had bugged me, no matter how hard I tried to not let them.

"Fair enough," Archie said. "But I don't know what the note is talking about specifically."

"We were…a little wild," Coop admitted. "I may or may not have gotten drunk more than once."

Ian grimaced. "Definitely more than once. We were all there for that particular pool party." The pictures. He winced a little as he met my gaze. "Sorry."

"I'm not mad," I told him. "I'd have to be a hypocrite to be angry about it." Jake hadn't said a word, and after last night, I wasn't going to press him. "You guys seem to think this is because of you."

"The Instagram thing was," Ian said quietly. "The note more or less says it is, since they want to make you think we did something objectionable."

"Or maybe whoever it is has no idea that we have tried to be honest," Coop said. "Even when it hurts."

"The car thing," Jake said finally, "crossed a major line. The rest of this is shit, but the car thing. They're taking their anger out on you. They want to make you hurt, and that's not okay."

"No," Archie agreed. "It's not."

"That said, we'll put our heads together," Ian said. "We'll figure this out."

Propping my chin on my hand, I chewed on my bottom lip. "I'm really wishing I'd sucked it up and gotten in your faces last spring at the moment."

"Me too," came from four different mouths at once with such vehemence, I had to laugh.

One by one, they cracked up along with me. The levity lasted until we got to the car and my phone buzzed. A photo popped up on the screen, and I nearly groaned because I did not want to deal with another slam from someone anonymous.

Only it wasn't from someone anonymous.

I stopped walking abruptly, and Ian gripped my hips when he nearly plowed into me. "Hey…"

The image on the screen was a woman's hand with an engagement ring on, and it was from my mom.

The message said,

Mom

Be home tomorrow. Be free, you're having dinner with Eddie and me.

Oh, I was going to be sick.

Chapter Nineteen

VICIOUS LITTLE VOICES

The silence in the car back to school weighed on me. It had to weigh on Archie, too. His only reaction to the picture and the message was a snort. "Since it's my date night, I'm going with you."

Honestly? I wasn't going to say no. I didn't want to face our parents on this subject.

"Keep us in the loop," Coop said, the sympathy tangling with worry in his eyes adding to the cramps in my gut. Jake and I walked to Study Hall together, signed in, then diverted to the library. My desire to study was almost nil.

But if I didn't, I would fall even further behind. The card Madame had given me burned in my back pocket. Jake didn't try to give me comforting words, instead, he hooked an ankle around mine or pressed his thigh against me. When he claimed one of my hands to hold, I gripped so tight, I worried I would leave nail indentations.

He didn't complain once.

After study hall, he walked me to sixth and promised to pick me up before we had to go to Mr. G's. I barely noticed anything in my TA period, I was too busy turning the last few days over in my mind. Every thought churned like a sour pill dissolving in my brain.

Bad meatloaf.

Archie.

Jake.

Instagram.

Archie's mom.

Ian.

The note on my essay.

The letters from Mr. Thorns.

Coop.

The note in my locker.

My car.

It was like being stuck on the equivalent of a mental mix master at rush hour. I couldn't get past the good or the bad. When the cramps got worse, I asked the teacher to get out early and I diverted to the nearest bathroom.

The last thing I needed was… yep.

Dammit.

I checked my backpack, at least I always kept emergency supplies in a zipped inner pocket. I was early, then again, I hadn't really been paying attention to the calendar. But I shouldn't be starting until Sunday.

Hurrying, I wanted to deal with this and get back out of here before Jake realized I slipped out of class without an escort. A, I appreciated what they were doing, it was sweet and B, the last time I talked about my period with *any* of them was right around the time it started.

That had gone epically not well.

Just never having that conversation again.

Period.

I almost snorted at the bad mental pun, when the door to the hall opened and I winced. I didn't want to be discovered, it was bad enough the damn thing started at school. At least I was inside the stall at the end, harder to notice.

"I can't believe they suspended her. Just like that."

Internally, I slammed my head against a wall.

Sharon.

"She's the nicest person ever, but no, hurt the pampered princess' feelings, and boom, you're yesterday's news."

"Well, to be fair," Maria sighed. "Laura kind of admitted she did it in a fit of pique. After the car thing…"

Car thing.

Wait.

Laura?

"She left her a candygram on her stupid essay prompt. As far as I'm concerned, she wasn't wrong. Coop and Laura were back together, and boom, he dumps her for the four-way slut princess."

"Sharon," Maria chastised her.

"What? You don't like the word, doesn't mean I can't use it. Besides, I didn't think you liked her anymore either."

Even understanding where the vitriol came from didn't make it any less painful.

"I don't hate her," Maria said, and I had to blink back tears at the weariness in her voice. "She's not the one who screwed up."

"So what, you're saying *I* did?" Sharon demanded.

"No," the other girl sighed. "I mean—the Instagram thing was cruel."

"Fuck her," Sharon said. "They are. If she thought she could just walk off with Bubba…"

"Sharon, damn girl, listen to yourself. Bubba went after her, not the other way around."

"Not the way I see it." There was a slam of a door, then flush of a toilet. Great, I was listening to this argument while they were peeing. I didn't move though, staying still and silent was my best defense at the moment.

"First," Maria said, another stall slamming. "She's not *new*. She's always been there."

"Yes, I know, and they've all had a crush on her, but the princess was too deaf, dumb, and stupid to notice." Hate flooded every word, and yeah, they stung. "I *don't* care, Maria. I don't care what she knew or didn't know. I care that she finally went away, and then *came back*."

The sink turned on.

"I finally got him. I spent all year on getting him, just like you wanted Jake. She was gone, and they were right there."

"Jake and I didn't break up because she came back."

Tipping my head back, I blinked away tears.

"You're not together because she's in the way—if you told him…"

"I'm not," Maria said. "So don't say another word, or I'll pop you in that mean mouth."

Silence ripped through the room.

"You need to let it go," she continued after a minute, the sound of paper towels tearing out of the dispenser. "I mean it. Don't bring it up and leave Frankie alone. At this point, you think any of them would touch you with a ten foot pole?"

"Then I have nothing to lose," Sharon stated. "But her highness does, and maybe it's time someone knocked her down a peg."

"Yeah well, leave me out of it," Maria said. "I mean it. You want to get arrested for vandalizing her car, be my guest. My beef isn't with her—I feel kind of sorry for her. Cause they're going to tear her apart like dogs with a bone."

Sharon had…? Anger flared through me, burning through some of the hurt. *Sharon* had done that to my car?

"And for the record," Sharon announced. "I *wish* I'd thought to do that to her car. The look on her face was awesome."

Bitch.

The door closed behind them, cutting off whatever Maria's response was.

I finished cleaning up and then slipped out of the stall to wash my hands. The bell rang as I stood there. Sharon definitely did the Instagram thing. Confirmed. She didn't do it to my car, though. As much hate was in her voice, she would definitely have taken credit for it.

Her anger wasn't because Bubba asked me to Homecoming. That could have been the trigger. But it wasn't about that, it was because I'd *come back*.

Pushing away from the counter, I left the bathroom. Arms folded, I made my way toward Jake, who was looking in the classroom with a frown. The scowl only deepened when he caught sight of me coming from the other direction.

"You were supposed to wait…"

"I had to go to the bathroom," I said, keeping my voice low. But I didn't unfold my arms. I was cold all over, the cramps were damn uncomfortable, and I had questions.

Again.

What was it Maria was supposed to tell Jake that would change his mind? I couldn't see it. Not really.

"Okay," he said, but when he went to hook an arm around me I shook my head. "What's wrong?"

Fastest way to make them take a step back. "Shark week."

"Damn," he whispered with a wince. But instead of leaving it alone, he said, "Can I do anything?"

Oh. "No, I'll be fine. Just want to get to Mr. G and get this over with."

"Need to hit your locker?"

Actually, I did, and Jake had already veered us in that direction. I swapped out my books. Half of them I didn't need to take home, so I didn't have to carry them. There was an envelope inside of my locker though, and Jake scowled at it.

The lettering on the front was familiar. Thorns.

Guess he discovered my car wasn't there. I tucked it into the backpack without opening it.

"Later?" I asked when Jake looked like he might object. Relieved when he relented easily enough, I shut my backpack up and went to sling it back on, but he caught it.

"I'll carry for you. Might be easier on… you know."

The corner of my mouth ticked up. "Thank you."

"Hey, whatever I can do to help."

So much for making them stop asking. My nerves were taut by the time we reached G's room.

"Hey," he said as we came in. "You guys can work on your reading, but, Frankie—I know there's a lot that's been going on, but I think you should go back and review those last two chapters."

Jake set my bag down next to my desk as I slid onto the seat. "Did I mess up something on the test?"

"The tests are a barometer to see where you are, if you were to take the exam today, that section wouldn't quite get to a 2 for your overall score."

My gut sank. If the cramps had been bad before, they were worse now.

"It's not a big deal," G continued. "Still early in the year. So go back through those last couple of chapters, and we'll do another test on Monday. Remember, this is a marathon, not a sprint."

Not even a 2.

Harvard required a 5 on AP tests. A 4 would get advanced standing, but not the credits I'd need to cut back the number of paid classes I'd have to take.

"I've got a meeting, so you two get to work and I'll see you both tomorrow." Then he was out of the room and it was just me and Jake.

G hadn't said Jake needed to go back over the last two chapters. I really should have just not come to school today. Maybe I'd skip tomorrow.

Between my grades and now that test score, what was I going to lose?

"Want me to quiz you after you read?" Jake offered. "It's been a crazy week."

"It's fine," I said. I wasn't going to cry. "I just need to focus, and I haven't been doing that."

My focus had been in shreds for days. I was barely getting to my homework in and around everything else. I could have done more last night after work, but I'd been with Jake, and that seemed way more important at the time.

It was still important.

"Hey," Jake's soft voice pulled my attention. He crouched next to my desk one hand on my leg. "Talk to me. That's one test, and sure, it sucks, but he's right, you're brilliant. You just need more time to read and maybe not me keeping you up all night."

I laughed a little. "Maybe…" I dug my book out of the backpack and then looked at the envelope.

"Jake, can I ask you a question?"

"Always." He hadn't moved away, so I shifted a little to face him.

"Would you have dated Maria if I'd not flaked last spring?"

Surprise flickered across his face. "We'd already kind of gone out a couple of times back then—usually in the group. Not really dates."

"Yeah, but you took her to the spring dance."

He sighed, but didn't look away. "Yeah, I did. It was kind of so we would both have someone to go with." He made a little click of sound and grimaced. "You stopped talking to us right around then. Got super busy and stuff. Maria was around…"

"So in other words, you asked her out because I was gone?"

"Well, when you put it like that," he sounded vaguely disgusted. "Why are you asking?"

"Something I heard Sharon say in the bathroom."

His eyes narrowed. "What did she say?"

"Why she's pissed at me." I flipped the book to the first chapter I needed to review. "She and Maria didn't know I was in there." Usually, I'd defend Sharon. I'd felt bad for her.

Kind of didn't anymore.

"She didn't do my car, or at least, that was what she said to Maria. Wish she'd done it because apparently, me seeing it was hilarious to her, and she's not even as mad that Ian asked me to Homecoming. She's pissed I came back after finally going away."

"Yeah well, fuck her." Vehemence punched up the last word.

"I'll pass."

He gawked for a moment, then a grin split his face as he laughed. "There she is—there's my baby girl."

I pressed a finger to his lips and shook my head. "Not at school, remember?"

Snorting, he stood and dragged his desk closer so he could sit next to me. "Yeah, yeah. I even know why for the rule, just not a fan, especially when you're hurting."

"I'm mad."

"What else did she say?"

I filled him in on the rest, including the mysterious whatever Maria might say to him that would change his mind. A part of me was testing him. I recognized it. I trusted Jake.

"I have no idea what she's talking about," he said. "And before you ask, no it has nothing to do with the news I don't want to jinx yet."

"Sorry," I said with a wince. "Trying to not ask is actually harder than you might think."

"Considering I'm sitting here not opening that letter because I want to know what it is, I totally get it." He put his hand over mine. "I mean it, Frankie. I don't know what they were talking about. More, I don't care. I'm right where I want to be. So, maybe they did get one thing right. I'm the ass that probably wouldn't have tried the dating thing with her if you'd still been there. But I was… I was pissed off that you just blew all of us off. Then wondering why I was still so hung up on someone who didn't see me."

That wasn't unfair.

"I'm sorry," I whispered. "I really didn't know."

"We know," he said. "And we were not exactly the best about showing it either. But we're here now, we're making it work."

We were.

"And Sharon hates my guts."

"Not defending her anymore?"

I touched my tongue to my upper lip before I shook my head. "No."

Then because he kept glancing at it, I slit the letter open.

Not even sure where to begin this note. The last few days have been terrible for you. I did leave a note on the car yesterday, but I don't think anything in it can be used against you. If someone does, don't worry. I'll take care of it.

I'd like to try and meet you again if you're up for it. I know last Saturday was bad, and this week hasn't improved much. If you want to, just wear a red shirt tomorrow. Cheesy, I know, but I think you could use a friend, and I'd like to be that friend.

"He wants to be your friend," Jake said slowly, the words grinding out between his teeth.

"So it seems… and in the interests of being honest, I'd had half an idea to write my own note and leave it on the car for him. To see if we could take a step back from these anonymous missives and meet."

"You did?" Wariness crept into his expression.

"I was going to, but I didn't, and I'm kind of glad I didn't since that would have been yesterday with my car." In all of it… "I forgot to tell you about Laura." I put the note down. Maybe I should tell Coop first.

"What about Laura?"

I deserved the startled look. I was kind of bouncing from subject to subject. "That was what they were talking about when they came in. The note on my essay prompt—it was Laura. Apparently, she was suspended today. I need to tell Coop." Scrubbing my hands over my face, I groaned. "But now I need to read."

"Hey." Jake caught one of my hands. "I'll tell Coop. You read that chapter, and I'll quiz you at the end? I'll read it again, too."

"You're not the one who screwed up your test."

"Well, I am the one who is part of the distracting," he said. "So let me help? And note, I'm not asking if you're going to wear that shirt tomorrow."

"Thank you, and I don't know. I don't know if everything hasn't gotten complicated, and tomorrow—yeah." Bad meatloaf for dinner.

Yay.

As promised, he let me read, but I just couldn't focus on the passages. My brain kept tracking back to the conversation in the bathroom, to the notes, and now to the letters. Mr. Thorns had made me smile the last couple of weeks, but with all the drama, did I really need to drag him into it?

It wasn't really fair to the guys, either.

Five minutes before the bell, I gave up and just packed away my books.

"We're going to fix this," Jake said quietly, and I chuckled.

Everything had been spiraling. "I have to fix me. Applications open in a week. I can't afford for my GPA to slip."

"It won't."

"You have a lot of faith in me."

"I know you," he reminded me as the bell rang, and then snagged my backpack before I could. "I know just how smart you are. You can do this."

The pep talk helped, some. So did finding Archie and Coop waiting for me at Archie's car. Ian was there, too. It was a good reminder. They were on my side.

I ended up filling Archie and Coop in on the ride home. They were both irritated about Laura, but Coop also seemed confused, and I felt bad being the one to tell him. Sharon didn't surprise them, but we'd all pretty much assumed she'd done the photos. The car thing still remained a mystery. One we weren't solving today.

Thankfully, Mom wasn't home when we got there. While her earlier message had said she'd be home Friday, there was the smallest amount of dread she'd be waiting for me. Right now, she was the last person I wanted to see.

Guilt assailed me the moment that thought took root. Unsurprisingly, the guys all showed up at Mason's with Archie and Coop following me, even after I turned down the ride. I needed the time in my car.

Cranking the music up as I drove helped chase away some of the bleaker thoughts.

Work. Then home to study. Then sleep. I needed to get my grades up and keep them there. No more excuses.

Staying focused at work was harder than it sounded. Normally, I just let the work distract me, but I found myself studying every teenage face that came in. Were they ones that covered my car in condoms? If Laura was the one who left the note on my essay, I'd bet money Sharon left the one in my locker. Though the guys didn't recognize the writing, it wasn't like I made a point of studying her penmanship.

When the girl herself showed up, I put on my big girl panties and waited on her, Maria, and their friends. I kept moving, even with the guys congregating in the corner after Jake and Ian got done with football. By the end of shift I was so tired, all I wanted to do was go home and crash. But I had at least two hours of homework to do, including getting some reading done for lit.

If this weekend was at all like the last one, I'd do nothing but fall further behind. Not acceptable.

The guys were waiting by my car when I came out. "Hey…" What was wrong?

"We've been talking," Archie began without preamble. Those words didn't always bode well. "Today worked, right?"

"You mean the escort from class to class?" I shrugged. "Yeah, it was fine. A little unfair to all of you having to come find me, but yeah, it was good."

"No notes in the locker?" Coop pressed. "Well, except for the wannabe boyfriend."

Ian smacked Coop against the chest with the back of his hand.

"Hey, it's a legit description," Coop argued.

"No, no other notes."

"So just the thing with the girls in the bathroom, and they didn't know you were there," Archie confirmed.

"Yeah, we talked about this earlier. Why are we going over it again?"

"Because we think we should do that regularly. One of us will come get you and Coop, right now it'll be me or Jake," Archie said. "We keep your car off campus, no one messes with it."

"And I'm working on getting a car," Coop admitted, and I wasn't the only one who gawked at him. "What? I have savings, I just never really needed one before."

I wasn't going to point out he didn't really need one now, he always rode with me or one of the guys. "That's great, but I can't just be dependent on you guys for rides. I do other things."

Not much, and arguably, four faintly skeptical expressions said the same. "Look, the only day that's tricky is Tuesdays," Ian offered. "I'm on my bike and I can take you, but Coop would have to ride with one of the others."

"And we can make it work," Archie said. "But until we figure this out, none of us want to risk you."

"Stop," I said, waving my hands. "There's no risking me. It's some crappy pranks and yes, do I want to slug the guy who did that to my car? Yes, I do. But I'm not changing another part of my life for anyone." Bad enough Mom wanted to do that for both of us. "I *really* don't want to talk about it anymore. Sharon hates me. Check. Laura got suspended for taking a swipe at me. Fine. Maria apparently doesn't hate me, so, yay me. But I have to study, I need to be focused on stuff that isn't this."

"We know," Jake said quietly, hands in his pockets. "That's why we want to make sure we can block out the noise. Your whole routine is shot."

Yes it was.

I blew out a breath. "I appreciate everything, guys, I really do. I know you have my back, but I need to go home and focus on me for a bit. I need to get this homework done."

"So no playdates," Archie said, not looking at me so much as at Coop and Jake.

We hadn't really discussed last night, and I kind of wanted to keep it that way. "If you don't mind, and we'll figure out dinner tomorrow?"

He made a low, disgusted noise. "We will, but I'm betting you money Edward cancels at the last minute, and we won't have to deal with either of them."

I really didn't know what to feel about that. Mom engaged? Just no. "Fingers crossed."

I got a gentle hug from each of them and a kiss from Archie and Ian, both light and affectionate. Jake just nuzzled a gentle one to my jaw, before whispering, "Sleep well, and I'm up if you need me. I can time stuff or whatever."

Sometimes, I wondered what I'd done right because the guys did get me, even when they didn't always seem to understand. Coop kept it light on the drive home. At the apartments, I checked Mom's spot automatically. It was empty. One of these days, I was just going to park there and be a rebel. It wasn't like she was using it.

Coop walked me to the door, and unlike the last three days, he didn't pin me there for a hot, devouring kiss so much as give me a careful hug and an even sweeter kiss. "Go on inside and lock up. Call me if you need me."

"Thanks, Coop—for everything."

"Anytime, you know that, and I'm sorry about Laura."

"Not your fault," I reminded him. "Even if you were a bit of a jerk."

"Yeah," he said with a grimace. "I'm working on that."

Another light kiss, and then I let myself in. I closed the door and locked it before leaning back and closing my eyes. The cramps coupled with the headache I currently nursed and my sore feet didn't make me want to do much. Shower, then I'd make a sandwich and get it done. It was only after I pushed off the door that I realized the cats hadn't come out to greet me.

That was… weird.

The single light in the kitchen was on, I always left the one over the stove lit when I'd be getting back after dark.

There was also a light in the living room on that I *hadn't* turned on before I left.

The living room was quiet otherwise, and there were no cats on the sofa. Where the hell were the cats? "Tiddles?" I called as I headed for the hallway. Of the three, he was always out to meet me.

The door to my room was closed, and in the half-light of the hallway, shadows elongating courtesy of the yellow lamp in the living room, I froze. It was like being in a horror movie.

I tugged my phone from my pocket and pulled up Coop's contact. He was closest. But I didn't hit connect. Maybe I shut the door on my way out? My bathroom door was closed too, and I never shut that when I left. Their litter box was in there.

As I pushed open the door to my room, the yowling of the cats immediately greeted me. Tabby raced out between my feet and straight to the bathroom door—which was closed. I pivoted and shoved that door open for her, too.

No way I shut the cats in my room.

Apprehension wrapped cool fingers around my spine as the door to my mom's room opened and her laughter floated out. "Let me just get us a drink…"

And there she was, wearing nothing but a t-shirt and her hair was a wreck and the door was open wide enough I had a perfect view of Mr. Standish—shirtless in Mom's bed.

I think I just threw up in my mouth.

Worse, my mom just grinned when she saw me. "Hey, baby. Sorry, keep the cats in your room tonight, okay? Eddie doesn't like them." She closed the door and headed for the kitchen.

Yep.

Horror movie.

Called it.

Chapter Twenty
AT THE BOTTOM OF EVERYTHING

I showered swiftly, not wanting to be out of my room longer than absolutely necessary. In fact, I didn't even want to be in my apartment. She'd seriously brought him here. Her car hadn't been in the lot, so he'd probably driven her. I ran a comb through my wet hair and left it to dry on its own. In my pajamas, I stuffed ear buds in and cranked up my music before leaving the bathroom.

I didn't want to even *accidentally* hear anything.

So. Gross.

In the kitchen, I made a sandwich, grabbed two sodas and a bottle of water, then a bag of chips. I wanted no excuses to have to come back out. Then I hoarded everything into my room and even grabbed the cat's litter box—I'd rather leave it in my bathroom, thank you very much—but if they had to be trapped with me, then I wasn't going to make them suffer.

Instead of sitting on the bed, I hunkered down on the floor on the far side of it, using the bed as a barrier between me and the door. Then I stared down at my phone.

I'd left the guys, what? Forty minutes earlier? If that? Torn between laughter, tears, and fury was not a good place to be. I should have grabbed the damn ice cream when I was in the kitchen. I'd finished the sandwich, and the unsettled feeling wasn't going away.

Music still cranked, I opened the text messages. My finger hovered from one to the others and back—finally, I went to the group text I had with them. It wasn't as active, unless we were planning something or checking on morning coffee.

Me

Anyone still up?

My phone pinged in rapid succession.

Coop

Yep, finishing paper.

Ian

Just watching a movie.

Jake

Told you I would be.

Archie

Yep. Trying to debug this robot program.

Relief sang through me, they were all there.

Me

Mom is here.

Several dots appeared as though someone was typing, but I wasn't finished.

Me

And your dad, Archie.

The dots stopped for a moment then:

Archie

You okay?

Coop

WTF? Her car wasn't there.

Ian

What do you need?

Jake

I can be there in 15.

Coop

I can be there in 2.

A little laugh worked its way up past the knot of tension.

Me

I don't know. I wasn't—they're in her room. They locked the cats in here. Still have homework. But I cannot focus.

Archie

Come here if you need to. Fuck, I can come get you.

A series of dittos followed.

As much as I wanted to say yes to all the offers—because seriously, the last place I wanted to be was here—I couldn't.

Me

I can't leave the cats.

Archie

Fine, then I'll come there.

Me

I don't know if that would help right now. Just… can someone help me get

Ian

Hang on.

My phone rang, cutting off the music, and I hit answer. "Hey," I said to Ian. I kept my voice low. I was pretty sure whatever they were doing, they weren't listening to me, but I really didn't want to find out.

"Hang on for a couple more seconds…" Then there were some beeps. "Jake's on." Another beep. "Archie." Finally… "And that's Coop."

"Hi."

"Hey, baby girl," Jake said. "What do you need to get done tonight, give us a list…"

And just like that, I had backup for my fraying concentration. I gave them the list of assignments. Just talking about it helped me organize it. I dragged my laptop and backpack closer and then wrote the list down on a notecard so I could cross them off as I went.

They stayed on the phone for the next two hours, occasionally commenting, always responding if I asked a question, and helping to keep me on track. By the time I finished the last sentence on the short French paper I had to turn in the next day, the clammy, crawly feeling and sick nausea had gone away.

The cramps were still there—yay—but I could survive those. My phone was nearly dead when we hung up. I got my backpack squared away, cleaned up my food trash and crept through the silent apartment to the kitchen to throw it away.

After a pitstop in the bathroom, I crawled into bed with my heating pad and put my phone on the charger.

Archie

It's going to be okay. Call, text, whatever you need, okay?

Jake

I'll be there early tomorrow, promise.

Coop

I'm right around the corner, you know that.

Ian

You're a rock star and my hero. The fact you shine even when everyone around you gets in the muck just makes me adore you more.

The messages buoyed me. I sent a kiss emoji and a night to each of them, then set the phone down on the nightstand. One by one, the cats all tumbled onto the bed to curl up with me, and I hugged Jake's pillow as I leaned into the heating pad.

Sleep proved elusive. My mind kept running in circles, like the cats doing rabbit races from topic to topic. The buzz of my phone pulled me upright to look at it. There was a message from Ian with the words *play me* under an audio file.

Tiddles complained when I snagged my ear buds and then hit play. The soft melody of his guitar combined with his voice made me grin. Two songs, a second one arrived as I was listening to the first.

I saved the files to my phone and then put them in a playlist. I listened to both of them twice before I answered his text.

Me

I love them. Thank you.

Ian

Wanted to give you a lullaby, sleep well.

Putting the songs on repeat, I curled up around Jake's pillow and the heating pad again as Ian sang me to sleep.

Tomorrow needed to be a better day.

By the time my alarm went off, I did not want to get up. The cats were quite vocal in their need for me to move though, and the fact I wanted to get out of the apartment before any of the other occupants woke up drove me.

Dressing in a hurry, I slipped on the borrowed t-shirt from Archie over a pair of shorts. The heat was back and likely would be for a few more days. I tied the t-shirt in the corner so it wouldn't hang down to my thighs. In the kitchen, I fed the cats and dropped in two pieces of bread to toast.

In the bathroom, I brushed my teeth then pulled my hair back into a braid. It was a mess of curls otherwise, and I didn't want to deal with it. I cleaned out the litter box and changed it, then wrestled with whether to leave it in my room or not.

I'd prefer not, but if she shut the cats up again, they needed access. Preferring they didn't have an accident, I left it, then grabbed a water bowl and dry food and put that in my room before grabbing my backpack.

It was barely six-forty and Jake wouldn't be there for at least another thirty minutes, though he had said early. I stood in the quiet of the kitchen and ate my toast and drank a cup of coffee before I took some pain relievers.

The cramps were worse today, but that had to be the stress. My stomach was in knots, too. The creak of the bedroom door opening intensified the unsettled feeling racing through my system. Mom appeared, and I almost sighed with relief.

Not that I wanted to see her, but she was so much better than…

Never mind.

Mr. Standish was right behind her.

At least they were both dressed.

Well, mostly dressed.

Mr. Standish had bare feet in my kitchen.

All of my appetite fled.

"Good morning, sweetheart," Mom said as she gave me a quick squeeze and a kiss on the cheek.

Who was she, and what had she done with my mother?

"Good morning, Frankie," Mr. Standish said, a wry smile on his face, and it was like a punch to the stomach. I forgot how much Archie looked like his dad. Or maybe I'd just blocked it out. He stood there awkwardly, and for a moment, I swore he was going to give me a hug.

Coffee cup in one hand and toast in the other, I retreated toward the table in the corner. My backpack was on, and if I could have phased right through the door, I would have. Too bad comic book powers didn't really exist.

"You're ready to go early," Mom said, pouring coffee for herself and then Mr. Standish like the three of us in the kitchen was a normal occurrence instead of some whacked out version of the *Twilight Zone*.

"Lots to do," I said, concentrating on eating each bite of the toast and not choking on it. Tiddles wound around my leg.

"You need to lock the cats up before you go, sweetie." Again with the endearments. Ugh. "I told you, Eddie isn't a fan."

"I'd just prefer not to get hair on everything." The gaze he settled on my cat was one of distaste.

"Yeah well, they live here," I reminded them. "Mr. Standish doesn't have to stay if he doesn't like them."

The words landed like a gauntlet, and my mother glared at me. "That was rude."

"Okay," I responded, then took a sip of my coffee. I wasn't apologizing. "It was also the truth."

"It's all right, Maddy," Mr. Standish said, running a hand down my mother's back, and ugh. I think I just threw up in my mouth again. "Frankie is right, the cats do live here for now. We may have to make other arrangements for them when we move you two."

"I know a good rescue…"

My jaw opened but no sound came out. I was not getting rid of my cats. Were they insane?

"We should talk at dinner tonight," Mr. Standish continued. "Frankie could use a new car, and we could look into that as well." He stole a look at me, and I think my face was frozen somewhere between *what the fuck* and *get out of my house*.

When he kissed my mother, I turned away. I really didn't want to watch that. The last bit of toast went down like a lump, and Tiddles stared up at me almost mournfully. No one was getting rid of my cats. If I had to get my own damn apartment, I'd figure it out. I had savings. I could make it work.

It wasn't like I didn't know how to look after myself.

My mother's fingers bit into my arm and jerked me around. "What the hell was that?" The hissed demand carried tremendous accusation.

"What the hell was what?" No way I would roll over on this one. As uncomfortable as all this made me, *she* was the one who brought him there. "Maybe I should ask you the same thing. Why is *he* here?"

"Because he's my fiancé," she snapped. "You'll be more respectful. He's willing to help you, Frankie. All you have to do is be nice."

"Help me?" She was joking, right?

"Yes. School. A car. He can make your life easier."

Easier.

Right.

"I don't want his money." I didn't want anyone's money.

"Fine, you don't have to take it, but you could at least do me the courtesy of being *happy* for me and supporting me. Sometimes, I wonder what I did that made you so damn selfish."

Me.

Selfish.

I pulled my arm out of her grasp. "Maybe you should look in a mirror." Not pulling my punches, I glared. "Maybe you should think about the fact in your *happiness* you're sinking someone else's marriage and someone else's family. You're not getting rid of my cats. You want to move in with him. You go right ahead. I'm not going anywhere."

"You know," she said. "When I was pregnant, I could have given you up for adoption."

Not the first time she'd ever said that to me.

"Maybe you should have, Mom, maybe then I'd have a real family."

The slap I saw coming a mile away, and it stung when it landed. Even when the tears sparked to my eyes, I refused to shed them.

"You ungrateful little—"

Someone knocked on the back door. Tiddles had vanished sometime around the moment we'd raised our voices. Now, Mom stared at me before she glanced at the door.

I backed away, then unlocked the door to find Coop standing there, eyes worried. His sandy blond hair was disheveled, like all he'd done was run his hand through the hair. His eyes narrowed, then he looked past me at my mother.

"Cooper," she said briefly, then looked at me. "Your friend can wait outside while you put up the cats." The expression she leveled at me promised a hell of a lot more trouble if I fought her on this.

"I'll be a minute," I told Coop.

"Want me to hold your backpack?" he asked, but that wasn't the real question. Was I okay was the question written all over his face, and no, I really wasn't.

I gave him a tight smile. "Sure. I'll just be a sec." I slipped out of the straps, and he took it and caught my hand. The squeeze he gave me reminded me I wasn't alone. After he stepped back, I closed the door.

"Frankie," my mother said. "When we go to dinner tonight, you will behave yourself. Am I clear?"

"Crystal."

"Eddie said he'd have a dress sent over for you, so I'll leave it in your room. Dress appropriately."

Fuck.

No.

"Whatever you say." I went to walk past her, but she lifted a hand, and I raised my arm ready to block that next hit. She'd gotten one slap, I wasn't taking another.

We locked gazes, and she frowned. "You really need to work on your attitude. I expect better from you."

For the first time in my life, I hated her. "Okay." I kept it as non-combative as I could. Truthfully, I didn't expect better from her. Sadly, this was my mother. She'd always been this woman. In all likelihood, if Archie was right, when this was over, my mother would be the one hurting.

And all I'd have were I told you so's and pieces to pick up.

"May I be excused? You wanted me to put the cats up."

With a sigh, she stepped aside and waved me away. It didn't surprise me the cats were already in my room. Tabby's tail stuck out from under the bed. Tory peered at me from inside the open closet door and Tiddles sat in the middle of my desk, tail lashing.

"Sorry, guys," I murmured. "I'll be home right after school. I promise." I double-checked the food, the water, and the litter, then shut the door before grabbing the trash bag with the used litter from my bathroom.

Thankfully, Mom wasn't in the kitchen anymore, and I made it outside without encountering either of them. Coop was right there when I came out, and I didn't care how it looked, I set the trash bag down before wrapping my arms around him.

He squeezed gently as he held me close. Eyes closed, I took a deep breath of him and the faint spiciness of his soap. He spread his hand out against my back before rubbing it in slow circles.

"Tell me what happened." It wasn't a question.

"I don't really want to talk about it."

And I didn't. This—I never liked talking about my mother. It was bad enough they all knew about her affair and the fact Mr. Standish had spent the night. A shudder rolled over me and despite the warm air, I was freezing.

Coop just held me while I tried to get it together. I didn't want to cry. I really didn't want to cry. Leaning on him helped, but it didn't take away the fact I still had to see them later that day.

And we couldn't keep standing here. If they came out—just no. When I pulled back, Coop tightened his arm and then studied my face. With very light fingers, he traced my cheekbone. It stung a little. She'd really gotten me.

His eyes narrowed, and he glared back at my apartment.

"Just let it go," I told him.

"No," he said, then pressed a gentle kiss to my forehead. "I'm tired of her hurting you."

"Right now, I just want to leave." Please don't make this a big deal. I didn't say it aloud, because I knew the answer. Coop pressed his lips to my forehead again and held there. Tension corded his arms as he sighed.

"Okay," he said, finally. "Okay." But he glanced back at the door, and I could almost read the need to knock on it again. Coop would fight my battles for me. It was easy to forget he didn't back down, even when he was so live and let live. That he let me talk him into it now was a gift.

Or maybe we were just delaying the inevitable.

Letting me go, he grabbed the trash bag with one hand and my backpack with the other. "Jake's almost here."

Early.

They were both super early, and I didn't have it in me to complain.

We headed toward the parking lot, and I debated just sliding into my car, but we had a plan. To be honest, as much as a part of me longed to run away, I didn't want to be alone.

The familiar yellow SUV pulled to a stop as we reached the parking lot.

"Go get in," Coop said. "I'm throwing this away."

He diverted toward the dumpster and didn't relinquish my backpack, so I just headed for Jake's car. He leaned over and pushed open the front passenger door. He searched my face with every bit of the intensity Coop had. The moment he latched onto the red mark on my cheek, his lips thinned.

"Who the fuck hit you?"

"It's nothing, okay?" I slid into the seat and did my best not grimace. The pain relievers hadn't kicked in for the cramps, and they were worse on day two than on day one. Hell, even my back hurt today. It would be better by tomorrow. Just had to make it through the day.

"No, it's not okay." He twisted in the seat as I buckled my seat belt. When he cupped my face, I leaned into the contact. "Who hit you, baby girl? Your mom or Archie's dad?"

"It wasn't Archie's dad," Coop answered as he let himself into the backseat and tossed the backpacks in. "That much I know."

"Coop."

"It's not the first time, Frankie," he countered. "You always cover for her."

I closed my eyes. "Please, just let it go."

There was silence, and when I opened my eyes, I found Jake staring behind me and I could almost read the war on his face.

"Let's just go to school?"

He dragged his gaze back to me. "How many times?"

"I'm not answering that. I don't want to talk about it."

"Enough," Coop supplied, and I groaned.

"Coop."

"Nope, I told you, not letting it go. I've let it go enough. You don't want to talk about it, fine. *I* won't force you. But I'm tired of what she does to you, Frankie. You always defend her…"

"She's my mom."

"She's…" Jake said, then seemed to bite off his next words before he leaned forward and kissed me. Like the hug with Coop earlier, I just leaned into the contact. The touch of his lips was gentle, sweet, and oh so careful as he licked his way in to tease my tongue. At my little sigh, he eased back and stared at me again. "I don't want her hitting you."

Neither did I.

"Can't change it," I said. "It's done. But thank you for caring."

His eyebrows tightened, and he shared an inexplicable look with Coop. Then he glanced back toward the apartments before giving me one more kiss. "We're not done with this." It sounded more like a promise. "Yes, I care."

"So do I," Coop said. "Of course, we care."

It was all a little too much, and I shifted in the seat. I ached inside and out. "Thank you."

"Silly girl," Coop muttered then tugged my braid gently. "You need more coffee if you need us to explain it to you."

Maybe I did.

Or maybe I just needed to get this day over and done with. I'd never been so relieved as I was when Jake pulled away. Even though I finally saw Mr. Standish's BMW. It was parked just a few slots to the left of my car. If I'd been paying attention the night before, I'd have known.

The sick feeling pitted my stomach again.

The silence in the car was so loud and thick, I could touch it. Jake didn't even have music on, so it wasn't hard to hear the buzzing of their phones. Mine had gone off, too, but I didn't want to dig it out of my pocket. Last night had been awful, but they'd all been great.

This morning had been so much worse.

Tonight?

Tonight, I had to go out to dinner with them, and Mr. Standish was buying me a dress?

Not a chance in hell would I wear it.

The sun shining seemed almost a middle finger from Mother Nature. Life sucks? Here, have some sunshine. I suppose it could also mean life wasn't that bad. At least, until you opened the door and got a face full of humidity—not so bad? Ha, just kidding.

My cheek still stung a little, and I hadn't looked in a mirror to see how bad it was and the closer we got to school… I flipped down the visor and pushed open the slide to look in the mirror.

It caught Coop's reflection and the white line of his mouth where his lips compressed. "It's not horrible," he told me. It wasn't. There was a red mark and there was no mistaking it was a hand.

Fuck.

I closed my eyes and leaned my head back as I slapped the visor shut. I didn't have cosmetics in my bag, I just didn't carry them. I could not go around school all day with a handprint. It would fade, but the fact I still had it said she'd definitely hit me as hard as it seemed.

The school was in sight, and I sat forward and dragged my phone out. Messages from Archie and Ian, general good mornings and both worried. The last one from Archie said Coop had already ratted out the slap.

Yeah. He was definitely not letting it go.

I both adored and despised him a little for being so stubborn about it. There was a reason I didn't talk about Mom. I never wanted them to look at me the way they were right now.

Scrolling past those messages, I found the one Rachel had sent to me and sent:

Me

Weird question, do you have some base and powder I could borrow?

Rachel

I even have concealer. What's up?

Me

Look like crap and need some help.

Rachel

Impossible, but I'll help. I'm at school, where are you?

Me

Pulling in the parking lot with Jake.

Rachel

Meet me in the girl's bathroom, theatre hall. It will be empty.

Me

Thank you.

Rachel

See you soon.

Jake parked and glanced from my phone to me. "You good?"

"I'm gonna meet Rachel and fix this." I motioned to my cheek. "I'll meet you guys in the cafeteria afterward, okay?"

"No," Jake said in the same breath as Coop did before Jake continued. "We'll walk you, then wait."

"Someone needs to tell the guys. And I won't be long." I was dying for coffee.

"It'll be cool," Coop said. "Guys are right there."

And sure enough, there was Ian and Archie, coffee cups in hand and both wearing worried expressions. Archie's turned far darker the moment he got a good look at me.

"She really fucking hit you?" It was such an echo of what Jake had said right down to the tone, I almost laughed.

Almost.

"I'm okay," I told him as he gave me the coffee. He started forward like he planned to hug me then drew back.

Fuck that.

I hugged him, and then his arms came around me and he hugged me close. "You are telling me what happened," he said against my ear. "Not here is fine, but after school and *before* dinner."

"Your dad is apparently buying me a dress," I answered him in the same low voice.

Archie snorted.

"I'm not wearing it," I warned him. "Like ever."

"I have no problems with that," he said, then pressed a gentle kiss to my cheek. "That right there I have a problem with." He loosened his hold, and then Ian was there he scooped me close.

I closed my eyes and held onto the coffee and Ian. "Thank you for the songs last night," I whispered. "They really helped."

"Good," he said. When he pulled back, he studied the red mark on my cheek. I should so have checked if it was showing before I left. I'd been in too much of a hurry to get out of there. "Just—Coop said you don't want to talk about it. She's done this before."

A part of me didn't want to answer, so I just stared at him. But that wasn't fair. Ian had recorded fucking lullabies for me to help me sleep. He didn't deserve me being a bitch about anything.

"Yes, but it's not like it happens all the time or every day. Now, I was just telling Jake and Coop, Rachel is going to loan me some make up so I can hide this, and I'm gonna meet her at the girl's bathroom in the theatre hall. No one is there right now."

Jake's expression had gone almost unreadable, but Archie's darkened further, and I didn't think that was possible. But all he said was, "Okay."

"I got her bag," Coop announced as they fell in around me like an escort.

It was both sweet and a little unnerving.

"I'm really capable of going to the…"

"Don't," Ian said, and he was the last one to snap of the four of them. Coop did it when it was just the two of us. Archie and Jake always did, they weren't shy. Ian tended to just be nicer. "We're escorting as much for us as for you, okay?" His tone gentled toward the end, and I lifted my hands to surrender the moment.

"Thanks, guys," I said. "Sometimes, it's just easier to pretend it didn't happen. Then I don't have to think about it. It's a lot harder when all of you know."

They seemed to chew that over as we headed inside. Jake took point, and we went down one of the quieter hallways toward the theatre rooms and black box theatre tucked away behind the auditorium.

"It's a lot easier to be all alone that way, too," Coop said. "Not my favorite."

And I knew that.

At the girl's bathroom, I pushed the doors in, leaving them in the hall to talk. Rachel leaned back against a sink, phone in hand when I walked in. She took one look at me and frowned. "Okay, when you said you needed to borrow make up, I thought you meant you had bags under your eyes. Which of those bitches hit you?"

Oh.

Boy.

"It wasn't anyone from school."

Her phone lowered. "One of the four idiots?"

I blew out a breath. "No, Rachel, it wasn't any of them and look, I appreciate the concern. I really do. I just want to cover this up so I don't have people staring at me all day. They've had enough reasons to do that lately." Crazily enough, she'd been the first one I thought to ask.

Tucking her phone away, she pulled a small cosmetics pouch out of her backpack and held it out to me.

"Thank you."

"You're welcome, you need a hand doing it? I'm not so bad at it." With a wince, she added, "Not that I'm implying you are."

"I didn't think you were," I admitted, then took a sip of the coffee before setting it down. "And yeah, it's been a while since I had to cover up something this big."

Rachel's eyes narrowed. "You've had to cover up something like this before?"

"Yeah, most recently hickeys." I really needed to just shut up, or I was going to end up revealing a lot of crap I didn't want to reveal.

Touching her tongue to her teeth, the other girl canted her head and said, "I told you I thought you could use a friend and that I'd like to be that friend." The words sent recognition sparking through me. "I understated it—you *need* a friend, and I am going to be that friend."

Wait.

What?

Rachel was Mr. Thorns?

The corner of her mouth kicked up, and then she touched her fingers to my sore cheek and began applying the coolness of the concealer. "Probably not the best time to drop the surprise on you," Rachel said. "I really wanted to tell you Saturday, but you looked so miserable."

I opened my mouth, then closed it again. Then… "You sent those roses."

"Yeah." Another smile, only this time with a hint of shyness. "I did. I've had a crush on you for a long time, and don't worry, I get it. You don't swing my way. A girl could hope and I did, but the more I tried to get to know you—the more I realized you needed a friend."

Facing her, I frowned. "You told me about the guys saying I was untouchable."

There wasn't an ounce of apology in her eyes. "Yes, I did. Because they were being jerks, and you didn't see it. Like I said—you needed a friend. I didn't mean for it to hurt you, or for you to shut down the way you did. But you barely seemed to notice the world over the summer."

She wasn't wrong.

"And for what it's worth," Rachel said. "Thanks for calling me when you needed help—even if it was just for make up tips."

It wasn't funny. It was all kind of sad in a way.

But I laughed, and the corners of Rachel's mouth curled up.

"Rach," I told her honestly. "If I did swing your way—I'd totally go for you."

Her smile grew, and she winked as she finished up the concealer, her touch light and almost effortless. "Guess I'll just have to settle for a bosom buddy—speaking of which, you have a great bosom and thanks for wearing the red shirt."

To be honest, I'd completely forgotten about the shirt.

Completely.

It had been a shit morning.

I'd worn Archie's shirt for comfort.

"Thanks for the roses, you have no idea how great they made me feel."

"Good." Another couple of touches, and she switched to the base. "Now sit still, and let's make you all sexy and shit for those four idiots—not that you need much help in that department."

My face heated, and I laughed.

Okay.

Rachel was Mr. Thorns and wanted to be my friend.

The guys were all outside waiting for me.

All of them had my back.

Maybe not such a shit morning, after all.

"I have no idea how to tell the guys," I admitted. "They really didn't like me getting those flowers."

Rachel smirked. "Good. Make them step up their game."

I laughed. "You're incorrigible."

"You don't know the half of it."

Yeah, maybe not so bad after all.

Chapter Twenty-One
REALITY CHECKS DON'T BOUNCE

Rachel's revelation added fresh spinout circles in my head, but at least these weren't wretched ones. The idea Rachel had liked me enough to go out of her way to make me feel good was one thing, but she hadn't been kidding about being attracted and I'll admit it, the idea flattered me and left me as stunned as when the guys admitted they wanted to date me.

She was right though. I needed a friend. The whole time she fixed my face, she kept up a small running patter of conversation. Including asking me about Homecoming. When I told her Cheryl had already demanded I go dress shopping with her, Rachel grinned.

"Good, Cheryl's got a good eye. I'm not bad, but—I'd want to dress you for me and not them." Her wink pulled another laugh from me.

"Okay, you flirting with me is going to take some getting used to."

Dropping her chin to her chest, Rachel let out a sigh. "This is the other reason I told you about the untouchable thing. I've been flirting with you for months, and you really never saw it."

Wait. What? "Is that why you'd start those nutty debates?"

She shrugged. "Maybe. Sometimes I just liked to rile you up. Though—I really did need help with the poetry homework, and I do appreciate it." Tipping her head critically, she studied me and then took a step back. "I think that works, can barely tell you have it on and you can't see the reddened skin. What do you think?"

A glance in the mirror, and I let out a relieved sigh. "You're really good at this."

"No, I'm not. But most of my stuff at least matches your skin tone." She packed her stuff away, and I grabbed my coffee.

"Seriously, thank you."

"Glad to help. Can I go rock your guys now?"

"You keep calling them my guys." It was a little on the uncomfortable side. For that matter, she'd said them instead of Ian earlier, too.

Another dramatic sigh, and Rachel shook her head. "Okay, so which of them are you pretending to date? Cause I know all of them want to date you, and I'm pretty sure based on what I've seen, you're into all of them." Cosmetic bag stored away and her backpack strap over her shoulder, she folded her arms and stared at me. "Don't worry. I'm definitely not judging."

I groaned. "It's complicated."

"The best things in life are complicated." Pushing away from the other sink, she hooked her arm through mine and we headed for the door. She pulled it open with a flourish. "Here she is guys, looking better than ever."

All four of them turned in our direction, even as their conversation cut off abruptly. Coop glanced from me to Rachel, then back again. "Looks good," he said slowly. "You still look like you, too."

I felt a bit better about everything. I hadn't been kidding about not wanting anyone to stare at me. "All Rachel, she's a life saver."

"Happy to help," she said, her arm still hooked through mine. "By the way boys, to save Frankie the angst, I'm the person who sent the roses and the letters."

If I had the foresight to lift my phone, I'd have been able to catch four, almost comical expressions varying from disbelief all the way to downright suspicion.

"Huh," Archie said after a beat. "Well, you've had a crush on her almost as long as I have."

"Wait—*you're* Mr. Thorns," Coop stated, eyebrows gathered in a fierce frown.

"Mr. Thorns?" She cocked her head and looked at me.

I shrugged. "I didn't know your name, and you gave me roses, so… yeah. Thorns."

"How very Jane Austen of you." Once upon a time, that dry remark might have irked me, but today, I only grinned. Because of all the bombshells of the last twenty-four hours—Hell, of the last *week!*—Rachel's was the easiest to swallow.

"Thank you," I said with a salute of my coffee.

Jake didn't say anything for a long moment, then seemed to nod to himself before he eyed Rachel. "All right… she's taken though. You got that, right?"

With an indelicate snort, Rachel squeezed my arm. "As long as you four lunkheads don't fuck it up any more than you already have."

"Wait… you were the one who told her we made her untouchable." Coop was still wrapping his head around it.

"Yep." Rachel gave them a little wave with her fingers. "So be aware, I'm watching you. I like Frankie, she needs a friend, and I fit the bill nicely. So, she wins, you don't. Keep it clean and don't screw up, and I won't have to destroy you. Toodles." She set off down the hallway, and I had to bite my lip to keep from laughing. Light tone or not, Rachel had looked deadly serious. About half a dozen steps away, she turned and lifted her thumb and pinky toward her head like she was making a phone call. "You need me, just call. And if you ever get tired of them being dicks, lemme know."

Ian snorted, then swung his head to look at me. "She's Mr. Thorns."

I lifted my shoulders. "I didn't realize."

"And you wore red," Coop said slowly, as if he was still playing catch up. "You wanted him to come find you."

"You know what, I kind of forgot. It's been a crazy morning. I just wore Archie's shirt."

That gave them a momentary pause and alone, in the empty hall, it was kind of peaceful, and I needed the minute. "Well then," Archie said with a grin. "I like how it looks on you. You should wear all my shirts."

Jake groaned and gave him a shove. "You suck." Then he glanced at me. "But feel free to raid my closet." Then his grin grew a little bit wider. Maybe he remembered me in his boxers, I wasn't asking.

Not right here.

"You okay?" Ian asked, hooking an arm over my shoulders. Coop still had my backpack.

Honestly, my emotions had been all over the place, but I was mostly okay right now. "I think so. I feel kind of bad because Rachel put herself out there, but she did it just to make me smile, and we've always been so…"

"Volatile?" Archie suggested.

"Maybe?" I winced. "I owe her though."

"Yeah?" Jake slanted a look at me. "Why? Because she gave you a reason to ditch us for months? Or she's prone to romantic gestures that make us look terrible?"

Coop snorted. "Jake's having a moment. He can't punch the competition."

No, but Jake could thump him. The playful shove pulled another smile. It had all been so grim. Now… "Because she did me a favor, more than once, and she's not asking for anything in return." That meant a lot.

"Cool," Ian said, then glanced down the hallway before he pressed a kiss to my temple. "Then let's focus on that. And don't fall off the face of the Earth after that dinner tonight. We're all going to be worried."

I glanced at Archie, and he nodded. "Don't worry. I'm going. We'll keep you in the loop."

"Good luck at the game, tonight, too. I wish I could say I'm sorry I won't be there. I would like to support you."

"But you hate football," Jake said easily. "It's all good. Gonna be a boring game anyway. I'm not playing."

"Hey," Ian said. "Don't be an ass."

"But I'm so good at it," Jake retaliated, and I grinned again. Coop held out my bag to Archie.

Even as we split up to head to our classes, I managed to hold onto some of my recovered mood. Archie bumped my shoulder gently. "I'm taking you and Coop home, then we'll see where they want to meet for dinner. I'm assuming you don't want to ride with them?"

"Fuck no," I said aloud, and he nodded.

"Cats or no cats, if they are there tonight, you aren't staying."

"Archie… Mom said we'd have to rehome the cats when we moved in with him and I—I pushed back. That's why she slapped me."

He frowned. "And you're worried if you're not there, they'll just get rid of them?"

"Right now, I have no idea what they're going to do."

"We'll figure it out," he said. "I promise."

I really wanted to believe him.

So. Much.

If Mom got rid of my cats…

I couldn't even contemplate it.

By seventh period, I was over the day and school. My focus had still been scattered, but I managed to pull it together for two quizzes and the French test I'd completely forgotten we were having.

There was an epic fail.

Luckily, I didn't choke on the test. The guys were champions at distraction. I had an escort for every class, and this time when I had to slip into the bathroom before lunch, Coop just waited in the hall. The cramps improved, some. The closer we got toward dinnertime, though, the worse they grew.

Fortunately, Mr. G just left us to read, and I'd finished that re-read of the chapters already, so Jake quizzed me. The distraction only lasted so long. My phone buzzed five minutes before the bell with a message from Mom with the time for dinner and the restaurant. They would be picking me up at six at the house. Oh, and she'd left the dress *Eddie* got for me on my door.

Jake grimaced when he read the text. "That just reads fucking creepy."

He was not wrong.

I fired a response back that said I'd meet them at the restaurant. Hopefully, they wouldn't be there when I got home.

The single *K* in response wasn't comforting.

Jake walked me out to the parking lot, and it was weird that we didn't head to where my car was but toward Archie's. Coop and Ian were already there with Archie waiting. We had to keep the goodbyes brief, but I wished them both luck on the game whether Jake was sitting it out or not.

"Take care of her," Ian said to Archie.

"I planned on it, we'll check in later."

"I promise," I said. "This time, I really will check in and not forget. I've been crap about it."

"You've been distracted, baby girl," Jake said quietly, the corner of his mouth kicking up. "As long as we know you're okay."

There wasn't much else to say in the crowded lot, so I gave them quick hugs, then slid into the car. Coop leaned forward between the seats as Archie headed out of the lot.

"Do you know where you're going?"

"My mom said Rosewood. The reservation is for seven."

"That's all the way on the edge of Fort Worth."

"I know," I said.

"And exclusive," Archie commented with a wry twist of his mouth. "Edward's going all out."

"Well, I told them I'd meet them. So I'm kind of hoping they're not at the house."

"Wanna give me your extra key in case I need to check on the cats for you tonight?" Coop offered, and I twisted to look at him.

"Will you?"

"Not a problem. I don't want you worrying about them."

"You guys probably think I'm being stupid. They're cats, they'll be fine if I just leave them water and food. Mom made me lock them in my room this morning, so I moved the litter box, but…"

"It's not stupid," Archie told me, one hand on my thigh. "Seriously, Frankie, you love your cats. You're allowed to worry and right now, there's a lot about this situation that makes me uncomfortable. The thing with your cats is not it."

"Nope, you love the little furballs. So grab the key and give it to me, and I'll swing by. Then if you skip out and stay at Archie's tonight, I'll sneak in and make sure they're okay."

"Thank you." When we got to the apartments, the very first thing I did once we were out of the car was to hug Coop. He wrapped me up in a firm, if gentle hug. I didn't care about the heat or the mugginess.

Coop cupped the back of my head and rubbed a hand between my shoulder blades as I pressed my face to his throat. I sighed, leaning there for a long moment.

"Take all the time you need," Archie said. "I mean, I don't mind standing here, all by myself, not getting hugged for being a superhero like Coop because he promised to take care of your pussy."

There was an absolute beat of silence, then Coop snickered and I couldn't stop the laughter welling up.

"You are awful," I told Archie as I turned my head, but didn't pull away from Coop.

Archie met my gaze with a grin. "I am, but then I like taking care of your pussy, singular or plural.”

Giggling, I held onto Coop, and he chortled.

“Keep it up, I can stand here and hold her all night.”

“You’d do it, too,” Archie commented, sounding more amused than anything. And as tempting an offer as that might be, I wanted some downtime before we had to deal with our parents, and Archie and I should talk. We really hadn’t had time to discuss the latest without others around, and he seemed to be as guarded about it as I was—at least, I thought he was. Maybe he talked to the guys when I wasn’t there.

In fairness, he might be avoiding saying unkind things about my mom to my face.

Not that I could fault him for the unkind things or the not wanting to say them to my face. It wasn’t like I wanted to call his father creepy to his face. Especially not when I could see how much Archie looked like him.

Shoving that uncomfortable thought away, I gave Coop another squeeze before pulling back and doing a quick search of the parking lot. Archie wrapped his hand around my nape and massaged it gently.

“He’s not here. I don’t see any of his cars.”

Relief spilled through me. Mom’s car was absent, too.

“Don’t worry,” Archie said. “You do not have to deal with them on your own.”

I was not a coward, but this morning was just another example of how bad this could get for everyone. Mom did not handle it well when things went sideways. Everything about this situation could go sideways.

After getting the key, Coop gave me a light kiss before glancing past me to Archie. “Take care of her.”

“I intend to,” he said, just the barest hint of irritation in his voice. Then Coop gave me another kiss ahead of leaving. I closed the door behind him and leaned against it. Archie stood in the middle of my living room, hands in his pockets for a beat before abruptly turning on his heel and heading down the hallway to my room. The door opened, and Tory streaked out into the living room and bounded from the coffee table to the back of the sofa where she stared at me, tail lashing.

When I reached the bedroom, he stared at the dress on the door and I leaned against his back. Closing my eyes, I just took a deep breath and hugged him from behind. With his hands over mine, he said, "We can cancel going out with them."

"It will just make it worse," I told him.

"I'm pretty sure your mother slapping you so hard she left a mark is already worse." The lightness in his tone was deceptive. "You don't want to talk about it. I know. You don't want to discuss that she hurt you, and I'm pretty sure she has before. I get it. Your mom is off limits, but hurting you is not okay."

"She isn't abusive abusive," I said, fumbling for a defense. "Saying she hits me is like accusing her of something."

The conversation was easier if I didn't look in his eyes. Did that make me a coward?

"There's all kinds of abuse, Frankie." The stroke of his thumb against the back of my hand soothed. "Will you let us—let me in so I can help?"

When I went to pull away, he caught my hand and turned. Archie frowned.

"I know I'm pushing. Coop is right, you need to be pushed on this."

"It's going to be hard enough going to that dinner tonight. Hard enough because you don't think it's real, do you? The engagement?"

"I think Edward's playing a game." He shrugged. "Getting engaged while you're still married isn't exactly stellar planning. But that's their problem. Not ours."

"Except it is my problem. I'm all my mom has. I'm… I'm the one who has to pick up the pieces."

He sighed. "You know our parents are supposed to take care of us, not the other way around, right?"

If we had Ian's parents, we would have that. Or if we had Coop's mom or Jake's. Their dads weren't great, but they weren't awful, awful, even if Coop really didn't like his and Jake remained pissed at his.

"Yeah? So why did we get the short end of the stick?"

"I have no idea," Archie admitted, then tugged me in close. "How are you feeling?"

"Tired. Achy. Kind of dreading tonight, but we have to go."

He sighed. I knew he didn't get it. Maybe none of them would. But it had just been me and Mom forever. They had extended families, but we only had each other. She wasn't perfect.

"I wish…" But I couldn't.

"What do you wish?"

"I wish it could be real for her. That she could be happy." Then when I went to college, I wouldn't have to worry about her. "But that's not fair to you."

"Not really fair to you either." He trailed his fingers down to my wrist, then traced the bracelet I'd worn. I didn't wear it every day, but like his shirt, I'd needed the comfort today.

Blowing out a breath, he said, "Okay, I brought clothes to change into so I'm going to go grab those. Take a shower, do what you can to relax and get ready. Can I get you anything?"

He was being so solicitous, and I tilted my head back. "You here is pretty great."

A wink, and he pressed a light kiss to my lips. "Does anything else make the cramps better?"

I made a face. We were not having this conversation.

"Hey, it's a thing that happens and if you're going to be uncomfortable, I'd like some clues on how to fix it."

"Well, not talking about it is a good start, and heating pads help, sometimes just making myself relax."

"Got it. Want me to feed the cats on my way to the car?"

"You don't have to."

"I want to," he insisted. "Go take care of you, let me take care of everything else."

The guys didn't usually coddle me. I'd never really needed coddling. Or maybe, more accurately, I'd never wanted coddling. I'd always just wanted to be one of them. But they'd all been coddling me today in different ways, and I kind of liked it—a little.

"Thank you, Archie."

The next hour passed by too quickly. I got my shower in and changed into a simple black dress, ignoring the purchase hanging on my door. It looked like a designer brand name, and it was just weird that his dad bought me a dress.

Archie dressed in a nice button down and slacks, he'd added a tie but skipped the jacket. "I can put it on when we get there."

"That's pretty dressy."

"Rosewood requires a jacket and tie for dinner service," he advised. Oh, that sounded terribly formal.

"I'm going to hate this place."

"Probably," he said. "But the food is good."

"Should I leave the cats out?"

"We can call Coop if you need to shut them back in. For now, let them have their apartment back." He trailed his fingers down my arm. "You know, you could have left them in your room last night. They would have been okay."

"It wasn't just about leaving them, if I'd slipped out—Mom would have been pissed and it would have been a thing."

Maybe even worse than it had already been.

"And this is my home. I'm supposed to be safe here, right?"

"Yeah. You are."

We texted the guys that we were on the way, and Coop said to let him know about the cats. The drive ended up being nice, even though it took us an hour to get there, it was nice just to sit with Archie. We listened to music, he held my hand, and I managed to relax a little. Not that it helped because as soon as we pulled up to the valet, my stomach was in knots all over again.

Archie pulled on his suit coat before he interlaced our fingers and guided me inside. "We're joining Edward Standish," he told the hostess.

Apparently, they had already arrived because we were shown to the table where the hostess and another waiter hurriedly added another place setting. It had only been set for three.

"Edward. Ms. Curtis," Archie said in a cool, brisk tone like this happened to us all the time. When I would have let go of him, he tightened his grip, keeping me firmly next to him until the new place setting was arranged, then he pulled my chair out, putting me on the far side away from my mom and his father.

"Archie," his father said with a frown while Mom shot me a reproachful look. "I wasn't aware you'd been invited."

"Well gosh, Edward, I'd have thought a family man like yourself would want to tell your son about your wedding plans—or maybe your divorce plans, or are you doubling up and getting a two for one?"

Oh boy.

"Good evening," our waiter said before his father could respond. He set two wine glasses on the table for Mr. Standish and my mom, then filled them before leaving the bottle in a chilling bucket. "What can I get you two to drink?"

Archie cut a look at me. "Coke or tea?"

"Coke." Hopefully that would settle the fresh knots in my stomach.

"Make that two," Archie told the waiter. "And a farmer's green salad for Frankie and a crab cake, she and I can share."

"Of course, would you care to order your appetizers?" The waiter looked at our parents, but his father merely shook his head, and my mother reached for her wine glass. "I'll be back shortly."

Then the waiter was gone.

"Archie, you weren't invited to this dinner, but since you're here, you could at least have the grace to show the manners you were raised with."

"Manners, those are more Muriel's purview," Archie said as he leaned back and put a hand on the back of my chair. The brush of his thumb between my shoulder blades helped. "You've always been the guy who wants to cut through the bullshit."

Mr. Standish scowled. "Don't make this a scene. I can just as easily cut you off."

"Sure, go ahead. I don't need your money. You forget, Grandfather still likes me." Archie smiled as though he could have said more, but he didn't, and the waiter returned with our drinks and a salad. Archie motioned for him to put it in front of me. "Go ahead and dig in, I know you're starving, and it could be a while before we get to the main course."

If we got that far…

He didn't actually say it, but it came across loud and clear.

"The crab cake will be out directly, would you like me to go over the specials?"

I took a sip of my Coke as Archie and his father glared daggers at each other. Well, more like Archie's dad glared at him and Archie wore a smirk. The knots in my gut had knots, and they were all doing a tug-of-war.

"Maybe that would help," my mother said a moment before her foot impacted mine.

I managed to not snort my drink and set it down. "Yes, please."

As the waiter went over the specials, my mother tapped a finger against the table. She was ticked. I was spoiling her evening. Guilt vied with a bit of vindictiveness. Maybe I shouldn't be trying to get even, but I sure as hell hadn't asked for this.

Nothing the waiter listed sounded like real food. It all sounded too fancy for words, and you couldn't pay me to eat duck foie gras. Steak tartare was basically raw meat. The minute he mentioned charred octopus, I was pretty sure my appetite checked out.

Nope.

Nope.

And oh my god, no.

"The scallops are good," Archie said. "We could split a plate of those and either the wagyu steak or the venison loin. Trust me, you'll like them."

I did trust him. "That sounds great."

One by one, we gave our orders, Archie and I would be splitting the plate between us. Another server brought out the crab cake, and I unfolded my napkin—a black one, they'd replaced the white napkin with a black one since I had on a black dress—and picked up a fork. Maybe if I stuffed food in my mouth, I could continue to avoid this dreadfully uncomfortable situation.

After the waiter left, my mother pinned a look on me. "What happened to the lovely dress Eddie left for you to wear?"

"Maddy," 'Eddie' said, and I did not gag on my food.

"It was a little too much lace," I admitted. And white. A lot of white. Even if I hadn't taken it out of the clear plastic bag. "I had this dress, and it's nice enough." Then I took another bite because I didn't want to talk about it.

"Besides, Edward shouldn't be buying Frankie clothes, Ms. Curtis. It's weird. He does that for his mistresses, not for his family. I know he doesn't do it for his wife."

Oh. I was going to die.

"For the love of God, Archie…" Mr. Standish went red, and his mouth compressed.

"Yeah, we don't do that in our house, Edward. You taught me that a long time ago. The only commandments we have are do unto ourselves what we wanna do."

"Archie." My mom waded into this morass and I stared down at the salad, uncertain of whether to laugh or to cry. This was a train wreck. I wasn't even driving the train, I was hanging off the back of it debating whether I should jump. "I understand this is probably difficult for you."

"Nope, Ms. Curtis," Archie said, perfectly polite, and the hand he had at my back moved as he shifted to sit forward, and then that hand found mine in my lap and gripped it. "You're not his first mistress. You're not even the first one I've met. Not really difficult at all. What is difficult is being polite to you after you slapped Frankie around and treated her like crap. What is difficult is being respectful when you threaten her, abandon her, and generally make her feel like it's her job to suffer in order for you to be happy." He picked up his drink then motioned from Mom to his dad. "This? This is a phase. Trust me, he can't afford the divorce."

Silence crashed down over the table, and I stuffed another bite of salad in my mouth. It probably cost twenty dollars. It probably tasted fantastic, but I barely noticed it as I paused only long enough to take a drink of the Coke and wash it down. My nails had to be digging into Archie's hand.

"I didn't want to do this over dinner," Mr. Standish said after a protracted silence while my mother drilled a glare into me. I didn't dare look at her. Maybe I shouldn't have let Archie say anything. On the other hand, I didn't disagree with him. "But since you've left me little choice…" The older man let out a long-suffering sigh. "Your mother is relocating to France for the next year. We are taking this time to get our affairs in order."

Archie raised his brows. "Relocating and getting affairs in order isn't a divorce, Edward. You two lived apart for two years when I was six and another year when I twelve. The revolving door of women has never actually stopped swinging. Maybe if you settled that down, she'd want to live with you."

"And maybe I don't want to live with her any longer. Maddy and I have been together for nearly a year now."

A year?

I stared at my mother.

I swore she smirked.

"In her absence, I'm moving Frankie and her mother into the house. You two are about to become siblings, but you're more than old enough to handle the change."

My stomach bottomed out.

"You do realize that house belongs to Muriel," Archie reminded him. "Not that I mind Frankie moving in. Plenty of room in my wing."

"Your mother isn't going to be living there. Maddy will be. I expect you to get your act together. You don't mind being cut off? Then you can be the one who moves out," Mr. Standish said.

"You know what. That's a great idea. I even know an apartment that's about to be available."

Archie glanced at me.

"Wanna be roomies?"

"Enough," Mr. Standish said as he slapped his hand against the table. "This dinner was about making sure Frankie understood the opportunities now available to her, and for me to welcome them to the family, not for you to work out your juvenile temper tantrum."

"Sure thing. Frankie, you wanna be my sister?"

I stared at him. "No."

"Yeah, me neither. Step-sister or not, I'm not feeling it." He looked at his dad. "Anything else we need to cover?"

"Frankie," my mother said, standing abruptly. "Come with me."

"No," Archie answered, his hand still on mine as he moved my mostly empty salad plate and set the crab cake in front of me. "If you can't be blunt with her in front of me—because as you'll notice Edward and I have no boundaries— you don't get to drag her off and yell at her. I'm here because I'm *Frankie's* friend. You're not going to hurt her again." Then he glanced at me. "That's really good. I have a feeling we're not going to make it to the main course, so go ahead and eat that, yeah?"

I stared at him, eyes wide. He was really doing this, and I didn't know whether to kiss him or smack him. Maybe both. But he wasn't backing down.

"Frankie," my mother said again, and I glanced at her. Locking my gaze on her, I dug my fingers into Archie's hand and sucked in a deep breath.

"I'm good right here. I'd tell Archie what you said anyway, and you and

Mr. Standish are engaged, so, no secrets, right?"

The look in her eyes promised retribution.

Well, I'd really torn it now. But I had Archie at my back, and he was right… I really didn't want to go find somewhere my mother could slap and rail at me for not having her side in this. I wanted her to be happy, but so much about this was just wrong.

"Maddy," Mr. Standish caught her hand. "Maybe we've gone about this the wrong way…"

She sank into her chair. Her expression was so stricken, my heart squeezed.

"We have sprung this on them rather abruptly." Mr. Standish sounded all kinds of reasonable. "Maybe let's start over at the beginning…and with the goals." Then Mr. Standish focused on me. "I know it's just been you and your mom, and I know you're protective. She's very protective of you, too."

Archie snorted, but Mr. Standish ignored him.

"This is really important to her, and it's even more important that she has your support." He leaned forward. "And there are a lot of benefits here for you, too. Like the brand new car waiting for you outside."

Brand new car.

Was he for real?

"And we're done," Archie pulled away his napkin and stood, then took hold of my chair. "C'mon…"

I glanced up at him then at my mom. I could read the *don't you dare* in her eyes.

"Frankie's not for sale, Edward. You two have a lovely dinner. You really do seem well-suited to each other."

I couldn't even get the words out as Archie hustled me out of the restaurant. The valet went to get the car, but not fast enough. My mother was outside and she caught my arm. The bite of her fingers hurt. "Frankie, we need to talk."

"Not here, Mom," I told her as Archie moved to get between us. "Please…I don't want to have this fight."

"Why are you doing this? Do you want me to be unhappy?"

"No, but I also don't think this is what you think it is. It's not just about you. You want to change everything in my life, get rid of my cats, and expect me to just stand here and say yay? Why? Because he has money? I don't want his money."

"Let her go, Ms. Curtis." The warning in Archie's voice seemed to give Mom pause, and she let me go. The fact we also had something of an audience in the other valets who were present also sank in.

"Archie," my mom turned to him, from furious to imploring in a heartbeat. "If you would just be more open to it, you and Frankie are close. You surely can't object to having her around more."

"Not even in the slightest, but Ms. Curtis, I know my dad. This is not going to end well for you. I wish I could make you see it. Frankie's worried about you, and she doesn't want you hurt. But all you can see is what you want, and that's pretty normal for the people in Edward's world. You don't get to hurt Frankie in the process, we are close and I am going to protect her, even if you won't."

"You're ruining everything." My mother's tone turned almost mournful. Then Mr. Standish came out.

"Come along, Maddy. Let the children go home and have their temper tantrum. We can celebrate privately." He wrapped an arm around my mother like he really cared, then he looked at me. "I hope you reconsider, young lady. I am well aware of everything your mother has had to give up for you. It would be a consideration if you could be bothered to do at least a little kindness back."

"Fuck off, *Eddie*," Archie said with a tight smile. Thankfully, his car pulled up and he opened the passenger door for me before the valet had even hopped out of the driver's seat.

The fact his tires squealed when he accelerated actually helped the semi-sick feeling in my stomach. Reaching over, I caught his hand, and he gripped mine as he drove.

"Sorry, Frankie," he said. "I thought I'd make it longer before he pissed me off."

"No," I said. "You don't have to be sorry. I thought you were amazing. You said all the things I was thinking, and you didn't even bat an eyelash."

"Oh, I batted a few. This whole thing is just fishy as hell. I don't know what game he's playing, but I don't want you in the middle of it."

It wasn't exactly where I wanted to be either.

"Did you mean it about the roomies thing?"

"Hell yes, I meant it. We wanted to get a place all together for college. We could totally start now, and then you don't have to worry about your cats."

I sighed.

My phone buzzed, and I let go of Archie long enough to pull it out of the bag I'd brought with me. The message was from my mother.

Mom

You and I need to talk. I did not appreciate your behavior tonight. I understand your friends might be a bad influence, but it was unacceptable to treat Eddie that way.

It didn't bode well.

"I'm thinking ice cream," Archie said as I closed the message and glanced at him. "Text Coop and the guys? By the time we get back, the game will be winding down."

"You didn't really get to eat," I reminded him.

"Yeah," he said. "The wagyu steak there is to die for. But don't worry, I'll make sure we get to have it another time. When we can enjoy it. So—ice cream?"

"I could go for some ice cream."

"Then text the guys. I think we could all use some."

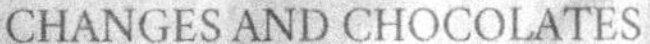

Chapter Twenty-Two

GOOD INTENTIONS

IAN

The game was brutal, but only because we were lacking part of our defense. Jake's power on the field couldn't be matched by the kid bootstrapped into his place. No offense to Tommy, he just didn't have it—yet. Still, we eked by with a win, scoring points in the last seconds of the game. This was our last home game for a few weeks, too. After Homecoming, if we could score a couple more wins, we were headed straight for playoffs, and we'd be taking the field through Thanksgiving.

If not, then we could wrap the season. At this point, I was ready to call it now. I still enjoyed the game, but between practices and the games themselves, I lost a lot of time with Frankie and the guys. Jake's interest had begun to wane, as well. When he got benched for the next two games, he hadn't even cared.

Between us, we'd checked out all the schools in the northeast with viable football scholarships that would allow us to also study our chosen interests, none of them were close enough to Harvard to matter. There wasn't a doubt in either of our minds that Frankie wouldn't get in, and where she went, I planned to follow.

Maybe that made me a bit of a joke to some, but I didn't care. I knew where I wanted to be. She'd been my best friend for years, even before she revealed she did actually want to date, I hadn't wanted there to be some huge distance between us.

I didn't waste a lot of time in the shower, just washed the sweat and dirt off then headed to my locker for my clothes. My uniform was in a bag, I'd get it cleaned over the weekend like I did after every game. Jake leaned against the locker next to mine.

"Frankie and Arch are almost back, they got caught in traffic. I'm gonna go pick up Coop and meet them at the Pit Stop."

"That was fast," I dragged on my jeans and raised my brows. We didn't spend a lot of time discussing any of them in the locker room. Too many ears.

"Yeah," was all Jake said, but his guarded expression spoke volumes. The fact Archie and Frankie had gone to have dinner with their newly engaged parents had promised to be a shitshow as far as they were concerned. Especially after what went down with her mother. Jake had been pissed, and Coop, for all his calm, had been equally furious. It wasn't news to any of us that Ms. Curtis wasn't stable, but her typically neglectful behavior masking actual abuse was not something we discussed, much less with Frankie.

Her defensiveness over her mother made sense. Once, and only once, had my parents discussed them where I could hear them. I hadn't even meant to listen, but Dad had expressed deep reservations to Mom about Frankie's situation, listing some classic hallmarks for abuse he saw in her behavior from her need to please others to the fact she didn't speak up to defend herself. It wasn't ego, he warned, it was the fact she didn't think she deserved the defense.

"Too often," he said. "Kids in her situation, they don't see that it can be any better or they deserve any better. So they defend what they have and pretend the rest doesn't matter. It's an obstinate blindness they need to survive."

Those words haunted me, to be honest. I also couldn't see what the hell he'd meant, not until that night at Frankie's when Jake knocked Coop through her coffee table and she unloaded on us. All these years, Frankie rarely got pissed off enough to rail at us for our behavior. To be honest, as much as it stung, we deserved it.

Once I was dressed, I slung my bag over my shoulder and followed Jake out of the locker room. The parking lot was still emptying from the game, but we avoided the clusters of other players, cheerleaders, band kids and more that formed as friends got together.

There'd be a huge rush for Mason's—another reason to be glad Frankie didn't work on Friday nights. After practice Wednesday and Thursday were bad enough. Fridays were a zoo.

Sharon glanced at us from a cluster of her friends, and I met her stare. When she tried to smile, I didn't return it. At the moment, I had no idea what I'd ever seen in her. A pretty face and a great ass didn't do much for a crappy personality. Not after she'd attacked Frankie. When she finally dropped her gaze, I nodded. The sooner she learned I wasn't *ever* looking to her again, the better.

We broke up *before* Frankie, anyway.

Digging my phone out, I glanced at the messages. Frankie had sent one to the group chat with us, like she had the night before about her mother and Mr. Standish being at her place. I wished she'd let one of us come get her or just come to one of our places. The handprint on her face had been…

"She's all right, Archie's probably driving which is why he isn't saying anything," Jake said as we headed out to where he'd parked. My motorcycle wasn't that far. "But she did say Archie was a badass."

I laughed at the faint snort in Jake's words. "What, you don't think he can be a badass?"

"No, he's capable of it. Most of the time he's just—the guy who takes what he wants, you know?" At his SUV, he said, "Wanna throw your stuff in the back? I can drop it off tonight or tomorrow for you."

"Thanks, man." I put my gear in, but kept my backpack. Then sent a text to say we were on our way to the Pit. "You getting Coop?"

"Yep, he's waiting." Jake rolled his head from side to side, but he didn't make a move to get in the SUV.

"You wanna talk before we go?" There weren't a lot of other reasons to linger in the lot. No one was parked near us, so we at least had some privacy.

"I don't know," Jake admitted. "Part of me thinks we could have avoided a lot of this."

I shrugged. "There's a lot of what ifs and shouldas or couldas, thing is, we didn't." Not that I had to ask him what he meant. "We started it, if you think about it."

"You mean I did." Jake pinned a look on me.

"If I meant you, I would have said you. I'm not a mute. I could have told you to knock that shit off when you started giving any guy who looked at her the stink eye. I could have gotten in the way when Archie basically started making it clear no one was allowed to ask her out. I could have said something when you punched that other kid. I didn't. So when I say *we* started it, I meant we."

With a snort and a shake of his head, Jake sighed. "You always gotta be the level-headed, perfect one."

"Hardly. If I were so perfect, I wouldn't have played the hint game, I'd have gone straight to her and told her how I felt."

"Well, you kind of did. You asked her to Homecoming before the rest of us could get our heads out of our asses."

"Archie was already trying to date her without her knowing they were dating." A fact Jake and I had discussed when he claimed Friday nights and staked out his territory. "He wasn't going to slow down. You needed a minute, but I had no doubt where you would take your chances the minute you caught your breath. And I wasn't wrong."

Jake spent the night there the week before, kept her out most of the night on Sunday and then Wednesday? Yeah, he was there all night again. The minute I read Coop's message, I got it. Archie got her in bed first, Jake got her next, and

I turned her down.

"Man, you know it's not like that."

Folding my arms, I leaned back against the bike seat. "Then what is it like, Jake? We're all going to try and get her in bed and then expect her to choose? How does that not lead to hard feelings? How does that not in the end turn out to be awful for her? She deserves better than that. She sure as hell deserves better from us."

"I'm not going to make her choose," Jake stated flatly. "Do I like that Archie isn't going to back off? Or you or Coop? No. Can I live with it? Yeah. But I told her, only you guys. No one else."

How the hell was that supposed to work? "This is nuts. Seriously, nuts. We're going to screw this all up for her because we're selfish."

"What are you talking about?"

"I'm talking about last night, she couldn't focus, we had to stay on the phone with her, remind her what was next, talk to her about assignments, and keep her eye on the prize. When was the last time Frankie needed *anyone* to help her study? We slow her down. I know I do. Hell, I took a damn AP Calculus class just so I could hang out with her. And because I knew she'd bootstrap me through it." And I wasn't proud of it, but I wouldn't drop, and I wouldn't let her down.

"Well, we broke it. We fix it. But it's not just us, it's the fucking notes and the crap with her car and her mom."

Notes. I rubbed my hands over my face. Rachel Manning had a thing for our girl and showed us all up with those roses. But they'd made Frankie smile. "Hey… we need to do something nice for her."

"Yeah, it's why we're gonna pick up Coop's lazy ass and go meet them for ice cream."

"No, jerk, I meant something nice for Frankie, like those roses. Something that's just about her and makes her feel good." She'd liked the songs I sent her the night before, I could do more of those.

"Let's figure something out." Jake reached for the driver's side door, then paused. "Bubba... man, you're not really pissed about the other night are you?"

"Did you have sex with her?" It was the most blunt I'd been.

"You punched Archie when she told you about him," Jake said slowly, facing me. "Need to do that to me?"

"Debating it." I'd punched Archie because he'd taken advantage of what she didn't know and pushed. There was no way he hadn't pushed. I got it, she didn't regret her choice, and I was glad for *her* there were no regrets. But Archie deserved the punch in the mouth.

"Then get it out of your system, because what she and I share is between us. I'm not going to drag you if you do or if Coop does or if she and Archie are again. That's personal, if she wants to talk about it or *you* do. Fine. I'm still your friend, I'll still listen. But I'm not backing off, Bubba, and if you want to fight over her, I'll fight you. I don't want to, but I will."

Yeah. That was pretty much what I figured. "Just take care of her," I said slowly. "Don't... do anything she ends up regretting."

"What the hell do you think I'm going to do?" Jake glared at me.

"I don't know, we didn't mean to hurt her before, and we did. So just be careful." It was the very least we could do.

Jake glanced past me for a moment, eyes narrowing and I turned. Maria was standing next to a car, phone in her hand looking over at us. When she turned her back, I sighed. Shit like this was getting us nowhere. Sharon had already gone after Frankie. Who knew what Maria or the other girls would pull? And why the hell had they decided to do it now? Frankie had been in our circle from the beginning, long before them, and she'd be there long after them, too.

Friends first.

It was the one thing that seemed to give her reservations about dating us, so I kept myself fixed to that point. I was going to *date* her and be her friend and prove to her I could.

It was the only way to do it.

JAKE

"Let's go," I told Bubba, and it came out a lot gruffer than I intended, but fuck it. He was a big boy. Not like he wasn't used to me snapping. It took everything I had not to march over and demand Maria tell me what the hell was going on.

Sure, Frankie said she'd defended Frankie to Sharon, but that didn't change the fact she likely knew more than she was saying. At the same time, I didn't want to get into it with her. Meeting her at the diner last Sunday had been bad enough. The fact someone took a picture of it and immediately posted it just added to crap falling on Frankie's head.

I wouldn't do that to her. Not again.

So, I left it alone.

After sending a message to Coop to let him know I was on the way, I headed out. Bubba would head straight to the Pit. Fine. Sitting out the game sucked, but it hadn't been as bad as they probably thought it would be. I'd already qualified as one of the top three finalists for a scholarship I had forgotten I'd applied for. It meant I was getting at least ten thousand for school and possibly up to a hundred thousand.

As soon as it locked, I was taking Frankie out to celebrate, but I didn't want to jinx it. I also didn't want to rub her face in it because I was pretty sure she'd applied for that scholarship, too. After the other day with G and the fact he said she scored low on that practice test. Her face. I was never going to forget that disappointment. The others hadn't seen it, but I had.

Part of why I wanted Archie to shut the hell up about it. I should never have told him, except he'd been there when I opened the letter. No, I didn't want to jinx anything, and I didn't want her to feel bad.

She was amazing, but she was taking hit after hit, and it was pissing me off. The Rachel thing might be funny later. Maybe. Still wrapping my mind around the fact another girl had made us look like a bunch of idiots *after* she set

Frankie up to basically walk away from us over the summer.

Yeah, I couldn't totally blame Rachel for that. We deserved Frankie's ire, but I could blame Rachel for telling Frankie when she damn well had to know it would hurt Frankie's feelings.

Again, that was on us.

Coop was in the parking lot when I got there. His expression was tense as he had the passenger door open and slid inside before I'd even fully stopped. "What's eating you?"

"I am struggling with my intense dislike for her mother," Coop admitted. "And when I say struggling, I mean, I've known her mother as long as I've known her, and the woman is a selfish, self-centered flake at times, but I always thought she cared more."

"People are who they are," I told him with a shrug. My dad was a stand up guy that people admired and always pointed to—look at how honorable he was, distinguished service, the military loved him, blah blah blah. Yeah, he was so great, he constantly left Mom to do all the heavy lifting, and when she wanted to go back to the States rather than live in Germany, he told her that he and the girlfriend would be fine if she wanted to do that.

That conversation haunted me, even when Mom insisted it hadn't been true. The problems between her and Dad were just bigger than the caring. He'd never had an affair, she tried to tell me, but that was also because she didn't want me to blame Dad. I didn't care. If he could say something like that to hurt her, then he could go straight to Hell. Mom had always been there, Dad couldn't say that.

"That's mature," Coop commented, and I shrugged.

"It is what it is," I said before turning around and scanning the parking lot on my way out.

"Her mom's car isn't here and neither is Archie's dad's, I looked. I also went by and checked on her cats. Figured she'd like to know they were all fine."

"Did you send her pictures?" I had to know because that sounded like a

Coop thing to do.

"I send her cat videos, of course I sent her pictures." He grinned, and I laughed. It wasn't that far to the Pit. My phone rang and it was Becca's number, so I hit answer.

"What's up, Squirt?"

"Mom wants you to bring milk and bread on your way home after the game."

I snorted. No she didn't, but I played along. "Sure, if I come home. I'll bring it."

"*If* you come home?" Becca squeaked. "Dude you better come home, you keep spending school nights away, Mom's gonna kick your ass."

"A, it's not a school night, and B, she already knows I might be crashing with the guys and Frankie tonight. We got lots to do." I grinned as Becca swore. "If Mom told you to go get it and you forgot it, that's on you."

"Dammit."

"But since I'm a nice big brother, I will grab it tonight or tomorrow morning, whenever I'm heading home."

"Thank you!" After a beat, she said, "Since you're in a giving mood, how do you feel about pizza?"

"I feel like you have your own money, bye." I hung up on her squeak, and Coop laughed.

"Little sisters."

"Man, you have one, I have three. When you get three, talk to me about little sisters." I loved them all, even when I wished Mom had drowned them at birth. But the girls were all independent and feisty. Becca was getting more like Frankie every day, which was a good thing. I wanted her to be tough.

"Yeah, still—Archie and Bubba don't get it." No, they didn't.

"Hey," I said slowly, what Bubba had said earlier kept niggling in the back of my mind. "Question for you."

"Shoot."

"Wednesday night didn't bother you, did it?"

He coughed. "You mean when you spent the night with Frankie?"

"Yeah, that Wednesday." Hopefully, he wouldn't try to make a joke about it.

Coop shrugged. "I wasn't thrilled, but she seemed pretty happy, and you didn't get all pissy when I kissed her goodnight or good morning. So—while I might have been jealous, I wasn't mad."

Cool. "Okay."

"Why?"

"Just—Bubba said something, and it's chewing on me."

"That she's going to have to choose eventually and when she does, that's gonna end up hurting some of us?" The question was so close to the mark of what Bubba said, I frowned.

"Yeah, but I don't see why she has to choose."

"You don't want her to choose you?" Skeptical didn't begin to cover it.

"Of course, I want her to choose me. I'm not an idiot. But—I don't mind if she doesn't." Apparently, I was weird.

"Life doesn't work that way," Coop said. "I mean, it would be nice if it did. We get the girl, we're still friends, and we can go on with our life. But… you know. People have expectations. Frankie has them, too. She's never dated before. We're it so far, and we've been doing such a great job."

Yeah, okay, that last bit of sarcasm. We did deserve it. "It hasn't all been horrible." Far from it.

"For us, maybe," Coop said slowly. "I worry about her."

"Why?" What else did he know?

"Just… she's not acting like her. She's totally off her game. The stress is getting to her, and I can see it. So right now, my focus is making things as easy as possible for her."

"I can get behind that."

"Good," Coop said. "Cause next week on my birthday, I really want her to have fun and not be a stressed out mess who needs a puppy pile hug."

I laughed. "Puppy pile hugs can be fun." It had been the night we all piled onto her bed and watched movies together. The only one not there had been Bubba. "What are the chances the idiot parents come back to her place tonight?"

"You know, I used to wish her mother was around, and now I'm kind of hoping she isn't."

Yeah. Me too.

Maybe we should all make plans to crash at Frankie's tonight. We'd make a hell of a barrier, and I was really tired of people making an end-run around us. She didn't need to take any more hits.

Ever.

COOP

At the Pit, I was out of the SUV before Jake even threw it in park. The agitation had been like an itch between my shoulder blades since I left Frankie with Archie to get ready and go out to dinner with their parents. The whole week had been a mess really. From the genuine worry in her voice over the idea her mom would get rid of the cats to the fact people had trashed her car to that damn red mark on her face that morning.

It wasn't the first time Ms. Curtis hit Frankie. In fact, I was pretty sure she'd done it a few times before. I'd seen it—once. We'd been ten, or maybe it was eleven. Frankie and I had been in and out of the apartments all day, sometimes at my place and sometimes at hers. We'd played video games, watched movies, and raided the ice cream in my freezer—cookies and cream, damn, that had been good. It had been hot as hell outside, and neither of us had actually wanted to go swimming.

When Frankie's mom got home though, she found out Frankie had forgotten to take something out of the freezer. I couldn't even remember what it was Frankie was supposed to have taken out, but her mom just unloaded on her.

It had been an ugly thing, and when Frankie tried to stand up for herself, Ms. Curtis had slapped her so hard, it had echoed in the kitchen. I must have made a noise because then, Ms. Curtis ordered me out of the house. I didn't see Frankie for four days after that, even though I went by every day and knocked.

When she did come out next, she didn't mention it at all, pretended it hadn't happened. I let it go. What did I know? I was just glad to have my buddy back. But seeing that red mark on her face, it reminded me of it all over again.

It wasn't busy inside the Pit. I picked out Frankie and the guys easily enough; they were sacked away in the big circle booth in the back corner. Frankie had a giant banana split in front of her. So that meant it had definitely gone bad.

Ice cream was her go to comfort food.

I swung through the line and ordered a double dip cone in a bowl and paid for it. Jake was right behind me, and he ordered pretty much the same thing. Ice cream in hand, I headed for the booth. Frankie's green eyes were shadowed and tired, but her smile was real.

"Hey," she said, and even her voice sounded tired. Why couldn't her mom just give her a break? I felt for Archie, too, but he acted like this was no big deal to him. All his focus was on Frankie, too.

"Hey, you look like crap," I told her cheerfully, and her grin grew warmer as Bubba glared at me.

"I look better than you," she retorted. There was my girl.

"Alas, that's not hard," Archie said. "Everyone looks better than Coop. The question is, does she look better than me?"

I snorted, and Frankie laughed. It was worth it, particularly when Bubba and Jake chorused a "Yes" right along with me.

Frankie's eyes warmed, and something in my gut unlocked. Okay. That was better. She dug a spoonful of chocolate ice cream, what looked like caramel syrup, some whip cream and more nuts than should be legal on something like that up to eat, and I sighed a little.

She always made little orgasm faces when she ate ice cream, and I was pretty sure she had no idea. Having now seen her orgasm face though, I could say with certainty that she *really* liked ice cream.

"See," Archie said, as he glanced at Frankie. "They like you better than me."

"Obviously," she retorted. "Apparently, you like me better than them, but I'm not falling into this trap of who do I like better."

No, she would never do that to us. "No one's asking you to," I said before Archie could make another smart-ass comment, but all he did was point to me.

"What he said."

"Thanks," she said with a sigh, then took another bite. She was decimating that banana split. My ice cream was good, but the fact she was so singularly focused worried me.

"How was the game?" she asked abruptly.

"We won," Bubba told her. "Barely. Guy they have subbing in for Jake isn't that good."

"He was fine," Jake said. "And Bubba did a nice save in the last quarter, don't let him play you. We won, and he helped set that play up."

Bubba shrugged. "It was the team, we had a good play, *we* made it."

"But winning is good, you're 4 and 1, right?"

"Technically," Jake said.

"That makes you second in the division." The fact she even knew that earned more than one pair of raised eyebrows. "Don't look so impressed, I do follow the wins and losses, and Archie told me earlier."

Jake laughed and Bubba grinned. "Fair enough," I said. "But the minute you start knowing stats, I start worrying the world has gone upside down."

I kind of regretted saying that because her eyes went all shadowed again, and that was killing me. I hated when she was unhappy, and I didn't hate much. Even when I dreaded dealing with the tension around Mom and Dad, I didn't hate them or it; I just didn't want to deal with it. When Frankie was unhappy, the world just seemed like a darker place.

She always had everything so put together. It was the face she showed the world. I was proud of our girl in a way I couldn't express to the others. More because I knew that face was a mask, but one she could wear because she was so good at what she did.

When she floundered or struggled, so did I, because I wanted to fix it for her, and I wasn't sure how. We could take on the bullies at school, that wasn't even an issue. Take her car to the detail place and clean up the obnoxious mess on it? No problem. Hell, Jake punched the one asshole who slut sneezed, and Laura had been suspended for her crap. We could help with that.

But the thing with her mom? I had no idea how to fix that situation. Push too hard where her mom was concerned, and Frankie would shut down. It didn't seem possible to push back without Frankie trying to defend her.

"The world is already kind of upside down." She glanced at Archie. "And you still haven't had anything resembling food."

"Yeah, I'm thinking after ice cream, we get pizza and pick out some absolutely terrible movies to watch." He trailed a finger down her arm, and the corner of her mouth tilted up again.

"Actually," I said. "That's not a bad idea. Jake mentioned something like that earlier." Totally making that shit up, I threw a look at Jake.

With a lift of his chin, he caught the toss and said, "Yeah, we can all pile on your bed, eat pizza, drink sodas, watch movies. Whatever you want."

Her expression turned worried. "I don't know if they went back there."

"So?" Bubba actually joined in. "You live there too, and there's more of us. We can even be quiet."

"Might make them want to go somewhere else," Archie said, his tone musing. "Either way, it's about you. Would that make you feel better? You can keep an eye on your cats and relax in your bed. We'll hang out, stuff you with pizza, and make you laugh. I volunteer Coop to even take out the trash after."

I rolled my eyes, but I didn't argue because the corners of her mouth tipped again. "For what it's worth, they weren't there when Jake got me."

"Thank you for the cat pictures, the tail one was really cute." Her smile warmed, even as she looked thoughtful. "Though, I don't know if we'll all fit on my bed."

"We'll figure it out," Bubba said. "Sitting on the floor never killed anyone. What do you want to do?"

"Not talk about problems, watch movies that make us laugh and groan, and eat pineapple pizza."

"Cool," Jake said. "Anyone need to clear it with the 'rents that we might end up crashing at Frankie's?"

ARCHIE

Sharing my date night wasn't high on my list of things I wanted to do, but Frankie needed all of us. Dinner with the parents had been a disaster before we got there. I'd half-expected it to implode—hoped really that Edward would cancel at the last minute because it was what he did—before we even had to make the drive. Unfortunately, we didn't get that lucky.

The fact he had actually given Ms. Curtis a ring was bad enough, but to continue with the farce of they were getting married? And he planned to move Frankie and her mom into our house? I didn't mind the idea of Frankie living with me. Quite the opposite, but she wasn't up for life with Edward Standish and all the bullshit that entailed. Year together or not, his mistresses had a habit of vanishing the moment he got bored.

The fact he bought Frankie a dress bothered me more than I'd told her. I hadn't been kidding about the fact he bought clothes for the women he dated or kept. Frankie wasn't going on that list.

Ever.

The very idea was disgusting.

So whatever game he planned to play, I was taking Frankie off the board. The ice cream and the guys helped to lift her mood. Back at her apartment, I was more than grateful to discover a distinct absence of our parents. I was all set to go another round with my dad if I had to. Thankfully, for Frankie's sake, that proved unnecessary.

We figured out the seating in her room, and it ended up with most of us on the floor on cushions, sprawled around each other, boxes of pizza open—and the TV we stole from the living room set up in the corner.

Frankie leaned against Bubba as we scrolled through the choices on Netflix, and I glanced at my phone. No word from Mom on her sudden French relocation. Jeremy, however, confirmed she'd had her trunks sent.

So at least that much of Edward's story might be based in fact.

What the hell was he doing?

A toe tapped my leg, and I glanced over to find Frankie watching me. She curled her toes against my thigh, and I put my hand over her foot and grinned. She mouthed *you okay?* and I nodded. I was okay. Surrounded by my best friends and allowed to kiss her the way I'd always wanted to?

I was more than okay.

Everything else, we'd figure out later.

Chapter Twenty-Three

WE ALL FALL DOWN

By the end of the first movie, I was full, sleepy, and almost content. All the rough edges had been sanded away by the fact the guys just hung out. It was almost like old times, only—better. I'd changed into sleep shorts and a tank top after we'd gotten home, they were down to boxers and t-shirts and queuing up the next movie. I'd started off the first movie leaning against Ian, ended up curled up next to Coop for the second with my head pillowed against his stomach. Jake had been rubbing my feet, and I must have fallen asleep there.

When I woke up, I was sandwiched in bed between Coop on one side and Jake on the other. The cat walking across me irked my bladder, and I smothered a yawn as I tried to figure out how to get up. A faint snore escaped Coop, matching one coming from farther away, and I leaned up to look. Archie was sprawled on his back amongst two of the cushions with a blanket over him, and Tory sleeping on his chest.

The fact he'd gone out of his way to make sure I wasn't alone last night and they all distracted me hadn't been lost on me. Tiddles glanced at me from the foot of the bed, but there was no sign of Tabby.

Where was Ian?

There was a blanket and pillow next to one of the other couch cushions, but no Ian. Tiddles suddenly streaked out of the room with Tory right behind him at the distinctive sound of a can opening. Easing out of the bed, I managed to not wake up Coop or Jake.

After pausing in the bathroom to deal with my bladder and brush my teeth, I padded into the kitchen to find Ian leaning against the kitchen counter staring at my fridge.

Following his gaze, I looked at the photo of the five of us that was hanging by a magnet. It had been there for years. I had a better copy in my room, but I'd plunked this on the fridge that summer between freshman and sophomore years. We'd taken it the last day of school.

He glanced at me as I came in. "You ever wish you could go back and be those kids again?"

"No," I said slowly. "Not that I minded being them when we were, but I'd much rather be looking at the end of high school than the beginning."

"Fair." When he stretched out an arm, I narrowed the distance and curled right up to him as he wrapped that arm around me and pressed a kiss to my temple. "How you feeling?"

"Not bad," I admitted. "Better than I thought I would." The cramps had faded, the irritation under my skin had reduced, and the singular dread from the day before had given way to a kind of apathy. I was at a loss as to what to do about Mom and Mr. Standish. "Feeling lucky."

"Yeah?" He glanced down at me, and I smiled.

"Yeah, you guys all came. You're all here. We're still friends, and as crazy as everything has been… I feel closer to all of you."

He nodded slowly, then tightened his arm and rested his cheek against my hair. "Good. You know we're always going to be here for you, no matter what, right?"

I frowned a little. "I do know that, and I'm there for you." As bumpy a road as the last few weeks had been, and as bad as last Saturday had been, I did know they were there for me. "Ian, are you okay?"

"Yeah," he said. "I'm fine. Just thinking about all the stuff we have to do." He didn't sound fine. I wiggled a little until he loosened his arm so I could look up at him. "Angel, I'm fine," he said quietly, then dropped a kiss on my nose. It was probably supposed to just be a light, teasing kiss, but I rose up on my tip toes, and he hesitated a moment before his mouth closed on mine.

I sighed into the kiss, it was slow and sweet. He asked for nothing and gave everything. Cupping his face, I marveled at the bristle of stubble along his jaw, even as his lips massaged mine. The first stroke of his tongue teased against mine, and I sighed. Peppermint and Ian.

I wasn't the only one who brushed my teeth. His fingers tightened against my sides, and he pulled back a moment. "Frankie…"

"Hey," Coop said as he shuffled into the kitchen. "Anyone make coffee or something?" A yawn elongated and stretched every word.

Something tightened in Ian's expression, but he just gave me a squeeze before he said, "No, but I can." He was already turning away before I could ask what was wrong. Then Coop curled an arm around my middle and pulled me back against him.

"Morning," he murmured and nuzzled a kiss to my cheek. The bristle of his stubble stung a bit, but I sighed at the heat of him wrapped around me. Tilting my head back, I started to answer, but he was already kissing me. If I'd been delighted by Ian's kiss, I thrilled to Coop's. It was equal parts comforting and teasing. He nipped my lower lip at the end and sighed. "Now, it's a good morning."

The slam of the filter basket startled more than just me. Tiddles bolted away from his now empty food bowl. Coop loosened his hold, and we both glanced at Ian. He wasn't looking at us, but his back was stiff.

Maybe the no kissing thing should extend to when we were all together.

Coop and Jake hadn't seemed to mind, but I didn't want to upset Ian. I pulled away, and it was Coop who frowned this time.

"Why are you people awake?" Archie shuffled into the kitchen, and I got a sleepy warm hug and another kiss, this one on the corner of my mouth, before he murmured into my hair, "Better one after I brush my teeth, promise."

I laughed and hugged him.

"Fed the cats," Ian said. "Got the coffee started. Figure we can all eat at home rather than dig through Frankie's fridge. In fact, I'm gonna go get dressed." Then he was out of the kitchen.

Archie leaned back and tracked Ian's passage with a frown. "What put a bug up his ass?"

"I think we did," Coop mused, then he tugged my hair. "You wanna shower?"

"I should. I have to work in a couple of hours." Should probably do some homework, too.

"Okay, we'll get the TV back where it goes."

"After coffee," Archie said, leaning back against a counter and keeping his arms looped around me until I settled with my back to his chest. "And after I get some cuddle time. You assholes stole the bed with her."

"Hey, you snooze, you lose." Coop grinned, absolutely unrepentant. He winked at me. "You sleep okay?"

"I did, thank you." The smell of coffee filled the kitchen, and honestly, I was ready to drink about a gallon of it. My brain was still in sluggish mode. Last night had been… brutal. But the guys—the guys had made it better. "I'm going to check on Ian."

A kiss to my nape, and Archie let me go.

I was almost to my bedroom when Jake said, "Man, what are you doing?"

"I'm getting dressed," Ian answered. "She's fine. She has you three, and you're all being cuddly. I need to go home and get some stuff done."

"Don't be like this, Bubba." Jake countered.

"Be like what?" But there was something in his voice, Jake was right. Something cool and reserved. Ian was never cold. "I'm fine. She's good. We came over to make sure she wasn't alone, she's definitely not alone."

"So, what? You just take off in a pissy mood?"

Silence greeted that remark, then Ian snorted, "Stealing your thunder? You and Archie are the only two who get to have a bad mood?"

"What the fuck—no. What the hell is going on with you?"

"Nothing," Ian replied. "Just have some stuff to do today, and she has work. Not going to get in the way. You guys are all here."

"C'mon, Bubba…"

"Look," he said, turning as he zipped up his jeans and that was when he saw me leaning against the doorframe. He sighed, then raked a hand through his hair. "I'm not being any way. I just have some homework to do, and I promised my mom I'd run some errands."

"Okay, but I think we should all talk if you're this uncomfortable." I'd told them all from the beginning I didn't want to lose my friendships, and I didn't want them turning on each other. To be honest, I'd thought it would be Jake or Archie, they were so damn possessive, but maybe I didn't think it all the way through.

"We don't have to talk, Frankie," Ian told me. "Seriously, it's all good."

"Then why does it feel like it's not all good for you at the moment?" We'd made a lot of the last few days about me, but I wasn't the only person in this group.

His shoulders dipped, and Jake shoved off the bed. "I'll let you two talk." Then he squeezed past me after a quick kiss.

Padding into the room, I sat on the end of my bed and looked at him. "Talk to me?"

Ian dropped to sit next to me and exhaled. "I'm not mad. I'm not upset. But it's… it's a little harder to watch you with everyone and know they are all pushing you, and sooner or later, it's going to hurt some of us, but it will definitely hurt you.”

“Because I’m dating everyone?” I had to be sure.

“Yeah, and not just because of what the asshats are doing, Frankie. We’re all crazy about you,” he continued, then turned sideways to face me. “The thing is…crazy has limits. I’ve watched you aching this week from finding out we knew about your mom to their plan to deal with Mathieu.”

It had been a week. Exactly a week since then. It felt like eighty years.

“The shit Sharon pulled, and Laura… the fact we still don’t know who did that to your car. That you have to deal with your mom and Archie’s dad, and whatever that ends up meaning. Throw Jake and Archie pushing you…”

“You keep saying their pushing me,” I cut in, twisting to face him too, and our knees brushed. “They’re not.”

“Yes they are,” he said flatly. “I’m not saying you don’t have the right to say yes to whatever you want. I just—I want you to focus on you, and I think that’s getting lost in all of this.”

“I am focusing on me, all we talk about is me. I know the dating thing is new, and I wasn’t trying to… I don’t want you to think I don’t like you because I…I had sex with them. I wanted to with you but you…”

“That’s my point,” Ian said slowly. “You’re new to all of this. Maybe we’re a bunch of assholes because we rushed when we thought we might lose you to some other guy. But I don’t want you to regret a moment, and everything that has been happening, it just makes it all so intense. I want you to want to take those steps, and I want to be the guy you can depend on. I want you to feel valued. I never want you to feel like we expect anything.”

My stomach sank. “I don’t think you expect anything. I’ll be honest, I don’t think any of you do. No one has made me do anything I didn’t want, Ian.”

His expression tensed.

“But that’s the problem, isn’t it?” I wanted them, too. “Because I want to date all of you.”

“It’s not a problem.” That was another lie. One he couldn’t even meet my gaze to say. Scrubbing his hands against his face, he groaned. "Frankie…where do you see this going? All of us?"

"At the moment?"

"Now? A month from now? Six months from now?"

"I don't know." It was the truth. "You guys are my best friends. I don't want to lose any of you."

"I know you don't, Angel. Trust me, I'm not going anywhere but…"

That horrible word.

"But I think that maybe we need to slow this down. I'll still take you to Homecoming. Still do that right, and if you want to keep having whatever with the guys, that's okay, cause that's your call. But I think you and me, we need to maybe step it back a little."

"Did I do something wrong?"

"God no, I think it's me," he admitted. "I think I worry about you too much." He tucked a finger under my chin. Yet, despite his smile, the sinking feeling didn't go away. "I never want to hurt you. I never want you to feel like you have to make a choice between me and the guys, or us and anything. You've got so much on your plate. I'm just going to lighten the load a little."

This felt an awful lot like he was breaking up with me.

"Rachel was right, you need a friend. Maybe more than you need yet another boyfriend, and… you know Jake and Archie. They want everything, and they're going to kill themselves to make sure you get it. I meant it when I said this isn't about you, I promise. I just need to figure some things out."

But not him.

My eyes burned. "Maybe we could all slow down then…if it means you won't… you won't go."

"I just said I'm not going anywhere. We'll do Homecoming, I'm going to do that right for you. We'll see where it goes from there, okay?" He tried for another smile. "Maybe if I back off some, Sharon will leave you alone, and it will get some of the others to shut up. Win win. Keep you safe, and it's not like you're not going to see me. Still need to get through calculus, and who else is going to listen to me put together my audition tape?"

The lump in my throat made it hard to swallow. Lifting my hand to his cheek, I leaned forward and kissed him. I didn't have the words to tell him I didn't want him to back off, not ones that didn't sound selfish or greedy. He was telling me what he needed, but then he kept saying he was doing it for me.

At first, he stilled against my lips, then he cradled my face and deepened the kiss. A long, slow brush of his tongue against mine sent a tangle of feeling through me, until he finally leaned his head back. "I'll see you later. Tell Coop that you have to like the dress, not just him, okay?" Then another light kiss, and he was gone. Up and moving as he left the apartment.

There were startled voices in the other room—more than one angry—then the back door closed with a solid thump. I sat there trying to piece together what just happened.

"Don't worry about him," Jake said as he appeared in the room. He grabbed his clothes and dressed hurriedly. "I'm going to talk to him." Pausing a beat, he eyed me. "Are you okay?"

"I'm—yeah, I'm fine." It was a lie, but I wasn't quite sure how I was. "Don't—don't make him feel bad."

"Frankie, Bubba's just got a bee up his ass. He cares about you."

"I know, but don't make him feel bad. If he can't do this with me dating everyone, then he can't." Which meant maybe I shouldn't be. "I told you I wasn't sure how this was going to work. I don't want you guys to fight."

"Sometimes, we need to have our heads knocked together." He crouched in front of me. "You going to be okay while I go track him down and see what's going on with him?"

I got my shit together, I had big girl panties. I could put them on. "I'll be fine. I gotta work." With a little shrug, I touched his cheek. "Homework and stuff…then dress shopping tonight."

It was the absolute last thing I wanted to do.

The. Absolute. Last.

"Get something pretty, course, you're going to be a knockout in anything." He gave me a quick kiss. "I'll see you at Mason's later, I'll drag Bubba in. Everything will be great. You'll see."

Then he was out, and it wasn't long before the backdoor thudded closed behind him. I stood up and glanced around the disheveled room. The television still needed to go back and the couch cushions. Needing to move, I made the bed.

"Hey," Coop said. "I brought you coffee." He held out the cup, and he was by himself. "Archie's on the phone with Jeremy, he hasn't left."

I nodded. "Thanks."

"Want a hand?"

"Need to move the TV."

"We can do that," he said, but his expression was guarded. "Are you okay?"

"I'm undecided," I admitted. "Ian's upset, but I think he's trying not to be."

"Jake will talk to him," Coop said. "I can call him later, too."

Sipping the coffee, I turned those words over in my head. "Coop, should I have said no to dating all of you?"

He grimaced.

"No," Archie said from the doorway. "You shouldn't have said no. There's nothing wrong with dating all of us."

Just like last week when Jake reminded me we had done nothing wrong. I was dating all of them. Except… "I don't think I'm really dating Ian, anymore."

"Give him time," Archie said. "It's been a tense few days, and he's thinking long game. He wants to protect you. That's not a guy who doesn't want to see you."

"Except he's right."

Coop sighed.

"Sooner or later I have to choose, right?"

Arms folded, Archie leaned against the doorframe. "I'm not asking you to choose. Are you?" He looked at Coop.

"No," Coop said slowly. "But to be fair—we've all kind of been slicing up your time because we're all a little greedy and want more with you. Maybe that's not fair to *you*."

"Shit," Archie said. "Really? That's the route you're going?"

"I'm calling it like I see it," Coop retorted. "Frankie's got a lot on her plate, and we're making it more difficult. Ian sees that, and I get where he's coming from."

"So you want to back off, too?" Suddenly the coffee tasted like ash.

"Back off might be too big a description, but…make it easier for you? Yeah. I'm always going to be here for you, but I think making sure you aren't getting nailed from all directions is more important than scratching some itch we all have."

Scratching an itch?

He grimaced. "Hearing that out loud makes it sound a lot worse than it is. Really—just don't feel like we need rush, how is that?"

From his position in the door, Archie's expression was a cross between pained and irritated. "I think it sounds like a bunch of crap."

"Not helpful," Coop told him, and I sighed. "Hey, look, it's Saturday morning and you've barely had coffee. We don't have to make these kinds of decisions. Archie and I will get the TV back in the living room, and then you can start getting ready for work. If you want, I'll go make waffles. I still remember where the waffle iron is."

I didn't want to make anyone do something they didn't want to do. Maybe I should be focusing on other things.

"For what it's worth, I think they're both idiots, and I'm not going any-fucking-where." Archie's staunch declaration made me smile a little.

"And you call me dramatic," Coop feigned fanning himself. "I do declare…"

And I laughed.

When Coop winked at me, the smile I had this time was real.

Lots of changes. Maybe too many.

But maybe what I needed to do was show the guys I did want them the way they kept showing me.

"Waffles would be great," I said. "Don't forget, you're going dress shopping with me tonight."

"Hubba hubba, we can play music on our phones and film a dress montage scene."

Okay.

Now that was funny.

"Don't you dare!"

"Oh well," Coop said as he and Archie lifted the television. "Now I have to."

As they wrestled it out of the room and left me alone, I stared around the emptying room. Less than an hour ago, we'd all been here and if not fine, at least together.

Staying together was more important than anything else. If dating all of them was going to be a problem…

…then maybe I needed to rethink that, too.

Some changes weren't worth losing or hurting my friends.

Ever.

I cared about them too much to hurt them.

Frankie and the boys return in *Keys and Kisses*.

To keep up with Heather and all her series join her reader's group:

https://www.facebook.com/groups/HeathersPack/

About Heather Long

USA Today bestselling author, Heather Long, likes long walks in the park, science fiction, superheroes, Marines, and men who aren't douche bags. Her books are filled with heroes and heroines tangled in romance as hot as Texas summertime. From paranormal historical westerns to contemporary military romance, Heather might switch genres, but one thing is true in all of her stories—her characters drive the books. When she's not wrangling her menagerie of animals, she devotes her time to family and friends she considers family. She believes if you like your heroes so real you could lick the grit off their chest, and your heroines so likable, you're sure you've been friends with women just like them, you'll enjoy her worlds as much as she does.

Follow Heather & Sign up for her newsletter:

www.heatherlong.net

Also by Heather Long

UNTOUCHABLE

Rules and Roses

Changes and Chocolates

Keys and Kisses

Whispers and Wishes

Hangovers and Holidays

Brazen and Breathless

Trials and Tiaras

Graduation and Gifts

Defiance and Dedication

82ND STREET VANDALS

Savage Vandal

Vicious Rebel

Ruthless Traitor

Dirty Devil

ALWAYS A MARINE SERIES

Once Her Man, Always Her Man

Retreat Hell! She Just Got Here

Tell It to the Marine

Proud to Serve Her

Her Marine

No Regrets, No Surrender

The Marine Cowboy

The Two and the Proud

A Marine and a Gentleman

Combat Barbie

Whiskey Tango Foxtrot

What Part of Marine Don't You Understand?

A Marine Affair

Marine Ever After

Marine in the Wind

Marine with Benefits

A Marine of Plenty

A Candle for a Marine

Marine under the Mistletoe

Have Yourself a Marine Christmas

Lest Old Marines Be Forgot

Her Marine Bodyguard

Smoke & Marines

BRAVO TEAM WOLF

When Danger Bites

Bitten Under Fire

BOOMERS
The Judas Contact
Deadly Genesis
Unstoppable
Chance Monroe
Earth Witches Aren't Easy
Plan Witch from Out of Town
Bad Witch Rising
Her Elite Assets
Featuring:
Pure Copper
Target: Tungsten
Asset: Arsenic
Fevered Hearts
Marshal of Hel Dorado
Brave are the Lonely
Micah & Mrs. Miller
A Fistful of Dreams
Raising Kane
Wanted: Fevered or Alive
Wild and Fevered
The Quick & The Fevered
A Man Called Wyatt
Going Royal
Some Like It Royal
Some Like It Scandalous
Some Like It Deadly
Some Like it Secret
Some Like it Easy
Her Marine Prince

Blocked

HEART OF THE NEBULA
Queenmaker

Deal Breaker

Throne Taker

LONE STAR LEATHERNECKS
Semper Fi Cowboy

As You Were, Cowboy

MADISON, THE WITCH HUNTER
Every Witch Way But Floosey's

MAGIC & MAYHEM
The Witch Singer

Bridget's Witch's Diary

The Witched Away Bride

Mongrels

Mongrels, Mischief & Mayhem

SHACKLED SOULS
Succubus Chained

Succubus Unchained

Succubus Blessed

SPACE COWBOY
Space Cowboy Survival Guide

WOLVES OF WILLOW BEND
Wolf at Law

Wolf Bite

Caged Wolf

Wolf Claim

Wolf Next Door

Rogue Wolf

Bayou Wolf

Untamed Wolf

Wolf with Benefits

River Wolf

Single Wicked Wolf

Desert Wolf

Snow Wolf

Wolf on Board

Holly Jolly Wolf

Shadow Wolf

His Moonstruck Wolf

Thunder Wolf

Ghost Wolf

Outlaw Wolves

Wolf Unleashed

www.ingramcontent.com/pod-product-compliance
Lightning Source LLC
Chambersburg PA
CBHW060631310726
48982CB00003B/740